High Tide in St Ives

CORA DEVINE

Morva Press

Published by Morva Press
ISBN 978-1-9160565-2-7

ALSO BY CORA DEVINE:

A Sea-Change
The Wreck
The Turning Tide
Something Rich and Strange
The Fogou

coradevine.co.uk

CONTENTS

AUTHOR'S NOTE

The old lifeboat which Kit has restored in the book is loosely based on the *James Stevens No. 10*, which served St Ives between 1900 and 1933. When her days of duty were over, she disappeared for a while, but was eventually rescued and restored. For several years she could be seen in St Ives Bay, running trips to The Carracks, or 'Seal Island'. Some years ago, I heard the boat had been submerged and wrecked during a storm in the Hayle Estuary, where she was moored. This seemed a tragic end for such a beautiful old vessel with so much history, so I thought I would bring her back to life. Since writing the novel, I have discovered that she was not completely destroyed after all, and has once again been made seaworthy. With luck, we will see this historic lifeboat a regular in the bay once more.

The original series of twenty lifeboats was purchased by the Royal National Lifeboat Institution (RNLI) following a bequest by businessman James Stevens. To avoid confusion with any of the few lifeboats that are still in existence, I have named Kit's boat the *James Stevens No. 21*, a boat that never actually existed, and blessed with fittings and dimensions that serve the story more than they do historical accuracy.

The Barquentine, or 'The Barque', is also an imaginary place, located 'somewhere' between Fore Street and the harbour; but the name is based on part of a listed building at Westcott's Quay, recently used as an art gallery. There is some evidence that it may have once been a tea room or bar in the 1960s, but much about this establishment remains an enigma.

Almost because of this, it seemed fitting to revive its name, at least, for the drinking den where the characters congregate.

Pudding Bag Lane, later named Capel Court, used to be behind The Sloop Inn, where the car park is now. Around 1935, the local council, in their wisdom, demolished it in an effort to 'clear the slums'. Thankfully these endeavours were curtailed, otherwise much of the Downalong (or Down'long) area would not be as we know and love it today. I have used the name for the fictional alley near Porthmeor beach, where Senara discovers the old pilchard cellar and net loft, but I am sorry to say that they too, do not exist in reality. That said, St Ives holds many secrets; so, who knows, when exploring the back streets of Downalong, what you might find?

This novel was conceived and largely written before the outbreak of Covid-19, and so I decided to keep it set in those better times, that I hope we will all fully return to soon.

Cora Devine

HIGH TIDE

IN

ST IVES

Prelude

It came as a complete surprise to Senara to discover that she was an eagle. And yet perversely, it also made perfect sense.

Of course she was an eagle. How she had not known this before was both shocking and deeply amusing. But now that she was an eagle, everything locked into place. She had profound understanding. The world stretched out below her in majestic colour as she soared over snow-capped mountains, a whole history of knowledge and instinct effortlessly embedded in her consciousness.

And now she was flying far out over the sparkling sea—*a sea eagle?* —with the wind buffeting and ruffling her feathers. But she was not cold, and there was no doubt or fear. All was beautiful in the world above the vast expanse of the ocean. She was alone and yet not alone, being part of all things and all time.

And then she was gliding lower, where she could see the heave and swell of the water. Above a boat now; a small white boat with two sails. She thought they were red sails. She could not see the sailor, but had an intuitive knowledge of his presence and her heart was gladdened by the unspoken sense of companionship...

CHAPTER 1

Transition

Cold, hard, ground.

Her cheek lay upon the cold hard ground and felt wet where she had drooled a little. Her eyes tried to make sense of the marbled tiles. That awful smell that she had found so nauseating permeated her senses; a combination of deep-fried pastry and noxious meaty filling; of doughnuts and coffee and car fumes, and the linger of wee from the underground. And worst of all was the noise; the incessant, driving, cacophonous hiss of the people. There were so many of them; all busy and full of care, and their voices lifted and combined to a maddening, loud whisper.

'I think she's coming round,' said a woman's voice.

'You all right, love?' A man this time.

Three faces, unfamiliar, hovered above her head.

'What happened?' Senara's voice was dry and hoarse. And then it came: the deep pang of regret for no longer being an eagle.

'You fainted, love,' said the man: *cockney accent, remarkably cheery under the circumstances*. 'Flat out, you was. One minute you was standing there, next thing we know, you're on the floor!'

Of course. Paddington station. The forecourt. Again, the awful disappointment at no longer flying over snow-capped mountains and out to sea. Senara sat up gingerly, and instinctively felt for the small woven shoulder bag, which thankfully was still at her side, and then looked around for her rucksack.

'Look, if she's all right now, I really have to go.' A brown-eyed young man looked restlessly at the other rescuers.

And then Senara remembered. She had been standing on the forecourt staring anxiously at the ever-changing flap display. The train was due to depart soon, but the platform had yet to be announced. A mob had assembled, all equally scrutinising the departures board, and there would surely be a scrum at the ticket gate. The faint had come on so suddenly that she had only had time for the words: 'I think I'm about to...' before falling limply towards the young man, quite possibly into his arms, like some doll-like heroine from an old silent movie. No wonder Brown-eyes looked embarrassed. He was too young, too self-consciously cool for heroics.

'Yeah, yeah, off you go,' instructed the cockney man. 'Gonna be late me-self after this palaver.'

Brown-eyes shuffled off, but not without a small shy look of appreciation towards Senara. Oh well; at least she still *had it*, even whilst dribbling.

'Yeah, you're all right now, ain't you darlin'? Nah, don't get up too quick, take it easy. Just need some decent nosh I reckon, looking at you.' The London accent sounded parodic, and startlingly alien, like a long-forgotten memory.

'It's okay, I've got your rucksack,' said her third saviour, a dark-haired woman with troubled but kind eyes. 'Do you think you can stand?'

The woman looked about Senara's age, but smartly-dressed in a tailored black suit and white silk blouse. There was a nervousness to her voice, as if she thought Senara might bite her, despite her help. Perhaps she considered her deranged, or an addict. Senara thought guiltily of the sleeping homeless people that she had passed by on her way to the tube station, shamefully wary of their presence. What if they too had fainted? Nobody cared; they were to be avoided; stepped over; ignored.

'Thanks, I feel fine, now,' Senara mumbled as she struggled to her feet, although in truth she was still a little light-headed.

She should have eaten of course. But she had stared at the glut of burritos and muffins and baguettes on offer and had felt queasy. An attempt at a muddy coffee with all the flavour of dust had been abandoned. And it hadn't helped that she had been out late last night with Teddy, and the boys from Oz, in Earls Court. One last farewell drink had inevitably turned into several too many. But above all else, Senara was convinced that it had been the air, or rather the lack of it, that had caused her collapse. The clean skies of Greece had left her unprepared for the sudden exposure to the warm wind and claustrophobia of the London Underground, and the pollution of the streets above.

'There you go; yeah, you're all right. Get some grub inside you love, look after yerself...take care now...' the cartoon cockney backed away into the crowds muttering random clichés as he went.

'Can I get you some water? Actually...' the dark-haired woman produced a small bottle from her bag, '...have this. I can easily get another from the buffet car later.'

Senara took the water gratefully and attempted to reinstate some level of health with a few long, refreshing glugs. She was shivering in the thin khaki shorts and slight broderie anglaise shirt. And then the relevance of the woman's words sank in, and she felt the panic rise.

'The train!' she cried. 'Did I miss it? The 10.06 to Penzance?'

Senara's hand touched her bag again, where her cheap advance ticket lay, potentially now useless.

'Not quite,' smiled the dark-haired woman. 'We'll just about make it if we hurry. That is, of course, if you're sure you're okay? I'm catching the same train,' she added, at seeing Senara's puzzled expression.

Senara's eyes darted frantically to the departures board, and saw that the train was indeed boarding, with just three minutes to spare.

'We'd better run,' she said.

Then swinging her rucksack with professional ease onto her back, she broke into a fast, long-legged lope towards the barrier. Her rescuer trotted along as quickly as she could a few paces behind, but struggled in impractical heels and with her large wheeled suitcase. As doors slammed and whistles blew, Senara finally located the carriage. Relaxing a little, she turned to thank her unexpected companion, hoping to put the morning's horrible incident behind her.

'Well, this is mine; thank you so much for your help,' Senara held out her hand in farewell. 'You were very kind to stay and risk missing the train.' But the woman did not take her grasp.

'Carriage D; mine too!' she said cheerfully, if appearing a little panicked herself now, as the Great Western Railway train performed its ritualistic last-chance machinations. Senara moved inside the gangway in order to let the woman board, but felt somewhat dismayed. She was not ungrateful, but had no desire to continue the association. Senara silently located her seat, and threw her rucksack deftly onto the overhead rack. The dark-haired woman struggled to balance her heavy suitcase on top of the existing stack at the end of the carriage, and then clutching her hand luggage, made her way anxiously along the rows of seats, scanning the numbers as she went. When she found it, to Senara's relief, the woman's reservation was a couple of rows ahead of her own on the other side of the aisle; too far for conversation. And the carriage was relatively packed, so there would be none of that amiable seat-swapping nonsense that had gone on aboard the cheap flight from Athens.

Just to be sure, Senara threw her handbag onto her designated seat by the window, but sat in the one next to it, naughtily hoping to prevent another passenger from sitting there. All the same, as the engines revved and the guard raised his flag and blew his whistle one last time, Senara responded to the woman's nervous backward glance with a smile and a nod. When the woman turned away again, all Senara could see was the curve of her thigh, the black skirt and tights, and sophisticated, heeled shoes. Senara regarded her own footwear and once more felt like an alien. She wore the most basic of Greek sandals: a sole of leather strapped to her foot by a criss-crossing cord of soft suede that was then wound and tied around her ankles. Her bare nut-brown feet and toes had been beaten clean; exfoliated by years of sea and sand. Senara could not conceive of ever again wearing a constricting pair of nylon tights.

As the train finally began to slowly pull away from the Paddington platform, she shifted across to the window seat, laid her head against the window, and closed her eyes.

Five years. Five years of her life gone, and what had she to show for it, except for an admittedly hardcore tan? Yes, she had bathed in the beauty of clear azure seas, and luxuriated, sweating, in the intense heat. Her life had been an idyllic round of sunshine, good food, wine, music, and dancing. There had also been unhappiness; but in honesty, she couldn't say that Nikos had broken her heart irrevocably. But rather, his rejection had signalled the end of the party, and Senara had found herself suddenly corralled; politely excluded from his circle of friends. Except, that was, for dear Teddy, of course. In fact, it had been Teddy's enthusiasm to visit England, and London in particular; his chiding and incessant pleading to that end that had cemented Senara's decision to finally return. And where was he now, her good friend Theodoros? Shacked up for the duration in Earls Court with a bunch of hard-living Australians, that's where. The boys from Oz were fellow travellers who had visited their island, and she might have lingered longer with them all herself, had her finances allowed. But London was just a staging post for Senara. She did not consider herself English, but Cornish; and home was still a long way off.

* * *

A few rows ahead of Senara, Malory Black shifted uneasily in her seat and checked the contents of her hand luggage for the umpteenth time. Tickets, emergency cash, and a tattered wad of printed information; all there, and not, in fact, ferreted away by pixies when she wasn't looking. She sought out the books that she had carefully selected for the journey and placed them on the fold-down table in front of her. A basic *Guide to Cornwall* from the high street newsagent, and a soft-backed notebook. She looked with particular affection at her battered copy of Masefield's *Salt Water Ballads*. It had perhaps played more of a role than she might have cared to admit in her long-fantasied, romantic notion to run away to the sea. *To the Lighthouse* may have been a more pretentious choice, since she had not been able to get along with Virginia Woolf as a schoolgirl. But she was rather in love with the *idea* of it, and so felt sure that the book would now make its secrets evident to her. This five-and-a-half-hour journey was to be a time of poetic reflection on the adventure that lay ahead, and she had chosen her inspiration carefully.

Unfortunately, it appeared that she would not be allowed to gaze wistfully out of the window in quiet contemplation, since the grumpy-looking businessman in the seat next to her held his copy of The Financial Times spread wide and aloft, blocking her own meagre view. Malory seethed that this be-suited and obvious philistine had scored the window seat; especially since he showed no interest as the fast-departing hangars and industrial estates on the outskirts of the city swiftly gave way to the green fields of pastoral England. She rummaged in her bag again for a pen—well she *might* be inspired to make notes—and once again touched her hand to the tickets, her purse. The businessman made silent irritated movements to show his displeasure at her close fretful proximity. She looked back to where the pretty blonde who had fainted sat alone, and wondered if she should move and talk to her? It might take her mind off things...

But she didn't want to talk to anyone. She wanted to think her thoughts and dream her dreams, and it was all being spoilt.

Relax, Malory, she told herself. *It's done now. You are on the train and you will just have to see it through*. Oh my god, she was on the train. She had very nearly missed it, and for a minute had been tempted to think it an omen; a sign that she should turn around and forget the whole madcap notion. But she was on the train. It was nothing. People changed their lives all the time. She was just re-locating that was all; going to live in Cornwall for a while. And if it didn't work out then she could just come back again. She had options. Nobody could actually make her stay. But her heart lurched at the thought of that first strange night that lay ahead. Would she shop for basic supplies and eat alone in the small, alien, flat that awaited her? Or dare she venture out for a meal and a drink, equally alone?

It had been some years since Malory had stepped forth to brave the world, and it saddened her that her life had taken such a prosaic path. After all, the girl of her youth had been an expectant, eager, and yes, adventurous spirit. She had climbed Ben Nevis for heaven's sake, and Snowdon too. She had paddled canoes around the lakes of Cumbria and camped under the stars. She had backpacked around the Mediterranean without a care for the next day; confident, hopeful, and *alive*. But somewhere along the way she had become cowed and unsure. It sometimes felt that she was cursed to endure an unfulfilled life. It began with her name: *Malory*. Well, there was no escaping its roots. Like malaise or malady, it signified foreboding. Even her surname, *Black*, hinted at the macabre. But she was on the train. She had taken a step into the unknown for the first time in years. And as she was propelled at top speed far away from London and all that she knew, Malory shivered in excitement and fear.

* * *

At Reading, the carriage was invaded by crowds of passengers, and polite altercations ensued over reserved seats that had been illicitly appropriated. A young man who had been scanning the aisles, and clearly anxious not to have to stand in the space between carriages all the way to Cornwall, with the overflowing rubbish bins and the toilet doors in constant use, suddenly smiled at Senara.

'Is this seat taken?' he asked whilst simultaneously glancing at the seat reservation display. It would have been hard for Senara to lie, and besides, he had an inoffensive enough look about him. And observing the pale face of a beleaguered-looking man with an open can of cider in his hand also looking around for a seat, it looked as though her solitude might have been interrupted by someone far less appealing. Meekly returning the smile, she removed her bag from the adjacent seat and allowed the man to occupy the confined space next to her.

Malory Black, delighted that the grumpy businessman had left the train, and noticing that it was not booked for the rest of the journey, shuffled across to the window seat. This was better. Now she would be able to lose herself in the green fields of England; hopefully to spy one of the giant white horse images carved into the chalk hills of Wiltshire; to gaze dreamily upon the boats on the River Exe...

However, her space was immediately invaded. A woman, who had boarded with her two young daughters, shouted at one of them to grab the seats in front of her. And then glaring at Malory with an evil eye, shoved the other child into the seat beside her.

The train had barely left Reading before the girl in front turned kneeling on her chair to face Malory, and peered at her eagerly before speaking:

'What's your name?'

'Um, it's Malory.'

'Ma-lor-y.' The child repeated as though consciously downloading the information. 'My name's Lottie. My sister's name is Lexie. Malory glanced to her right, where little Lexie sat too close, pudgy-faced and staring vacantly at her.

'We're going to Cornwall,' continued Lottie, as Lexie distractedly leant against Malory's arm. 'Malory, are you going to Cornwall?'

'Erm, yes.'

'We're going to Cornwall too. Malory, how old are you? Do you have a boyfriend, Malory? I've got a boyfriend.'

The child could not have been more than about twelve. Malory answered politely and looked to their mother for some assistance, some supervision. But the woman was intoning loudly into her mobile phone about how they had caught the train and yes, it *had* just left Reading; the little buggers had been up all night and she was going to swipe one of them before long. They'd had sausage rolls and coke at the station, but she'd left her fags on the table. The mother stood up in the aisle as if to receive a better signal or, as Malory suspected, to better provide a greater audience with the benefit of hearing the meticulous details of her trip thus far. The back of her silver bomber jacket was stitched fancifully with the words 'Hard Bitch'. Lexie's eyelids drooped, and her head nodded as she began to lean more heavily on Malory's arm.

'Malory, why don't you have a boyfriend?' Lottie's candid gaze assessed Malory's appearance, as she rested her chin on folded arms on the chair back. 'I've had loads of boyfriends. But I really love Joey. Have you got any gum, Malory?'

'Er, no,' Malory desperately fumbled through the pages of *To the Lighthouse*.

'I've got some gum. Do you want some? Malory...'

Clearly it was going to be an even longer journey than anticipated.

* * *

'I'm *so* glad I picked the right seat!' The young man in the seat next to Senara turned and whispered in the direction of her ear. His eyes danced brightly in the direction of the unfortunate Malory, before turning to alight on Senara's own. She shyly met his affable grin and could not help but smile back.

He was plain-looking. Not tall enough and too slight of build to normally be attractive to her. He had a long thin nose and sandy, curly hair that he kept cropped close. He whispered again, 'I have a feeling we are going to be subject to Hard Bitch's story for the duration...'

Sure enough, Hard Bitch was frantically stabbing out yet another mobile number with immaculately manicured nails, before beginning the story again. *...yeah, they'd caught the train. Steve had taken the car, but there was no room for them after they'd packed all the suitcases and stuff. The little buggers were driving her mad and she was going to swipe one of them in a minute...*

'I wonder which one she means to swipe?' said Senara under her breath to the young man. 'Do you think there's a judicial process or is it a random swipe?'

As the train sped further across the lush Wiltshire landscape, Senara and the young man both settled into reading their books, doing their best, as were the other immediate passengers, to ignore the increasingly frightful performance and interrogation going on a few rows away. Occasionally one or other of them made a comment on the view, and the man offered to fetch Senara a coffee from the buffet car. At first, she was hesitant. She knew the rules about strangers and drinks. But the man looked so respectable, and harmless. Already missing the laid-back camaraderie of the European crowd in Greece, she decided to trust.

'I'm Brian, by the way,' he said upon his return, holding out the paper cup to her.

'Senara,' she replied, expecting it to elicit the usual response, and her practised answer. But Brian did not pronounce it unusual.

'After St Senara?' he asked. 'From the church at Zennor?'

'That's right,' she said, impressed. 'You must be Cornish, then.'

'No, but I live in Truro. And I've visited Penwith many times.'

They struck up a casual, non-committal conversation, peppered with updates and sniggers on the antics of Hard Bitch and her family. By the time they had left Exeter, Lottie was pronouncing loudly how the dark-haired woman was quite pretty really, but should try wearing a shorter skirt. Senara and Brian struggled to contain their suppressed mirth; clutching their stomachs and weeping silent, joyous tears.

* * *

Shortly after passing the length of the River Exe and Dawlish Warren, the train was immediately and spectacularly by the water's edge, as it passed along the South Devon Railway sea wall. The tide was high and the waves appeared to lap right at the carriage window. Malory could bear it no longer. She had already missed the White Horse of Westbury. Excusing herself, she squeezed past the dormant child next to her, feigning deafness to Lottie's demand:

'Malory; where are you going, Malory?'

She was met with sympathetic looks from other passengers as she made her way unsteadily along the length of the rocking, jolting carriage. In the small bending, twisting corridor between the cars she found that the window in the exit door was open, and the sweet smell of the sea breeze filled her nostrils and lifted her spirits. As the train skirted along the tide's very edge and plunged through tunnels in the sea cliffs, Malory wondered at Brunel's imagination and sheer audacity to have built these few miles of track. Light glittered on the grey English Channel, and a family, armed with buckets and spades, walked along the sea wall in the May afternoon warmth. The children turned and waved at the passing train. It was a scene of pure English seaside nostalgia, and finally Malory had a sense of having left London behind for another world entirely. She took several deep breaths of salty air and for the first time that day, a small smile crept onto her lips.

And then, with seemingly equal impulse, the train suddenly left the coast's edge and headed back inland. In no hurry to return to her seat, Malory wandered further up the train to the buffet car, where she idled away some time in the queue, before ordering an unappetizing-looking sandwich and a small individual-sized bottle of champagne. Then remembering her plight, she quickly ordered an additional bottle for when she would have to eventually return to her seat. She remained in the buffet car as she munched half-heartedly on her sandwich, watching as the idyllic fields of Newton Abbot and Totnes, and the high peaks of Dartmoor gave way to the grey-housed terraces and dockyards of Plymouth.

You were never far from somewhere, she thought.

There were still cities, with all their industry and commerce, even in the midst of bucolic Devon. She made her way back to her spot by the open window and was irked to see that a couple of teenagers now lurked there, but thankfully they did not seem interested in the view, but were content to sit on their bags, rocking gently with the rhythm of the train, and texting on their phones. Malory repositioned herself by the door as before.

And then the banks of the River Tamar were in view, and without warning, the train abruptly, and with practised ease, dropped its speed to a crawl. Peering as far as she dared through the open window, Malory saw they were approaching the Royal Albert Bridge, which spanned the breadth of the Tamar between Devon and Cornwall.

'*...almost entirely separated from the rest of England by the Tamar*,' Malory recalled from her *Guide to Cornwall*.

She raised her eyes to read, as the inscription in stone 'I. K. BRUNEL, ENGINEER, 1859' passed slowly overhead. The train creaked and rolled past the iron trusses of the bridge at an unnaturally careful pace, bringing a peculiar silence. Malory looked down far below her at the giddying sight of the many small sailing boats; their masts twinkling in the afternoon sun. She saw the front carriages curl away in front of her, as the long train made its processional crossing from Devon into Cornwall. And although reason told her the slow amble across the water was obviously a safety precaution, there was something ceremonial implied in the majestic, respectfully slow passage from one world into the next.

'Bye, London,' she whispered to herself as she twisted the cork on the champagne bottle, and then glugged from its neck.

Having safely eased its length across the water to Saltash, the train immediately picked up speed again, and Malory was just in time to see the boarded sign flying past that read: 'Welcome to Cornwall', and repeated underneath in an ancient language 'Kernow a'gas dynergh'.

* * *

A few carriages back Senara fell silent, and as if sensing her change in mood, her temporary companion became diplomatically engrossed in his book. Senara shuddered as the conductor announced in turn over the loudspeaker, the connecting stations: *Liskeard for Looe, Par for Newquay, Truro for Falmouth...* The train journey became more laborious now, stopping more frequently after the fast escape from London. Green fields and yellow gorse, small towns with quaint railway stations, forests, rivers and moors; it was all familiar. But this was not yet Senara's Cornwall. There was still a long way to go before they reached the west; the west of

Senara's childhood and formative years. The *wild* west. And yet time appeared to quicken as her destination loomed ever nearer. She stared sullenly from the window and her heart was full.

Gradually, the train emptied of passengers. The man called Brian left the train at Truro. As he stretched for his bag on the luggage rack overhead, Lottie could be overheard loudly asking that poor woman, who had returned to her seat, for a sip of her champagne. He wished Senara good luck for the rest of the journey, delivered with a knowing smile and a wink, and then he was gone. Senara hastily replaced her bag on the vacated chair. She was unlikely to be so lucky should another passenger join her. She paused at the word: *lucky*...

Was she unlucky in love? Or did she just make bad decisions? She thought about the man who had just left the train. He was friendly, charming, utterly likeable. Why could she never find herself someone like that? Someone nice, someone... *Normal.* She daydreamed for a while of how it would be to have a relationship not marked by drama, trauma, or heartbreak; but instead, a stable, easy friendship. She thought of all the pleasant but ordinary suitors she had firmly, if kindly, rejected in the past; choosing instead the more dangerously attractive types. Like Nikos. Like Grady O'Keefe.

Senara felt the icy chill of adrenalin course her veins at the thought of him, and her hand raised compulsively, to fiddle nervously with the top of her right ear.

Even now, after all these years, Senara was apprehensive at the thought of their paths crossing again. Quickly, she cleared her mind of his lurking shadow and vowed in future to consider any plain and normal admirers who might happen to come her way.

* * *

Hard Bitch and her wretched offspring alighted from the train at Camborne. Lottie looked dejected at being forced to leave her new best friend, and despite her relief, Malory found it strangely affecting. The remaining passengers stopped short of breaking into a cheer, but Malory could sense their empathy as she regained her personal space. She tried to collect her thoughts, which were now somewhat blunted by the champagne. *Almost there.* Her time for contemplation was to be short.

* * *

Senara and Malory were amongst a handful of passengers who left the Penzance train at St Erth. Temporarily confused, Malory opted to follow the others as they crossed the old-fashioned canopied footbridge that led across to the other platforms, struggling to haul her heavy suitcase up and down the steps. The departed train left the quaint station silent and still in the May afternoon, and Malory noticed the birdsong, and the hedgerow flowers, coloured fuchsia and tangerine. And there were palm trees. Malory gaped at the strange, exotic sight as the leaves gently rustled in the warm breeze.

An L-shaped granite ticket office and café cradled the terminal branch line, which was separated from the main line by an old semaphore signal box that stood towards the East. But there was no sign yet of the connecting train, and Malory took a moment to browse the old railway posters in the café. They promised 'Glorious Sands', 'Ideal Bathing', and other delights of the Cornish Riviera. The unpretentious café had proper wooden tables and chairs, and sold fresh tea in pots, with cake. It was a world apart from London stations with their pre-packaged food, and livid plastic or cold metal seating. She glanced at her phone: another five minutes until the train arrived.

She bought some postcards from the café, and then wandered into the spacious ticket office and found the sparsely decorated ladies' bathroom. There was nobody about, and her heels echoed loudly on the floor tiles. In the silence of the bathroom, she stared at her reflection in the mirror. She knew no one. Malory, who knew all about loneliness, had never felt more isolated.

She emerged again in time to see the small train approach the junction and stop gently before the terminal buffers. She found herself once again boarding a carriage alongside the girl with the glorious long hair, who had fainted, way back in Paddington; in another world.

Senara smiled awkwardly in recognition. 'Sit on the right-hand side of the carriage,' she advised.

'Oh?' said Malory in puzzlement.

'You'll see..' said Senara.

Obediently, Malory found a forward-facing seat by the window. Senara sat down opposite her, out of politeness for their earlier connection.

The little train wasted no time. Immediately the few passengers were on board, it set off again, returning along the line that had brought it. The two women sat quietly, each engrossed in their own thoughts as they gazed at the view of the Hayle estuary, and the variety of birds picking around the salt marshes at Lelant. And then the mouth of the estuary appeared with the bay beyond.

Malory was on her feet. Her fingers were spread on the barrier of the carriage window and her expression could not have been more childlike had she had her nose pressed against the glass. Senara raised a weary eyebrow, but even she, despite her acquaintance, had to acknowledge the spectacle of the scenery as the train rolled past Porthkidney Sands; a vast stretch of empty, pristine beach. Water the colour of the palest green sea-glass lapped at the white-gold shore, turning azure in the deeper water, and then stretching towards the horizon, an intense cobalt blue. Godrevy lighthouse appeared in the distance on its island rock, a defending knight against the ocean.

'But... This is so beautiful,' Malory said aloud. 'I can't believe it's England...'

'It's not,' said Senara, instinctively, before remembering to smile, to show no animosity. But Malory caught enough of a glint in the sky-blue eyes to understand: Cornwall was a nation; a land apart.

The train passed through the grass-covered sand dunes, and then on towards Carbis Bay, hugging the edge of the cliffs. Precipitous headlands of dense green foliage plunged to meet the sea in craggy rocks and caves, and sailboats dotted the dreamlike bay. Finally, their destination was in sight. Malory sat down again and took in the vision of the fast-approaching, and final promontory. The *Guide to Cornwall* had described it as the 'jewel in Cornwall's crown', but in this case, the hackneyed phrase did justice to the reality. Senara, after one cursory look, turned in her seat with her back to the sight, and took a deep breath.

Shortly afterwards, the two women walked in silence together along the single platform that led to the car park overlooking Porthminster Beach; Senara lost in thought, and Malory still muted by the view; by the sheer assault on her senses. They stopped by the wall near the station entrance, overlooking The Warren, and the colourful parasols on the outside decking of the Pedn Olva Hotel. Before them was the curved line of the harbour, and the small peninsula of land that stretched precariously out into the ocean. A patchwork clutter of buildings vied for space in these lowlands known as 'Downalong', and piled up in terraces on Barnoon Hill to the west. Slate rooftops, yellowed with lichen, contrasted against the vast blue sky. And all around, the ocean gleamed, dazzling and perfect against golden beaches.

It was a mirage; a magical town built on sand, that would surely be reclaimed by the sea and the mists. For the second time that day, Malory smiled; a genuine heartfelt smile. Maybe it was going to be all right.

Senara took in the scene with different eyes. It was magnificent, of course, but the familiarity swept away the previous five years in an instant.

St Ives. Stunning, spectacular St Ives. But every crooked corner, and narrow cobbled street; every rock on the beach, or boat in the harbour, was known to her; was held deep down in the core of her. It was all still here, like a painting; unchanging, preserved.

'My name's Malory.'

The woman who had seemingly stalked her all the way from London was holding out her hand to Senara, in a most formal and old-fashioned manner.

'Senara.' She took the grasp briefly and gave a light-hearted tug.

'Lovely name,' said Malory, the ill-boded one. When Senara did not respond, she grabbed the handle of her wheeled suitcase again. 'Well, I'm off. Don't suppose you've been here before? I need to find Fore Street. Well, the High Street first, to pick up some keys. I thought I'd got it all worked out on Google maps, but now I'm here it all looks so confusing.'

Senara gave a wry smile. 'Yes, I've been here before.'

She gave Malory directions to the estate agents: '...straight down Tregenna Hill, past Skidden Hill and Street-an-Pol...'

Malory nodded conscientiously throughout, but was captivated by the exotic names.

Senara glanced surreptitiously once more at Malory's too-high heels, and wondered at how inappropriate they were. How would she cope on the hills or the cobbled stones of Fore Street? She'd twist an ankle if she wasn't careful. They wished each other goodbye and then parted suddenly, abruptly. Senara turned briefly to observe Malory's departing figure, foolishly dressed in figure-hugging pencil-skirt and tights—in *May!*—and dragging the cumbersome trolley suitcase. Then she turned in the opposite direction towards the granite steps that lead down to The Warren.

'Picturesque' was a word applied to much of St Ives, and The Warren was no exception. Many of the small cottages lining what had once been the site of a tin mine on the rocky Pedn Olva outcrop, were now either holiday lets or small but charming bed and breakfast houses. Senara strolled down the narrow street with a heart heavy with regret. Every step took her one further into the past, and one more away from her break for freedom. Each step unravelled the past five years in Greece and took her back to everything that she knew and understood—and everything that she had tried to escape from.

As she neared the harbour and the strong briny smell of the seaweed hit her, she was jolted unwillingly to another time. There were so many memories; people she knew. It would be quite a feat if she were to complete her homeward-bound trek unrecognised, and undisturbed by salutation.

Yet surprisingly, she passed un-accosted along Lambeth Walk before the Church, past the lifeboat house, and then Wharf Road, where any number of unseen eyes could be upon her from the numerous bars and cafés. Then came the most dangerous part; past The Barquentine, or 'The Barque', as the gang used to call it. She wondered if they all still gathered there... It was situated on the first floor above a shop, and Senara kept her head down as she passed beneath its distinctive windows.

Further hazard awaited at The Sloop Inn, the ancient harbourside pub. On a sunny afternoon like this, many would be gathered on the seats outside. She was surprised to have made it this far without being seen; without being stopped by some well-meaning, but know-it-all local, who would announce her return to one and all. She slunk quickly past the pub, and made her way through the labyrinthine back streets of Downalong towards home.

And then she was there. As she stood under the much-photographed street sign, Senara hesitated and lifted her eyes to the same words that she had stood beneath five years ago and sworn her goodbyes.

Teetotal Street.

The chastising Wesleyan admonishment brought back a host of memories that she had haughtily aspired to escape from. And now, like the bad girl that she was, she was back, tail between her legs, looking for help. But worse than that, as Senara gazed at the sign, she realised that nothing had changed; and that her heart was still filled with the same disturbing feeling:

That there was something missing.

CHAPTER 2

The Barque

In a darkened nook of The Barquentine, Dan Hosking stared at his pint of Doom thinking that the name perfectly summarised his mood.

'I'm woebegone,' he said.

'It's your own fault, you know,' said Kit, without looking at him, but staring straight ahead and sipping on his own glass of beer.

'How's that?' said Dan gloomily. 'What am I doing wrong? They all seem great to start with. I reckon I'm just one of life's losers.'

'You should be more discerning,' said Kit. 'A woman only has to look at you, and you go bounding after her like a lovesick puppy. You don't stop to think: What's she like? Will we get on? Do we have common interests?'

'But I know what I like...' protested Dan.

'Yes, you do. You know what you like to look at. And then you stop thinking.'

'You're harsh, Kitto.'

'He's right though,' Dan's brother Zack piped in with a wink. 'Add to that, you fancy anything and anyone.'

'I do not!'

'You do,' Kit and Zack chorused together.

'That last one was a freak,' continued Zack. 'Don't think I've ever seen such rouged cheeks. And the way she, sort of, drew her eyebrows on. She looked like some kind of scary doll.'

'Well, I thought she was cute,' said Dan unconvincingly. There was a pause as they all took another glug of beer or stared aimlessly around the dark wood-panelled bar.

'Except she did use to creep out of bed like, really early,' mused Dan. 'To do...well I don't know what. But I don't think I ever saw what she really looked like.'

'Ha! And do you remember the one from the summer disco?' Zack grinned. 'What a psycho.'

'She was not!' Dan spluttered. 'Well, not to start with anyway. And it was nice to be wanted. It was sweet that she called all the time to check I was all right. But, yeah okay, texting Mum daily, telling her what we'd been up to was a bit random. And I will admit, calling the lifeboat out that time was unforgiveable.'

Kit and Zack did not snigger or grin this time but said nothing. They were both volunteer lifeboatmen, and pretending to be stranded in a dinghy in two-foot of calm water was no joke.

'What you need,' said Kit eventually, 'is a set of rules. You are seemingly so overcome with latent desire, that you are incapable of making sensible judgments.'

'Now it's getting interesting!' Zack said, slamming his beer glass down on the wooden table. 'You're right Kitto, he needs help; needs to learn the basics. Oy, Tamsin!' Zack raised his burly arm towards their friend who worked behind the bar. 'Got a pen and paper? We need to make Dan a list here...'

'I'm kind of busy right now,' said Tamsin, as she pulled at the beer handle. But then, with a thought to the huddle of expectant visitors standing before her at the bar added, 'But I'll be right with you...*my luvvers*!' and winked at her three mates.

Seeing that John, the bar manager, was similarly occupied, Zack grumbled and returned to his beer.

'Well, I was thinking more of Dan compiling his own thoughts,' said Kit. 'You know, try to learn from past experience.'

'Oh, give over,' scoffed Zack. 'That's the trouble; he never learns from his past mistakes; he keeps repeating them over and over, and adding new ones just to complicate matters. Seriously, he needs help.'

'I'm right *here*,' mumbled Dan.

'Hmm, maybe,' said Kit, ignoring him and rubbing his beard. But he looked unsure. 'I still think these things should be organic; instinctive. When I said a set of rules, I meant a mental one; one that can be adjusted and adapted. Making written lists is a bit, well, formulaic. It's too rigid; doesn't allow for spontaneity.'

'I thought we were agreed that spontaneity is exactly Dan's problem,' said Zack. He turned and yelled towards the bar area again. 'Tamsin! Pen and paper please, my love?'

When Tamsin glared again, Zack leapt up from his stool, cheerfully barged his way past the tourists, and draped himself across the bar. When she could stand his irritatingly beaming grin no longer, Tamsin took a moment to throw a notepad and pen in his direction, before returning to her customers. Swiftly re-seated, Zack slapped and rubbed his hands together and looked expectantly at Kit.

'Right, what shall we call it?'

'Eh?' said Kit.

'It's got to have a title. Give it more… I dunno, seriousness. Importance…'

'Gravitas?' suggested Kit.

'That's it. Gravitas,' said Zack, jabbing his pen in the air in Kit's direction. 'Can't just write a *list*; a list with no title, that'd get forgotten about.'

Kit's sardonic, raised eyebrow was lost on him.

'I didn't think you were actually serious!' Dan piped in, and looking worried.

'Shush, I'm thinking...' said Zack. 'Ah, got it!' He bent over the notepad and scribbled three words in capital letters which he then emphatically underlined. For gravitas.

Kit and Dan craned their heads to read the title.

It said: *WHAT MEN WANT*.

'Ha!' said Kit with a grin. 'Succinct.'

'What Men Want?' Dan looked dubious. 'Where exactly is this headed?'

'It's like that film. You know, *What Women Want*, only in reverse,' explained Zack.

'Or, "What does a woman want?" as Freud asked first,' said Kit. 'But never mind, carry on. Don't reckon Freud knew anyway.'

'This will be *our* turn. Let's make a list of what we men want from a woman,' said Zack.

'But you're happily married!' said Dan. 'You only have to write one word: *Mandy*.'

Zack did not answer but kept his eyes steadily on the expectant white page before him. Then carefully, he wrote:

1. Must be hot.

'No, no, you can't write that, much too vague,' said Kit. 'That won't help Dan at all. You're going to have to be more specific. And besides, beauty is in the eye of the beholder and all that.'

'I don't mean beautiful, I mean hot,' said Zack. 'Beautiful was going to be my number 2.'

'Look, if you want this to read like some sexist tripe from a slavering lad's mag, then go ahead,' said Kit. 'But this could be an opportunity to examine what you really want from a relationship. This could develop into a significantly profound exploration, if you let it.'

Zack and Dan's eyes met; they could never be sure if Kit was taking the piss.

'Look at it this way,' continued Kit. 'Think of all the things you *don't* want from a woman, and work from there... Although I still have my doubts about encouraging this.'

'I don't want her to nag,' said Zack, scribbling furiously.

'You're *married*,' Dan reminded Zack again, with some disdain. 'I thought this was supposed to be for me.'

The others continued, disregarding him.

'Okay, well that's a starting point,' said Kit. 'Work it back. What you really mean is that you *do* want someone you can have open and honest discussion with; where you don't feel that you're always running away.'

'I do?' Zack scowled.

'Yes,' Kit sighed. 'Write it down, if you're going to.' Observing the brothers' confusion, Kit grabbed the notepad and pen and crossing out Zack's entries, quickly wrote:

1. Openness and honesty.

When he was met with looks of disappointment, he relented and added:

2. Sexually appealing.

They were men, after all.

'Can she wear mini-skirts and low-cut tops?' asked Dan hopefully, draining his pint and starting to look a little flushed.

'No!' Kit shook his head in despair. 'That's *too* specific.'

'But... I really like breasts. And legs....' Dan moped.

Three of the visitors who had been at the bar sat down at the opposing long table and smiled and nodded at the locals.

'Alright lads?' one of them called amiably. Kit flicked a long-lashed look at their jaunty sea-faring caps and spanking new fisherman's jumpers, but nodded back, alongside the others' begrudging, grunting replies.

'Talking breast or leg man, are we?' said another one of the intruders. 'Never can decide myself...' He leered.

'How about,' said Zack, ignoring him, 'she can reveal either her cleavage, or her legs, but not both at the same time? No tarts.'

Kit sighed, but on the notepad, he changed the last entry to read: '*Sexually appealing, but classy.*'

'And should I go for blondes, brunettes, or redheads?' Dan asked.

Kit looked at Dan's candid big-eyed expression and realised that he was not joking. He shook his head again and his deep-voiced chuckle turned heads at the bar. Why was he taking this so seriously? Dan was hopeless. It couldn't hurt to help him out a bit. Kit considered for another moment, then said,

'I tell you what, mate, get me another drink and *I* will write the list. But you must promise to stick to it. It might seem tough, but I fear it's the only way forward. Well?'

Dan frowned. 'Can't Astrid just set me up with one of her mates? Wouldn't that be easier?'

'No. No blind dates; asking for disaster,' said Kit firmly. 'And besides, I don't want my girlfriend complaining that you've broken the heart of one of her best friends when it all goes horribly wrong.'

Lurching slightly but filled with ale-fuelled bonhomie, Dan slapped Kit on the back as he rose.

'Okay then, it's a deal. You write the list, and I'll stick to it. You've never had trouble finding the ladies so I guess you know what's what... Another pint, Zacky?'

As Dan approached the counter, Tamsin Doble was already pulling the first of three more pints of Doom Bar. He smiled that unsure, self-conscious half-smile of his, and Tamsin thought that if it were up to her, she would shred that stupid list they were making. Tamsin knew exactly what it was that Dan Hosking needed, the great lumbering fool; and it wasn't one of Astrid Martin's flaky friends.

The black wood-panelled door of the bar opened and a younger man, breezed in. He was casually dressed in skinny black jeans and a grey T-shirt, but carried himself with the confidence of a rock star. He bore a canvas backpack, carelessly slung over one shoulder. With hands in pockets and a leisurely back-kick of his heel, the door was banged shut again. Despite immediately noticing the three be-capped sailing-types at one table, Jago Berryman knew the rules: keep the back bar as private as possible, for as long as possible. Inevitably as the season progressed, it would become filled up with tourists, and too busy to even contemplate. But for the moment, any further invaders might be intimidated by the firmly shut door and the consequent eyes upon them if they dared to enter.

'Hi guys,' said Jago cheerfully, to Kit and Zack. 'How do I find you all on this wonderful day?' Then spotting Dan at the bar called, 'Grab me an OJ while you're there, would you mate? With ice.'

'Someone's stoked,' said Zack.

'You are not wrong, my friend,' said Jago, straddling the bench at their table, and throwing his bag on the floor. 'It was all clean glassy peelers on Mother 'Meor this morning. So, after some excellent surfing, I am at one with the world today. Although...'

'Let me guess, itching to get back in the water already,' laughed Zack.

Jago grimaced. 'I've heard there's some swell happening down south this evening, might try to get on it... What's Kit up to?' he said, observing Kit hunched over a notepad and apparently deep in thought.

'Writing a list,' explained Zack. 'A list of essential qualities; trying to steer Dan away from evil women; set him on course for true love.'

'Oh right, you mean like a mythical woman,' Jago joked. 'But a list? It's a bit clinical, isn't it?'

'Trust me, he needs to learn. He's a grown man already,' Kit muttered without looking up.

'Yeah, thanks for recognising that fact...' said Dan, returning from the bar with the drinks, 'though you'd hardly know it the way you lot treat me...'

'Well, she ought to be a surfer...' said Jago, between sips of orange juice. '...And look hot in a wetsuit, of course.'

'Believe it or not, there is a world that exists outside of surfing,' said Kit, finally looking up. 'There are fine, well-balanced people who have never surfed and never will. They are still worthy of consideration.'

Jago's expression was one of wounded disillusionment. 'What's happened to you, Brother? You used to be the coolest dude around these parts. You hardly even surf nowadays...'

'Yes, I do,' said Kit quietly.

'Yeah, but not like you used to. You could have been a pro. Now you just mess about on boats all day like...like it's not in your blood anymore!'

Kit abandoned the notepad and leant into the back of the wooden settle, observing his friend's look of incomprehension with amusement.

'Those boats happen to be my livelihood,' he said. 'I don't accuse you of messing about with your barrow,' he added, referring to the portable stall that Jago used for street trading.

'But you're losing it, Kit. Seriously you need to get back in the water.'

'Jago, you make it sound like I never surf. And I am on the water, every day. Just think of a boat as an extended surfboard...'

'Ah no; it's not the same,' said Jago. 'On a boat, you're not *in* the water. You're spending the whole time trying *not* to be in the water. You can't be at one with the waves.'

'I'm with the young fellow,' interjected one of the sailing types. 'Once surfing's in your blood it's there to stay. I'm hooked, myself.'

'Hey,' said Jago, suddenly defensive. 'You don't know who you're talking to. Kit is a legend, a soul surfer of the highest order. That's why...' he turned to stare pointedly at Kit again, 'it's such a bummer that he doesn't appear to care anymore.'

'I do care,' said Kit softly, with a smile.

'This man,' continued Jago, ignoring him and turning to admonish the incomer again, 'was so cool he used to surf naked. And I don't mean in the warm waters of like, Bali, or Costa Rica, but right here in Cornwall.'

Kit looked amused.

'No kidding?' said the sailor-type. 'There's really no need you know. They've made great advances in wetsuit technology these days...'

His friends sniggered into their drinks.

Kit eyed the man appraisingly. He was middle-aged, but lean and well-groomed in the way that only came from money and pampering. He knew his name was Olly, but he was well-known around town as Olly-down-from-London; a second-home owner and regular visitor. His superior tone and jolly sense of entitlement was grating, but otherwise he had a pleasant enough manner, and there was no reason to judge him anything but decent in character.

'I didn't *always* surf naked, that's a myth,' he said, grinning. 'There was that one time, but that was for charity.'

'Ha! I distinctly remember when I was younger you lot all going off for summer moonlight sessions,' Jago continued his berating. 'You and Senara and the gang. And if you weren't completely naked, you were near as. At one with the water... See?'

Kit laughed again. 'That may be true... I think there was a heatwave at the time.'

'Well, all the same, I'm sticking to my wetsuit, chaps,' said Olly, raising his glass of beer in salute.

'What board do you ride?' Kit asked, by way of appeasement.

He told them.

Their merriment was barely contained.

'All the gear...' said Zack into his pint.

'...but no idea,' finished Jago.

It was enough for the trio of Londoners to let some small degree of irritation ruffle their confidence.

'Well, you locals will always know best, I'm sure,' said Olly. 'And I don't suppose for a minute that jealousy or resentment comes into it. Personally, I see no shame in being able to afford the best equipment. I like to think it enhances my performance on the water.'

'*Performance*?' Kit spluttered, his smile now incredulous, yet still amicable. 'There is no room for freedom in *performance*. That's why I was never interested in being a pro. Surfing is for the soul, not for competition.'

'Yeah, that's true...' said Jago thoughtfully. 'But what about the greats, like Kelly Slater? Not to mention all the local lads who've got sponsorship...'

'Sure, good luck to them,' said Kit. 'They're making a living out of what we love. But for the rest of us; well for me at least...'

'As I thought...' interrupted Olly, looking at his friends in turn. He didn't have to say it again; the implication was there in his tone: the conviction that they were jealous.

Jago looked hopefully at Kit, willing him to be incensed. For once. But when he spoke, Kit's voice was measured and his smile remained fixed. Only a barely perceptible raising of his voice ensured that the men on the other table would hear him.

'To answer your question, Jago, of course I still love surfing. It just seems to me that for something that is supposed to be so free-spirited, it's become increasingly infested with an awful element of snobbery and commercialism. John Betjeman surfing an old wooden belly-board in the North Atlantic, wearing nothing more than a pair of shorts; now *that's* free. Investing a small fortune in high-tech neoprene is not. Mixing things up a bit is good, for sure. Explore different boards; go retro, old school; try new progressive. But keep in mind the *stoke*. The minute you start competing with the next guy over boards and suits, you don't understand what it's about.'

Jago beamed happily. *Of course Kit was not lost.* How indeed could he have doubted him?

'So, you're saying,' said Olly, 'that if I offered you my board right now, for free, you wouldn't take it? Even knowing how much it's worth?'

'No,' said Kit.

Olly made a 'pfft' sound, his eyes scornful with disbelief.

'What it's worth,' Kit continued calmly, 'is subjective. What you paid for it, irrelevant. I currently have nine boards in my quiver; each one selected for its merits. I love my boards; but I couldn't even tell you what I paid for them, sometimes if anything. That has no bearing; it is incidental.'

'Nine boards, eh?' Olly grinned crookedly, and Kit knew instantly that he was making a mental note to expand his own collection.

'But numbers are competitive, too,' added Kit. 'Like I said, it doesn't matter if it's one ole' belly board or a shop full of sticks, so long as each one has meaning or purpose.'

'Well, this is all a bit spiritual for me,' Olly smiled in a pacifying way. 'It's just a sport, as far as I'm concerned.'

'And *that*, is precisely, where you don't get it,' said Jago.

'Well, there's room for us all in the ocean anyway,' said Olly. 'Now, how about a drink, lads? My shout?'

'No, there isn't,' muttered Jago under his breath. 'And don't be dropping in on *my* wave with your great big fancy board.'

The wooden door to the bar burst open again, and they all looked up to check out the brave interloper. A grubby overcoat, despite the sunny weather, coupled with fingerless gloves and signature tweed trilby hat, complete with feather, instantly confirmed the newcomer as known, if not entirely desirable. Bill Negus was a local 'eccentric'; a self-professed playwright, poet, and artist, who was indeed sometimes found lurking around the fringes of the September Festival. But he was more usually situated on a barstool in The Barque, regaling gullible tourists with his tales of grandeur. His entrance, as ever, entailed more fuss than was necessary, as he protractedly removed coat, hat, and scarf, and grumpily eyed each of the clientele in turn as if to assess how he would deliver this day's performance. Nevertheless, on this occasion, it served the purpose of quashing the brewing argument.

'Mister Curnow,' he addressed Kit in loud theatrical tones, 'I do believe I espied a shoal of mackerel to the direct North-North-East of Smeaton's Pier. If you choose to leave them for the seals whilst you consume ale, I can only suppose your environmental leanings to be operative this day.'

He proceeded to fold his overcoat into an unnecessarily small bundle, with brow knitted, and lips pursed in disapproval.

'Afternoon, Bill,' said Kit brightly in response. Others mumbled similar greetings.

Olly got up and greeted the older man with a handshake. 'Bill! Good to see you again, my friend. Just arrived today! Great to be back. I was just about to get a round of drinks. Can I persuade you...? Port, isn't it?'

Bill took his hand and nodded gravely. Just the barest smile of recognition curled at one corner of his lip. Happy at such an immediate result, he situated himself in an ungainly fashion on a high stool at one end of the bar, his over-folded coat resting on his lap and his arms crossed on top of that. He would be there for the night, if he was lucky.

'Mister Berryman,' he announced from his perch to where Jago sat. 'I had not heard word that your sister was returning to us?'

Dan nudged Jago to grab his attention.

'Young Senara. *Your* old friend, Mister Curnow,' continued Bill loftily. 'I saw her myself in the harbour less than an hour ago. She was very, very brown.' With a look of distaste, he raised Olly's proffered glass of port to his lips and partook elegantly.

'Is that right, Jago?' said Kit. 'Is Snow back?'

'Not that I know about,' Jago answered. 'But then that would be just like her. Are you sure it was Senara, Bill?'

'Yesss,' said Bill in a drawn-out manner, and nodding wearily. 'Long-legged filly of a girl. All that loose blonde hair. And as I said, most tanned. I'm not sure it's at all becoming.'

Digesting the information, Jago reached for his backpack and rummaged inside for his phone. Sure enough, when he found it amongst the sketchbooks and pencils, there was both a missed call and a message from his sister.

'Looks like Bill's right,' he said. 'Senara's back in town. She's at the house right now. I'd better go.' He departed amidst murmurings of puzzlement and farewell.

'Well, there's a thing,' said Dan, once he had gone. 'Almost thought we'd never see her again.'

'Set the cat amongst the pigeons, that will,' said Zack.

'Sure will,' said someone else, as the consensus hummed around the bar. Even Tamsin, enjoying a rare break in custom, was slouched upon the counter, nodding gravely.

'Nonsense,' said Kit. 'Don't go dragging up idle gossip, now. It's all over and in the past, and not very interesting to begin with.'

But even Kit was intrigued: So... Senara was back.

A sudden influx of further customers signalled an end to their quiet session, and Kit, Zack, and Dan picked their way through the crowd, stopping to say goodbye to Tamsin and John. Outside in the warm sunshine, as they parted ways, it was Zack who suddenly remembered. Dashing back inside, he squeezed past the congregation at the bar, leaned across the newly installed occupants of the long table, and retrieved the notepad. Once outside again he paused to skip down the list that Kit had prepared for his brother, and chuckled to himself.

'Well now,' he said aloud. 'This should be entertaining...'

CHAPTER 3

Malory

Before anything else, Malory carefully unpacked the bowl from its bubble wrap and placed it on the deep sill of the shop window, right in the centre. Then she pulled up a nearby wooden chair and sat for a minute in contemplation, as people passed up and down Fore Street outside.

The stoneware bowl was simple in design; made of plain clay, but with a chocolate-coloured glaze on the inside. It was a squat cone shape with a curved rim and small pedestal. Too small to be of much use as a fruit bowl, it was, however, a charming objet d'art. When she had found it at the Portobello Road market, she had felt instinctively drawn to the bowl's pure style and beauty. The stallholder had been ignorant as to its origins, but Malory fancied it was an original Bernard Leach. The only clue to its provenance was a curved symbol etched into the base, shaped almost like a triskelion, but unevenly so, and with an extra twist on one of the curlicues. Malory could not decipher it, but knew, somehow, that she had to have the bowl. And now, placed on the window sill in St Ives, it felt right.

'Yeah, you'd better be right,' said Malory aloud, to the bowl. 'It's your fault I'm here.'

She had found the deli on Fore Street on the way to the shop, and had bought basic supplies and fresh local produce of fruit, artisan bread, and cheeses called Yarg and Trelawney. But she only nibbled at them, feeling compelled to go outside and explore. She thought she might visit The Sloop Inn on the harbour front; a suggestion from the *Guide to Cornwall.* A large, stiff drink might just help her relax. She changed quickly from her travelling clothes, into a simple, tailored summer dress and pretty, heeled sandals, then headed out in the direction of the harbour.

But she did not get far, before she was tempted by the lure of a narrow, cobbled alleyway that, judging by a tantalising glimpse of blue water, appeared to be another route down to the front. Intrigued, she passed down some stone steps until, halfway along, she paused at a pair of tall and narrow wooden doors, built into the granite wall. They were painted the same bright blue as the sea-view beyond, and appeared to have no handles, but only finger-holes by which to open them. Above the doors, a sign was painted with an illustration of an antiquated sailing ship, and written in cursive letters that alluded to old pirate maps, were the words: 'The Barquentine'.

Malory stood looking in curiosity at the sign, wondering what lay beyond. It was a strange, hidden-away place to put anything that required custom. Indeed, there were no menus or such placed on the exterior to imply what business took place there. Perhaps it was a dwelling, she thought, already delighted to have found such quirkiness only steps away from the shop.

As she stood admiring the sign, the doors kicked open, and a young man, clearly in a hurry, almost fell on top of her. He caught her arms briefly to stop her from toppling in her heels.

'Whoa,' he said. 'Steady there.'

He was tall and broad-shouldered; strong-looking, without being brawny. He wore black jeans, a faded grey T-shirt that revealed a variety of tattoos on his arms, and a backpack. He stood aside, blocking the way to the harbour, and held one of the blue doors open. He gestured with his other arm fancifully, indicating a flight of wooden steps that led up inside the building. A soft breeze drifted up the alleyway from the sea, gently tousling his already dishevelled hair.

'Well?' he said. 'Are you going in, or aren't you?'

He looked at her with steady, sea-blue eyes. There was something deadpan in his manner of speech that left Malory feeling flustered; as if she were the biggest fool to ever walk the planet.

'Yes. Of course,' she said. 'Thank you.'

Why else would she be lurking aimlessly in a narrow alleyway? There was nothing for it now. She would have to enter the mysterious building, which for all she knew was a drug den or a brothel; should indeed such things exist in salubrious St Ives. But the thought was enough to make her hesitate, and the man's expression became quizzical. He squinted his eyes in a droll manner, and a sardonic half-smile pulled at the corner of his mouth.

It was extremely agitating. Particularly since Malory knew that she was behaving like a tourist; an ingenue; a newbie...

She nodded quickly as if to thank him again, and then scurried up the stairs with as much intention as she could muster. When she was halfway up, she heard the blue doors slam shut again behind her.

At the top of the stairs there was a tiny landing, with doors leading to each side. One door was painted with the word 'Fore' and the other 'Aft'. The former was opened, and she saw a large, bright room filled with people drinking and eating. The décor resembled the deck of a boat, with long slatted benches to sit on, and lifebuoys and anchors for decoration. It was noisy and bustling, and there did not appear to be a quiet corner for a lone woman to slide into, inconspicuously.

The other door, marked 'Aft' was painted black and was firmly shut. But she could hear murmurings on the other side suggesting another bar area.

'Aft it is, then,' said Malory under her breath.

This bar was much smaller than the other, and the black-painted wood panelling on the walls made it feel all the more snug, and intimate. The walls were adorned with antique prints of sailing ships, whales, and other marine creatures. Malory loved it immediately. It felt as though she had entered below deck of an old galleon ship. Leaded glass windows overlooked the harbour, and St Ives Bay glinted in the early evening sunlight.

But that's silly, thought Malory loftily. Surely this bar, facing out to sea, should be 'Fore', and the other one 'Aft'?

She spotted a vacant table, by a bay window that had been made into a cushioned settle. Quickly, she claimed the spot with her cardigan, and from her bag, a notebook and pen, which she laid upon the table. The notebook was a trick that she had devised over the years, not just for the purpose of securing a seat, but to look purposeful in the event that anyone should question or oppose her temerity at being a woman, alone, and in a pub. She knew it was shameful, and that she should not need the excuse of being absorbed in some written work. But Malory had spent too long enduring casual sexism in the City bars of London.

Some men sat at two long tables nearby, but otherwise it was not very busy. Malory headed for the bar. To her chagrin, the barman ignored her, instead serving other—male—customers before her. As more people began to arrive and fill the bar area, Malory considered her options. She could make a loud announcement that it was her turn, or she could pick up her things and slope away. Just then, the men who had been sitting at the table next to hers got up to leave. One of them stopped beside Malory at the counter, leaned over it, and called to the barmaid who had been busy restocking the fridge.

'Hey Tamsin,' he said. 'This maid is next.' He indicated Malory with a nod of his head.

As the barmaid quickly approached, Malory subtly scanned the profile of the man standing next to her. She took in the bearded, tanned face, and long, wavy hair. the He was strikingly handsome; in a weathered, Viking, kind of way.

'Thanks,' she muttered, nervously, when he caught her eye.

'Enjoy your drink,' he said, smiling, before hurrying out after his companions.

Malory could only wonder if the whole of St Ives was populated by all manner of attractive men.

'Cheers, Kit,' and 'See you later, guys,' the barmaid called Tamsin called after the departing men, before turning her attention to Malory.

'I apologise for the wait,' she said, pointedly. 'What can I get you?'

The barman looked up in surprise. 'Oh, I'm sorry,' he said. 'I thought you two were together?' He eyed the man he was serving, who stood nearby.

The man grinned, and turned to look at Malory. 'Unfortunately, not,' he said, appraising her.

Malory tried not to visibly recoil in embarrassment.

'Just because a woman stands at a bar,' Tamsin berated the barman, 'you assume she must be with a man? Honestly, John.' She rolled her eyes.

The barman called John looked abashed. 'I didn't mean... I wouldn't usually... It's just...'

'Go on...' said the barmaid, waiting with hand on hip.

'I'll just have a glass of white wine please,' said Malory timidly, hoping to diffuse the situation. 'Whatever you have that you recommend.'

Tamsin moved to the fridge and took out a bottle of wine. On her return, she glowered at John as she poured Malory's drink. 'Cat got your tongue?'

'Forgive me,' said John, to Malory. 'It's just that you looked like... Well, a Londoner. Olly was getting a round in, and I thought you were part of his group.'

The man next to Malory at the bar gave a jovial laugh.

An older man sitting on a stool at the end of the counter loudly pronounced: 'You can always tell. Londoners, that is. Just like Olly, here.'

Malory was mortified, but the man named Olly leaned in closer to her, with a practised smile. 'Don't pay any attention to old Bill,' he said. 'And let me get your drink anyway.'

'Oh, that's totally unnecessary,' said Malory quickly. Then turning to John, said: 'It was just a mistake.'

Tamsin made a scoffing sound, as she took Malory's payment.

John grinned nervously. 'You'd never know I was the boss, right? You'd think Tamsin was in charge.'

'You may be the boss, but I *am* in charge,' said Tamsin drily.

Malory gave thanks and returned to her seat. Ignoring the interested looks she still received from Olly and some of the others, she soon began to relax as she took in her surroundings, and the view from the window. The bar was cosy and inviting, and John, despite his initial mistake, had been apologetic and friendly. And the town, at first sight, appeared as beautiful as her research—and hopes—had suggested.

She stole a glance at 'Old Bill' in the corner, and wondered if she too, would indeed, grow old here. Perhaps, in years to come, this might become her 'spot' in the corner of the bar. She would be tolerated as a local oddball, a character. 'Old

Mal' they would call her. And when she was long gone, this seat by the window would become known as 'Old Mal's Chair'. It was a curious thing, to arrive in a strange town, alone, and with no clue as to how your days would unfold.

'Excuse me, but would you mind if I joined you?' said a woman's voice, distracting Malory from the window and her thoughts. The woman stood before her, nervously clutching a half-pint of beer.

Malory hesitated. She had already had her solitude disrupted on the train. All she wanted was a *moment* of contemplative rapture, for heaven's sake.

But instinctively understanding the woman's plight, she smiled, and said, 'No. Of course not.'

Her new companion wasted no time in 'opening up'. Malory could only nod and smile as the words spilled out. It transpired that the woman was walking the coast path alone from St Ives to Newquay. This was the first night of her trek, and Malory tried not to gawp as she explained that she had not booked any accommodation en route. She had found a bed and breakfast upon arrival, and planned to similarly improvise for the entire journey. She was being *strong*, she said. Her husband had had an affair and she was determined not to wallow in misery and despair, but to strike out on a bold exploit.

'I understand,' said Malory.

But the woman paid little attention, only kept chattering, as if in doing so, she might convince herself of the rationale behind her mission. Malory wondered if the woman was some warped angel sent to mock her. For she too, had set out on an adventure with no rhyme nor reason attached, only a vague, nebulous idea that her destiny, or part of it, belonged in St Ives. It had started, strangely, with the bowl, and a series of synchronicities that had followed. A neighbour's child heard over the garden fence, reciting the old rhyme: *As I was going to St Ives…*; the copy of *To the Lighthouse* calling to her in the second-hand bookshop. When browsing the British Film Institute online, she happened upon an old Pathé documentary chronicling the lives of the St Ives colony of artists that had mesmerised her. In the Tate Britain gallery, she had lingered long before Peter Lanyon's painting *Wreck*, entranced by the colours of both sea and man, as they collided in forceful tumult; certain she could feel the sea wind, and hear the seagulls' cries.

Curiosity became investigation, became obsession. Instinctively, Malory knew there was something of import that had drawn her to St Ives. She just did not know what it was.

'So,' the woman was saying, 'I am determined to be brave, and to engage with all the locals I meet on my way. You…*are* a local, aren't you?'

Malory paused. *This*. This was what she would have to do, she realised. She too, would have to be courageous and grasp life with both hands, otherwise it might slip away into loneliness, disaster, and despair. She could not just sit in the corner and become Old Mal. She smiled.

'Yes,' she said. 'Yes, I suppose I am.'

CHAPTER 4

Teetotal Street

Jago had barely left the bar—almost knocking over that woman in his haste—when he received another call confirming that yes, his sister Senara was without a key, and sitting on the doorstep of the house in Teetotal Street. A few minutes later he found her with her back resting against the blue stable door, attracting dubious looks from passers-by.

'You're not in keeping with the image of St Ives, Senara,' he said. 'We don't do vagabonds in these pretty streets, you know...'

Senara grinned, despite her mood, happy to see her brother again after all this time. He had been out to visit once or twice with his mates, but she was still surprised to see that he had changed somewhat; grown older, she supposed. At twenty-five, he was no longer the near-teenager she had first left behind, but a young man in the prime of life. She jumped up and gratefully accepted the bear-hug. Jago gave good bear-hugs. He was part of that generation that were always embracing and sharing affection; that did not distinguish between male and female friends, but appeared to be having one long cheerful love-in. Just five years older, the rules and manners amongst Senara's own circle—with the exception of Teddy—were so different, she might have been from another epoch.

His brown hair was messy and outgrown, and she reached up to ruffle it affectionately.

'You're so tall now,' she said. 'I thought you'd stopped growing years ago.'

'You sound like Aunt Minnie. So, what gives, Honey?' he asked. 'But let's get you off the streets first...you're ruining the scenery.' He hefted the rucksack over one shoulder and unlocked the door to the small downstairs apartment.

'Top of the house rented out then?' enquired Senara, entering into the shaded gloom.

'Yup, a German couple; don't know why they need three bedrooms, but who am I to complain? There's a family in there at half-term, and then quite a few weeks booked after that. Solid in the summer holidays, of course.'

'I thought it would be,' said Senara, immediately colliding with, and almost dislodging, a surfboard upon entering. 'That's why I didn't clutter up the Carncrows Street entrance.'

But *damn it*, she was thinking, *no room for me here*.

The house was a classic fisherman's cottage of the Downalong part of St Ives. Three-storey, but small, narrow, and terraced. The official 'front' entrance stood on parallel Carncrows Street, but as she had suspected, Jago had let out the top part of the house, comprising of ground and upper floor levels, to holidaymakers. The rear entrance in Teetotal Street, which they had been more accustomed to using since childhood, led to a lower-ground floor, which their great-grandfather, Thomas Berryman, had used as a fish cellar. Jago had fashioned a trap door at the top of the stairwell between the old cellar and the upper floors, forming a separate dwelling for rental. He managed to live for a good part of the winter months—as long as he could afford really—in the whole house. But come the Spring, he would climb down to the cellar and secure the trap door for the duration. With the cottage already pokey, this descent to an even more confined space was always a trial. But then, he was out most of the time in the summer months, and it could be borne; the rental income was vital to enable his other endeavours.

Senara looked around the dusky room. The overhead fisherman's lamp was pretty, but did little to dispel the shadows. Long and narrow, this had been a large enough room when they were growing up and it had been converted to the family kitchen and dining area. Now cupboard and larder space had been stripped back to the bare essentials to make way for a seating area with just one sofa and one armchair. Some folding doors separated this space from Jago's bedroom, and small shower room with toilet; no bath. And everywhere there were surfboards, piled up against the wall or supported from the ceiling by wooden beams.

'You can have the bed, I guess,' said Jago, hurriedly tidying away surfing magazines and unwashed cups. 'I'll take the sofa. Wish I'd known you were coming Senara. You could have let me know. Just a text, even.'

'Thanks. And I'm sorry, you're right. It's been a bit full-on...'

It was a rubbish excuse and she knew it. The truth was that Senara had been in two minds all the way from Greece as to whether she wanted to return to St Ives. Even standing there with that woman by the wall near the station, part of her had still wanted to turn around. She might even have done so, had it not been for the fact of her impoverishment. And now that she was here...

'Oh Jago, I'm sorry for landing on you like this. I couldn't face Mum and Dad's; what would I do there? At least here I might get some work?'

'Well, you'd better be quick. Summer jobs are being snatched up fast.' He called from the sleeping area, where he was staring at the bedclothes.

Reading his mind Senara said: 'Don't worry, they'll do for tonight. And it should be me on the sofa, I don't mind roughing it, you know.'

'No, no, I couldn't call myself a gentleman if I did that,' said Jago, returning to face her. 'But perhaps we can swap on a weekly basis?' he said with a wink. 'Assuming you're back for a while?'

'I'm not going back to Antiparos if that's what you mean. But it's much smaller than I remember,' Senara frowned. 'We can't live down here like a couple of rats all summer.'

'I seem to manage most years,' Jago said grimly. 'Besides, if we're both hopefully out working all hours, it won't be so bad. And you can get your old room back in November.' He smiled a cheesy grin. 'We'll make the best of it.'

Dear, sweet Jago. Senara returned the smile. She was lucky to have anywhere at all to stay, in St Ives.

'So... No Nikos?' asked Jago cautiously, filling the kettle and lighting the gas stove.

'Over,' said Senara with finality.

'Ah,' Jago stared at the blue flames licking around the base of the old copper kettle.

'It's okay, I'm fine,' said Senara, throwing herself onto the sofa, and resting her head against its back. 'It came to a natural end. In as much as he was looking to get married, and suddenly I wasn't Greek enough.'

'Oh Sis...' began Jago.

'No, it's okay,' Senara waved a hand dismissively, yet her voice held a bitter undercurrent. 'Reckon I had a lucky escape. Can you imagine if we'd married and had children? I might have been trapped forever. Nikos has become suddenly orthodox. As my friend Teddy says, I would have become one of the 'unseen' wives, permanently barefoot and pregnant in the kitchen, whilst my husband went out shagging other men.'

'Eh? Is Nikos...?' Jago half-turned as he poured the boiled water into the teapot, spilling some on the countertop.

'No, not really...' said Senara grudgingly. 'It's just me being bitter. And I think some wishful thinking on Teddy's part...'

She accepted the cup of hot tea that Jago handed her, gratefully.

She could have elaborated. She could have explained how she had felt increasingly isolated and frozen out; how Nikos had become scornful and disapproving, where once he had claimed to adore her. When love no longer sustained, came the slow realisation that she had nothing without him. She lived in his house. She worked, for a pittance, cooking and waitressing, in his taverna. She had no savings left. His friends, initially so enamoured of her, had turned evasive and cool, in what seemed like direct correlation to the number of eligible young Greek women that his family paraded under his nose. Senara was no longer the adored; she was the awkward problem. She had worked herself stupid in the taverna kitchen, desperate to prove her worth; to earn her keep.

She could have told Jago about that last night when, exhausted and overwrought from an exceptionally busy day, she had snapped when Nikos had berated her publicly for a misdemeanour; how she had hurled the oily stuffed pepper, plate and all, in his direction, and then tearfully run off to the sound of his furious insults; taunts that declared she was not a real woman, but a useless, stupid, and vain Brit. The pride that had made her pack her bags that same night and seek refuge with Teddy, now also prevented her from revealing to her brother the extent of her humiliation. And yet faced with the oppressive containment of the small apartment, the sudden removal from the life to which she had become accustomed, seemed painfully real.

Jago sat watching her from the armchair, with his wide, bright eyes.

'Look, I know you just got here,' he said. 'But are you hungry? Only, I'm pretty sure Rosa is looking for a waitress at Driftwood. Kill two birds? You know the position will be filled soon enough.'

Senara sighed. It seemed she was destined for servility. But remembering how long it had been since she had eaten decent food, and the weakness that had brought on the faint, she suddenly felt ravenous.

'Are you kidding?' she said. 'I could murder a pizza right now. Are they still as good?'

'Better,' said Jago. 'It's all sourdough, crispy kale and fig vincotto these days. Although sometimes I really just want a big, fat, juicy, deep-pan, cheese-and-tomato, if you know what I mean...'

'Stop it!' cried Senara. 'I'm absolutely famished. Let's go, then.'

They grabbed their jackets and skipped out into the early evening, chattering madly as they darted through the narrow alleyways to the harbourside. But when they reached The Wharf, Senara stopped dead in her tracks.

'What's up?' said Jago. He followed Senara's line of vision to where Grady O'Keefe stood by the railings opposite The Sloop. As ever, he wore white overalls covered in plaster and carried a sketchbook under his arm.

'Right,' said Jago, before linking Senara's arm and forcing her to walk again. But he diverted their route up Fish Street, and away from Grady O'Keefe.

But it was no use. Grady had spotted Senara. And as his cool grey eyes met hers, a smile crept upon his lips.

CHAPTER 5

Salt Maidens

'You need to go and visit Aunt Minnie,' said Jago to Senara the next morning. 'She won't like that you're back and she didn't hear about it first.'

'Yeah, I guess,' said Senara sleepily from the bed, and cradling the cup of coffee that Jago had handed her. Her befuddled mind was still processing the events of the previous day. She was somewhat in shock to have run into Grady so soon, but then remembered that this was St Ives, and that there was no shallow end of the pool in which to plunge. However, celebratory cocktails with Jago at Driftwood had helped restore her composure, and Rosa had obligingly offered her a few shifts waitressing.

'Come on,' said Jago. 'Sup up, and I'll go with you.'

'Urgh, what's the rush?' said Senara. 'It's so early.'

'I want to get a surf in before earning a crust,' said Jago.

'I don't know why I even asked,' said Senara. 'But will she be up?'

Jago's brow furrowed in mock consternation.

'Of course!' he beamed.

Their great-aunt Minnie lived only minutes away, but in such a tucked-away corner, even for St Ives, that it would be difficult to find for the uninitiated. From the street outside, large painted wooden doors suggested a boathouse, or even a garage. But on entering, one encountered a secret yard, that served the back-entrances of several cottages and lofts, and where surfboards were stored, and laundry hung out to dry.

Senara and Jago darted up the cast-iron steps to Aunt Minnie's home and studio.

'I'm amazed she can still get up these stairs,' said Senara. 'She's in her eighties.'

'She's fit as a fiddle,' said Jago. 'Still painting. And still drinks at The Castle Inn once a week with her mates.'

The front door had once been painted dark purple, and then green, but the layers of paint had flaked away to form an abstract pattern, that almost looked deliberate. Either way, Minnie refused to let Jago repaint it for her, because she liked the effect. They were welcomed in with hugs, and coos of delight by the elderly lady, and immediately offered tea. Minnie wore a painting smock over jeans, sandals on her feet, and had tied her long silver hair in a plait that trailed down her back.

Senara took in the studio apartment that had not changed any more than Minnie had. The bare floorboards were painted the blue-green colour of sea glass, and the furniture was dated, but simple and comfortable. Everywhere, on the walls, or stacked up in a corner, were her own abstract paintings, and those by others she had known, back in the days when the St Ives colony had been at the forefront of the arts scene. Senara often wondered what treasures had been casually received, to be left scattered around the shambolic home.

Minnie Quick had been born in St Ives, but having some Irish blood, brazenly claimed descendance from Saint Ia, herself, for whom the town, sometimes called St Eia, was named.

'Saint Ia came over the sea from Ireland floating on a leaf,' she reminded them, before laughing. 'A leaf! Can you imagine that? But it means I may well be an Irish princess. You too, for that matter,' she nodded at Senara, with a wink. 'You know, you're the spitting image of Nell. She was my own great-aunt.

I have her picture somewhere.' Minnie moved to the desk, which sat under heaving shelves of books relating to art. 'It's very old. I'm lucky to possess it.'

As Minnie rummaged through the desk drawer, Senara and Jago exchanged looks, but said nothing. They had heard the story of Aunt Nell many times before. Finding the precious black and white photograph, Minnie showed them once again the group gathering of apron-clad women, posing uncomfortably for the formal picture.

'There she is, see?' said Minnie, pointing to a young woman in the front row. 'And that's my own grandmother, her sister, next to her.'

Senara could not tell, from the faded photo, if Nell indeed, truly resembled her. Yet there was something in the dark expression in her eyes, that resonated.

'You see,' said Minnie. 'Spitting image.'

Senara smiled and nodded.

'She had a terrible tragic story, though,' said Minnie, and Senara again met Jago's eyes, prepared to hear the story once more.

'She was a salt-maiden,' continued Minnie. 'Worked down at Porthmeor, when it was all fish factories, back then. Pilchard Palaces, they called them. When the fish came off the dippers, she'd be there with her sister and the other maidens, ready to salt the pilchards for storing. But she was in love, you see, with one of the seine boat fishermen. Loved him fiercely, madly, she did. Only trouble was,' Minnie emitted a small chuckle, 'he was married, so she had to bite her tongue. She kept her feelings to herself, happy just seeing him close by. Or at least, as happy as she could be.'

Senara and Jago listened patiently as Aunt Minnie retold the story of bygone times. How once, late on a muggy day, the huer's cry went out. The weather looked ominous, as though a storm was brewing, but still the seine boats took to the sea.

'They were hungry, you see?' said Minnie. 'They needed the fish, and the money to survive.'

The story went that the clouds began to swirl menacingly in the sky, and the waves grew rougher, until a huge storm arose. The townsfolk began to fear for the lives of the fishermen, and Nell became consumed with agony to realise that her love was one of them. She spent all night on the pier, staring out to sea, desperately awaiting a sign of the return of the boats. But it was of no use. By dawn, news came that one of the boats had perished, and that her love was amongst those that were lost.

'Well, of course, Nellie was grief-stricken,' said Minnie. 'But the terrible thing was, that she could never tell a soul about her heartache, for he was not hers to grieve. She buried her sorrow deep, and died young of a broken heart...'

'Of course, there's a major flaw in that story,' said Jago later, as they left the loft studio.

'I know,' sighed Senara. 'You say this every time.'

It didn't stop Jago from persisting. 'If Nell never told a soul about her heartbreak, how do we know any of it is true?'

'Just because she never told anyone,' said Senara, 'doesn't mean that nobody *knew*...'

CHAPTER 6

Seagulls

Malory jammed the pillow over her ears as the ungodly racket continued relentlessly. She tried to imagine what kind of creature could possibly feel the need to make so much noise at sunrise. When she could bear it no longer, she stirred in the bed and peered around her as the strange room came into focus. Woodchip wallpaper painted a pale—what was that colour? —salmon?

Sick. That's what it was; a pallid, lumpy shade of vomit. Although the paint company probably called it something like 'Wild Trout' or 'Taramasalata'. The room was small and there was a prevailing odour that felt wrong. But there was a half-glazed door that led out onto a small roof-terrace 'garden', and in the distance, beyond the jumble of rooftops, was the sea.

Malory left the bed and stumbled sleepily in her pyjamas towards this source of inspiration; of hope. She turned the key in the lock and stepped out, barefoot, onto the terrace. The previous owners, in their wisdom, had covered the square space with a fake grass 'lawn', and some equally plastic flowers hung in baskets from the railings that enclosed it. There was just about room for a couple of chairs and a small table, but it was the views that gave the space its potential. To one side she could see across the rooftops, yellow with lichen, to the deep blue of where the ocean met the sky. She knew, from her studies, that there was a large beach that way, and the desire to explore stirred again in Malory's heart. To the other side, the view was over Fore Street, and beyond that the harbour, with the pier and its two lighthouses stretching out into water that sparkled in the rising sun's rays. She watched as a lone fishing boat chugged out into the bay. All around her, scattered across the rooftops, and completely unbothered by her presence, an assembly of seagulls squawked their artless chorus as they greeted the new day. Malory stood amongst them, the reluctant queen of an unruly tribe. She surveyed her rude subjects from her rooftop perch and wondered what on earth she had done.

The flat was arranged over two floors above the shop. The bedroom, a bathroom, and the roof terrace on top; and a simple lounge and kitchen below. The shop itself was relatively spacious, comprising two adjoining spaces, marked by a raised floor at the back end, where she appeared to have inherited a desk, an armchair, and a vintage-looking plan chest; and there was a small storeroom and bathroom beyond that. The lease had included the existing stock of art supplies: canvasses, sketchbooks, and an overwhelming array of pencils, brushes, and paints. Malory had not been to an art shop since high school, and had no retail experience whatsoever. It would take a while to acquaint herself with the products, not to mention the more daunting task of pretending that she knew what she was doing. It was not the art gallery that she dreamed of one day owning, but it was a start. And so, Malory Black arose that morning amidst a cacophony of noise, and to life as the new tenant of Atlantic Arts.

Her brief foray the night before had enlightened her of at least one thing: that heels and cobblestones did not go together. She looked at the clothes in her wardrobe as if they had become alien overnight, and belonged to someone else entirely; a stranger. She paused. It was bizarre to suddenly not know how to dress oneself. Malory would have considered herself quite sophisticated; a *fashionista*, even. She knew how to pull together an on-trend look; how to match accessories. But right now, nothing appeared right. Eventually, she decided on cropped jeans, a plain T-shirt, and a chunky, grandad-style cardigan that swamped her small, trim physique. She pulled on a pair of canvas shoes and observed her reflection in the mirror. The dressed-down clothes looked incongruous with the expensive jewellery. She touched the ends of her hair, soft and conditioned, and back to its real colour now. For many years in London, she had been a blonde.

In fact, she had been *that* blonde, impeccably and unashamedly bottle-bleached. To be anything else, she had thought at the time, would have amounted to nothing less than bad grooming. She had dyed and waxed and preened with the best of them. She had flitted between the gym and the beauty salon, and wilfully deprived herself of delicious, joyous food in order to maintain an acceptable size and shape. But the recent haircut had got rid of the last of the brown dye, and her natural dark shade had been restored. She had not yet applied the usual veneer of make-up, and peering closer at her bare olive skin, Malory saw in the mirror that the bridge of her nose had the faintest sprinkling of freckles. *Who was she?*

A strange, amorphous gloom crept over her. In frustration, Malory grabbed her keys and stuffed some cash into her back pocket, then hurried from the pokey flat. Slowly, she made her way along Fore Street, with the intention of finding the large beach that she knew was called Porthmeor.

Malory's investigations prior to arriving in St Ives had been thorough. She quickly found The Digey, a narrow cobbled street of very old and pretty fisherman's cottages, and could not resist peeking in through windows and open doorways.

Adorned with cheerful and quirky furnishings, it was clear that many of the cottages had had their original charm subverted to match the needs of the modern holidaymaker or second-home owner. Malory was sure she remembered a time when to stay in a fisherman's cottage meant an escape to a simple, unsophisticated lifestyle. But everything now, it seemed, was required to be 'luxury', or 'boutique', whatever that meant.

More like gentrified to death... she thought.

Yet, where the dwellings were unspoilt by extravagance, she felt a real sense of the past. The cottages were small and opened directly to the cobblestones, having been built at a time when gardens and parking spaces were not even a consideration. Some had stone steps that led up to a front door, and Malory knew, from her intense swotting sessions before moving, that the basement levels would have been used for storing fishing nets, and for pressing pilchards. In an open upstairs window, a towel draped over the sill, and nearby, hooked to a handy drainpipe, a wetsuit dangled, drying in the breeze. Even narrower alleys projected off sideways, with names like Rose Lane and Love Lane... It was all very romantic. An archaic granite arch marked the entrance to Hicks Court; an intriguing square of further, hidden dwellings; all, so far as she could make out, small and huddled together as if for protection, for warmth.

The cobbled stones underfoot were strewn with sand, blown in by the wind. And sunlight, warm against her back, skittered through the morning shadows, casting a magical light. Malory ambled along, increasingly enchanted. And then, at the junction with Back Road West, she stopped, abruptly. There was Alfred Wallis's cottage, where Ben Nicholson and Christopher Wood had stumbled upon the naïve painter; and beyond that, the walkway that led down to Porthmeor Studios.

Malory fancied that she could see the young Wilhelmina Barns-Graham—or Willie, as the artist had been known in life—stride up the walkway in her painting overalls, and walk right towards her, looking her straight in the eye.

Soon, Willie, thought Malory. *Soon.*

She would find a way to explore the art studios at some point. But for now, she was drawn to a different spectacle. At the end of The Digey, she could see a fraction of a wall, beyond which the world appeared to end, and only the deep blue of the sea rose against the skyline. Something stirred in her, like a remembrance, or déjà vu. She hastened on again, until she stood by the sea wall and could take in all the glory of Porthmeor Beach.

Here, out of the sheltered alleys, she felt the sea-wind in her face. Huge waves came rushing, in long surf lines to the shore, where they smashed dramatically against the sand, and receded again in a froth of foam and scattered shells. Large granite rocks appeared here and there, with smaller black ones dispersed along the tideline like precious stones; but for the most part, the beach was pristine and empty. All of Malory's extensive, geeky studies came to life before her eyes. To the west was the headland of Carrick Du, dominated by the distinctively shaped rock known as Man's Head. To the East was Pendinas, or The Island, as it was more simply known. It was not actually an island at all, but the site of an ancient promontory fort, connected to the mainland by an isthmus. Malory felt compelled to walk along the shoreline; to feel the sand with the bare skin of her feet, and to wade in the clear water.

She took off her shoes by the sea wall and ventured down some steps onto the beach. It was early, and apart from staff preparing to open the beach café, there were very few people about. A solitary worker collected rubbish with a litter-picker, and further along, the surf school made preparations for the day's classes. She strolled along the sand, breathing in the fresh sea air and listening to the roar of the waves. Malory experienced a fierce sensation of elemental energy emanating from the ocean, and the surrounding granite rocks. It was exhilarating, and breathtakingly beautiful. Above the beach, the Tate gallery building loomed imposingly, like some grand ocean liner. Yet Malory knew that it had been built on the site of what was once a gas factory. She knew that where the sea wall continued along the stretch of beach towards The Island, it had once housed the many pilchard processing factories, or pilchard palaces, as they were sometimes called. Back then, despite the subsistence it offered, the sea was something to be respected and feared. The buildings would have faced away from the ocean, their backs braced to the sea to gird against its worst moods. But now, with sea views considered a luxury, all windows of the converted apartments and studios faced the ocean.

No one would dream now, thought Malory, *of placing a gas factory on such a prestigious landscape.*

She roamed aimlessly at the water's edge, letting the waves flow over her bare feet. She could see that there was another café at the west end of the beach, and thought she might get a coffee. But she reached an area where passage became difficult. Here, the turning tide crashed against a crop of rocks and receded again with a pull that she felt was too strong, and that might pull her over. Frowning, Malory assessed the rocks. They were not too high; she should be able to clamber over. Carefully, with her shoes in one hand, she climbed up upon an accessible-looking slab, and then edged her way through the cluster, feeling her way with her other hand. Before long, she came upon a dip in the formation, where a sandy pool was formed by a circle of surrounding rock. The easiest route was to traverse it and then climb up again on the other side. Malory splashed down into the shallow pool.

'Mornin'' said a voice with a subtle Cornish accent. 'Looking like a nice one, an' all.'

Malory turned to see someone grinning amiably at her. It was the young man from the night before; the one who had bumped into her when he had charged out of The Barquentine. He wore—or rather half-wore—a wetsuit, but it was unzipped, and the top half dangled from his waist, so that his arms and torso were completely bare. Malory tried not to stare at the large tattoo of an octopus on his chest. Its arms curled around his ribcage, up to his shoulders, and tantalisingly, towards his midriff. Spotting some clothes and a towel secreted on a rock ledge, she could only assume that she had interrupted him dressing.

'I'm sorry,' she said. 'I didn't know anyone was here.'

He looked askance at her. 'You think you've picked a private spot on the beach to change, and the whole world decides to drop by.' He picked up a surfboard from the sand and propped it against the rock, examining it for dings and dents.

'Hardly the whole world!' said Malory.

'It is a big beach, though,' said the man. 'Lots of other rocks. You have to go out of your way to get behind this one. I guess you just couldn't resist my naked beauty.'

She looked at him in horror and disbelief. 'I told you, I didn't notice you!'

'Of course not,' he said. 'Although... Didn't you run into me yesterday too? Kind of suspicious.'

Malory saw the merriment in his eyes, but felt foolish all the same.

'I'll go then,' she said, 'and leave you in peace.'

'There's no need to get a strop on,' he said. 'Show's over anyhow.' He pulled his arms into the wetsuit and deftly reached behind to tug at the long cord that pulled the zip up. 'You already missed the best part...' He smiled wickedly.

Malory felt somewhat amazed at how he spoke to her; as if he had always known her.

'Wow. You really like yourself, don't you?' she stammered in fury and frustration.

'Nothing wrong with that,' he said.

'Is that so?' said Malory. 'Some might call it a flaw. A defect, even. A blot on the landscape of personality.'

He laughed. 'Someone got out the wrong side of the bed.'

'As a matter of fact, I did,' said Malory. 'On the wrong side of the country, if you must know. And how the hell does anybody sleep here anyway, with those seagulls making all that noise?'

'Ah, got woken by the dawn chorus, did you? It's not so bad; you'll get used to it. Just visiting?'

'No, not visiting...' Malory forced the words; 'I live here now. I've just moved. It's probably all a big mistake. And it's a *terrible* noise! A complete racket.'

'Sounds like you've got a nest nearby. Where are you living?'

She told him.

'The art shop? Interesting... And yep. Most likely a nest somewhere in the rooftops there,' he said. 'Better get used to it.'

'Do you mean it's always going to be that noisy? Oh my god...'

'Nah, just when the chicks are young. It'll quieten off a bit soon. At least till next year...'

'Oh no. What have I done?'

'No worries. Just feed them some rice. Watch them swell and blow up. At least, that's what we were told as kids.'

'But... But that's disgusting!'

The young man grinned maliciously. 'Kind of is.'

'And cruel! How could you?'

'It's great fun,' he said meeting her eyes unflinchingly. 'Feathers *everywhere*.'

Malory stared back at him, aware of the oddness of standing in a puddle with a stranger, having this outlandish conversation.

'I'm sorry, but that's appalling. What kind of person would do such a thing?'

'The kind of person who gets a lie-in, I reckon.'

Malory shook her head in disbelief. It was disconcerting that he was so good-looking and yet so obviously twisted.

'Who *are* you?' she found herself saying aloud.

He looked at her in curiosity for a second, then held his hand out for her to shake.

'I'm Jago.'

Malory could not help but respond. She had been brought up to be scrupulously polite. She took his hand. Strangely disturbed by his touch, she quickly let go again.

'Jago,' she repeated. 'Just Jago?'

'What more do you need? I'm Jago; everyone knows me; ask around. But since you're dying to know, it's Jago Berryman. And you are?'

'I'm Malory. Malory Black.'

'That's like a villain name or something. You know, proper *James Bond* baddie. Or like, *Malory Black and The Mysterons*,' he beamed. 'But if you've finished chatting, I've got some waves to catch.'

Malory looked through a gap in the rocks at the huge swell and pounding breakers. 'You're going in? Into *that?*'

'That's the general idea. I don't get dressed up in rubber just 'cos I'm weird or something.'

'But blowing up seagulls is fine,' said Malory.

He laughed. 'Hey, relax. I was just kidding you about that...' He winked. 'Or was I...?'

Malory was aware that she was staring again. What to make of him?

'Well don't let me keep you,' she said. 'I've got some fiendish world domination plots to hatch anyway.'

She moved towards the other side of the rockpool, and began to clamber up again. Jago Berryman picked up his surfboard and followed, effortlessly balancing on foot, while she clawed and clung to the rocks with her spare hand. Malory had the uneasy feeling that he was watching her, and worse, that she was holding him up. She reached the other side of the rock cluster and jumped down again, near where a stream fell from the cliff and carved a path through the sand. She splashed across and made towards the café. Jago jumped down behind her, but headed off in the direction of the sea.

'I'll see you around then,' he called after her.

'Maybe,' she called back.

Maybe. How pathetic. She cursed herself for her lack of wit as she struggled up the rising bank of sand, desperately trying not to stumble and fall as each footstep sank into the soft powder. All the while she thought she could feel Jago's eyes burning into her back—or more particularly, her backside—as she made her ungainly way up the beach. But when she reached the top near the café, she chanced a leisurely backward glance, only to see Jago Berryman running athletically towards the water's edge, with his surfboard under his arm. She watched as he plunged into the oncoming waves, and then prone on his board, paddle out to sea.

CHAPTER 7

Smeaton's Pier

Senara stopped by St Leonard's, the tiny fishermen's chapel at the entrance to the pier, and stared at the message on her phone. It was Twitter, informing her that she had a new follower. Initially disinterested, she checked out the profile anyway. It very quickly dawned on her that it was Brian, the man from the train. The profile did not reveal his occupation, only a desire to live life to the full. His pictures were of country landscapes, mountain biking, and hang-gliders. Puzzled, she wondered how he had managed to find her, but then supposed it was her unusual name. And she might have mentioned that she was headed to St Ives? She couldn't remember. Idly, she followed back, before replacing the phone in her pocket.

Continuing her stroll along Smeaton's Pier, she basked in the morning sunshine, taking in the sea air, and the views. She was shortly to start her first shift at Driftwood, but for now, relished the time and space to reflect. She passed the old ship's anchor, embedded in the cobbles, a remnant from the wreck of the *Cintra*, and a reminder of the terrible gales and stormy seas that had claimed so many lives around these rocky shores. Small birds, called Turnstones, perched along the granite sea wall, and hopped around her feet, endlessly foraging. Leaning against the railings, she idled for a moment, observing the crowds gathered to sit in the sun on the old stone pier head that had once served the Rampers, the doomed wooden pier. At low tide you could still see the remnant stumps of black, seaweed-slimed wooden posts; a memorial to its lost fight with the sea.

She went on beyond the stout original lighthouse, along the nineteenth-century extension, where memories lay heaped with the lobster pots and dormant in the fishermen's huts. At the end of the pier, she stopped near the 'new' lighthouse and surveyed the scenery. The sea glittered in the sunshine, with distant peaks of surf, or 'white horses', that danced in the wind. On the other side of St Ives Bay, three miles of golden sand and dunes stretched all the way from Hayle to Godrevy, where the island lighthouse warned of the perilous black rocks that lay unseen.

Senara turned towards the other side of the pier, and leaned against the railings near the steps. Across the water, she recognised, by their distinctive green colour, Zack and Dan Hosking's small fleet of self-drive boats for hire. Once this harbour would have been filled with seine boats and the masts and sails of luggers, but now it sheltered dozens of pleasure boats, dinghies, and gigs. Yet still, near the harbour wall, there remained fishing boats; for although the days of seine fishing were long gone, it was still a working pier.

The view was idyllic; sublimely so. But Senara was consumed with perverse emotions. Rather than enjoy the beauty, she could only feel an overwhelming sense of failure and defeat, coupled with an anxiety stemming from the previous evening's encounter with Grady.

A teenage boy stood nearby, calling for any last takers for a boat trip to 'Seal Island'. It was the name given to tourists for the rocky islands off Treveal Cliff, more properly called *The Carracks*, and where seals were known to bask. The boat moored directly beneath her was being loaded with passengers. It was an old-fashioned lifeboat painted a bright sea-blue, with distinctive red stripes. The boatman was reaching to help the last of them, a worried-looking woman, board from the wet granite steps that led down from the pier. He held her hand as she stepped onto the unsteady vessel, then guided her, carefully supporting with strong arms, to sit amongst the other passengers. Recognising him, Senara watched as the boatman subtly assessed the numbers. Then he did that thing—*that annoying thing*—that he did... He strode around the rocking boat; skipping, where there was space, across the wooden planks that served as seats; balancing effortlessly in his chunky boots, whilst the passengers tightly gripped the benches or clung nervously to the gunwales.

It was Kit.

If only he would fall in. Just once... thought Senara, grinning evilly to herself.

At that moment, he looked up and spotted her. Instantaneously, his usual nonchalant expression broke into a huge grin. Shielding his eyes against the sun, he waved and beckoned to her to come down. Senara returned the smile but shook her head in apology. She would have to go to work soon; no time for boat trips. And she wasn't sure she was ready for Kit showing off his sea-legs just yet.

His smile faded a little, and he looked disappointed, almost crestfallen... But Senara knew him better than that. He called instructions to his teenage helper to come down and safeguard the waiting passengers, then leaping from the boat, he bounded up the stone steps to the top of the sea wall. He moved towards her with the grin restored.

He hasn't changed, she thought as he approached. Same old Kit with the lazy manner. He wore a scruffy boiler suit with the sleeves rolled up to reveal his tanned arms. His long wavy hair, which started out a light-brown, had been sun-bleached blonde, with sparks of red and threads of gold. *Like*

Cúchulainn; Senara thought, remembering Aunt Minnie's proclamation upon encountering Kit as a young man:

'He's like Cúchulainn himself, rising up to meet the hound, with that hair. 'Ansum too. We'll have to keep our daughters away from that one,' she had said, with a chuckle.

Today, he had tamed this mane by tying back the front part, like a little girl's style, to keep it from blowing across his eyes in the wind.

He grabbed her in a hug that lifted her off the ground. 'Hey, Snow. I heard you were back!'

Senara giggled. 'Put me down, Kit!'

He obliged. 'It's good to see you again. Why didn't you say you were coming home?'

'It's a long story. And besides; you never came to visit. You promised you would.'

'Yeah, I know,' he said. 'I'm sorry. Time just carries us along, doesn't it?'

'I love the new boat,' said Senara. 'Is it yours? Do you still have the *Silver Star*?' she added, referring to Kit's fishing boat.

'I do,' he said. 'Right over there,' he pointed to where the boat was moored. 'She's definitely still seaworthy. But this one's been a labour of love. It's the *James Stevens No. 21*, part of the old lifeboat fleet. I found her rotting away in the estuary and took it upon myself to restore her. She was a rowboat, originally, but I've fitted an engine. She's a good-looking vessel, and the tourists love her.'

'It is a beautiful boat,' agreed Senara. 'Good for you. And how's the music scene? Are you still playing the acoustic folk stuff?'

'Yeah, of course,' said Kit. 'Still writing and playing; gigging the usual circuit of festivals, when I can; same as Jago's band.'

'That's great.' Senara smiled.

Kit looked at her studiously. 'Come for a drink tonight at The Barque; catch up with the gang.'

Senara frowned. 'Oh, I don't know... I'm not sure I'd be welcome.'

'Don't be daft. And you can't hide, Senara, not in St Ives.'

She looked him in the eyes. 'I...guess you're not angry with me anymore.'

'Oh Snow. I was never angry with you, I was just...' he hesitated.

Senara groaned. 'Oh my god... You were going to say disappointed, weren't you?'

Kit laughed. 'Maybe...'

'Are you my dad, now?' But Senara was laughing too. 'Well, we'll see. I've got to go to work in a bit; I've got a shift at Driftwood, so I'll probably be too tired. But it's good to see you too. We'll catch up soon, I promise.'

He looked away, as if in frustration, or perhaps impatience, then abruptly returned his gaze. 'Snow...'

'You'd better go,' she interrupted. 'Your customers are waiting.'

'They're fine,' he said. 'You worry too much. Always have.'

'You've left them bobbing around with some kid!'

'That's Tom Barber. I think he knows his way around a boat.'

'You're kidding,' cried Senara. Tom Barber had practically grown up on his father's fishing boat. 'But he was just a little child!'

'As we all were, my love. Like I said, time goes on whether we like it or not.'

Senara looked at his face. Yes, it was perhaps more weather-beaten. He still had the same scar that traversed his forehead to his cheek, from where his surfboard had nearly knocked him out, long ago. And the other one, smaller, on his eyebrow, from an escapade even further back in time. There might have been a few creases around his green eyes, but they still shone with the same spirit and intelligence. It was still Kit.

'I hear you finally settled down,' she said.

He grinned lopsidedly. 'Yeah, I guess so. Her name's Astrid. You'll have to meet her.'

'I'm sure I will, soon enough. But I really have to go.' She touched his arm, and then leaned in to place a polite kiss on his cheek. 'We'll speak again, soon.'

Kit watched her departing figure for a few seconds, and then returning his attention to the waiting customers, hurried back down the pier steps to the boat. Quickly, he worked in tandem with Tom to loosen the ropes and then strode once more across the benches, silently and expertly checking that everyone was okay. Satisfied, he reached the helm and started the engine. To the unsuspecting passengers, safe in the protection of the sea wall, it appeared a beautiful, calm and clear morning; and they began to relax, and chat, in a leisurely manner, as Kit carefully steered the boat out of the harbour.

With the wind in his face now, and his hair flying, Kit smiled before calling to the captive tourists. 'Might be a bit rough out in the bay...'

CHAPTER 8

Seal Island

Kit stopped the engine and let the boat settle on the heaving ocean by The Carracks. It had been a bumpy ride. He could see the relief on the tourists' faces, although none looked like they might actually throw up. Thankfully there were a few seals there today, and the passengers happily snapped pictures on their cameras and phones. Kit was always bemused at how they never considered that they were floating on a powerful force of nature, and that whilst he had lifejackets for *them*, their devices might not survive any calamities. Never one to talk much to his customers, apart from the necessary safety instructions, or to answer questions, he stood silently at the helm and let them get on with it. Looking back towards the land, he spied a couple of walkers worming their way along the coast path; but otherwise, the granite rocks and zawns of Trevega and Treveal Cliffs were still, silent, and timeless. Apart from the tourists' chatter, the only sounds were of gulls flying overhead, and the usual, hypnotic song of the sea breaking against the foot of the cliffs. *Mordros*, they called it; *the sound of the sea.*

It had been good to see Senara again. They had been friends since childhood, their lives carelessly entwined by chance. He still remembered that day at junior school, when he had been entranced by the teacher's introduction of the new pupil, Senara Holly Berryman, who had transferred from another school. Mishearing through his daydream, Kit had stopped doodling on his exercise book, suddenly interested that there was such a person in the world as 'Holly Berry Snowman'. The first thing that struck him—or anyone really—was her hair. A startling white-blonde, it flowed past her shoulders, covering her small frame like a blanket of driven snow. By chance, it was actually snowing that day, rare for the Cornish winter. Senara stood framed by the window and the cascade of snowflakes outside. Pure and ethereal, she could have been The Snow Queen's daughter.

Later, in the playground, Kit had thrown snowballs at her. 'Snowman! Snowman!' he jeered.

'You're a mean boy, Kit Curnow,' Senara had shouted back. 'That's *not* my name!'

But then she had stooped and cupped together an icy missile of her own and hurled it back at him, striking him on the cheek with a ferocity that surprised him.

Somehow the wild Cornish winters melded with memories of still, hot summers. As the years passed, and they turned into teenagers, Kit would spend idle days with Senara and Jago on their uncle's farm at Zennor, running with the small brown rabbits across the fields, or swimming at nearby Pendour Cove. The steep, overgrown cliffs made it inaccessible from the coast path, but Kit, being Kit, had found a way. There was a narrow, beaten track that led down to nearby Veor Cove, and if you had the courage, you could swim around the rocks to Pendour. He remembered how they used to play a game, whereupon spotting walkers on the coast path at Zennor Head, they would stand motionless in the sea, staring in the direction of the intruders, so that anyone spying them would be curious, and then baffled, as the trio simultaneously dived underwater and swam around the rocks to hide. Perhaps the walkers might hear their laughter carried on the wind, and, if they'd heard the story of The Mermaid of

Zennor, be half-convinced that they had stumbled upon some strange sea people. Or so the youngsters liked to imagine.

The story told that the mermaid had fallen in love with Mathey Trewella after hearing his beautiful singing voice in church, and had enticed him to her watery home. Sometimes Kit would sing loudly, from his hiding place, an old-fashioned hymn; all the more to convince those hearing his voice rise up from the cove, that it was indeed the ghost of the doomed Mathey...

When she got bored of swimming and exploring the caves with the boys, Senara would sit atop of a perpendicular rock, like the mermaid Morvoren herself, with her long hair blowing in the sea wind. Only instead of a mirror and comb, she held a harmonica, and played to her audience of seals, dolphins and fish.

How long ago that was, thought Kit now, as he watched the hikers disappear around the headland. Those days no longer felt real, but golden, and mythical; like a dream. Reluctantly, he confronted the matter that was bothering him. Of course, he had been sincere when he had suggested that Senara meet Astrid. It was impossible to think that she would not, being one of his oldest friends. But what Kit had not made clear, was that Astrid was a close confidant of Pepper's...

He told himself that there was nothing to worry about, and that Astrid would rise above it all. Yet there was something else niggling him, that he could not quite light upon. It had something to do with what Senara had said, about his 'settling down'. He had never thought about it in those terms before, but rather had drifted into things. It bothered him that Senara had put a label on it, and this in turn made him feel guilty for his objection. It wasn't Astrid's fault, he reminded himself; she had been a victim of circumstance.

The wind picked up some more, and the boat rolled on the ocean swell. One or two of his passengers looked a little anxious and scrambled back to their seats. Others zipped up their jackets and scanned the skies for rainclouds.

Time to go. Kit called instructions to the boatload, and once they had all settled down, he restarted the engine.

'Be easier-going on the way back,' he called loudly to the tourists, 'with the wind and the waves behind us.'

The gratitude on the faces of the passengers was palpable.

Kit grinned slyly to himself. As he manoeuvred the boat into position, he called again: 'Let me know if any of them fall off the sides, Tommy.'

'Aye, Aye, Cap'n,' Tom replied with a salute.

The passengers looked aghast, and began to mutter frantically amongst each other. What did he mean? Could that happen? Where did he say the lifejackets were?

Kit beamed innocuously while the tourists looked frantically at the increasingly high waves, their knuckles whitening as they clung ever-harder to the gunwales.

He was overthinking things, that was all. He'd feel much more comfortable once Astrid and Senara met; then they would each better understand how things were. His serenity restored; Kit addressed the passengers once more.

'Hold on tight, now,' he shouted, as he put the engine into full throttle. 'Should be a fun ride...'

CHAPTER 9

What Men Want.

1. Openness and honesty
2. Sexual appeal, but classy. Natural beauty is preferable. No ironed hair/fake nails. No fake anything. Avoid the fake
3. Kindness. Avoid cruelty, bitching and gossip
4. Intelligence. Educated and well-read; but open-minded and free-thinking
5. Loyal/trustworthy
6. A correlating sense of humour
7. Most definitely non-possessive – freedom is vital for the soul
8. Creative. Should have at least one creative passion; e.g., write, paint, draw, play music, garden, grow, make, etc.
9. A free spirit. Happy to be in nature and the elements. Not afraid to get hands dirty
10. Spiritual. A sense of wonder, but discerning. Avoid dubious beliefs; e.g., witchcraft, aliens, lizard people, magic crystals, general woo-woo

The three men sat at one of the tables outside The Sloop. Fishing boats danced before them in the harbour, as the tide rolled in. The evening was bright still, but chill enough that they all wore thick jumpers or hoodies. Their expressions varied from amused to befuddled as they silently regarded the notebook on the table.

'I'll tell you what's missing,' Dan muttered sulkily. 'It ought to say, "*Must like beer*", that's what.'

Dan had recently ventured on a date that was beyond, and some might say, above, any experience he had had before, and prompted entirely by the list of rules before him. The fortunate woman was Marta Miller, a local artist with the real credentials of gallery representation and "a proper studio and everything".

The three of them had been at Porthmeor one evening, enjoying the sunset and a cold beer downstairs at the beach café, when they had spotted her. She had been sitting alone at one of the benches, drinking hot chocolate and reading what looked like an exhibition catalogue. It was thick, glossy, and expensive-looking.

'She looks educated,' Zack had said, although his tone was more one of disapproval, almost begrudging.

'And she's an artist,' said Kit. 'She exhibited in town recently. So, she's creative.'

'I suppose she's not bad looking, either,' Dan had mumbled, observing Marta's flawless skin and pretty legs that emerged from under the plain, shapeless shift dress. 'But what about the dyed red hair though? That most definitely is not natural. Doesn't pass the test. Oh well.'

'It's not a test,' sighed Kit. 'Think of the list more as guidance, rather than rigid regulations.'

'Oh, I see,' said Dan. 'So, you're saying you can twist the rules to make me do whatever you say.'

'I'm saying, she meets some of the criteria. No one is perfect, and you won't find out the rest of it until you get to know her. So, go for it.'

'Okay, okay,' said Dan, getting up nervously. 'But you two don't want to know what Tamsin has to say about this 'list' rigmarole.'

'Tamsin?' said Zack. 'What's it got to do with Tamsin? Now go on!'

Dan had never really thought that Marta would agree to the date, but, egged on by Kit and Zack, was compelled to show willing, if only to get them off his back for five minutes. But after studying him pensively for a second or two through her arty, red horn-rimmed spectacles, she had, surprisingly, said yes.

'The hot chocolate, that should have been my first clue,' said Dan, mournfully. 'Who goes to see the sunset without sipping on a beer, or a cocktail? A glass of wine at least?'

'Just about everyone,' laughed Kit. 'I'm partial to a hot chocolate myself.'

'Fair enough,' said Dan. 'But we arranged to meet right here, outside the pub. I naturally assumed we'd be going in, but she refused. Doesn't drink, she says. It muddles her clarity of thought or something. Likes to be clear-headed at all times, she says.'

'That's good,' said Kit. 'Shows discipline. And individual thinking.'

'So, what happened?' asked Zack.

'Well, it was a bit awkward, just standing there. I was gasping for a beer and all. But anyway, I asked her what *she'd* like to do, thinking she'd say, "Let's go see a movie", or something. But no. She says an artist mate of hers is having a "private view" that night, and could we go to that?'

'Well, that's not so bad,' said Zack. 'Usually there's wine or champagne at those bashes, right? At least that must have taken the edge off.'

'You'd think, right?' said Dan. 'We got to the place, and it's this big empty studio, and it was completely dark. There was no booze. No snacks. There were only about eight people there in all—including the artist—and they...'

Dan paused momentarily to stem the flow of painful memories with a clenched fist to his mouth.

'They shut us in,' he continued, bravely. 'In the dark. And we all had to sit in silence and watch a weird film.'

'So, that's...*kind of* like a movie?' said Kit, hopefully.

Dan sighed heavily. 'No... *Not* a movie. A work of art. Installation they call it. I had no idea what on earth was going on. And then it got worse.'

Kit chuckled. 'I can see where this is going.'

'After about twenty minutes, which felt more like twenty hours, the film, which was all these images of dolls half-buried in soil, and rotten leaves and mouldy food and that,—really disturbing stuff,—well, it stopped abruptly and some spotlights came on around the room. We were made—with no warning, mind; no options;—made to cavort around the room making shadow shapes against the wall with our bodies. While the artist filmed the whole thing. It was *so* undignified.'

Zack looked puzzled. 'But...*why?*'

Dan spoke with mock loftiness: 'Because we became part of the installation. Something to do with chaos and the ephemeral nature of life. Or something.'

Kit exploded with laughter. 'Couldn't you have snuck out?'

'I thought of that,' said Dan. 'But when I cavorted to where the door was, the artist stood there with his camera, giving me a stern look, so I had to carry on cavorting.'

Kit was in hysterics. 'I must admit, I *would* pay real money to see that.'

'They were all getting into it,' continued Dan. 'The others that is. Marta was busting some freaky moves, and not one, not one of them seemed to think it was embarrassing, or funny. I wanted to laugh out loud but somehow didn't think it'd go down too well. Anyway, I eventually escaped after what felt like about two days, took her home, said all the usual niceties, and then hurried back to the pub just in time for last orders. Tamsin was working and I told her all about it. She says the list is daft and sexist nonsense.'

'She's probably right,' said Kit, wryly.

'How did you cavort then?' asked Zack, looking at his brother suspiciously. They were both big, hefty lads. 'Go on, give us a show.'

'No chance,' said Dan. 'What happened in the dark studio stays in the dark studio. It is to be forever banished from memory.'

'But not the artist's video installation,' said Kit.

They were still grinning at poor Dan's mortification when Grady O'Keefe strolled by. He raised an arm to them in gesture and called out cheerfully:

'Hello lads, starting early on the ale again, I see. Wish I could join you, but...' he tapped the sketchbook in his other hand. 'Busy! Things to create.' He turned, walking backwards now, 'I'll catch you another time.'

Then spinning on his heel again, he continued his jaunty pace along The Wharf towards Fore Street. The three friends watched him go.

'Dickhead,' said Dan.

'Wanker,' said Zack.

The brothers looked at Kit expectantly.

'Oh, come now,' said Kit. 'We don't have to do this every time. It's childish.'

'Yes, we do,' said Zack flatly. 'We *always* do it.'

'And he is,' said Dan. 'You know he is. Patronising git. "*Things to create!*"' he mimicked.

'You've seen his sculptures,' said Zack. 'Long columns of lumpy plaster. Dumpy little turds of clay. What does he know about a hard day's work? Pretentious tuss.'

'He's Pepper's husband,' said Kit. 'We should restrain ourselves; it's disrespectful.'

'Disrespectful?' said Zack. 'After what he did himself? The business with Senara?'

Kit frowned. They were right. Senara had taken the blame, for the most part, whilst Grady had emerged relatively unscathed. He had maintained his relationship with Pepper, whereas Senara had fled. The man pranced around town seemingly bereft of remorse. But worse than that, there was an arrogance about him; as if he found their concerns trivial, their disquietude amusing.

'Look, I dislike the guy as much as you,' he said. 'Probably more so. I just think we should, you know... Rise above it.'

Dan looked at Kit, dumbfounded, then said emphatically: 'He's a dickhead.'

'Wanker,' nodded Zack.

They both looked at Kit again.

Kit shook his head in resignation. They weren't going to let up.

'Nob,' he conceded with a grin.

CHAPTER 10

Driftwood

Senara took a moment from her duties to look across the harbour from the front patio of Driftwood. The pizzeria was ideally situated—notwithstanding the steady flow of traffic that passed along the wharf—for taking in the picturesque views, and these few outside tables were highly sought after. Senara had worked here previously, before Greece, and the familiar scene made it all the more strange to be back; to find herself suddenly transported and waitressing once more in Rosa's pizzeria, and no longer in the heat of Nikos's taverna; to be accosted not with the scent of bougainvillea, but of seaweed.

Strange too, to be single again, with no sign of romance on the cards for her. Perhaps it was just as well. Her track record was hardly encouraging. The only person who appeared to be remotely interested in her was Brian, that man she had met on the train. He had recently followed her on Instagram too, and had taken to messaging her privately. He was 'just saying hi', he said, and 'of course' he remembered her. Perhaps they could meet for coffee if he was ever in St Ives?

'Cool,' she had replied, but not without pause. She was sure she was not the sort of person to strike up an online relationship, but in this instance, they had actually met before. Her hesitance, she knew, was because she was not immediately attracted to him, and this made her feel bad. Given her woeful history, she knew that she should perhaps take a chance on a different type. And he was only suggesting coffee, after all.

She sighed, and began to clear the vacated table of its abandoned clutter of plates, glasses, and bottles. The other outside tables were all taken, and none of their occupants appeared likely to be giving up their prized seats any time soon, but lingered over bottles of wine and post-meal cheese boards.

'Hello,' said a voice from the pavement. It was the other person from the train; the woman called Malory. 'How are you?' she said.

'I'm great, thanks,' said Senara with a smile. She was aware that she had not been overly friendly when they had first met. She had been self-absorbed and introverted, and now felt a pang of guilt. 'No more fainting fits, at least.'

'Glad to hear it,' said Malory. 'This looks like a nice place. I suppose you'd recommend it if you work here?'

'Yeah, it's amazing,' said Senara. 'The pizzas are to die for. But there are other options. Pasta and salads, mostly.'

Malory looked hesitant, almost nervous. 'I don't suppose that table will be free now?'

Senara took a quick look around at the internal part of the café, wondering as she did why this Malory always seemed so reticent. They were already quite busy for lunchtime, and there was a couple waiting to be seated. They were eyeing the patio spot covetously, jittery with expectation. It *was* one of the best tables.

'Sure,' she said. 'In fact,' Senara reached into her apron pocket and whisked out a card printed with the word 'RESERVED'. 'Just to be sure. Come on in,' she beckoned.

Malory made her way to the café entrance, skirted past the unfortunate waiting couple, and then wove her way through the seated diners to the outside space.

'Thank you,' she said. 'That was kind of you.'

'Not at all,' said Senara. 'Besides, I owe you.'

'You really don't,' said Malory. 'I was just there. I only did what anyone else would have.'

'I'm not so sure about that,' said Senara grimly. 'But thank you; for looking after me. I'm glad you were there. Now, will anyone be joining you?'

Malory's expression changed, and there it was again. That *look*. 'No, it's just me, I'm afraid.'

And then Senara understood. 'Not a problem, I'll just finish clearing these things away and then be back with your menu. Can I bring you a drink?'

'Yes, that would be great,' said Malory. 'A white wine, please. The house one will be fine.'

'Okay. One white wine, coming up. Enjoy the view!'

By the time Senara returned with the wine and the menu, Malory had removed her cap and sunglasses, and appeared to have relaxed a little. The lifeboat house was a short distance along the wharf and she was watching the manoeuvres of the crew.

'Thank you,' Malory said, taking the menu. 'What's going on? With the lifeboat, I mean.' She had recognised one of the crew as the man—the Viking—who had helped her in The Barquentine.

Senara looked and saw Kit and other lifeboatmen on the slipway in full gear, making ready the inshore lifeboat. 'Oh. It looks like they're launching,' she said pensively. 'I hope it's nothing serious.'

'They're all volunteers, aren't they?' said Malory. 'They really ought to be paid. I mean, it's so hazardous, isn't it? Doesn't seem right somehow.'

'Oh, I don't know,' said Senara. 'In some ways, I think it's a good thing. I mean, I know it feels wrong, because of the danger involved, but that's kind of the point. Because it's voluntary, you get the right type. You know, people with the right...*mettle.*'

'Oh I see,' said Malory. 'It requires a certain character. And courage, of course.'

'Exactly,' said Senara. 'And there's so much training involved. It demands commitment. They won't take just *anyone...*' she said waving to someone passing on the street '...Like this guy, for instance.'

Malory looked on in disbelief, as the man called Jago sauntered towards them, and leaned casually on the patio railings.

'Afternoon ladies,' he said. 'Did I hear you disparage my good name?'

'I was just explaining how only the finest volunteer for the lifeboat crew,' said Senara.

Jago grimaced. 'Don't you start,' he said. 'Kit is always pestering me to sign up.'

'As if they'd have you,' said Senara. Then seeing Malory's slightly shocked expression, added: 'It's okay; he's my brother. I love him really.'

'Your brother?' said Malory.

But her surprise was ignored as they all watched the inshore lifeboat speed across the water and disappear beyond the pier.

Jago suddenly climbed over the railings and sat down in the chair opposite Malory. 'I'll have a beer Sis, since you're taking orders. A nice cold lager.'

'Jago! You can't just intrude on the customers. Go and have a beer in The Barque,' said Senara.

'Malory doesn't mind, do you Malory?' said Jago. 'I'm starving too. Chuck us the menu when you're done.'

Senara pointed her pen at each of them in turn. 'You two know each other?'

'We've met,' said Malory.

Senara looked at each of them again curiously, but before she could ascertain more, she felt the soft nudge of a bottom brush against her own. Customers on the adjacent table had finally departed, and Rosa, the café's owner, had come to clear the dishes onto a tray. Having squeezed past Senara, she turned and slouched, casually resting her hand on the back of Jago's chair.

The other waitresses at Driftwood were, without exception, young, fresh-faced, and slender. Most of them were beach-blonde, with strong, lean, and tanned surfer's legs that looked good in the short black skirts of their uniform. Rosa was striking in as much as she broke this mould. She was older, for a start, although Senara could not have said exactly how old. She only knew that she had moved down to St Ives at least ten years earlier, with her then young daughter, Giovanna. After only one previous visit, she had been smitten; and had thrown all her passion into growing her business.

Unlike the other waitresses, Rosa wore a tea dress; black with a print of small red flowers, and an apron. Her hair was a startling mass of uncontrollable long ginger curls, that did not immediately reveal her Italian heritage. She spoke with a London accent, her voice deep and husky from cigarettes, which were stolen in bursts between custom, in the alley at the back of the restaurant. Her figure was rounded from a life of merry abandon; the love of good food and wine. As she frequently announced, 'People who say I should lose weight? They can go eff themselves. Nobody is gonna tell me I take up too much space on this planet.'

Rosa took the situation in, curious about the stranger at the table who appeared self-conscious. But then turned her attention to Jago.

'Back again?' she said. 'Thank goodness for you, keeping me in business.'

'Happy to oblige,' said Jago. 'Although it is completely ruining *me*.'

'What a beautiful day it is too,' said Rosa. 'Perfect for pizza and wine. I don't believe we've met?' She returned her sharp eye to the newcomer.

'This is Malory,' said Jago, as if she were an old friend. 'She's just moved here. Malory, meet Rosa, the owner. You'll get a seriously great pizza here, trust me.'

'Ah, I didn't realise you'd moved here,' said Senara. 'So, how do you like St Ives?'

'It's beautiful,' said Malory. 'But I'm still settling in.'

'Yeah, how *is* the dawn chorus?' said Jago. 'You getting any sleep yet?'

'Well, it's still kind of rowdy, but I'm getting used to it. And yes, actually, I'm sleeping much better. Too well, in fact. I can barely awake some days.'

'Ah,' nodded Rosa knowingly. 'That'll be the air.'

'The sea air,' explained Senara. 'It's so fresh. It takes a bit of getting used to. I've been struggling to adjust myself, since I got back. It makes me dream more. Deep, weird dreams that seem real.'

'That's it, exactly!' cried Malory. 'I dream all the time now, and more than that, I remember them. Whereas I don't recall remembering my dreams in London.' She paused. 'How strange is that, now that I come to think about it?'

'I dream *all* the time,' said Jago.

'Just a couple of nights ago,' continued Malory, 'I dreamed...'

She looked around at the expectant faces, suddenly unsure. ‘Don’t laugh, but I dreamt that Keanu Reeves was my flatmate.’

‘Yeah, I’ve had that dream…’ said Rosa wryly.

‘No, no, it wasn’t like *that*. He was just my flatmate. In a completely platonic, ordinary kind of way. And for a moment after I woke up, I totally believed it was true. And I was almost laughing aloud at the absurdity. Not that Keanu was my flatmate, you understand, but that I could possibly forget about something like that! That I would take such a thing for granted. I mean…how could you?’

‘I don’t think it’s something I would forget,’ said Senara, laughing.

‘And then,’ Malory was grinning too now, as if finally relaxing. ‘It slowly dawned on me how crazy it was that he chose to live with me, in what is possibly the most unappealing, most un-chic flat in the whole of St Ives!’

‘Especially with the resident seagull colony,’ said Jago.

‘Quite,’ said Malory, ‘I mean, I’ve peeked in a few windows. There’s some serious swank going on here.’

She smiled at Jago, before quickly looking down again into her drink, swirling it idly in her hand.

‘Oh well,’ she said. ‘It was nice while it lasted. Keanu appears to have moved out now.’

‘Anyhow,’ said Rosa, as if tearing herself away from a dream of Keanu. ‘Don’t like to break up the party,’ she said. ‘But there are customers waiting…’

‘Of course,’ said Senara. ‘Sure. I’m on it.’

As Rosa picked up her tray and returned to the kitchen at the back of the restaurant, Senara turned to Malory, who had barely had a chance to look at the menu. ‘Do you know what’d you’d like? Or shall I come back?’

'Have the Caprina e Barbabietola,' said Jago. 'Goat's cheese, beetroot, butternut squash, onion. Delicious.'

'I don't like goat's cheese,' said Malory.

'What?' said Jago, incredulously, and grabbing the menu. 'That's insane. You could maybe ask for it without, but it wouldn't be the same. Let's see then...' he scoured the list of pizzas. 'How about the Ortolana?'

'No,' said Malory. 'I think I'll have the Buffalito. If that's all right with you?'

'Okay,' said Jago, slowly. 'A respectable choice. Simple but classic.'

'But with added pine nuts and sultanas,' said Malory.

'Sultanas?' said Jago, frowning. 'Urgh.'

'And a wedge of lemon on the side.'

'What is wrong with you?' said Jago.

'It's *my* pizza!' said Malory.

'Jago!' hissed Senara, with a warning look at her brother, followed by an apologetic one for Malory. 'I'll give you more time. And don't be afraid to tell him to go away.' She turned and headed back inside.

'Don't forget the beer,' Jago called after her.

While Senara was fetching the bottle of lager from the fridge, she noticed Rosa, who stood behind the till, giving her a wide-eyed look and a nod of the head towards the restaurant.

Okay, okay, I said I was on it, thought Senara, and then hurried back with Jago's drink. Amazingly, in the short time that she had been gone, Malory had not only accepted Jago's presence, but been persuaded to share a pizza with him. Senara shook her head at her brother's insolence, but aware of Rosa's impatience, took the order without further admonishment. When she reached the order desk, Rosa once again gave her a meaningful look and a tilt of the head towards one of the restaurant tables. There were two women seated with a couple of young children, and the one facing her glared at Senara with a venomous look. The children were probably hungry and impatient, Senara assumed. She had been a waitress long enough to know the signs. Parents did not have the luxury of lingering over drinks before their orders arrived, but rather, intended leisurely meals were galloped through thanks to restless offspring. She took her order pad from her apron pocket and dashed towards the table in question. In her hurry, she did not see Rosa's look of alarm.

Senara approached the two women at the table with a smile. 'Sorry to keep you waiting. Can I get you some drinks?'

The first woman, brown-haired and bare-faced, continued to glower at Senara wordlessly, as one of the children, a little boy of about two years old, climbed upon her lap and started to jig, while the woman attempted to contain and balance him. The other child, a girl who could not have been much older, was systematically tearing up the children's menu into long paper strips. Senara turned to the other woman hopefully. The second woman was pretty, in a hippy sort of way, in a floaty loose dress. She had very straight blonde hair, precisely applied make-up, and wore an array of silver jewellery.

'I think we'd like another waitress,' said the second woman, in a cold tone.

For a second Senara was stunned, not understanding. 'I'm sorry,' she said. 'Is there something wrong?'

The blonde woman turned to look at her companion, who still wrestled with the little boy. 'What do you think? Shall we go elsewhere?'

'I apologise again for the wait,' stammered Senara, 'As you can see, we're very busy. But I'll personally make sure your food arrives...' her voice trailed off as she looked into the eyes of the brown-haired woman.

And then she knew. She had not at first seen through the guise of mousy-coloured hair cut into a practical chin-length style; the pale, jaded expression, and black, functional clothes.

'Pepper?' she gasped, even as the flush raced through her veins.

The woman continued to stare at her; her usually pretty features hardened and cold. 'I heard you were back. Surprised you had the nerve to show your face again.'

Ridiculously, Senara fought the urge to laugh at the clichéd comment. But even as she recoiled from the attack, even as she felt her legs begin to tremble with nerves, she could not help but gape in amazement. The Pepper she knew bore no resemblance to this dowdy, embattled-looking woman. Pepper had been the archetypal surfer-chick, with long, wavy, blonde hair. She rocked around town in little Roxy dresses, flip-flops, and nalu beads. Back in the day, Senara and Pepper had been almost inseparable, hanging out at the beach and surfing. Some even said that they were like twins, hard to tell apart; although Pepper's hair was not natural, like Senara's, but bleached; and Senara's long legs made her the taller of the two. But otherwise, they had become recognised and regarded as a pair. And so, it was a shock to see the transformation that her former friend had undergone.

Senara looked again at the two little children and realized that they must be *his*. They were Grady's children. As the little girl looked at her in curiosity, Senara saw his grey eyes. The impact hit Senara like a punch in the stomach; all her guilt and regret compounded into one.

'Let's go, Astrid,' said Pepper, loud enough to turn heads.

The two women stood and began to pack up the children's paraphernalia. Senara looked on in fresh horror at the mention of the blonde woman's name. Could this be the same Astrid? Kit's girlfriend?

'But I want pizza!' cried the little girl.

'Sorry, Molly. We'll get pizza somewhere else,' said Pepper.

'But I like it *here...*'

Senara stood by, foolish and inert as she watched them go.

'I'm sorry...' she heard herself say. Then again, her voice catching pitifully, 'I'm *sorry.*'

But the small party was already walking away, leaving Senara to face the looks from the other customers, who had observed the scene. On the patio, Jago was too far away, and engrossed in conversation with Malory, to notice her distress. But from those nearby, she saw in their eyes judgment, annoyance, and downright glee. Turned to stone, she might have stood there all day had Rosa not come and guided her back to the safety of the kitchen.

There, she put a comforting arm around Senara's shoulder. 'I tried to warn you. She came in while you were still on the patio.'

Everyone knows, thought Senara. *Everyone. Even Rosa.* Instinctively, she put her hands up to cover her face.

Rosa spoke gently: 'Perhaps you should take the rest of the shift off. I can cover your tables.'

'No. I'm...I'm fine,' said Senara.

But even as she protested, the shock and the shame engulfed her, and shaking uncontrollably, she collapsed into tears.

CHAPTER 11

On the Rocks

Dan Hosking cursed as his foot slipped on the jagged wet rocks again. Once more that day he wondered why he had agreed to this...

It had been decided by communal vote that he should give Marta another chance. It hardly seemed fair to Dan, since of the three of them in the reckoning, he was the only one to actually have to go on the date. So, he felt with some aggrievance that his vote should count for more; should carry more weight. But Kit and Zack had persuaded him that Marta was worth another chance.

'It's not like there's anything wrong with her,' Kit had said. 'And I have to say, your first date was at least amusing, if you would only look at it like that.'

'Yeah, and she's still fit,' added Zack, as they'd huddled together in The Barquentine over pints.

'I suppose,' had been Dan's only argument.

Yet when it had come to making the phone call, he had come over in a sweat of apprehension. What if he'd left it too late and she was upset that he hadn't called before now? What if she thought him a total loser, and talked of him scathingly to her mates? Perhaps she was dating someone else? It was a ray of hope. Yes, she might be dating someone else; bound to be, a pretty girl like that.

But Marta had sounded, if not quite eager, perfectly content to see him again.

'Yeah sure,' she had said, matter-of-factly, 'I was going to drive down to Gwynver tomorrow if you'd like to come?'

'Gwynver?' Dan had mused. He should be working, but even as this excuse formed in his mind, he knew Zack would say that it was quiet, not being the weekend, and that he could take off. And Gwynver was beautiful, of course. But...

'There won't be any surfing involved?' he'd queried.

Dan knew that the beach was a favourite surfing haunt of Kit and Jago. Despite being in the boat-hire business, Dan didn't really like the water. Could barely even swim, if the truth was told. And the coves and 'secret spots' of Penwith were notoriously inhabited by a tribe of super-fit and sometimes territorial surfers. None of it did Dan's anxiety any good, and he'd rubbed his paunch nervously.

But Marta had laughed, which was a good sign, and that had relaxed him a bit. 'No, no surfing. I promise.'

The drive down to Gwynver had been pleasant enough, careering along the winding moorland road in Marta's cute and trendy pickup truck. They had admired the scenery and concurred that the day was most pleasant, and that the sea was indeed a very distinct shade of blue—although the distant 'white horses' of waves breaking far out at sea should have foretold of what was to come. But it was only when Dan stood facing the bracing sea wind coming off the Atlantic Ocean, and with no obvious means of escape, that he began to have serious doubts about the whole situation.

The waves today were "pumping", he noted with some pride at his knowledge of the vernacular. High ridges of terrifying grey-green mountains of water thundered into spumes of breaking foam, that crashed into the rocks they stood upon, with all the force of the mighty ocean. It did not look remotely enticing to Dan, but predictably, an adrenalin-charged line-up of hardcore surfers was out. They rode the hollows—the 'green rooms'—of the waves, and flipped aerials off the lip, before leaping, with panache, into the churning sea.

It was all too much for Dan.

'It's okay,' said Marta. 'We're only going to paint them. *En plein air*, as it were.'

When they had arrived, and parked somewhere at the top of the cliff, Marta had produced a couple of drawing boards from the back of the truck, to which she had taped some paper. She had handed these to Dan, who had failed to see the significance at the time,—at least, it couldn't have anything to do with *him*—and instructed him to carry them down to the beach. But now as he perched on the slippery rocks, it all became clear. Marta reached into the satchel that she always carried and hauled out some brushes, watercolour paints, and a small cannister of water.

'Ah, no, you see; I'm not the artistic type,' Dan spluttered. 'Never have been. But you go ahead. I'll just watch.'

He steeled himself against the wind as his eyes turned wistfully along the coastline towards Sennen Cove, where The Old Success Inn lay; where there would be shelter, and a pint.

'Nonsense,' said Marta. 'Anyone can be a creator. Too many people have it knocked out of them at school, when they are told they cannot draw by some equally repressed and resentful teacher.'

'So... I'm *repressed?*' said Dan, with a puzzled look.

Marta dismissed him with a wave of her hand. 'It's just a question of practice. How can you ever know what you can achieve, if you don't try?'

'No, really,' protested Dan. 'I'm rubbish. Truly...'

But Marta merely tutted and handed him a paintbrush. With a heavy sigh, he acquiesced.

Looking around, Dan saw that there wasn't even anywhere to sit down. The rocks were all wet and covered in yellow lichen, or sharp mussel shells, or barnacles. Following Marta's lead, he clenched the drawing board on top of one forearm, whilst simultaneously attempting to balance his own large frame on his precarious foothold. It was extremely uncomfortable.

But Marta looked as though she was in raptures as she dipped her brush and began to paint.

'Try to capture the dynamic juxtaposition of surfer and wave,' she yelled against the burgeoning wind and resounding sea.

Dan shivered in his T-shirt and wished he'd brought his hoody from the truck. Too late now. If he ventured upon the climb back up the cliff, there was a good chance he would not come back. He gave one last desperate look around, but with no salvation in sight, thought he might as well give it a go.

First, he painted a large panel of blue across the top of his paper. This took him a good while, as he battled against the strengthening wind, that whipped against his board. He tightened his grip and painted another panel of green for the sea. In an act of daring, he added some white splodges to represent the breaking waves. Then carefully, he drew a little matchstick-figure surfer—well they *were* a long way away—atop of a bright red surfboard. Emboldened now, he carefully added some round blobs in brown paint to represent the cluster of rocks. And then, in a spasmodic fit of artistry—and because he had noticed the lichen—he dabbed some yellow spots onto the brown blobs.

Getting carried away with himself now, he picked out some black paint and attempted to draw the mussels on the rocks. He took a while to do this, becoming absorbed in the process. He even began to think that this must be what it felt like, to be a *real* artist. But then he stopped to observe what he had done, to look at the picture as a whole, and realized that it had all gone horribly wrong. The mussels were way too big and were getting all mixed up with the rocks. Perhaps he should have used a smaller brush?...

It was too late. His fledgling artistic practice withered and died along with his discouragement. Fed up now, he glanced across to where Marta worked busily.

What the... What the hell was she doing?

Marta had squatted down on the rocks and was dabbing her brush into a puddle of seawater left behind by the tide and was not only using it to wet her paint, but splattering it randomly across her picture. And she didn't appear to have even got around to the sky, as her painting was just a mass of black and grey patterns and lines. Noticing that he had stopped, she got up and daintily picked her way across to him with an encouraging smile.

'How's it going?' she said cheerfully. But her expression changed when she saw his picture.

'It's finished,' said Dan.

'Really?' said Marta. Rather too sternly, Dan thought. She looked at him expectantly. When he started to look upset, she softened a little. 'Have you thought about the sky?' she said.

Well, she *was one to talk.*

'Is it really blue?' Marta continued.

'Well...*yeah*,' said Dan, starting to feel a bit miffed.

'Is it?' she pressed.

Dan continued to look sulky. This must be one of those trick questions.

'If you are going to make a representational image then you have to learn to depict what you are actually observing,' said Marta, 'and not what you think to be there. Do you understand?'

'Not really,' muttered Dan. 'But it's not *black* anyway, like you've painted it, I know that much. Not unless it's supposed to be night-time.'

Marta wore a patient expression. 'I have not chosen to represent the likeness of the scene, but rather capture the essence, the spirit of the place; the energy of the waves and the dance of the surfers combined. The shapes that they make.'

'I told you I wasn't an artist,' said Dan.

Marta look unexpectedly cheerful again. 'Keep at it, you'll get there,' she said encouragingly. 'I like what you've done with the rocks, those black ones look sort of menacing.'

Dan thought once more of the comfort of The Old Success. But it didn't look like Marta was ready to leave yet, so he resigned himself to one more attempt at his painting, even though he thought it was finished. And then when she was done, he'd persuade her to take him for a pint to recover. Even as he conjured up this encouraging thought, the tide, which had been gradually incoming, suddenly surged without warning across the rocks. Dan struggled to keep a foothold as the water cascaded past him, soaking his trainers and the bottom of his jeans. The water receded with just as much force, and he wobbled again.

Swearing, he shouted a warning to Marta. 'We'd better get out of here before...'

It was too late. The ocean had already reared and begun a second incursion. This time the current was too strong and knocked Dan from his feet. He landed hard against the rock, spluttering as the freezing water engulfed him, wrenching the drawing board from his arms. It was carried away on the bubbling stream like a piece of driftwood. He struggled to a sitting position, and looked again towards Marta, in some concern.

But Marta was squatting again, miraculously unscathed, on a large, level piece of rock. Seemingly unaware of his predicament, she had deliberately submerged her painting in a rockpool left by the surge, and was dragging it back and forth through the salty waters.

'Isn't this great?' she called, without looking back at him, her voice carried on the wind. 'The sea will dictate the flow and pattern of the marks! It's a collaboration between nature and man!'

Dan watched as his painting was carried away, beaten and torn by the rocks and the tide.

'In that case, mine should be a bleddy masterpiece,' he muttered under his breath.

CHAPTER 12

Kit

Kit Curnow let himself into the old fish cellar underneath his house. He opened the top half of the stable door to let in the fresh evening air and propped his surfboard against the wall with the others. The lifeboat shout earlier had been difficult and stressful. Some teenagers who had been drinking on an old, unseaworthy dinghy had not realised how far they had strayed to sea, or indeed the peril that they were in. It had taken some persuasion to convince them to return with the lifeboat. He had been grateful, later on, for the surf, that had left him renewed, and invigorated.

Unlike most of the neighbouring holiday lets, Kit had not had the cellar converted into a 'tastefully refurbished' kitchen-diner, but rather kept it much as it had always been, and used it for storing his fishing gear and boards. He stripped naked, then carrying the wetsuit with him, padded barefoot across the slate tiles towards the back of the cellar. A half-glazed door led out onto a small covered balcony—only a ledge really—that nevertheless overlooked Bamaluz Beach, and a view of the bay across to the lighthouse. Only the balcony wall ensured his modesty, as he stepped under the outdoor shower that he had fitted. He turned the dial and drenched himself in the powerful blast of water. Running his fingers through his long hair, he rinsed the salt water from his body.

It never completely worked. There was always a lingering essence of the sea. In truth, Kit did not feel quite normal if his skin did not have that saltwater feeling—as if it had been pumiced and buffed, and he was ever-so-slightly dehydrated, and dazed from sunshine. But Astrid didn't like it when his hair was 'sticky', as she put it, after a surf. His living as a fisherman, was cause for equal objection.

'You stink of fish,' she berated him regularly. 'Why can't you get another job? I don't understand why you want to be surrounded by dead fish all day.'

She had, he admitted, a point. There were times when he considered his options, for fishing was not an easy game, especially since he operated on a small, sustainable scale. And he had, on more than one occasion, been offered a position at the surf school. But Astrid opposed this plan too, on the grounds of it being equally insecure and seasonal. If he had but known, her true disapproval lay in the fact that his strong lean muscles would be permanently on show in a wetsuit, and his tanned, good-looking face and winning smile on display for every giggly beachgoer. But Astrid did not say this. No, it was a 'proper' job that she prescribed for him; one with a 'future', whatever that meant.

He eyed the new bar of soap that had been strategically placed on the shelf for him to use. It was chocolate coloured, and permeated with flecks of red. He picked it up and sniffed cautiously. Sure enough, it smelled of chocolate, coconut, and—what was that?—strawberry? Kit wouldn't have minded something herbal or citrussy like bergamot, or an earthy, masculine sandalwood. But Astrid always devised that he should smell sweet and edible. Nevertheless, he began to soap his body dutifully with the bar, singing loudly as he did. He turned to overlook the sea, just in time to catch a boatload of tourists pass by beneath, drawn to the source of the sea shanty. Each of them stared, drop-jawed and agog at his beautiful nakedness. He grinned and waved. When someone wolf-whistled, he saluted, and bowed with a theatrical flourish.

* * *

Kit left his wetsuit rinsed and hanging to dry on the outside ledge and then, naked but for a towel fastened around his waist, locked up the cellar again. Casually, he walked barefoot the short distance along Wheal Dream to the exterior staircase with ornate wrought-iron railings, that led to the upper house. As ever, he attracted the attention of passers-by. A middle-aged woman eyed him sideways with a grin, flagrantly ogling his toned, tanned physique, as he leisurely climbed the stone steps. Her husband squirmed in an equal measure of shame and envy.

He entered into the small living room, dominated by a granite fireplace, which Astrid had adorned with a row of candles. He dropped his keys on the table that she had bought, influenced by her interest in all things South Asian. The wooden base was carved in the shape of an elephant, and she had placed it to one side of the hearth, which irritated Kit. There was nothing wrong with the table, as such; only that Kit felt it out of character against the beauty of the stone fireplace.

As usual, he slipped on the patterned cloth—a relic from her travels in India—that she had lain, covering the stripped wooden floorboards that he had carefully restored and sealed in yacht varnish.

'Are you sure it's not a tablecloth?' he had asked her at the time. 'It's got no grip.'

And as usual, he dodged the crystals hanging in the kitchen doorway. Pink quartz was for love, said Astrid, and blue quartz for calm and harmony.

“There’s nothing calming about being hit on the head with a stone,” Kit had said upon his first encounter.

Astrid was in the kitchen preparing a meal.

‘Steak again?’ asked Kit. ‘There’s fresh mackerel in the fridge, you know.’

‘You can have that,’ said Astrid. ‘I didn’t fancy it.’ She appeared to be preparing some kind of sauce in the blender.

Kit opened a bag of nuts and munched on them as he observed her. The worktop was littered with broken eggshells, bottles of vinegar and lemon, and a tub of dried herbs.

‘What’s that you’re making?’ he said. ‘And I thought you were going out to lunch with Pepper today? You still hungry?’

‘Bearnaise sauce. And that was the plan,’ said Astrid. ‘But it didn’t work out. Pepper got the children takeaway fish and chips instead, and took them home.’

‘That’s a shame,’ said Kit, looking again at the gargantuan steak on a plate on the counter. ‘Hey, use some fresh tarragon from the balcony. Got to say though, you eat a lot of dead animals for someone so into karma.’

‘How is it different from eating fish? And I need the protein,’ she said huffily, her back still turned to him. ‘The animal’s strength gives me strength. So long as I honour it, it will not object to me being nourished by its power.’

She took the steak and began to pummel it with a small mallet.

‘Bullshit,’ said Kit laughing, between mouthfuls of peanut.

Astrid finally turned to face him. She sighed patiently, as though confronting a child. ‘Please Kit, put some clothes on. Why do you parade around the streets like that? It’s exhibitionist.’

‘No, it’s not,’ said Kit smiling. He abandoned the nuts and encircled her small waist with his powerful arms. ‘I’m just comfortable with myself. Why should anyone care? Why do you care?'

'It's embarrassing,' she said, turning from his embrace and back to beating up the poor dead cow that had died to give her strength.

'Okay, what's up?' said Kit. He had planned to tell Astrid about the shout, but sensed her mood to be unreceptive. 'You've clearly got the hump about something.'

'I met your friend Senara today,' said Astrid. 'At Driftwood, with Pepper. She was waitressing.'

'Yes. I told you she'd got a job there, didn't I?'

'Maybe. Anyhow, I didn't like her.'

'Why?' said Kit, looking concerned. 'What happened?'

'Not much,' said Astrid. 'We left; refused to let her serve us.'

Kit's smile dropped away, and his features set into an unusual look of dismay. His voice sounded grave when he spoke. 'Wait, so... You *ambushed* her?'

Astrid gave a little shrug as she continued to prepare the steak.

Kit swore under his breath. 'Well, that's just great. Very mature.'

He strode to the fridge and took out a bottle of cold beer. He opened it and drank straight from the bottle.

Astrid threw down the meat mallet and turned to face him with arms crossed.

'Was it mature of her to sleep with her best friend's husband?' she demanded.

'They weren't married back then,' said Kit. 'But no, it wasn't right. She made a mistake, Astrid. She's a good person who made a mistake. And you know what Grady's like.'

'She knew what she was doing.'

'And he didn't? He was almost a decade older than both of them.'

'Why do you always stick up for this woman?' Astrid looked at him in suspicion. 'What really happened between you?'

'Nothing,' said Kit. 'I've told you; we go way back. We're old friends that's all. You would see that she's really lovely if you gave her a chance.'

'I don't want her anywhere near our relationship. I don't want you to associate with her.'

'That's ridiculous,' said Kit.

'Really? Do you blame me?' Astrid raised her voice. 'What if she makes a play for you?'

Kit finally lost patience. 'I'm bored of this. It's gossip, Astrid, and I'm not going to join in your playground bullying. Please, Astrid, get to know her. You'll see I'm right.'

Astrid turned on the blender that contained the bearnaise sauce, drowning out his argument.

Kit took his beer and went upstairs to the bedroom to change into jeans and a knitted jumper. When he returned, he saw that Astrid had gone to eat her steak in the living room in front of the television. He stepped out through the kitchen door to the sun terrace. This was a larger, square-shaped balcony that overhung the one with the shower below. The terrace had a small table and two chairs where you could sit and watch the sun rise over the bay, but mostly the space was taken up by his herbs, which he grew from seed or cutting. He had made some tiered shelving which took up most of one side of the balcony, placed to receive the most sunlight. Elsewhere, there was a propagator filled with seedling tomato plants, and scattered around, small trees of lemon, bay, and a hopeful olive.

Astrid complained about the lack of space—she wanted more room for her yoga mat and sun lounger. But this was one territory that Kit insisted remain his own. He walked to the balcony wall and stared towards the lighthouse at Godrevy in the distance. He supped his beer and tried to calm himself, as the colours in the sky slowly dimmed and changed. Soon the sun would be setting behind the headland over on Porthmeor Beach, and here on the harbour side of the Downalong peninsula, the moon would light up the darkening sea. Often, he would sit here, late into the night, gazing upon the canopy of stars and listening to the ever-present sound of the sea.

It was a place that made it hard to imagine that there was any trouble in the world. He sighed and reminded himself of how lucky he was.

His equilibrium restored, he finished the beer and then went to fill the watering can from the outside tap. From the kitchen window, he could see through into the living room. Astrid appeared to have finished eating, and now held her mobile to one ear and made quiet intonations to the caller. But Kit knew, without doubt, that it was Pepper.

Kit felt the frustration rise in him again, but quickly turned away to carefully water his plants. The grateful aromas of rosemary, basil, and oregano greeted him as he moved along the terrace, inspecting each plant in turn. By the time he was finished, he felt better again. But he did not go back to re-join Astrid. Instead, he crept into the vacated, darkening kitchen and stole another beer from the fridge. By the sound of ambient music coming from the living room, he ascertained that Astrid was restoring her own balance with a bout of meditation.

He picked up his guitar from where it was propped up on the kitchen bench, then went outside again and pulled up one of the chairs. With his feet upon the other one, he looked to the night sky and tried to relax, as he gently strummed the chords to an old folk song. But he felt downhearted about the way things had gone. If only Astrid had met Senara through him, and not Pepper. Kit had spent his whole life avoiding conflict, bad feeling, and anything that might cause stress. He believed, with a passion, in being laid back, and easy-going. But Senara had only been home for five minutes, and already was the cause of a rift between Astrid and himself. He tried to work his way around the uneasy feeling that threatened to disrupt his serenity; but if he was to be just, it could not be evaded:

What if Astrid was right, and Senara was trouble?

CHAPTER 13

Choux Buns

It was a dreamy, sweltering day in May. Sitting at her desk in Atlantic Arts, Malory once again raised her eyes to view the opposite side of Fore Street. There he was again; that man standing in the doorway of the small gallery that bore the name, 'Grady O'Keefe'. She assumed that this must be the man himself. He was muscular and lean for his age—around forty, she thought—and wore his silver hair cropped short. Dressed in faded blue jeans and a tight black T-shirt that flattered his shape, he leaned casually against the doorframe with his arms folded, and watched the world go by. And every so often he would raise his eyes to stare unashamedly through the window to where Malory sat, a smile permanently on his face.

But Malory could tell even at this distance that it was his eyes that were his real power. Steady, inscrutable, and piercing, their grey-blue colour set off against the deep tan of his face.

Well, Mr O'Keefe, thought Malory. *Aren't you the big man to be reckoned with*? She looked down at the papers on the desk in front of her and pretended to be engrossed, until he got bored and went back inside. But Malory wasn't really thinking about figures and profits. She was wondering why she had allowed herself to be railroaded into sharing a pizza dinner with Jago Berryman. She had discovered that, apart from his love of surfing, he played guitar in a local band.

'Here's one of our flyers,' he had said, pulling a crumpled piece of paper from his pocket. 'Cosmic Ray and the Neutrinos. You should come and see us play, sometime.'

Of course he played in a band. He looked every inch the part. She had to admit it had felt good to have company, and it was true that she needed to make friends. But a guitar-playing surfer?

It was ridiculous. He was being a nuisance. And if he did not have such an earnest, carefree expression, and engaging forthright manner; if he wasn't so damn cheeky, and his hair did not fall a certain way across his eyes; then she might almost accuse him of harassment.

A noise from outside in the street distracted her. She heard the clatter of wheels on the cobbles, and then, as if she had summoned him with her thoughts, her eyes met the sight of Jago Berryman, parking some sort of barrow in front of her shop. Malory had noticed the tribe of street pedlars, hair braiders, and buskers who traded in the harbour and along Fore Street, and was not remotely surprised to discover that Jago was one of them.

He was once again stripped to the waist, dressed in only board shorts, flip-flops, and a straw hat. Today, bracelets of leather and macramé were knotted around his wrists, and about his neck, what looked like a shark's tooth attached to a leather thong.

Malory rolled her eyes. It was all such a cliché. Except she remembered that she too had once been like this... Once, in another world of carefree backpacking and before...well, everything else. Once again Malory had the strangest feeling; a yearning for who she once was, or might have been. And who was she now? How did she fit into the world?

Jago stood with his back to the window, his attention fixed on the passing tourists. Malory sighed. He was infuriating.

True, he had not acknowledged her presence this time, but it still felt like he was deliberately pestering her. She got up and stormed outside. She stood there for a minute, hands on hips, whilst Jago completely ignored her. Instead, he continued to flirt with a couple of blushing young girls, apparently with the intent of selling them necklaces like the one he wore. His barrow was a sort of wooden contraption on wheels, with handles for pushing. It was bedecked with items of jewellery, and on a high rail hung more straw hats and flip-flops.

Eventually, his sale made, Jago finally acknowledged Malory's presence.

'Afternoon,' he said. 'Beautiful day. You ought to get down to the beach. Perhaps I can interest you in a hat to keep the sun off?'

'What do you think you're doing?' said Malory. 'Those stupid hats are completely blocking my window. I'm trying to run a business here.'

'*I'm* trying to run a business here,' said Jago, leaning with one arm raised upon the barrow rail and looking at her steadily.

Malory looked at the display of wares dismissively. 'What? With this tat?'

Jago frowned. 'Well, that's rude.'

'Well, it *is* tat,' said Malory, laughing. She picked up a macramé bracelet and inspected it. In honesty, it wasn't that bad. But probably machine-made, or manufactured in some sweatshop somewhere. Nothing like the ones that she used to make by hand, and sell somewhere in a lost magical land in the Mediterranean. 'But more to the point, you're affecting my trade; driving away customers. Probably. Are you even allowed to do this? Is it legal?'

Jago grinned. 'Well, get you, Miss High and Mighty. I'm pretty sure anyone who wants to buy art stuff will buy art stuff.

They're not going to be scared off at the corner because...' and here he feigned mock horror, '...Oh no! There's a street seller outside! And it is legal, actually. I have a licence. But don't worry I won't be here all day. Have to keep moving.'

'How do you even make any money selling this stuff anyway? Are people really that gullible?'

Jago gave her a steely glare. 'Thanks for belittling my livelihood. Maybe when you've been in St Ives a little longer, you'll realise that many of us have to do more than one thing to survive; especially since tourism dies off in the winter. It's called diversification.'

Malory winced at the sarcasm. 'I know what diversification is.'

'Then perhaps you'll understand that this is good business, with the thousands of tourists we get in summer.'

He turned to fetch something from a bag hanging from the stall. He took out a lunch box and opened it. Inside were what looked like some sort of pastry bites.

'Savoury choux bun?' he asked coolly, and proffering the snacks to her. 'Blue cheese and watercress. Amazing.'

Choux buns? What on earth was he doing with choux buns? It felt so incongruous. Confused, Malory took one anyway. She held it in the flat palm of her hand, not quite sure why she was sharing his lunch.

'I've got beetroot balls, if you prefer?' said Jago.

'You've got wha...? No, don't tell me! I don't want to know about your...your *beetroot balls!*' said Malory, feeling flushed. 'I'm supposed to be working.'

'Suit yourself. Anyhow...' continued Jago, looking at her intently whilst munching on one of the buns.

'Yes?' said Malory.

'This isn't what I really do,' he said.

'Yes, I know, you're in a band. You told me,' sighed Malory.

'No, not that. That's mostly just for fun. What I really am...' Jago stood up straight, '...is an artist.'

'An artist?' Malory chuckled. 'You?'

Jago gave her a look, then turned to take some cash from another passing tourist for one of the hats. He placed it personally on the girl's head. 'Looks great,' he smiled. 'Enjoy the sunshine!'

He turned to Malory again. 'Why not me?'

'You didn't mention it over pizza...'

'You didn't ask.'

'Okay,' said Malory, laughing. 'I believe you. What sort of art? Comic books? Graffiti?' She eyed the octopus on his chest. 'Tattoos?'

For the first time, Malory sensed that she had gone too far. Jago looked at her this time with real annoyance.

'Nothing wrong with any of those things,' he said.

'No, of course not, you're right,' Malory replied, suddenly ashamed.

'If you don't mind, I've got customers.'

'Right,' said Malory. 'Me too.'

There was nothing else to say. Malory could only return to the shop and pray that she actually had some custom soon, to justify her haughtiness. But when Jago quickly picked up his barrow handles and moved on, she allowed herself to wallow in some justified self-loathing. She looked at the choux bun that she still held in her hand. Shrugging, she took a bite.

'Oh my god...' she gasped aloud, after tasting the morsel, and staring at the rest of the bun incredulously.

Flavoursome and light, Malory thought it might be the most delicious thing she had ever tasted.

CHAPTER 14

Salt Water

It had been a long time since Senara had carried her surfboard across Porthmeor beach. She had forgotten how heavy and unwieldy the baby-blue longboard was, but still relished the sensation, and the feel of it under her arm, as she recalled all the fun sessions that she and this board had had in happier times. Senara had always preferred mellow waves, and the elegant, stylish glide of a longboard, over the more frenzied aerials and fast turns allowed by shorter surfboards.

She felt apprehensive, still shaken by the encounter with Pepper, but encouraged by the words of Brian, who had been messaging her. She wasn't sure why she had begun to confide in him—was she that desperate for a friend? But now that he had stopped suggesting that they meet, Senara felt less pressured, and had even started to look forward to his nightly messages, offering kindness, support, and advice. Brian, who she had discovered was a copywriter of some sort, always seemed to know the right thing to say, and it was his motivational guidance that had cemented her resolve today.

You're depriving yourself of something you love, he had messaged.

When she reached the water's edge, she put the board down to assess the waves. It was early morning, before the lifeguards arrived, and despite the sunshine, the beach was near-empty. Where gentle waves lapped at the shore, the water was the colour of pale jade. Further out, the sea became a dark navy-blue that met the horizon with a sky the colour of her board. She could tell instinctively that soon the turning tide and an offshore wind might conspire to turn these waves into small glassy peelers.

She had to get to grips with this. It was time to surf again. On Antiparos she had mucked about on a belly-board a few times on Sunset Beach, but never did get around to making that trip to Tinos, where, it was rumoured, the calm Aegean threw up a few waves; or to nearby Naxos to at least try wind-surfing. But now she knew it was imperative that she regain some of the life force that she had once drawn from surfing. She could not let these awful feelings consume her again—the guilt and self-hatred that had damaged her so deeply before. Five years ago, Senara had walked around in a state of constant pain. She awoke in pain, and fell asleep in pain. It felt as though her innards had been removed and replaced with heavy steel; her heart with a rock. Senara had always taken to the sea when her soul was troubled, but after the fall-out with Pepper, even surfing had lost its healing power. Where once she would have paddled out to a line-up of mutual fellowship, suddenly she faced hostile looks and isolation. The whole world hated her, it seemed, and in the end, she had run away.

Yet she had been sure, at the beginning, that there had been something between herself and Grady; something real, and magical.

She could remember the exact moment that she had first set eyes on him. She had been standing at the sea wall with Pepper, checking out the waves at Porthmeor, trying to decide if it was worth a paddle out. For some reason she had turned just as a large, noisy motorbike came cruising around the corner. At the bend in the road where Senara stood, the rider slowed the bike down almost to a standstill, and then pulling up his old-fashioned goggles, he had looked right at her.

Even now Senara felt the remnants of the frisson of delicious excitement. Because he had really *looked* at her, and those grey eyes with their steady intent had registered a flare of appreciation. Grady O'Keefe had smiled at her, and then revved the engine of his bike, before picking up speed again, and screeching up Porthmeor Hill. He had literally ridden into town, and into her life, like a knight on a black steed.

Or a gunslinger looking for trouble, Senara thought ruefully now, embarrassed at her stupid naivety.

But at the time she had been thrilled at the exchange; had been sure that they had made a connection. It did not take long before the whole town identified him as the latest artist, or in this case, sculptor, to move to town. In the days and weeks that followed, it seemed that he haunted Senara's footsteps. He was there on Porthmeor Beach, drinking coffee at the café, and inscrutable in dark sunglasses as she made her way up the sand with her surfboard. He appeared in the bookshop, smiling brazenly at her over the piles of books stacked on the table between them, as she pretended to be absorbed by *Stories of the Sea*.

He had finally tracked her down, it seemed, to Driftwood, where she worked. He became a regular morning visitor before he began his day in the studio, even if he only ever ordered a black coffee. He always preferred to sit outside with his coffee because he smoked, and Senara remembered, to her shame, how cool she had thought this at the time. In fact, she had thought everything about him was cool. The motorbike, the buzz cut hair, the dark shades, and the tight black T-shirts that enhanced his strong, muscular arms. At first, she had been so nervous in his presence that she could barely serve him. She would try not to stumble as her legs quaked when she picked her way through the seemingly endless mass of tables, and desperately try not to drop or spill the expresso that rattled on its tiny saucer. But he *always* flirted with her, she was sure.

And then there was New Year's Eve, when St Ives became one big street party. It was customary for townsfolk and visitors alike, to don fancy dress as they crawled the bars and cafés, culminating with fireworks on Porthminster Beach.

'Let's just go as mermaids this year,' Senara had said to Pepper. 'I've always wanted to be a mermaid.'

'Not very original,' Pepper had replied.

'I know, but who cares about that?' said Senara. 'It's about fun, in the end, isn't it?'

'I suppose so,' said Pepper. Then grinning added: 'We would look hot, though, wouldn't we?'

'Exactly,' said Senara, beaming, and secretly thinking about Grady.

Senara had avoided the dubious online mermaid fishtails that did not actually allow walking, but instead made her own 'tail', a long, clinging skirt fashioned from pale green satin and chiffon, embellished with curling rows of sequins in pale blue, green, and pink. The skirt started at the hip, revealing her stomach, and ended with a small train at her feet. It only remained to decorate a bikini top with sequins and shells, and her outfit was done. She would freeze, but it would be worth it.

'That's seriously gorgeous,' Pepper had said. 'You have to make me one!'

And so, Senara had gone to work again, with only days to spare until New Year's Eve, but agreed that it would work all the better if they had matching outfits. Once Pepper's costume was ready, it was only left on the night to do their make-up and hair.

They spray-painted their long blonde locks in stripes of green and blue, and used glittered make-up on their eyes, lips, and body. When they were ready, they had cracked open cheap champagne, and saluted each other before heading out into the night.

'To us,' said Pepper.

'To us,' repeated Senara. 'The hottest mermaids in St Ives Bay.'

It was much later, in the scrum of one of the pubs on Fore Street, that Senara had begun to feel disheartened. There was still an hour to go until midnight, but so far, her efforts at siren-seduction appeared to have been wasted. Kit had shown up, with Zack and Dan.

'What are you supposed to be?' she had asked, regarding their put-together costumes, that vaguely resembled ancient Greeks.

'We're *The Odyssey*,' said Dan.

'*The* Odyssey?' laughed Pepper. 'What, all of you?'

'More specifically, we're *on* an odyssey,' said Kit. 'We're ancient mariners.'

'Which one of you is Odysseus?' Senara had shouted over the loud music. She never did find out.

Zack went to join his wife and her friends at a table, and Dan tried to hit on a girl dressed as some sort of sexy piskie. Pepper was attempting to communicate with Kit at the bar, her mouth held close to his bent ear, and her hand resting on his chest for balance in the jostling crowd.

Needing some air, Senara fumbled her way through the throng to the street outside. It was just as packed, but at least she could breathe in the cool sea air. She moved away from the crowded entrance to the pub, and then, slightly woozy from alcohol and fresh air, dropped her phone. Before she could retrieve it, a man in a caped costume and sporting a fake sword, bent to pick it up, then returned it to her with a bow. He appeared to be dressed as Zorro, but even in the dark street, Senara recognised the enigmatic eyes behind the mask. He stood upright, and moving closer, touched her gently on the cheek.

'So beautiful,' he said.

When she did not withdraw, he leant forwards and kissed her on the lips, pulling her closer to his body. Senara could not believe it was happening; this was exactly as she had imagined it would be, but was now suddenly real. She responded to Grady's kiss eagerly. But too soon, he had withdrawn from the embrace, and with a melodramatic swirl of his cape, vanished into the night.

Now, as she watched the breaking waves, Senara wished again that she had spoken of the encounter straight away. But it was Pepper who announced her intentions first. In one of their close conspiratorial chats as they sat huddled together on the beach, Pepper had declared, out of the blue, it felt, how she 'had the hots', for that Grady O'Keefe, the new artist in town. Of course, Senara had agreed, and confirmed that she too was attracted to him. But it was too late. She had broken the rules and kept her desire hidden too long. The bond with Pepper demanded that she should know all Senara's secrets, but Senara had wanted to keep this to herself, to nurture and nourish it close to her heart.

And so, she had been devastated not long after, to discover Pepper and Grady kissing in a dark corner of a party. Confusion and despair followed when they appeared to be dating. This was not how the story was supposed to go. Senara had believed herself to be in love, and had felt sure the attraction was mutual. But as Pepper and Grady became an item, she was forced to hide her misery.

Only you didn't hide it very well, did you girl? She berated herself. *You should have just let it go...*

If only she could change the past, just as she had now changed her mind about Grady. But the story remained; would always remain, tainting her life.

Yet there was one thing she could do, and that was to get back in the water.

Haters are gonna hate, Brian had messaged. *You can only do you, and who needs false friends anyway?*

Senara lifted her board and strode into the oncoming waves with purpose.

CHAPTER 15

The Girls

Later that day, at the other end of the beach, in the section portioned off by the lifeguards' flags as safe for swimmers and bodyboarders, Malory too stood gazing at the breaking waves in trepidation. She had hired a bodyboard from one of the surf shops in Fore Street, but had forgone the ordeal of hiring a wetsuit, for now, intimidated by the variety and her lack of knowledge. Feeling naked, but not wishing to get changed on the beach, she had walked in a swimsuit and board shorts the short distance from her flat, and along The Digey to Porthmeor, her bare feet tender against the cobbles and gritty roadside paths. To passers-by, she may have looked the part; as if she knew exactly what she was doing, and not in fact having an inner battle with her ego.

You have to do it, she told herself. *You* want *to do it. Little children do it, so stop being such a wuss.*

Malory had enjoyed walks along the beach, and around The Island, but somehow it wasn't enough. The St Ives vibe of being in, or on, the water at all times, made her feel somehow inadequate. As she watched the surfers float and slide and fly on the waves, she was filled with a desire that she had not known existed. It gnawed at her. She longed to be part of it, even in a small way.

Standing now with the lifeguards' eyes hot on her back, there was no turning back. Knowing that without a wetsuit the water would be freezing, Malory steeled herself. She had swum in the sea before, she reminded herself, not just in the

Med, but in the stark, south coast waters of Brighton and Bournemouth. It would be good for her, she reasoned; she would adjust.

The first icy fingers of ocean that curled around her feet almost made her change her mind. But the sun was warm on her shoulders, so she stopped deliberating and paddled determinedly into deeper water, gasping in shock as the cold sea embraced her. When she was waist-deep, and suitably distanced from other surfers, she turned with the board facing the shore, and awaited an appropriate wave. It took a few attempts to get the timing right, to catch the breaker at the right moment, and not just float on the swell. But then suddenly, she was off; flying on the surf towards the shore, then turning excitedly to immediately wade out for more, and yet more... In the quiet moments that she waited, with the sun's heat on her face, Malory looked out towards the town and the moors beyond, with the strangest feeling of being present.

I am here now, she thought, as though recording the moment for its import. *I am in the sea at St Ives, riding the ocean waves.*

Despite her exertion, the cold eventually became too much to bear. But when Malory finally strode from the sea, there was a wide grin on her face. As the sunshine warmed her skin, she felt more alive than she had done for a long time, exhilarated by the exercise and the cleansing power of the cold ocean.

Maybe this is what I'm here for. To surf..., she thought as she picked her way back up the beach. How different this was from the first time she had stumbled up its banks, imagining Jago Berryman's eyes on her. Now, following her immersion in its salt waters, she felt initiated, and somehow more belonging, of the place. Immediately she laughed at her pretence; at the idea that she could become a surfer, like *him*. No, there was something else yet to reveal itself to Malory, an unseen lure that fluttered around her consciousness, but that she could not define. There were no clues, but rather feelings, as she wandered the streets of St Ives.

In her mind's eye she saw the young Virginia Woolf, then Stephen, half-asleep in her childhood nursery at Talland House, listening in ecstasy to the waves breaking; or walking the path down to Porthminster beach, her senses and spirit enraptured by the intensity of the surrounding nature.

On Barnoon Hill, she saw Barbara Hepworth touching a hand to the stone wall of Trewyn House garden, about to discover her perfect sculpture studio hidden within.

In Bethesda Place, where Daphne du Maurier lodged on her visits, she could hear the merry laughter of the author and her painter sister Jeanne, as they strode together down to the harbour.

Then of course, there was Willie, boldly hanging out with the boys, as part of The Crypt Group in the former Mariners Church off Norway Square; or plotting with Barbara and the others in The Castle Inn, to form The Penwith Society of Arts.

Having visited most of the galleries in town, it seemed strange to Malory that although she loved the artwork of Lanyon and Heron and Wynter, it was the women whose presence she felt lingering in the streets of St Ives. So much so, that she had taken to calling them *The Girls*.

It was The Girls: Virginia, Barbara, Daphne, Willie; who seemed to want to tell her something; to offer some elusive encouragement that she could not grasp.

Yet after getting in the sea, Malory felt that she was a step nearer to the mystery. She had thrown off the cloak of timidity, the reticence of her London ways, and ridden the waves. It was a changed Malory who walked back up The

Digey to her odd new home. She still felt exposed, but in a different way. There was a new creature emerging from the shell of her former self, but the question remained: *What would she do?*

CHAPTER 16

The Net Loft

The surf had been a good thing. Senara had slept well after the physical workout, and the saltwater waves had somewhat eased her troubled soul. Instead of the more usual discordant dreams, she had dreamt that she was gliding on her surfboard, but high above the sea, and she was searching for something. In the morning, it reminded Senara that once, she had been an eagle, flying over the ocean, and she thought how strange the experience had been. It had felt more real than any dream, as if in her faint she had leapt into another body in a parallel world. But more than that, she had experienced an intangible, ineffable feeling. The closest she could get to describing it was... *Joy*. All she did know, was that she wanted the feeling again, instead of the disquietude that accompanied her every waking day.

The next morning the sea was flat, so Senara could not surf again, as she had hoped, before her afternoon shift at Driftwood. Instead, she took a walk along the coast path towards Clodgy Point. Beyond Carrick Du, the path cut through dense vegetation; verdant, and lush with wildflowers. Halfway along, she clambered up to sit on a rock, a favourite spot since childhood. Despite occasional passers-by, it still gave Senara a sense of peace out here, for it was ancient and unchanging. The same rock, the same sounds from the flora, the trickle of a hidden, overgrown stream nearby. The further you went from St Ives, the more the noise of people and cars became replaced by the hum of nature. This was the domain of beetles, butterflies, kittiwakes and fulmars. Today, with the sea quiet, the path became alive with the buzz of insects, the call of seabirds, and the mournful wail of a grey seal, carried on the air. She sat on the rock and looked out over the mesmerising, bright blue sea.

Then she took out her mobile and stared at it. How could something so inoffensive instil a rush of fear in her? For she knew that she should call Pepper. Or text her at the least, although the idea felt cowardly. She should not hide, but meet the source of her anguish head on. Senara decided on a middle way.

She tapped out a message to Pepper, suggesting that they meet. That way, Senara reasoned, she would not escape any punishment still owed her, and neither could hide behind the one-way apology of a text message. She pressed send, and waited, but the phone remained silent, accusatory.

Senara returned her attention to the beauty surrounding her, desperate to dissolve her melancholy. But her treacherous mind kept replaying the conversations with Pepper all those years ago; the shouts and accusations; the tears and name-calling. She had sought, not forgiveness, but understanding; had attempted to explain to Pepper the string of events that had led to her irrational and traitorous behaviour. Yet Pepper had, with one comment, rendered her excuses invalid.

'You know, I was there too, that day,' Pepper had said, referring to the time that Grady had ridden into town on his mechanical steed. 'Why do you always think everything is about you?'

And she was right. Pepper had been standing right beside her. Senara, in her arrogance and vanity had felt that Grady only had eyes for her, and that they had bonded. But there had been two of them standing by the sea wall that day. The awful truth of the matter served to twist Senara's version of events, until she could no longer trust it. Of course. Of course, she had imagined it all. *Pepper had been there too.*

When the phone finally bleeped, disrupting her reverie, it made Senara jump; a jolt of panic piercing her heart.

But It was Kit: *Where are you? We still need to catch up. I've got a couple of free hours. Coffee?*

For an instant Senara smiled. But it was short-lived. Updated by Jago, she had been dismayed to discover that Pepper's friend was indeed the same Astrid who lived with Kit.

His girlfriend.

She still found it hard to accept the concept. Kit, who had always been so hard to pin down; the eternal free spirit, averse to shackles, appeared to have met his match. At that moment Senara dearly longed to see him. Kit was a friendly face amongst all the whispering and gossip. But to hang out with him, however innocuous, would surely only court suspicion.

He sent another message: *I know what happened at Driftwood. Come talk to me Snow. Everything will work itself out. X*

Even as the stirrings of elation sprang in her heart, the tears welled again. Kit meant well, but how could she ever be forgiven? Yet he was her oldest friend, before Pepper ever came on the scene. Was she supposed to give him up?

They arranged to meet at Norway Square. She found him amongst the shrubs and hydrangeas seated with his arms outstretched along the back of a bench, and an ancient ginger cat snoozing proprietorially on his lap.

'Captain!' cried Senara, recognising the creature, and stroking its head. 'I can't believe this poor old thing is still alive.'

'Yep,' said Kit. 'Still prowling the same old haunts. Probably got at least half a dozen owners feeding him.'

'Bless him,' said Senara, taking the seat next to Kit on the bench, uncomfortably aware that his arm was now almost embracing her. She sat stiffly, trying not to make bodily contact. What if someone should see?

He kissed her anyway; the usual polite greeting of a peck on the cheek. 'What have you been up to, on this beautiful day?'

'Walking the coast path,' said Senara.

'On your own?'

Senara looked down. 'Yes.'

'I see. You were ruminating, weren't you?'

'Can a person not spend time alone without being suspected of being weird?' protested Senara.

'You were though, weren't you?' said Kit. 'I know you. Churning it all over and imagining everything to be bigger and darker than it is. Forget the past, Snow. Live in the here and now.'

'Your girlfriend hates me. Pepper hates me.'

'Astrid doesn't hate you; she just doesn't know you. All she knows is rumour. But I'm sorry it had to happen like that. I wish you could have met through me, instead.'

'It wouldn't have made any difference. She's Pepper's friend. And she has good reason to despise me.' Senara turned away to hide the emotion in her eyes. 'I should never have come back.'

Kit put both arms around her and hugged her, disturbing the cat, who nevertheless refused to budge from its comfortable position.

'I can't stand all this bloody misery!' he said.

Releasing her, he gently removed the old cat from his lap, placing it carefully back on the bench. Then standing, he pulled Senara up by the arms. 'Come on, let's go for a walk, find somewhere for a coffee.'

They wove their way through the backstreets, instinctively knowing every alley and short-cut. Senara took in the assortment of small independent businesses they passed; art galleries, potteries and tea-rooms, both old and new.

Suddenly Senara stopped and grabbed Kit's arm. 'Wait a minute...'

She walked over to view an estate agent sign that had been attached to a narrow alleyway, that might otherwise have been overlooked. There was no street name assigned to the lane, but locals knew it as Pudding Bag Lane, because you could only go "in one way and out the same". Senara stared at the sign. It was a local agency, and she knew the owner to be Bob Prowse; a friend of her father's.

It read: *For Sale: Licensed Business Premises*. Below this were a couple of photos of a neglected-looking space with a bar.

'Isn't this Isadora Francis's place?' said Senara. 'You know, the artist. She used to live and work in an old net loft around here.'

'Yeah, you might be right,' said Kit. 'I heard she died.'

'No!' cried Senara. 'Dora Francis died? That's really sad.'

'Comes to us all, my love,' said Kit. 'Had a full life though, I'd say.'

'She did. And this *must* be the place. My Aunt Minnie said she had her own private bar in her studio. All the local artists used to congregate and argue about the direction of abstraction, and whatnot. Or so the stories go.'

'I hate it when these old places come up for sale,' said Kit. 'You just know they'll get snapped up by someone with too much money and no sense of history, and turned into yet another luxury holiday home. It's a crying shame.'

'Yes, but this is being sold as a business, not a holiday let. Come on, let's go and take a look.'

'Why?' said Kit, raising his arms in despair.

But Senara was already heading further down the narrow confines of Pudding Bag Lane. She turned her head back towards him and said, 'Here and now, Kit. Here and now...'

They reached a small hidden courtyard where the backs of several buildings convened, and a secret tunnel led down to a tall wooden gate leading, presumably, to the beach.

'I never knew that was there!' said Senara. 'How could I ever have missed it?'

'So much for 'in one way and out the same',' muttered Kit.

Granite steps led up to the first floor of an old stone building, where some double doors and a window were painted the same colour as the gate to the beach, a worn and peeling dark green. The doors were open and they could hear voices within. Without a word Senara ran up the stairs and marched inside. Puzzled, Kit followed her.

They disturbed a middle-aged couple, and a flustered looking young man in a suit with a clipboard.

'Can I help you?' said the besuited man, presumably the estate agent.

'Yes,' said Senara. 'We've come to view the property.'

'Do you have an appointment?' said the agent, looking disgruntled and flicking through the notes on his clipboard.

'No... But I know Bob. He's a good friend of the family. He won't mind.'

'It's highly irregular,' said the agent. 'Viewings are by strict appointment only, and as you can see, I already have an interested party.' The middle-aged couple smiled awkwardly. 'Perhaps you could ring the office and make an appointment to come back another time?'

'Don't be silly, we're here now,' said Senara. 'But if you want to call Bob and ask him, I'm sure it will be okay. Tell him it's Senara. Although if I know Bob, he *will* mind being disturbed if he's on the golf course. Anyhow, we won't be long, you carry on.' She looked at the other couple with a dazzling smile. '*You* don't mind, do you?'

'No, no, not at all,' and 'No problem, fine with me,' the couple muttered and made demonstrative hand gestures.

'Great!' said Senara, then turned to the agent. 'You see, not a problem.' Then she quickly wandered off before he could protest. Kit followed her at his languid pace, gazing at her in amusement as she took in the premises.

'What?' said Senara. 'Why are you looking at me?'

'I was just thinking... It was good to see you back.'

'What do you mean?' she asked.

'The old Senara. Before you became a fountain of doom.'

'Very funny,' said Senara and walked off again.

It was a long room, originally designed for the making of fishing nets, or storing sails. There was an old, neglected wood-burning stove, and above them the exposed row of ceiling joists were dusty with cobwebs. The bare floorboards were scratched and scarred where the varnish had long been worn from them. At one end was a bar area and behind that a small greasy kitchen. To one side there were basic bathroom facilities, and at the very back, there was a smaller room where the dividing wall was set with glass panes, to allow in light from the larger space. The building might have been dark and grim but for a series of small windows set into the thick granite wall, and at the other end of the room, one large window magically framed a view of Porthmeor Beach, and the vast Atlantic beyond.

'It's perfect,' Senara whispered to Kit as they stood taking in the view.

'For what?' said Kit.

She turned to face him. 'I really need this place, Kit. I've always wanted to run my own café... A proper surf shack. And this space is just perfect. It hasn't been over-modernised. It has that relaxed vibe I'm after. You could even have sand on the floor...'

'Wait, wait...' said Kit. 'A surf shack? You want to open a surf shack, here?'

'Why not?' said Senara. 'Think about it, Kit. I've spent most of my adult life cooking and serving. It's practically all I'm good for! But I want somewhere to call my own, and this place would be just right. I can feel it. It has all the history and atmosphere. You said yourself...' Senara lowered her voice so that the other couple making their own inspection might not hear her, '...that it'll be ruined; turned into something awful if it's not appreciated. And look...' She dragged Kit over to a faded poster on the wall.

'See?' said Senara.

'Well, well,' said Kit, regarding the old advertisement. 'The Surfer's Store... So, Dora was into surfing? Who knew?'

The Surfer's Store was the first ever surf shop in the country, and it had opened right there in St Ives, in The Digey.

'You see,' said Senara. 'It's a sign.'

Kit shook his head, cynically. 'You're too romantic Snow. It's just a tatty old poster.'

Senara ignored him. 'I mean, I can't afford it, of course, but if I *could* somehow raise the money... Don't you think it's a good idea?'

Kit stood with his arms folded and studied the shabby, run down premises again. Then he looked Senara straight in the eye. 'I think it's a terrible idea.'

'Oh,' Senara faltered.

Kit sighed. 'Well for a start, no one will find you. Few people have heard of Pudding Bag Lane and even fewer know where it is.'

'I could put up a sign,' said Senara. 'And advertise.'

'It would still be like a secret spot,' he said, referring to the term for surf breaks that were kept hidden from the visiting hordes. 'You can't see it anywhere from the street. You'd have virtually no passing trade. Only those in the know would visit.'

'Well...that could work,' said Senara. 'It could be all the better for being a secret spot. It would only attract the surfing community...'

'Wrong again,' said Kit. He turned to gesture out of the window, and the view of waves and sand. 'For one thing, you have no direct access onto the beach. For another, most surfers, as you know, park above West Beach. That way they get to check out the waves from the cliff top. Then they can get changed in their vans and head straight down into the water. And where are you and your surf shack placed in this scenario? Nowhere. Hidden away down the other end of the beach. And even if you weren't, don't forget surfers wear wetsuits! They're not going to be carrying the money for a quick burger and a beer. You haven't thought this through at all.'

Senara looked petulant. 'Well, it doesn't matter if my customers aren't real surfers. They can be tourists and wannabes for all I care. They still have the dream of surfing, and appreciate the culture. And anyway, who said anything about burgers? This will be a vegetarian surf shack.'

Kit stared at her for a second in disbelief, before breaking into loud hearty laughter. The other couple and estate agent turned to look at them, the latter disapprovingly.

'Are you serious?' said Kit, barely able to contain his amusement. 'You want to serve lentils and lettuce to surfers? Surfers who need energy to paddle out? Who come out of the sea noodle-armed and ready to devour a horse? Surfers need protein, Senara, and carbs. Have you heard of a Hawaiian breakfast? Rice, eggs, and lots of meat... What are you planning to serve? Muesli?'

'I have a few ideas,' said Senara huffily. 'And you'd be surprised how much protein power there is in plant food.'

'Again, seriously? You really believe all that guff?'

'Of course. And I'm a surfer, aren't I? And what about Kelly Slater? He practically lives on chia seeds. Anyhow, it's a moot point since I...'

She glanced at the estate agent, and lowered her voice again.

'...since I don't have the money anyway,' she hissed. 'But it's so frustrating. I can see it all in my mind's eye. This whole place is just... It's just *me*.'

'I'll give you that,' said Kit with a nod to the faded surroundings. 'Seems just about crazy enough.'

'I have to say I'm disappointed,' said Senara. 'I thought you'd be more supportive.'

Kit placed his hands firmly on her shoulders and locked her eyes again.

'Senara,' he said. 'You would go under in a week.'

CHAPTER 17

An Artist

The best thing about St Ives, Malory decided, was the unexpected discovery that she now craved being outdoors all the time. Every morning she awoke charged with a compulsion to be up and outside as soon as possible, lest she should miss any of the beauty that appeared around every corner, ever-changing with the weather and the light. On working days, she rose with the sun, and made coffee in a portable cup. Then, taking it with her, she would walk the full length of Porthmeor Beach, and up and around The Island, where the Atlantic waves journeyed in from the horizon to crash on the dark rocks below. Afterwards, she would wind her way back through the narrow streets of cottages to the harbour where she would watch the fishermen return from an early catch, before making her way back up Fore Street to the shop.

But this sudden desire for the outdoors was also the worst thing about St Ives, because after her morning stroll, she then had to spend the day confined to the shop. At least, that was, if she was serious about building a business. All day long a parade of people carrying surfboards and beach gear traipsed past her window. The changing light and the call of seabirds made her long to be beach-headed too.

Back in the leafy suburb on the outskirts of London, Malory had never craved the outdoor life. Going outside was a necessity for getting from A to B, and physical exercise came via the gym. There was a time once, when she would walk the bridle paths and parks nearby, but familiarity and boredom had soon set in.

But here there was so much to do and see; the coast path and the moors to explore, beaches at Porthminster, Carbis Bay and further beyond. She had purchased her own bodyboard and wetsuit, so that now she would always be ready for the waves without hesitance, or fear for the cold. And for the first time in her life, she toyed with the notion of a proper surf lesson. She promised herself that one day she would walk the length of beaches from the Hayle estuary 'to the lighthouse,' in homage to Virginia, whose novel she had finally begun to penetrate. Everywhere, others walked and ran and took kayaks to sea. They raced gig boats. Yet as ever, her enthusiasm was tainted with a sadness; for some adventures were better enjoyed when shared. Perhaps she would get a dog...

A now-familiar rattling sound alerted her to the street outside. Sure enough, it was Jago with his barrow. Malory sighed. There was no point in confronting him again. She had no desire to fall out with the locals over something so petty. Especially since custom that morning had been dismal even before his appearance.

In a state of semi-daydream, Malory found herself watching his movements as he chatted to passers-by. She had to admit that he had an easy manner, a flirtatious charm and a charisma that drew all walks of life to him. Malory had never felt that she wanted to be a boy, but suddenly felt consumed with something akin to jealousy. What was it like to be so likeable and confident? So beguiling and beautiful? Not that Malory was unattractive, she knew she wasn't; but his grace went beyond his physical appeal; he radiated from within.

She was so deep in her thoughts that it took her a while to realise that he was not selling the usual paraphernalia, but that his stall was completely covered with what looked like slim boards and.... Were those the backs of canvasses? Malory's curiosity got the better of her.

She went outside and stared at the new contents of the barrow. Instead of hats and flip-flops and jewellery, Jago had covered the entire stall in a range of small paintings. As she approached to inspect these new wares, he looked at her warily out of the corner of his eyes but said nothing. Malory quickly assessed the artwork. The small canvasses and boards were of varying size, none of which were framed, but she could tell were otherwise finished to a professional standard. She raised her lashes discreetly to meet his cautious eye, but he only looked away indifferently.

Malory continued her perusal in a state of some astonishment. These works had not been executed in the narrative comic-book style that she had expected, nor were they the usual scenes of blue seas, sand, and seagulls that appealed to tourists. She could tell straight away that they were worthy of serious consideration; that there was substance and intention behind them. Semi-abstract, they were bold and beguiling... Like their creator.

'So, I take it these are *your* paintings?' she said at last.

He looked at her askance. 'You gonna call them tat?'

Malory laughed, as much at her own snobbery, as at his cheek. He had clearly set this up to shame her, to show her up for her previous rudeness.

'No, I'm not,' she said, with a smile. 'They're good. *Really* good. But I'm sure you don't need me to tell you that.'

'Nope,' said Jago, leaning against the door frame of the shop, and giving the impression that he didn't give two hoots for her opinion.

Although clearly, thought Malory, *he did.*

'Listen,' she said. 'I apologise. I was horribly dismissive before, and you've succeeded in humbling me. But...if you can produce work like this, why do you bother with the other stuff? Why not just concentrate on selling your artwork?'

He eyed her with a faint smile of amusement.

'Well now, I just don't know,' he said, shaking his head in mock puzzlement. 'Might be tricky. What with the rain, and the high winds, and all the sand blowing around... Not to mention the seagull poo.'

'I don't mean on the stall,' said Malory, exasperated. 'I mean sell your paintings for a living, as you well know.'

He made a scoffing sound. 'These are just a selection of small paintings. Sketches, really. I have much larger works back in the studio. And I do sell them occasionally, actually. But as I said before, I need other sources of income.'

'So today you are just...'

'Making a point, yes.'

Malory looked at him thoughtfully. 'I have an idea. By way of apology, how would you like to put some of your paintings up for sale in the shop? It is an art shop after all, and the walls could do with livening up.'

When she saw his dubious expression, she wondered if she had insulted him again.

'Oh,' she said. 'Unless you already have gallery representation elsewhere?'

'How much?' said Jago.

'What do you mean?'

'Commission. How much commission do you want, if a painting sells from your shop?'

Malory smiled again. 'No commission. As I said it's an apology. Unless you become a big name of course, then we'll talk again...' She winked.

'In that case,' said Jago, 'you're on.'

He gazed at her steadily, in that way that made Malory so uncomfortable.

'So, where do you...where do you, like, work out of?' she gibbered. 'Did you say you had a studio? Where is it? Porthmeor?'

'Yeah, I wish,' said Jago, and for the first time Malory detected a note of deflation in his voice. 'There's lots of competition for Porthmeor Studios. But yeah, I have a studio. I tell you what... Give me your number and I'll show it to you one day, when you're free. You can have a private view.'

He raised an eyebrow suggestively.

Malory hesitated and tried not to blush; tried not to assume that this was anything more than a casual arrangement.

'Of course,' she said. 'I'd love to see your...' for some reason her brain could not find other words, '...bigger works.'

She squirmed when Jago grinned. Surely, he did not think she was flirting?

Between them they selected a few of the small paintings for Malory to hang in the gallery, for now, and discussed prices. As soon as they had exchanged numbers, Jago picked up his stall by the handles and promptly departed, only stopping to call back: 'I'll text you then.'

As soon as he was out of sight, Malory went back into the shop and allowed herself a small smile. A thrill of excitement coursed through her body, unbidden.

'What are you doing, Malory?' she muttered aloud, and with the terrifying feeling that somehow, she had ventured into dangerous waters. *Just who do you think you are?*

And so, she reminded herself of exactly that, and quelled all of the foolishness that stirred within her.

CHAPTER 18

Daisy

Dan Hosking settled at the bar of The Barque with his pint of Doom. Sometimes he preferred it when his mates weren't around to goad him, and he could just enjoy a beer and a packet of pork scratchings without them teasing him about his gluttony. Sometimes just to sit and indulge in pleasure, and look forward to tonight's television was all he wanted. Often when times were quiet like this, and Tamsin wasn't too busy behind the bar, she would help him complete the newspaper crossword. Not the cryptic one mind, but the quick-break one where you just had to answer the questions. Dan hated the cryptic crossword. It was no fun at all. Keep life simple, that was his motto.

'Okay, here's another one,' he called out. 'What's a collective name for flowers? I don't get it. It's just 'flowers', isn't it?'

'How many letters?' said Tamsin.

'Seven,' said Dan. 'I can only think 'meadow', but that doesn't fit.'

'Bouquet,' said Tamsin.

Dan frowned and perused the crossword, tapping each square with his pen. He did this twice, just to be sure. 'Yep, that works. Well done.'

'You're welcome,' said Tamsin.

Dan filled in the boxes carefully.

When he looked up, she was still watching him through mascara-painted lashes. Expertly applied eyeliner perfectly set off her dark brown eyes. Today her lipstick was a deep red to match the print of cherries on her tight dress. As ever, Tamsin wore her dark hair in a 1950's hairstyle held in place with a tortoiseshell comb. What was it she had called it once? A chignon?

'Alrighty then,' he said. 'Try this one. Smallest subatomic particle? Seven down, five letters.'

Tamsin glanced at the puzzle, which Dan had turned sideways on, for her to see.

'Quark,' she said. 'Although strictly speaking, the question should read smallest *known* particle.'

Once again Dan tapped out the boxes with his pen to see if the answer would fit. When he appeared confused, she said: 'That's q, u, a, r, k. Quark.'

'Well. You're right again, I believe Tamsin. You always were the clever one at school.'

Tamsin smiled at him. 'Oh, I don't know.'

'No, it's true. I remember you always came top in everything. You could have gone to university. How come you never did?'

'Dunno,' said Tamsin. 'I guess I like it here.' She turned away to serve another customer. Dan watched her curvaceous hips sway as she walked.

It was true though, he thought. Tamsin had been effortlessly clever in the classroom. But her interests lay in rockabilly music and an obsession with Marilyn Monroe. She insisted that she was perfectly content with, and suited for, bar work. It had reached the stage where people had almost forgotten that she was ever smart.

Tamsin returned to lean on the bar near Dan. He tried not to stare obviously at her cleavage, but focused on her interlocked fingers. Tamsin had the daintiest, most well-manicured hands. Today her long nails were painted a brilliant shiny red. Dan cast his eyes downwards upon the crossword.

‘So, what happened with you and that Marta Miller?’ said Tamsin. ‘You still dating?’

‘Sadly, no,’ said Dan. ‘I mean, she was lovely and all that. But I don’t think I’m cut out for the art scene.’

‘Bit out of your comfort zone, was it?’ said Tamsin.

‘Yeah, very much so,’ said Dan, as he scrambled about in the packet for another handful of pork scratchings. ‘Oh well. Wasn’t meant to be, I guess.’

He chomped down his snack, then drained the contents of his glass. ‘I’ll have another, when you’re ready please, Tamsin,’ he said, nodding towards the empty vessel.

Tamsin looked at him shrewdly, as she picked up the foamy glass and tottered to the pump handle in her heeled sandals. ‘So, what’d you do, just dump her then?’

‘Not exactly...’ said Dan shamefacedly, as Tamsin pulled a fresh draught of beer, then wiggled back with his drink replenished. ‘Cheers, put it on my tab, will you?’

Tamsin leaned her elbows on the bar and supported her chin in her hands. ‘Go on then. What happened?’

‘I’d rather not say,’ said Dan.

‘Oh, come on, it’s just *me*,’ said Tamsin. ‘And I did help you with your crossword.’

Dan stopped twiddling his thumbs and grabbed a slurp from his pint. ‘Like I said, I’m not made for this whole art thing. Don’t really understand it. It scares me. I feel like I’m always on edge; like I’m going to say or do something stupid.’

Tamsin raised her eyebrows at him. ‘Oh dear. What did you do?’

Dan sighed, deeply. ‘We were at the Tate. One of them exhibition things. Luckily, I didn’t have to buy a ticket ‘cos she’s a member and all that.’

'Who was the artist?'

'Oh, *I* don't know,' said Dan irritably. 'They don't have real names. Not like you and me. It was like, a one-word name.'

Tamsin suppressed a chuckle. 'I see. So, what was the art like?'

'Well, the paintings were all right, I suppose. Sort of colourful and textured. I wanted to touch one, but luckily Marta slapped my hand just in time, because you're not allowed to do that.'

'Of course not. But go on.'

'Well, you see, my hay fever had been playing up really bad. I'd forgotten to take my tablet that morning.'

'How old does a man have to be before he remembers he gets hay fever every summer?'

'I know, I know,' said Dan. 'But my mum always used to remind me to take a pill. Anyhow, I'd remembered to pick up some tissues on the way because my eyes were streaming and my nose full of snot.'

Tamsin pulled a face. 'Perhaps not the best day to visit an art exhibition?'

'On the contrary,' said Dan. 'I thought it would be good to get indoors. You know, away from all the nature. And I wore my sunglasses to protect my eyes.'

'Okay,' said Tamsin, rolling her eyes. 'So, what happened?'

'Well, we were walking around the exhibition rooms and Marta was explaining to me what each of the paintings were about,' said Dan. 'But I could barely see them at this point, I was suffering so much. Anyway, I'd been stuffing my used tissues in my pocket, but was getting through them pretty fast...'

'And?' said Tamsin. 'Hurry up, I'll have more customers in a minute.'

'I came across a bin and saw the opportunity to get rid of the tissues. So, I just pulled them out of my pocket and tried to stuff them in the bin. Only it wouldn't open properly. So, I started pushing the top of it really hard. It still wouldn't open so I just left the pile of tissues on top. That's when Marta notices what I'm up to, and rushes over whispering loudly at me, asking what on earth I think I'm doing?'

'What *were* you doing?' said Tamsin.

Dan sighed. 'Turns out it wasn't a bin after all. It was part of the exhibition. Another bloody installation. Marta was fuming. Said I had defiled a work of art. "But it looks like a bin," I said! So then, *she* said—still talking in that sort of, quiet shriek—"In the middle of the room? Who puts a bin in the middle of the room at a Tate exhibition?" So, I said, "Well, I don't know, but I had my sunglasses on, so that didn't help." So, *she* says, "Who wears sunglasses to an art exhibition?" And that, to cut a long and rather hideous story short, was pretty much that.'

Tamsin giggled. 'That is *so* you, Dan. And it serves you right. I've told you that list is nothing but trouble. It's just wrong from start to finish. Why are you dating women you have nothing in common with?'

'Because, I dated all the women I had something in common with, and it didn't work out. Probably because they were all like me...' he added sadly.

'Maybe you should've just cast your net in a different place,' said Tamsin.

Dan looked puzzled. 'What, you mean like... *Hayle?*'

The door of the bar swung open and a flurry of fresh customers came in. One of them was Olly-down-from-London. Tamsin shook her head in despair at Dan, and returned to her duties.

Dan moped. He'd have to finish the crossword by himself now, he supposed, as Tamsin and John swung into professional mode. But as Olly got the first round in, as usual, Dan noticed that today the group of friends was joined by a much younger girl, whom he had never seen before.

The girl wore a pretty, flowered dress that fell to mid-calf length and flat brown leather sandals. Little pink pearly buttons fastened what would otherwise have been a revealing neckline. She was slim but with strong sturdy legs. Her long chestnut hair turned golden as it reached all the way down to her bottom, which he could tell was shapely and pert under the sheer material of her dress. She wore no make-up, but her cheeks were flushed pink as though weathered from hardy exercise in the sun.

Dan gulped. *Bloody Hell.* He reached into his pocket and whipped out the notebook. Sheltering it with one hand, he scanned its contents with scrunched eyes. She was definitely a natural beauty, that was for sure. Demure of dress, yet still sexy. Pretending to be engrossed in the crossword, Dan shamelessly eavesdropped on the group.

'What can I get you, Daisy, my darling?' said Olly.

Dan furrowed his brow. She was far too young for Olly.

'I'll have a cider, Daddy,' said Daisy. 'A pint please. I'm parched after today.'

Dan's ears pricked up. Aha, so she was Olly's daughter! That made more sense. And a beautiful girl who liked a pint? It was too good.

But since 'drinks pints' was sadly still not on the list, he supposed he would have to investigate further.

'Hey there,' Olly suddenly called out. 'It's Zack, isn't it?'

'Um, no,' mumbled Dan. 'Zack's my brother. I'm Dan.'

'I thought it was one or the other of you,' said Olly. 'What can I get you?'

'Ah, I'm fine thanks,' said Dan, indicating his full pint. Noticing the list was still on the counter he slid it discreetly back into his pocket. 'It's er, Olly, right? Sorry, I didn't see you there...'

But ignoring Dan's mumbles, Olly spoke with authority: 'Nonsense, always room for another,' he said, and gestured to Tamsin to pull yet another pint.

'Well thank you kindly,' said Dan. 'Very decent of you.' Then in a fit of bravery, he spoke directly to Daisy. 'I er, don't believe we've been introduced?'

Wow. Kit and Zack would be proud of him if they had been there to witness such suavity. Yet he was somewhat relieved that they weren't.

'Hi, I'm Daisy,' she said with a beaming smile, revealing small and perfect white teeth. 'I just got here.'

'I'm Dan,' repeated Dan. 'Um, just got here?'

'Daisy has come down from Bristol,' said Olly.

'Bristol?' said Dan.

'Uni,' said Daisy.

'That's...nice,' said Dan. 'And, um, what do you study?'

'Theatre,' said Daisy. 'It's awesome!'

'Really?' said Dan. 'That sounds interesting.' He thumbed the notebook in his pocket. *Yes! She was creative!*

'Yeah, it really is,' said Daisy. I get to act, write, and direct; and y'know, just all aspects of performance. And the theatre scene in Briz is just like, y'know, sooo amazing.'

Dan loved the way she repeatedly tucked her hair behind her ear. And he thought she had the brightest eyes he had ever seen.

'Dan and his brother work on the boats,' said Olly, joining in.

'Wow. Amazing. Awesome,' said Daisy. 'We've just been out sailing on Daddy's boat. Is yours berthed here too?'

'Er, not exactly,' said Dan. 'I'm more in the business of...chartering. Kind of.'

'Cool. We've been out on the water like, *all* day,' said Daisy, clearly excited at this fact.

Desperate to avoid admitting he didn't like water, let alone own a yacht, Dan changed the subject. 'So...how long are you here for, Daisy?'

'Oh, I'm here for the summer,' she answered brightly.

'And you'll be staying in St Ives?'

'Yeah, for sure. Mostly on Mummy's farm. But I'll hang with Daddy at the beach house while he's down from London.'

'Mummy's farm?' said Dan.

'Yeah, Mummy and William live at Hendra Maen; it's up near Amalveor.'

'And...Daddy has a beach house?'

'Yeah, on Porthmeor. It's pretty basic, y'know. But it's awesome. You should visit. Shouldn't he Daddy?'

'By all means,' said Olly.

'Awesome,' said Daisy.

'Awesome,' said Dan.

Behind the bar, Tamsin harrumphed loudly, as she pulled another pint.

CHAPTER 19

Dreams

Senara went to see Bob Prowse, to little avail. He showed her the full details for Dora Francis's net loft, but despite a reasonable price for the lease and yearly rental, it was still beyond her means.

'You could sell that cottage of yours,' said Bob. 'I'd be willing to buy it myself, at the right price. The money would more than cover the leasehold on the net loft, and even put a deposit down on another house. There's lots of cheaper properties outside of St Ives.'

Senara knew too well how much Bob would love to get his hands on the house in Teetotal Street. He would gentrify it to the rafters, then either sell it at a profit, or charge double the holiday rent that Jago did.

'No, that's out of the question,' she said. 'It's not fair to Jago.' Technically, their parents had passed the house over to both of them, but Senara acknowledged that it was Jago who had lived in, and maintained it. 'Besides, where would we live? I'd never get a loan on my earnings, otherwise we could maybe mortgage the cottage itself. I probably can't even rent, given my lack of references.'

Senara thought ruefully of all those years working for Nikos. She had not considered them wasted years at the time, for she was young, the sun was shining, and all her needs were met. But back home in the United Kingdom she was barely solvent.

'If you were to sell, I could rent you both one of my flats in Hayle,' said Bob. 'We could skip the references, since I know you. Let's go crazy and say we skip the deposit too. It's something to think about, Senara.'

'Thank you, Bob, I will think about it,' Senara lied, knowing she would never put such a dilemma on Jago's shoulders. 'In the meantime, please promise me you won't sell this business to anyone else without telling me first. Give me a couple of weeks to figure things out?'

'I can't promise not to sell, my dear, but I will keep you informed,' said Bob. 'However, if you are not able to mortgage, or prepared to put your cottage on the market, I doubt very much that you'll raise the money.'

Senara left the estate agent's despondent, but not entirely defeated. It had not escaped her notice that Bob had not suggested that she approach her parents for a loan. His advice had been based, unsurprisingly, on his own interests, and desire to acquire another classic Downalong fisherman's cottage. But she was frustrated, all the same. She did not wish to concern her parents who had earned the right to their retirement without further risk, especially since they had already bestowed her and Jago the cottage. But to have the ambition, desire, and vision so clearly in her mind and heart, only to be thwarted by lack of means, was a miserable plight. Nevertheless, having persuaded Bob to loan her a set of keys, and at the risk of intensifying her disappointment, she ventured to visit the net loft alone.

Even as she clicked the door shut behind her, and took in the silent, shady room, she knew it was an exercise in torment. She could see everything in her mind's eye. It would all need cleaning up and some mending. But otherwise, the net loft's beauty lay in its absence of pretension. It still carried the resonance of its original intended use, despite Dora's installation of the bar. As such, she would keep refurbishment to a minimum, but imagined customers sharing one long communal table, like a medieval banqueting hall, and seated upon reclaimed wooden benches and stools. The furniture would be simple, basic; functional, yet beautiful. But there would be cushions and blankets for comfort. She would display Jago's surf paintings on whitewashed granite walls. On certain nights they would hold events; exhibitions, book launches and talks. She moved around, imagining where the coffee machine would go, or the juice bar. She imagined fairy lights draped from the rafters, candles strung along the central table, and the log burner fired up on wintery nights with the sea pounding below. It would be a tall ship coursing the ocean waves; a saviour raft from the storm outside.

Senara sat upon the window sill, and watched as the setting sun began its slow roll along the spine of the Carrick Du headland. Before long, it would slide off the rocks below Clodgy Point and into the ocean, in a blaze of spectacle and colour. She knew she should leave now and return the keys. But while she remained, the dream was real. For the time being, this place was hers. The future that she imagined was alive, and had not yet been usurped by an alternative reality.

In truth, Senara enjoyed the time alone, to be hidden away from the eyes that she felt were always upon her, with their silent accusations. Making plans and dreams was a welcome distraction from the constant cycle of painful, debilitating thoughts that crippled her from within. What was it, Kit had called it? *Ruminating*, that was it. And he was right, of course. Senara knew that her dark thoughts were the source of her pain, but it was like trying to escape quicksand. Every time she tried to haul herself out of the quagmire, some small thing would remind her of her crime, and she would be sucked back under again. But the inspiration that she had felt upon discovering this place had given her a hope and a vision so distracting, that for a while, she had almost forgotten to punish herself.

Brian, as ever, had been supportive. He had messaged her the night before, assuring her that the right place for her would eventually come along, and that he had faith in her talents and abilities.

Ha! You clearly don't know me that well, she had messaged back. *I'm pitifully inept at life.*

But secretly, she enjoyed, and was flattered by the constant attention and positive feedback from Brian. She had begun to feel a warm glow whenever his messages popped up, and they had started to end their chats with friendly digital kisses. She began to feel that there might be something there, something more... If she could but remember exactly what he looked like.

Eventually, as the room darkened around her, Senara forced herself to go. Standing by the door again, she took one last look around at the hushed space that surrounded her. She could see the twinkling lights, and hear the voices and the happy laughter that called to her from another dimension. The atmosphere was pregnant with possibility, silently awaiting permission—for *her* permission—to exist. If she walked away; if she abandoned her dreams; then this whole world would collapse, and another one entirely would continue. Senara felt that she might burst with the sadness.

Outside, standing in the shadowy confines at the top of the stone steps, she reluctantly locked the doors. Then she put one hand against the dusty glass pane, as if to communicate with the darkness within.

I'm sorry, she thought. *You would have been amazing. But you were a nice dream. For a while.*

CHAPTER 20

The Solitude Soul

In a dilapidated old boatyard in the Hayle estuary, Kit Curnow took a step back to look at the magnificent wooden boat and began to think for the first time, after months of hard work, that she might soon be ready to launch. Inspired by his restoration of the old lifeboat, he had once again, been tempted by this latest project. It was a lugger, an old St Ives 'Jumbo', the battered hulk of which he had tracked down to a boatyard in Falmouth, recognising its distinctive flat-bottomed hull. Designed that way in order that they might stay upright in the harbour at low tide, and having only been in existence for a short time, they were few and far between. So, having idly and wilfully searched for and found one online, Kit felt he could not subsequently ignore its existence.

Restoring the boat had been an intense and costly labour of love, but with typical terrier-like tenacity, he had kept at it, roping in Zack's help where necessary. In truth, he enjoyed the time away from the crowds, much in the way that he enjoyed his herb garden; or those still, early mornings out on the *Silver Star*, when it was just himself and the sea. It was a time for solitude and reflection.

If Kit were completely honest, one of the reasons that he continued his trade as a fisherman, despite his increasing concern for fish stocks and the environment, was the seclusion it afforded him. He made no more than a basic living from using hand cast nets and lines, but balance and harmony with nature were vital to his conscience and well-being. And being out on the water in the beauty of early morning, with the sun coming up over the ocean's horizon, was for him a meditative, almost spiritual experience. Being in nature, and with the means to acquire only what he needed to survive, stirred in him a primeval emotion of connectedness. This meditative spell also fell upon him when absorbed in creativity; when writing a song, or in the long hours spent restoring an old boat.

'And you are indeed becoming a beauty, my love,' he said quietly as he patted the bow with one hand. 'But what shall we name you?'

A bleep from the phone in the back pocket of his boiler suit distracted him. It was a text from Astrid: *Where are u? We need 2 talk.*

Kit smiled. He didn't understand why Astrid still abbreviated words which surely took no longer to type out in full.

He replied: *At the boatyard. I'll be home soon x.*

There was no reply. He'd had one eye on the tide in the estuary, hoping to catch a surf at Hawkes Point on the way home. But the urgent message—which lacked the usual stream of 'kisses'—and subsequent silence could only mean one thing. That he was in trouble...

He had told Astrid about meeting Senara for coffee, and she had not taken the news well. Before he could elaborate, she had left for a yoga class, and then headed over to Pepper's, no doubt for a wine-fuelled gossip. Things had been frosty between them since, but he couldn't imagine what new crime he might have committed.

Sighing, Kit finished and locked up, then walked the short distance to where he had parked the van. He knew it was a cliché, but the vintage camper van suited his needs perfectly. There was enough room in the back for his surfboards, and to change into a wetsuit. It was a place to sleep should he seek waves a bit further afield. The cooking facilities were sufficient to make a hot coffee after a cold surf, or scramble a couple of eggs if he had camped overnight. It was another private space that enabled his yearning for freedom.

He drove around the estuary, then joined the Old Coach Road, which carried him over Lelant Downs and through Halsetown, until he approached St Ives from the upper part of town. From there, he drove through the streets until he arrived in the Ayr district, where the Hosking family home was, and where they let him park the camper. Zack, his wife, and two young children lived in the house with their widowed mother. Dan had been moved to a log cabin they had constructed in the already small garden, a scheme which at first, he had protested. But Kit knew Dan had secretly come to love the place. The child in him enjoyed having his own space to play video games and watch as many movies as he liked, and to be able to live in the sort of mess where—he argued—everything was near to hand. Kit was aware that he himself was lucky to live in a Downalong property, but the old streets and houses had been built without consideration to such an imaginary thing as a motor car. He had a permit to park on Smeaton's Pier for his other vehicle, a shabby old truck that he used to transport fish, but with the remaining car parks always full in the summer, Kit was grateful for a home for the van.

After parking in the alley by the Hoskings' garage, he made his way down the hill. Today he decided to cut through Barnoon Cemetery, a sea of headstones and ancient stone crosses on the hillside overlooking Porthmeor beach. It had always struck him as a generous notion, to allow the deceased such a beautiful last resting place, with views across a golden shore. Here, the ever-changing ocean met the skyline, as if beckoning to still further adventure, and horizons yet to be met. Many of his ancestors were buried here, and the graveyard resonated with the presence of the past. But it was also a place that connected Kit to the sea, and to his fellow mariners.

As ever, he saluted as he loped past the grave of Alfred Wallis, the artist and fellow fisherman. Here also lay crewmen from the shipwreck of the SS *Alba*, which had foundered upon rocks near The Island, an incident which Wallis himself had painted. There were memorials to victims of the sinking of RMS *Titanic*, miners and quarrymen who had sought a new life in America. Here too, were the graves of lifeboatmen from the 1939 disaster, who had died risking their lives to save others. Kit always felt a melancholy respect in this place. It was born out of an affinity for his seafaring brothers, and sorrow at that sombre engraving, *Lost at Sea*. For he knew that he too, was not invulnerable to the ocean's capricious nature; that he too might meet his fate at her hand.

As he made his way downhill, he reflected once more upon the strange view of carved stone angels and Celtic crosses set against the magnificent backdrop of waves and surfers. Life went on, he supposed... And today it was looking fair, he thought ruefully, as he watched his comrades ride the peeling waves. It was torture, for a surfer, to spend so much time watching and waiting for the right conditions, only to have to go to work, or, as was his present dilemma, to have been summoned elsewhere. When he reached the bottom of the hill, he decided to walk along the beach anyway. If nothing else, he might be able to pass on some good news to his fellow surfers about the nature and size of the waves from an 'eyeball' perspective.

The surf school were out in force with their classes, and Kit waved at a couple of his friends as they spotted him on the shore. He took off his flip-flops and paddled along the shoreline, not just for the joy of getting wet, but to ascertain the water temperature. As he neared the east end of the beach, he stopped to watch as the waves rolled in, crashing against the rocks at The Island's edge, but otherwise seamlessly moving towards the shore in stately procession. It was tempting, and might have been fun on a longboard, he mused...but not worth a message to the group chat on his phone who would have downed tools, laptops, or even children, had he summoned them with three little words: *Boiler is Working...*

Most people ignored the strange-shaped black 'rocks' that appeared at extreme low tide near The Island. But closer inspection revealed that they were not rocks at all, but part of the barnacled and seaweed-strewn remains of the wreck of the *Alba*. Where the ship's boilers now sat entrenched, a sandbank had formed, and when conditions were right, this produced a heavy, right-hand barrel. Even Astrid would have understood if he had absconded to surf The Boiler, but it was not going to be today.

Remembering Astrid, he turned to make his way back up the beach away from the shore. But he was distracted again by something that had been baffling him. He scanned the line of buildings in front of him; the holiday apartments, converted pilchard cellars and salting houses, and the back of Porthmeor Studios that grew out of the old sea wall. Where was the wooden gate that led to that hidden courtyard, and to Dora Francis's old net loft, that Senara so coveted? Sure, there were some entrances that he knew of; doorways to the fishermen's cellars underneath the art studios, and a tunnel to the flats. But in all his life, he had never before noticed this particular entry to the beach, and he was curious.

He walked the length of buildings, frowning in puzzlement. He walked back again, all thoughts of Astrid forgotten, before stopping and staring in bewilderment. When he finally figured it out, he broke into a grin. *Of course*. The gate did not lead directly onto the sand, but was hidden, obscured by the converted buildings. Discovering the gap, he ventured through, and after another turn, he found it. A sign attached to the tattered green door read, 'Private, no entry.' Paying no attention, he lifted the old-fashioned iron latch and pushed. The gate resisted, long since settled into its resting place, before shuddering open to reveal the cool, sandy, shadowed tunnel that led to the net loft.

Carefully shutting the gate behind him, Kit ventured along the short tunnel, until he stood in a pool of warm sunlight that had found the enclosed, and secret, cobbled courtyard. The air was still and strangely quiet, like a place removed from time. He looked up at the door to the old building, and the place of Senara's hopes and dreams. Despite his criticism at the time, it was true that it had once been a gathering place of some renown, and so it was not impossible that it might be again. He wished now that he had not been so cynical. Senara could do with a helping hand; a boost to get her life back on track.

He walked up the steps and peered through the dusty window. The 'For Sale' sign was still up, and so he could reasonably assume that the property was still available. As he reviewed the dark interior, an idea slowly formed in his mind. It was to do with that back room behind the glass panels. As the images formed in his imagination, he became increasingly regretful. Perhaps Senara had been right. Perhaps there was more possibility to this old building than he had allowed. Yet, to his shame, he had scathingly dismissed her ideas.

His phone pinged again, dragging him back into the present. This time Astrid sent no more than an accusatory: *???*

He turned away from the net loft, and hurrying down the steps and along Pudding Bag Lane, he re-entered the hustle and bustle of the streets of St Ives.

It makes no difference anyway, he thought. Senara did not have the money, and neither did he. But right at that moment Kit dearly wished that he could help his friend. He wanted her back to her old self, happy and confident. He wanted to see her smile radiant again, and her eyes not filled with doubt and shame.

Back at the house, he searched the rooms looking for Astrid. He found her on the terrace, dressed in a bikini, and reclined on a sun lounger. Kit noticed that she had moved some of his pot plants—the olive and lemon trees—in order to place the lounger in the best sun spot. Kit would have rather his plants had benefitted from the afternoon rays, but not being able to read her mood behind the sunglasses, he held his tongue.

Habitually taking a beer from the fridge, he joined her outside. As usual, he surveyed the views over the bay and towards the lighthouse, before turning to lean casually against the balcony wall.

'So, what's up?' he said.

Astrid stared at him for a moment, still inscrutable behind the sunglasses. Then she stood up and, without a word, walked indoors. Sensing the atmosphere, Kit could still not help but admire her figure as she walked away. Her tiny waist and the way it curved into a perfectly shaped bottom was one of the first things that had attracted him. But Astrid returned from the shadows with her nakedness covered in a short kimono.

She did not sit down again but strode around the terrace restlessly. Finally, she removed the sunglasses and addressed him. 'Where have you been?'

'I told you, at the boatyard, working on the Jumbo.'

'That was ages ago...'

'Was I supposed to drop everything?' Kit said in exasperation. 'I had to finish up, and park the car...'

'You were seen,' she said.

'Seen?' said Kit, although paranoia began to tie knots in his usually serene demeanour.

'With Senara,' said Astrid.

'I told you, we met for coffee.'

'At Porthgwidden. You said you went to Porthgwidden.'

'And so we did.'

'This was in Norway Square. You were seen in Norway Square with your arms around her.'

* * *

Astrid was clearly upset. She poured out an incoherently bleated tale of how one of Pepper's friends had seen him in Norway Square in an embrace with Senara, and that she just knew there was something going on between them, and why had she been so trusting, when Pepper had warned her about Senara and...

'For god's sake,' said Kit. 'Does she have spies everywhere?'

'Not spies,' cried Astrid. 'Friends! And it's because she's *my* friend that she told me...'

'It was the same day. We met in Norway Square, yes, at first,' said Kit. 'And she was upset, because of what happened at Driftwood. What was I supposed to do?'

'What does it have to do with you? I still don't understand why you were even with her!' shouted Astrid.

'She's my friend,' said Kit, grimly. 'I saw Zack and Dan yesterday too, for a beer, if you need a reason for that too. It's the same thing....'

'No, it is *not* the same thing. Women like that...' Astrid's voice quivered with anger. 'Women like that manipulate men.'

'What do you mean, women like that?' Kit's tone was sombre.

'You know what I mean.' Astrid's eyes flashed. 'She uses her looks to get what she wants. She wanted Grady and it worked, didn't it? She betrayed her friend, and now she's after you.'

Kit sighed. 'She is not *after* me. And just because she's beautiful, doesn't make her a bad person. It doesn't mean she doesn't have feelings.'

'So, you do think she's beautiful?' Astrid could barely contain her rage.

'It's not really up for debate,' said Kit. 'And you're missing the point. What I'm saying is that I don't subscribe to your notion that all attractive-looking people are somehow...ugly on the inside. It's just not fair. And usually based on rumour put about by bitter, jealous, rivals.'

'Are you saying I'm just jealous? That this is my fault?'

'No... But Pepper is bitter, and unforgiving, at least where Senara is concerned. Grady, she's fine with. She even married the guy.'

'So, you're saying that Pepper's in the wrong, somehow? That she should forgive Senara for what she did?'

'I'm saying...' said Kit, softening, '...that this *vendetta* has nothing to do with us. I told you before, I'm not going to take sides or get involved in a witch-hunt.'

Astrid appeared to have run out of steam, and stood sulking, with arms folded, as she leant against the balcony wall.

Kit approached her and put his arms around her. 'Look, I'm sorry. I should have told you everything. We were just catching up, honestly. I haven't seen her for five years. The next time we meet up, you must come too.'

Astrid stared into his eyes, questioning, before appearing to relent. He felt the stiffness in her body relax into his embrace, as she rested her head briefly on his shoulder. Then looking at him again, she said, with the hint of a smile:

'That's a stupid idea. Pepper would kill me.'

Kit began to form the argument in his mind that their relationship should carry more importance than her friendship with Pepper; but before he had a chance to reply, Astrid reached her lips up to meet his, and wrapped one leg around his body. He could feel the heat of her sun-warmed body beneath the skimpy kimono as she kissed him passionately.

Kit was not a man who was generally up for confrontation. Given the way things had been going minutes before, he surmised that there was no way the conversation was going to end in a better scenario. He returned her kiss, feeling with his hands his way around the curves of her body. Then picking her up, he carried her upstairs to the bedroom.

CHAPTER 21

Dissonance

Malory held one of Jago's paintings up against the wall at the back of the shop, trying to decide a suitable placement. She felt that larger, more dramatic works would look better on the main expanse of plain whitewashed walls, but these smaller paintings would be done more justice in this nook at the back where the payment desk was. She wondered if Jago had been serious about showing her his studio. She had to admit curiosity, but equally felt irrationally uncomfortable about the whole idea, for reasons that she kept keenly repressed.

The bell above the door jangled, so Malory laid the painting carefully with the others on the plan chest, and turned to greet the customer. It was Grady O'Keefe.

He sauntered over to where she stood, then proffered a handshake.

'I thought it was time I introduced myself,' he said. 'I'm Grady. I have the shop and studio opposite.'

'Yes, I've noticed your shop,' said Malory, taking his outstretched hand politely. 'I'm Malory. Malory Black.'

'Delighted to meet you, Malory. As an artist I've long been a patron of Atlantic Arts,' said Grady. 'Alan Harvey, the previous owner, was a good pal of mine, before he retired. I see no reason why the relationship should not continue. Got to support local businesses, right?'

'Your custom is of course enormously valued,' said Malory. 'Is there anything I can do for you today?'

He had not let go of her hand.

'I'm quite sure there is,' he said, fixing those steel-grey eyes upon her own, a smile curling at the corner of his lips.

He finally released his grip and turned to look at the paintings arranged on top of the chest.

'Local artist?' he asked picking one up in a careless manner that unnerved Malory. She was responsible for Jago's paintings and had agreed to hang them, not let them be manhandled by customers.

'Yes,' she said, 'Jago Berryman. Perhaps you've heard of him?'

Grady chuckled, still staring at the painting. 'Yes, I know Jago. Still trying his hand at painting then? Well, well, well.'

'Is there something you require?' said Malory, gently removing the painting from Grady and placing it back on top of the chest.

He stared at her, still smiling, as if she were simple. Malory did not know why she felt somehow wrong-footed.

'Alan kept a list of my regular requirements,' said Grady, still wandering around the nook part of the shop with casual familiarity. 'Perhaps he left it with you?'

'Ah, yes, I think he did,' said Malory, carefully skirting around Grady to reach a position of more authority on the other side of the desk. She reached into a drawer and pulled out a ledger. Browsing through the names carefully written at the top of each page, she eventually found the list marked for Grady O'Keefe.

'Here we are,' said Malory. 'Is this all you'd like? I could probably find most of these items right now as we're not busy.'

'No, that's fine,' said Grady. 'I can pop back in a few days when you've packed them all ready for collection. And I'll need this order fulfilled every month. Will that be okay?'

'Of course,' said Malory. Although scanning the list she did not know why he did not purchase most of the items now. It was not extensive, or the items obscure; just sketchbooks, drawing pencils, charcoal and oil pastels. Only the bags of plaster would have to be ordered in.

'Perhaps I'll pick up a couple of the sketchbooks while I'm here,' said Grady, as though reading her mind.

'Okay; well, they're over here...' said Malory, moving back around the desk.

'I know where they are,' he said quickly, but remained in place, barring her way.

'Right. Well, I'll let you browse then.' Malory returned once more behind the desk, and sitting down, feigned renewed interest in the book that Alan Harvey had left.

The doorbell tinkled again, and Malory looked up in relief, grateful for another customer. But her initial consolation quickly turned to concern as she saw the newcomer turn ashen, and look as though she might faint again.

For it was Senara.

* * *

Senara had stood outside the bakery at the corner of The Digey for several minutes, trying to quell her nerves. She had promised to pick up some paints for Jago, but Atlantic Arts was directly opposite Grady's shop. She had managed, since her return, to evade him, but knew an encounter was inevitable sooner or later. She couldn't avoid Fore Street, after all. And to let Jago down for such a pathetic reason felt cowardly. He'd told Senara about Malory's offer to exhibit his paintings, and was busy in the studio.

Summoning her courage, she marched toward the art shop. Reaching apparent safety, she opened the door and stepped inside, only to be confronted by the presence of the very person she had hoped to avoid. With her heart thumping, she stopped dead in the doorway, fearing her legs would give way. Even as adrenalin raced through her body, she could neither fight nor take flight; only stand, her hand gripping the doorknob for support.

Grady looked at her with amusement. 'Hello, Senara,' he said.

Confused, Senara wondered vaguely if this was how it was going to go... That she would be required to make chit-chat, and act *normal*, despite the intensity of her emotions.

'Hello...' she parroted feebly, her voice timid and tremulous, and her mind cursing herself for speaking to him at all.

Malory stood up from behind the desk, and from the look in her eyes, could tell that Senara was in some distress.

'Ah, Senara,' said Malory. 'Good to see you. And great timing. You can help me decide how to hang Jago's paintings.' She beckoned Senara to the back of the shop.

Wordlessly, Senara obeyed.

'Take a seat,' said Malory, indicating the small armchair besides the plan chest. 'I'll just finish up with this customer, then I'll be with you.'

'Okay,' was all Senara could muster, but thankful for being able to sit down.

She watched as Malory returned to speak to Grady in professional tones. Something about materials and supplies. Senara didn't know,—didn't want to know,—didn't want to hear his voice, so relaxed and insouciant.

'Just charge these to my bill for when I collect the rest of the supplies,' Grady said, helping himself to a wad of sketchbooks.

Senara watched warily out of the corner of her eye, as Malory appeared to make a note of what Grady had pilfered in advance. And now he was shaking hands with Malory and saying how good it was to meet her, and that he would see her again soon.

Go. Just go... Senara willed, as Grady continued to make pleasantries.

It was only the entrance of another customer that appeared to finally prompt his exit, but not before he threw another expectant look towards the back of the shop where Senara sat.

What was he expecting, a cheery wave and goodbye? Senara fixed her eyes on the short list of paint colours on a scrunched-up piece of paper that she held in her sweaty palm, and did not look up until she heard the shop doorbell ring again, indicating his departure.

When Malory had finished serving the new customer, she turned to Senara. 'Cup of tea? You look like you could use one.'

'Or maybe something stronger...' muttered Senara, dismayed at the shake in her voice. 'But no, I'm fine thanks. Well, maybe some water? Then I just need to buy some paints for Jago.'

'Of course,' Malory popped into the small kitchen behind the shop floor and returned seconds later with a glass of water.

Senara took a few sips, and then eyed Malory, sardonically. 'Well, this feels familiar,' she said.

Malory smiled, understanding. 'I hope you don't mind me asking,' she said. 'But are you okay? When you first came into the shop you looked like... Pardon the cliché, but you looked like you'd seen a ghost.'

Senara groaned. 'Was it really so obvious?'

'I'm afraid so,' said Malory.

Senara threw her head against the back of the armchair. 'Oh, that's just great.'

'Again, I know it's none of my business,' said Malory. 'But I got the feeling it was something to do with *him*?' She nodded in the direction of Grady's shop.

'Yes, it was entirely to do with him,' said Senara.

'I see,' said Malory. As if intuiting not to probe further, she strolled over to look at Jago's paintings again. 'He's really rather good. Jago, I mean. I love how he subverts even a beautiful landscape, somehow puts his distinctive mark on it. This one, for example...'

She propped one of the paintings on the chest up against the wall. It was a depiction of granite rocks on a clifftop, overlooking a dramatic deep blue seascape. But Jago had also scrawled liberally in a deep raspberry colour that contrasted with the brilliant blues, the words 'Zennor Kiss', followed by the symbols: 'xx'.

'I've heard Zennor is lovely,' Malory continued quietly, still drinking in the painting. 'I'm planning to walk there soon, along the coast path.'

'It is,' said Senara, grateful for the change in subject. 'And the walk is stunningly beautiful on a still day. But you have to be careful if the winds are high. It gets very blowy up on the clifftops. And it's quite strenuous. Will take you the best part of a morning.'

'Really?' said Malory, I thought it was only about six or seven miles?'

Senara smiled, relieved to be smiling. 'Yeah, in Cornish miles! Feels more like ten once you've tackled all the steep inclines and descents. And the path can be very narrow and overgrown in places. And rocky. And close to the cliff edge. Sorry, I'm blathering.'

'I've been as far as Clodgy Point,' said Malory. 'That didn't seem so bad.'

'Oh, it's fine as far as Clodgy,' said Senara. 'But after that it gets tougher. Have you got some decent walking boots?'

Malory looked glum. 'I've got trainers. Will that not do?'

'I suppose...' said Senara. 'It depends. It can get very muddy and wet in parts even if there's not been much rain...' Seeing Malory's expression, she added: 'But we've had great weather lately, I'm sure it'll be mostly dry. Trainers should be fine. How about a map?'

'A map?' said Malory. 'I thought the path just followed the coastline. That it would be a one foot-in-front-of-the-other, sort of thing?'

'Well, yes,' said Senara. 'But once you leave St Ives, there is nothing between here and Zennor. If you run into trouble, you'll need to let someone know where you are, or use a map to find your way inland. At River Cove, for instance; there's a footpath thereabouts that will take you back to The Coffin Path, or eventually back to the road.'

'I see,' said Malory disheartened. 'I didn't realise it would be so complicated. I feel a bit foolish.'

'Oh,' said Senara, guiltily. 'I wasn't trying to put you off. You should still do it. It really is a beautiful walk, and with a beer awaiting you at The Tinner's Arms when you get there.'

'Maybe,' said Malory. She leaned against the plan chest with folded arms, and looked pensive. 'But perhaps I should give it more thought. Like you said, I could run into trouble, and... Well. I don't want to be one of *those* headlines. You know, "*Woman rescued from cliff fall*", or "*Woman falls down mine shaft*".' She sighed.

Senara saw the look again, that look that she had come to recognise; to associate with Malory. Yet Malory had been kind to her on more than one occasion; had rescued her from Grady just now, and had not pried for information. On impulse she said, 'How about if I go with you?'

'Really?' said Malory.

'Of course,' said Senara. 'I'm not saying you *shouldn't* go alone; that you can't do it. But I've walked it many, many times. I'll know exactly where we are, and you won't be alone if things go awry.'

Malory beamed, and Senara noticed immediately how it transformed her face. The constant undercurrent of anxiety disappeared and her light, her beauty, was revealed.

'I would love that!' said Malory. 'Are you sure?'

'Of course, I'm sure,' said Senara, smiling back. 'Only it works both ways. You'll have to rescue me if I do something stupid. Like, you know... *Faint.*'

Malory giggled. 'I hate to say it, but I almost thought you were about to again, just now.'

Senara laughed hysterically, happy for the release. 'Oh my god, me too.' She put her head in her hands. 'Thank goodness I didn't. I mean, can you imagine?'

They both chuckled, and feeling much better for it, Senara remembered the task in hand.

Malory quickly found Jago's oil paints: cobalt blue, alizarin crimson and cadmium yellow. 'Just three colours?' she asked.

'I think these are the ones he runs out of most of all, along with white. He says he can mix pretty much any colour he needs from those,' said Senara. 'I guess he knows what he's doing.'

'He certainly does,' said Malory, thoughtfully.

They exchanged numbers and decided upon a suitable day for the hike. Malory had hired Rosa's daughter, Giovanna, to work part-time in the shop, allowing her some valuable free time.

'So, I'll see you then,' said Senara. 'Unless of course the weather is bad. But I'll message you. And, um... Thank you. You know, for...'

'Don't mention it,' said Malory.

* * *

Senara left Atlantic Arts feeling much better; even somewhat emboldened. The opiate of laughter had worked its magic. She looked across to Grady's shop, where she could see him talking to a customer.

Laying on the charm, she thought. *Hauling in another poor sucker.*

It occurred to her that perhaps this was the way to go: to laugh at him; to laugh at herself and her failings. But as she turned away down Fore Street, and even as the sunshine dappled the cobblestones and bounced off the water in the harbour, the demon returned. Even on such a day of beauty and laughter and life, of budding friendship and plans, guilt stalked her.

As she wound her way through the milling crowd in the harbour, she thought she caught a glimpse of someone she recognised, as he turned to go up Fish Street by The Sloop.

'Brian?' she called out, unsure; but the man kept walking.

She hurried to catch up, but the stream of traffic turning into Fish Street blocked her passage. By the time she turned the corner, she could no longer see him. Had it been him? She checked her phone, but there were no messages; no suggestion that he was in town. Should she ask? She stared at the phone, uncertainly. A cloud covered the sun, casting the street in sudden gloom. Senara shivered. Meeting Grady had unsettled her, and now her mind was surely playing tricks. Brian had messaged her just last night, and had made no mention of being in St Ives. It couldn't have been him.

Senara pondered the situation with Brian as she slowly wandered back to Teetotal Street. Perhaps she was subconsciously hoping to see him, to find a friendly face in the crowd. Maybe it was a sign that they should develop their friendship further. The online scenario had been fun at first, but in honesty, Senara sometimes found it a bit strange. She didn't always understand his meaning. The night before, he had said that he had just finished eating, but felt 'unsatisfied'.

Hmmm. I feel the need for something sweet... he had messaged. *What do you suggest?*

I'm sweet... the words popped into Senara's head before she could stop them. It left her feeling somewhat alarmed. What was happening? Had he prompted her? Were they flirting now? There was something that felt discordant with their usual friendly banter.

Instead, she typed: *I dunno, got any biscuits?*

He had not replied, which left her perplexed.

It dawned on Senara that the nature of their friendship had limitations, and was ultimately going nowhere. Sometimes it felt unnatural; unhealthy even; and Senara felt that she should run away; should curb the regularity of their messages. Yet other times she felt a warm gratitude when the phone pinged, and she did not wish to injure someone who had been so supportive. In slow realisation, she saw that there was only one way to ascertain the true nature of the relationship; only one way to find out who exactly she was dealing with.

They would have to meet again.

CHAPTER 22

Cornish Pasties

The morning after his meeting with Daisy at the pub, Dan had awoken with a stonking hangover, but renewed hope in his heart. He could not quite believe his luck. Daisy did not only fit the bill, but was gorgeous too. And moreover, she had drunk him under the table, which had only increased his admiration.

They had started with cider; Dan swiftly abandoning his usual pint of Doom to be in the same place, the same mood, as the object of his desire. At some point in the evening—he couldn't quite recall how or why, but felt it was Olly's instigation—they had moved on to shots. Peach schnapps quickly evolved into tequila slammers, and he couldn't quite remember all the details of getting home. Parts of the evening's conversation were also blurry. But through the haze of drunkenness something had embedded itself in his memory; that she had invited him over on Saturday for drinks at Olly's beach house. Apparently, there was going to be some sort of gathering. And despite the fuzziness of his recollection, the one thing he was quite sure about, was that they had gotten along; that they had had fun. He spent the next day in a state of blissful euphoria, and not only because he was possibly still drunk.

But as the days wore on, his optimism faded, and doubts crept in. *She might not have meant it.* Had perhaps even forgotten all about it. By Friday night he felt driven to drown his insecurities with another drinking session at The Barque.

Part of him hoped that Daisy would be there again, and her disposition reinforce his initial delight. But apart from strangers, the bar was near-empty that night. Tamsin was not even working that shift, so there was no one to tell his woes to. He had sat there alone, and as drink followed drink, so his anxiety had increased.

In the morning he felt terrible. He stumbled to the bathroom and shakily reached into the medicine cupboard for the Dioralyte. It was a source of personal mortification for Dan that while he was rarely ever genuinely ill, he kept the precious packet of electrolytes handy for just such moments as this, when water alone was just not going to cut it. He moved unsteadily to the sink, then with trembling hand, filled a glass of water, emptied the packet, and then glugged greedily. Reluctantly, he examined his face in the bathroom mirror. Dark morning stubble and puffy eyes. He rubbed his chin habitually; still too much flesh hung around his neck, but they said he was a looker, regardless. Cuddly, women called him, or strong. Although if truth be told, he was more weight than strength.

"My big Cornish lads", his mother would say as she scooped another helping of mashed potato onto her sons' plates. For a while, in his brief rugby playing days, it had been an advantage, but a knee injury had put him off all that.

Dan knew he wasn't perfect; that he was, in many ways, flawed. Yet people didn't seem to mind. He got along with most of them. But in the cold, sober light of day, confronted with his addled reflection, he wondered once more if Daisy had changed her mind. It was quite possible that the morning after their meeting she had awoken with a groan, clutching her head, and wondering why she had invited a Neanderthal to Daddy's. He decided he would play it by ear. Best not to get his hopes up.

Reluctantly, he dragged himself to the harbour for work. It was a bright sunny morning, with no wind, and a sea flat as a pancake. Perfect weather for tourists to hire a self-drive boat and go exploring the bay. Zack was already there, by the little booth that they hired the boats out from, transporting lifejackets from the back of their shared Land Rover, which was temporarily parked on the slipway.

'Mornin'!' Zack called in an overly cheery manner.

'You could have waited,' grumbled Dan, disgruntled at having had to walk down the hill.

'Didn't expect to see you till midday,' said Zack, 'judging by the time you got in last night. Heard you banging around in the garden.' He chuckled. 'Good night, was it?'

'Not really,' Dan muttered. 'I do feel rough though, I'm not gonna lie.'

'Ah, a bit of sunshine and a pasty, you'll be fine,' said Zack.

Dan needed no further encouragement. Being of a highly suggestible nature, his stomach immediately felt incredibly empty and his mind turned to the thought of a scrumptious hot pasty. He felt in his shorts pocket for some cash, and without another word wandered off across the cobbled wharf to the pasty bakery.

Zack shook his head at his brother's departing figure. The bakery had barely just opened. He grinned, and called: 'Fetch me one an' all, will you?'

Zack turned to see Kit's truck pull up on the slipway. The back was stacked with cool-boxes.

Kit jumped out and strode to greet his friend. 'It's a fine morning!'

'It is indeed,' said Zack. 'The young 'un's fetching pasties if you're hungry.'

'Starving,' said Kit. He shouted across the street. 'Oy, Dan, one more!'

Dan grimaced as he stood at the bakery hatch, and fumbled in his pockets again.

'Good catch?' said Zack.

'Eh, not bad,' said Kit. 'Enough for my local customers. Not enough for Newlyn. Was beautiful out on the water this morning, though.'

'Get out early, did you? Go far?'

'Didn't intend to. Bleddy seal kept chasing me around and scaring away the fish.'

'Alfie?' said Zack.

Kit nodded. 'Of course. I tried off Porthmeor, but he found me there too. Had to keep circling the bay trying to shake him off.' He winked at Zack.

Kit did not add that upon his return to the harbour he had thrown the seal a couple of fish from his catch anyway. It was little wonder it tried to follow his boat everywhere.

Dan trotted back across the wharf with the pasties in brown paper bags, and they all sat down on the wooden slipway barrier to enjoy.

'Pasties for breakfast,' said Kit. 'Could we be any more Cornish?'

'Probably find ourselves on a picture postcard next summer,' said Zack.

'Can't beat it, though,' said Dan, squaring up for another bite. 'Proper job.'

'So, how's it going with you and your young lady?' said Zack.

For a second, Dan looked alarmed. Had they gotten wind of Daisy? But then he realised his brother had directed the question at Kit.

'All right, I guess,' said Kit. 'Why do you ask?'

'Well, I'm not one to listen to gossip,' said Zack. 'But Mandy said she heard you'd had a fight.'

Kit sighed. 'Gossip is exactly what it is. It's true we've had a few disagreements lately, but that's normal in any relationship, isn't it?'

'Made up though, have you?' said Zack.

Kit grinned and eyed up his pasty, assessing where to approach for the next gargantuan bite. 'Thing is... I can never resist those curves. How such a magnificent bum can emerge from such a tiny waist is beyond me. Women are amazing.'

Zack laughed. 'Yeah, you've always had a thing for a curvy lady.'

'I wouldn't say that, exactly,' said Kit.

'Yeah, remember that one time, at the New Year's Eve fancy dress?' said Zack. 'You followed that mermaid all the way down Fore Street...'

Kit looked uneasy. 'Oh, that. That was years ago.'

'All the way down Fore Street,' Zack chuckled. 'You couldn't see her face, only her back, with her little waist and curvy bum in her green mermaid dress. *That is the woman of my dreams*, you said. Pushed your way through the crowds to keep up, making us come too. Then you followed her into that bar only to discover...'

'When she turned around...' joined in Dan, enjoying that the amusement was at Kit's expense, for once.

'Only to discover when she turned around...' said Zack.

'That it was only Senara...' finished Dan.

The two brothers laughed heartily.

Kit was not the sort of person who blushed, but his composure was clearly disturbed. 'Well, she'd died her hair blue and green. How was I supposed to know?'

'You were about to hit on your best mate, Kitto. *The woman of your dreams*,' mocked Zack.

Kit rolled his eyes. They never let you forget anything in St Ives.

'I'll thank you not to tell that story in front of Astrid, anytime soon,' he said wryly, and took another bite of pasty.

At that moment Grady O'Keefe came strutting along the harbour front, as ever with a sketchbook in one hand and a pencil wedged behind his ear. When he saw the three men munching on their pasties, he smiled cursorily, but raising a dismissive hand, declared: 'No time! Working!'

Kit, Zack and Dan watched as he marched off towards the pier.

'Dickhead,' said Dan.

'Wanker,' said Zack.

'Nob,' said Kit.

'And nobody asked!' Zack called with an extra surge of boldness, at Grady's departing figure.

'I'd better get back to it,' said Kit, wiping his hands on the napkin provided, and moving to put the rubbish in the bin. 'Got to deliver these fish. Let me know if you get any ticket sales for the old lifeboat. If it stays like this, will be a joy to take her out later.'

'Will do,' said Zack. 'What's everyone doing tonight? Anything on?'

'Nothing planned,' said Kit. 'Beer? If Mandy doesn't mind losing you for an hour or two? Dan? You in?'

Dan looked uncomfortable. 'I might have something on...'

'Really?' said Kit. 'A date, perhaps?'

'Not exactly...' said Dan.

'Spill,' said Zack, moving to the ticket booth. 'We don't have time for guessing games, customers will be arriving soon.'

And so, reluctantly, Dan spilled the beans. He told them all about his meeting with Daisy, and the invite to Olly's beach house, but how he wasn't sure if it was sincere, or if he would go.

'Did you get her number?' asked Kit.

'Yes, but...'

'Then just call her, ask if the invite still stands. That way you'll know for sure and will stop tormenting yourself.'

'I can't,' said Dan. 'What if it's awkward? What if she doesn't remember me? What if she...rejects me?'

'Stop being fearful,' said Kit. 'She gave you her number, didn't she? But you haven't called her. Girls hate that.'

'I suppose...' said Dan.

The quandary was resolved by the appearance of Olly himself, taking a stroll around the harbour.

'Good morning, boys,' he said, joining them. 'Isn't it a splendid one? Perfect for messing around on a boat.'

They muttered and nodded in agreement.

'Don't forget the gathering, tonight,' he said, moving on his way again. 'At the beach house. It's *Ship Ashore*, down at Porthmeor. You know it? Come for sunset cocktails, All welcome.'

'So, that's settled. Looks like we're all invited?' said Zack once Olly had gone.

'Sounded so,' said Kit. 'But I've really got to get moving. These mackerel won't stay fresh forever.' He hurried to the van, then called, 'Let me know about the ticket sales, otherwise I'll see you later.'

Zack waited for Kit's van to depart, then turned to his brother and said, with a grin: 'So, looks like we get to meet your new girlfriend, then.'

Dan's heart sank. This was worse than ever. What chance did he stand of being all suave again, with Zack and Kit overseeing his every move? Sometimes Dan didn't think they wanted him to find a girlfriend at all. Sometimes he wondered if he was just one great big joke to them.

CHAPTER 23

Ghost Stories

Giovanna was proving to be an asset to Atlantic Arts. A quick learner, adaptable, and skilled in customer service, it was her third job in town that summer. As well as shifts in her mother's restaurant, she worked a couple of evenings in a bar in the town centre.

At first, Malory had been worried that it might be too much for her, but Giovanna assured her that compared to the stresses of waitressing or bar work, sitting in a shop all day was 'a doddle.' Once persuaded that the girl was not going to fall asleep at the desk, Malory was delighted to have some spare time to explore; to visit the art galleries and swim or play in the sea. She had still not taken proper surf lessons, but liked to think that soon she might be brave enough to overcome her inhibitions.

'Right, I'm off,' she said. 'You have my mobile number if you need me?'

'Yeah, it's all cool,' said Giovanna. 'Go. Enjoy your day. Will you go to the beach?'

'Maybe later,' said Malory. 'I have an appointment first... Actually, appointment sounds a bit arsy. I'm going to view some paintings, by the artist who painted those.' She pointed to the paintings hanging in the nook.

'Oh, they're by Jago, aren't they? I love him!' said Giovanna with passion.

'You do?' asked Malory, not sure if the girl was referring to the artist or his work. Perhaps she meant literally, that she loved him. Perhaps they were dating? It occurred to Malory in that instant that of course he would have a girlfriend. Why wouldn't he? An unwelcome feeling stirred within her.

'Oh, yes, everyone loves Jago,' said Giovanna matter-of-factly. 'He's dreamy. And such a great person.'

Malory smiled. 'I suppose he is a bit of a character.'

She left Giovanna in charge and headed apprehensively to the harbour, where she had arranged to meet this dreamy individual.

The harbour was packed with visitors, who walked too slowly, often in the road, encumbering the steady stream of traffic that moved along the wharf. Malory was a fast walker by nature, and found this ambling infuriating. She was quite sure that these people in their newly acquired surf T-shirts and rubber clogs, would not wander aimlessly along a busy road at home. Yet something about the holiday-vibe of café-bars and restaurants, of quaint boats in the harbour and street-sellers lining the wharf, apparently deemed the behaviour acceptable. And then they would stop, mid-dawdle, to stare at the selection of wares on offer from the various outlets. The pub looked appealing, but was the sun over the yardarm yet? Perhaps they wanted a pasty, a pancake, or an ice-cream? The traffic honked, and the seagulls watched from their high perches, ready to strike should any poor fool neglect to cover their food.

She saw him, across the throng of people, with some friends, laughing and joking in the sunshine. His stall was nearby, just one of a collection on The Wharf offering jewellery, souvenirs or henna tattoos. As usual, his hair was an appealing mess, and as usual, he was bare-chested. Malory shook her head; why did he always have to be half-naked? Then she stopped and watched, transfixed, as he leapt nimbly onto the wall by the old fisherman's huts, then ran along its short length, to perform a perfect somersault onto the sandy beach. Then just as deftly, he sprang up again, vaulting over the harbour rail, to the acclaim of his friends.

Malory wavered. There was something about him; something so athletic and lithe and... *Vital.* He had easy strength and energy, and possessed the careless beauty of youth. He exuded a natural confidence, and was loved by all, it seemed.

He reminded her of Sam.

And there it was. The source of her unease in Jago's company that she had tried to suppress. The reason why she should not—could not—nourish her complex feelings in his presence. Part of her wanted to turn and run, to go and hide in the safety of a more suitable activity. She should be at an art exhibition, or taking a cream tea in a harbour café, not making assignments with beautiful men.

She pulled herself together. He was waiting for her, after all, and she was supposed to be pretending to the world that she was a professional. She summoned her courage and approached the group of friends.

On seeing her, Jago waved, and—thankfully—put his shirt back on. He appeared to hand captaincy of the stall to one of his friends, before coming to greet her halfway. They stood outside the pasty shop, with the crowds teeming around them.

'Hi, how're you doing?' he said.

'I'm good,' said Malory, feigning a breezy nonchalance.

'Thanks for doing this,' he said. 'I'm chuffed that you want to see the rest of my work, but there's no obligation. You have to be completely honest if you change your mind about exhibiting the paintings.'

'Of course,' said Malory. 'I'm fully prepared to accept that the others were a fluke, and that you're really a talentless pretender.'

'Harsh!' He pulled a face, in mock offence. 'On the other hand, if you think they're amazing, you'll admit that too, right?'

'Would you care either way?'

Jago grinned; his perfect white teeth set off against the tanned face. 'Not really.'

'Let's just go, shall we?' said Malory.

They walked up Fish Street, and then eventually along Island Road. Malory was still getting used to the maze of narrow streets that made up the Downalong area of St Ives, making mental maps wherever she went, and thrilled to discover new and interesting corners and alleyways.

'So, you grew up here, in St Ives?' she said, as they strolled the lanes, through bursts of sunshine and shade.

'Yep, born and bred,' said Jago. 'Nowhere else I'd rather be. Heaven on Earth, it is.'

'Don't you ever wonder? I mean, what the rest of the world is like? What it's like to live in a city?'

He stopped momentarily to look at her in amusement. 'What do you mean? Do you think the little country boy has never seen the world?'

'Well, no, I...'

'I've travelled, I've seen things. Surfed in countries you've probably never heard of. But this place always draws me back. And I couldn't live in a city, for long. Sure, they have their appeal, but I'd miss... You know,' he turned to look at her. 'All the beauty.'

Malory felt a shiver twist its way down her spine.

'So where is it, then, this studio?' she said.

'It's just along here,' he gestured. 'But it's a bit of a secret, so I ask for your discretion.'

'Why is it a secret?'

'You'll see.'

He led her to a parade of fishermen's huts and lock-ups, which were noticeable in St Ives for the fact that they had not been renovated, or converted into something swanky, but rather remained fit for the purpose for which they were intended. Jago approached a door set in a granite wall and opened it with a key.

Malory followed him inside. She appeared to be in a storage room for fishing nets, lobster pots, and various other fishermen's tools. It was cluttered, dank and dim, and did not resemble the light and airy studio she had envisaged. For a second, she had a sense of caution. Why had she allowed this near-stranger to lure her into this secluded place? Why should she trust him, just because he was so damned charismatic?

'This way,' said Jago.

He led her though another door, a narrow corridor, and then finally into a larger square space. The room must have been ensconced in the heart of the buildings, for there were no windows in the surrounding walls; but large panes of glass in the gabled roof filled the studio with light. The walls had been painted bright white, and everywhere, hung or propped against them, were Jago's paintings. There was a small ceramic sink in one corner, with pots of drying paintbrushes on the draining board, and what looked like a decorator's table, covered in various paints, rags, oils and turpentines. Curiously, there were still signs of it being a fisherman's store, with nets and fishing rods taking up one corner.

'Well, this is...unexpected.' Said Malory.

'It belongs to my friend Kit. He's a fisherman. But he has cellar space in his own house and so lets me use this. The other fishermen turn a blind eye because technically Kit still uses it, and well, they all know me, I suppose.'

'But you're not really supposed to be here?' said Malory.

'Not really, no,' laughed Jago.

'You're lucky.'

'I guess so. But I don't like being hidden away like this. One of these days I hope to get myself a studio at Porthmeor. It's good to mingle with other artists. You know, keep track of what's going on in the community. Not to mention the prestige. But most of all I want those great big windows overlooking the ocean. I'll think I've died and gone to heaven if I ever get one of those spaces.'

She met his eyes. For the first time since she had met him, he appeared vulnerable. They were two people, alone in a secret place, hidden from the eyes of the world. She became very aware of the intensity of his gaze and his close, physical presence. She turned away to view the paintings.

As she wandered around, taking each one in, she could feel his eyes follow her, although he said nothing. The paintings were of a consistent style, but of varied subject matter. Some appeared surfing-related; but rather than a view from the shore, Jago's paintings described the feeling of being inside the green barrel of the breaking wave, or of duck-diving under it, in a vortex of water. Some were views of the landscape from the sea, but all were adorned with writings and lines of poetry; scribbled on with an acrylic pen, paint-brushed in romantic cursive letters, or stencilled with a spray can. Some lines were familiar to her—Masefield and Longfellow—but others she took to be his own words, of abstract meaning.

And then there were scenes from the land. Jago did not paint tourist-friendly images of boats in the harbour or seagulls; of blue skies and yellow beaches. Instead, he painted *them*; the tourists themselves, as he saw them from his barrow; crowds milling in all directions, rendered in a surreal, sometimes grotesque manner. And again, there were the inscribed words. One painting in hues of grey, blue, and his signature raspberry red, said 'Pasties and Pills'; others decreed 'Soul Surfers of Slough' and 'Weekend Warriors'.

They were rather rude.

But still, Malory could tell, compelling and dynamic. Rather like their creator...

'So?' said Jago after a while.

Malory turned to him. 'I love them. Do you really not have gallery representation?'

'To be honest, I'm not really sure how to go about it. I'm self-taught. Some of the galleries here are kind of intimidating if you're not in the inner circle. Even my Aunt Minnie, who's been painting all her life, feels like an outsider. But she's always encouraged me, anyway.'

'Quite right too,' said Malory. 'But I'm surprised. You don't strike me as being easily intimidated. I'm quite sure if you marched into any of the local galleries with one of these, it would spark interest. But let's get them out of here and into Atlantic Arts for a start. We can take it from there.'

'We?' said Jago with a sly grin.

Malory could feel the blush threaten to betray. 'I said I'd help you. If you like. I need to connect with the galleries in town anyway.'

'So, are you like, my agent, now?'

Malory laughed. 'Not exactly. More like... Ambassador.'

Jago smiled at her, warm and relaxed. 'All right then. Let's do this!'

Malory turned away from his gaze, and fixed her eyes instead upon a surfboard that stood propped up against the wall with the paintings. Under a shiny coat of resin, it had been painted with the same distinctive character of Jago's artwork.

'And you painted this too?' she asked.

'Not only painted it,' said Jago, 'I made it. A friend of mine is a shaper and he helped me out.'

'A shaper?' said Malory.

'Yeah. Sorry, it's a surfing term. Someone who makes surfboards by hand,' said Jago. 'There's a craft to it. I always wanted to make my own, and this here, is the result. I love it.' he said softly.

Malory saw the pride and joy on his face, as he lightly touched the surfboard.

'And do you use it?' she asked.

He looked at her with a puzzled, amused expression. 'Of course I do.'

'Really?' said Malory, squirming under his scrutiny. 'Only, it's a work of art in itself.'

'Maybe,' said Jago. 'But it has to go in the sea.'

'Oh, right,' said Malory. 'I get it. In the sea it becomes infused and permeated with the salt water and the elements.'

He looked at her once more as though she was crazy.

'It's a *surfboard*, Malory,' he grinned.

They left the building, and as Jago locked up, he said: 'So, do you know a lot about art then?'

'I like to think so. But like you, I'm self-taught. I once hoped to study History of Art, but life…' Malory looked away, out to sea, '…took a different direction.'

'It does that,' said Jago.

'I'd like my own gallery one day,' said Malory. 'It's sort of a dream of mine.'

'Seriously?' said Jago, smirking. 'Malory's Gallery?'

'Well, I wouldn't call it *that*,' Malory scoffed. 'But I'm particularly drawn to the work of the St Ives Colony. I think it's part of the reason why I came here.'

'Always makes me laugh when I hear it called that,' said Jago. 'A *colony of artists*. I just envisage them all squatting on the rooftops, squawking and flapping their arms.'

Malory laughed.

'You should meet Aunt Minnie,' said Jago. 'She remembers a lot of the artists and writers from back then. You know, from the...' he made parentheses signs in the air, '... *golden* era.'

'I'd like that,' said Malory.

'So, where do you come from then, mysterious Malory Black?' said Jago. 'I don't mean London; I mean, what's your story?'

Malory hesitated. 'I'd rather not talk about it.'

'Right,' said Jago, with an astute expression.

'Come with me,' he said, breaking the silence that threatened. 'Let me show you something.'

'More secret places?'

'Not quite.'

Malory followed Jago through the car park by The Island.

He stopped and pointed. 'See that building there? The tall white one with the pointy roof?'

'Uh-huh,' said Malory.

'That's Sven Berlin's 'Tower'. Where he lived and painted. And partied, and squabbled with the other artists, or so go the tales.'

'Of course!' said Malory. 'It's in a painting, by Willie—' she smiled to herself, '—I mean *Wilhelmina* Barns-Graham. Although I don't think I'd have recognised it, the surroundings have changed so much.'

'Yeah, it's kinda diminished by the massive toilet block built next door,' said Jago, laughing. He looked at her curiously. 'Come on,' he said. 'Let's go for a walk.'

Before Malory could protest, he took off through the car park again, heading towards the path that led up to the top of

The Island. She followed in his wake. They climbed to the point of the hill where the coastguard watch was, and admired the views across the bay.

Malory could see Willie with her easel, painting the view of the sheds and Sven's Tower from the island.

Then Jago guided her to the steps that led down to the coast path that edged The Island. But halfway down, he stopped, and leaned against the metal handrail that also acted as a barrier.

'See over there?' he pointed. 'That high ledge? I've heard that Borlase Smart used to climb up there dragging a huge canvas and easel with him. And paints, of course.'

'Cumbersome,' said Malory, observing the narrow, beaten track below them, that became a scramble over precipitous rocks.

'Yeah, pretty tricky, when you consider the danger,' said Jago. 'But it's all about the view.'

'Crazy. I can't imagine many artists of today going to such lengths.' Malory looked at him. 'Although I suspect *you* might!'

'Hah! I may have,' Jago smirked. 'But you're right. It takes an insane kind of commitment. You do still get people fishing off those lower rocks, but if you're ever here at night and see a light moving slowly up and down to the sea from the ledge...' he pointed again, '...that'll be The Lady.'

'Who?' said Malory.

Jago continued to walk down the path, obliging Malory to follow once more.

'The Lady with the Lantern,' he said. 'Come on, I'll tell you all about it.'

He grabbed her hand and pulled her quickly down the rest of the steep descent. Malory had no choice but to let go of the iron handrail, and trust to his strong grip.

They reached the bottom of the slope where the path became flatter as it ran around the headland towards Porthmeor Beach. He pulled her to sit alongside him upon a wooden bench that overlooked the ocean. On the hill behind them, St Nicholas chapel rose on its perch, eternally on lookout for renegades and smugglers. Malory subtly extracted her hand from his, but he still sat very close. Wild flowers grew on the grassy verge that separated them from the cascade of black rocks that tumbled into the sea below. A scattering, warm wind gently tousled their hair.

Jago sat upright and raised a hand towards the sea in a contrived manner.

'Many years ago, during a terrible storm, there was a shipwreck off those rocks,' he began. 'The brave fishermen of St Ives manned a boat to go to its aid. They managed, with the help of ropes, to get close to the foundering ship, and began to transfer the sailors to their own boat. But it wasn't easy in the stormy waters. Now, there was a lady on board, with a young child, an infant. Terrified, she would not trust her baby to another's arms, although they tried to persuade her.'

'Why are you speaking like that?' giggled Malory. 'Do you often talk this way?'

'Shush,' said Jago, with a disapproving look. 'I'm telling a story.'

He cleared his throat theatrically, and continued.

'As the stricken boat collapsed around them, the remaining sailors tied a rope around her waist, and the fishermen hauled her through the wild waves, still with the babe in her arms. But alas, she fainted, and the child, slipping from her grasp, was lost to the sea. When she came to, she became consumed with grief, and falling into a deep despair, died of a broken heart. They buried her in Barnoon Cemetery. But it is said, that on stormy nights, she leaves her grave, crosses Porthmeor beach with a lantern, and searches the rocks over there, looking for her lost child. It is also said that her appearance portends a wreck...'

'A Ghost?' Malory looked at him and chuckled. 'You're telling me a ghost story? In all seriousness?'

'It's true,' said Jago, with mock severity. 'Seen the lights myself once. I can tell you, I got the chills. Never got off The Island so fast before.'

'It was probably just fishermen, you know,' said Malory. 'Your lights. That's if you saw them at all.'

'Of course, I saw them,' he said with a wounded expression. 'True; at first, I thought it was a boat on the water. But then it started to move up the side of the rocks. A strange orange glow, moving too fast and too smoothly for a fisherman clambering unsteadily with gear. Proper spooked me.'

'Okay,' said Malory. 'If you say so. To be honest...'

He looked at her, waiting.

'I've walked up here, alone, before. I love it. I sit on this very bench. I love to watch the sea, and the way it crashes against the rocks. I love that there is nothing ahead but ocean, all the way to North America...'

'Strictly speaking,' he said pointing straight ahead of them, 'If you go that way, you'd probably hit Ireland first...'

She gave him a reproachful look. 'Okay, well that way then,' she indicated the west. 'And you know, I'm taking into account the whole vastness of the Atlantic, not just our specific co-ordinates on this tiny headland!'

'Well, I don't know,' Jago shook his head. 'Specifics are important. Especially when headed out to sea. But please continue. You were being romantic...'

'And *you're* being facetious,' Malory giggled. 'But if I *may* continue, I will admit there's something other-worldly about being here, away from the crowds. I can sense it in the atmosphere. It's as though it is imbued in the rocks themselves.'

'What is?' Jago watched her curiously.

She met his eyes. 'The past. I can *feel* the past up here. All the history. The shipwrecks and smugglers, the artists and writers. Beyond that even. There is a sense of the primeval.'

'So, in other words... *Ghosts?*' said Jago with a grin.

Malory laughed. 'In a way, yes, I suppose so. I catch glimpses of them; of other times; in the corners of my mind. But I'm still not falling for your Lady with the Lantern story.'

'Tell you what,' said Jago, 'next time there's a storm approaching, we'll come up here at sunset; bring a flask of hot chocolate and a blanket. Then you'll see for yourself.'

Malory did not know what to say. The idea of watching a sunset under a blanket with him sounded incredibly intimate. He couldn't possibly be suggesting... A *date*? Could he? The idea terrified her. She should probably laugh it off.

'*We?*' she heard herself say, echoing his own, earlier question.

All of life fell silent, except for the sound of the sea, incessant as it swirled and splashed around the rockpools below. The breath of watery air made her feel exhilarated. And he was part of it all; part of this place; conjured up from its heart and baptised in its salt waters.

'Yes. We.' Jago put an arm around Malory's shoulders, then leaning forward, kissed her tenderly on the lips.

There was no time for Malory to protest. He had taken her completely by surprise, and it had happened. The moment had moved from the present to the past; was now already forming as a memory that could not be undone. He had kissed her. Jago Berryman had just kissed her on The Island in St Ives. And now he was staring at her with earnest intensity.

'I... Why did you do that?' stammered Malory.

Jago leaned back against the bench to face the sea, his face serious, as though he was wrestling with some decision. Then abruptly, he turned towards her again, and his eyes met hers.

'Malory,' he said. 'I think you know I like you. I've liked you ever since we met. So, I was wondering... I'd like to ask you out. Properly. You and me. What do you say?'

Malory stared at him for a moment in horror. The morning had gone well. She had enjoyed his company. But this was beyond any expectation. She stood up and stared out to sea for a moment, trying to compose her thoughts. But aware of the discomfort that she must be causing, she turned again and spoke quickly. Best to get it over with.

'I'm sorry Jago, I don't think that would be a good idea. I mean, you're a lovely guy. You really are. I just think...'

'What?' said Jago, a hurt expression creeping across his face.

'I just think you're too young for me.'

There. She had said it.

Jago propped his elbows on the back of the bench in a relaxed manner, and to her surprise, laughed.

'Is that all?' he said.

Flummoxed, Malory stuttered... 'Well, yes, but...'

'How old are you? Twenty-eight? Twenty-nine? I know you probably feel that's way older than me, but it's only a few years. What difference does it make? It's about how we get along. And we do get along, don't we? Come on Malory, give it a chance. One date. It's not like I'm asking you to marry me.'

She felt as though she was about to collapse. Her heart beat wildly and her body shook. She looked at him with his beautiful skin, his bright eyes and messy hair. She thought about being close to that body, to have him kiss her again... For a moment, she was deliriously tempted.

'I'm sorry,' she said. 'I can't. It just doesn't feel right.'

She turned and walked away, her legs like jelly.

She could sense him following. 'Malory, please...'

She stopped again to face him. She had to be firm, but her heart ached at the thought of hurting him. She touched his arm.

'I think it would be best if we kept things professional. Bring the paintings to the shop whenever you can. I meant what I said about endorsing them. I want to help you, I really do. But that's all. Please accept it.'

Silently, gravely, he nodded.

All Malory could do was remove her hand from the strong muscle of his arm, and then force herself to turn and walk away.

CHAPTER 24

Beach House

Senara and Giovanna stood in the centre of the vast room and openly gawped. The two girls had been hired independently to waitress for Olly at his house party, but had not been quite prepared for the glamour of the venue.

From outside, *Ship Ashore* had looked like any number of ordinary Downalong cottages, with thick stone walls and a stable door. Senara had passed it by many times without guessing at the splendour that lay within. But as Olly led them inside, she saw that it had been completely redesigned to an architect's vision of sophisticated, modern, seaside living. All the walls had been painted white, maximising the light. Downstairs there was a long corridor with a row of solid oak doors on one side, still smelling of fresh wood, and each with a porthole window. These were the bedrooms, and each had been given a name, printed onto an enamel sign fixed to the doors; *The Bosun's Nest*; *The Fo'c'sle*; *The Captain's Cabin...* When Senara peeped through one of the little round windows she saw dark grey painted floorboards, rustic, driftwood furniture and lime-green towels expertly folded on the beds.

On the other side of the hallway, a wooden staircase with a rope for a handrail led them up to the huge open-plan living space.

'Wow,' said Giovanna.

'Amazing,' said Senara.

'I'm glad you approve,' said Olly. 'We like it anyway. It's homely.'

Senara and Giovanna exchanged glances, wordlessly expressing their mutual thought: *How the other half live...* It was a sentiment only intensified by the fact that both of them had just finished their day jobs, yet still required further employment.

A wooden beamed, vaulted ceiling, again painted white, increased the feeling of light and space. High windows along the tops of the walls allowed privacy, but the room was dominated by the view at the end of the room, where floor-to-ceiling glass doors opened onto a balcony that overlooked the beach. A retro Ercol sofa and matching chairs, strewn with cushions in tasteful fabrics, exuded understated class. There was a children's corner with board games, books, and bean bags. *This is our second-home*, it all screamed. *This is how we live when we kick off our shoes and relax*. Yet nothing could disguise the smell of wealth and expense.

An enormous dining table, made from what looked like reclaimed ship's timbers took up another area, with seating for more than a dozen. A secondary seating area contained more comfortable large sofas gathered around a wood-burning stove. Sailing and surfing magazines sat in neat, untouched, piles on the coffee-table. The furnishings were all in subtle, faded shades of sky blue, sea-green, and rose-pink. Nooks and shelves were furnished with quirky models of seagulls or boats. But there was real artwork on the walls, in the form of huge, abstract canvasses. This was a world where the sun always shone, where everything was permanently shipshape, and there was always champagne in the fridge.

'It's beautiful,' said Senara, feeling both a sense of wonder, and a wistfulness for a life she would never have.

Olly guided the two girls to the kitchen area, where trays of canapes had been prepared, and rows of champagne and cocktail glasses lay in wait. Everything here was sleek and modern, and, in contrast to the muted hues of the living area, consisted of glossy red cabinets and brilliant white tiles, illuminated by strip lights. They needed no introduction to Noah, a local lad who, whilst not quite a mixologist, had been employed to prepare the cocktails, and Denny, an Australian chef who, like them, had been hired for the evening. They both knew Denny well, as he had been working in various St Ives restaurants for about ten years now, having had his world travels interrupted by the charms of a local girl, now his wife.

'Senara!' he said. 'Thought you'd scarpered for good.'

Senara smirked uneasily. She didn't trust Denny's cheesy grin and fake good humour. There was something in his eyes that she didn't trust. But the three had all worked together before in various establishments, and so easily fell into a professional mode. Denny instructed that after the canapes and champagne had been served, there would be baby-sized portions of traditional battered fish and chips, served in paper cones, complete with wooden fork. But of course, the batter would be made with a local ale, the chips thrice-fried, and all served with a choice of his signature organic apple cider vinaigrette, fresh tartar sauce, or special-recipe sieved tomato ketchup. The girls were instructed that when the food was ready, they were to place a slice of lemon atop of each construction, held in place with a cocktail stick sporting a little St Piran's flag on top. For those averse to fish, there were miniature pasties; and, apparently having exhausted the 'local' theme, chocolate churros to finish.

Senara made mental notes. The menu was simple, and with a Cornish flavour, but a bit tired, she thought. When she had her own restaurant, she too would refine her own recipes and sauces. She kept a scrapbook, filled with ideas; articles, drawings, photos, and scribbled potential menus. In Antiparos, she had already developed her own take on some of the taverna dishes. Nikos's family used methods of cooking that had been developed over many years of tradition, and of having to make do with what had been available; fresh fish, potatoes, green beans, huge beefsteak tomatoes, feta cheese, peppers, and rice. All sloshed in plenty of olive oil and flavoured with oregano or basil from the kitchen garden.

It was indeed, a healthful, delicious diet. But with supplies from the mainland now much easier to source, Senara had experimented imaginatively. She had put Puy lentils, feta, and balsamic roast tomatoes in the stuffed peppers, to lessen the portion of rice, so that the result was juicy and flavoursome. She had added sultanas, capers, and a dollop of pomegranate molasses to the dolmades to give them a sweet and salty kick. She steered clear of the meat dishes, but invented a vegetarian moussaka, using her thick red lentil spaghetti sauce in place of the lamb. Nikos, despite his initial scepticism, had allowed her to try some of these ideas out on the customers, as a 'special' of the day, and had reluctantly been forced to admit that her experiments were popular. Senara longed to get back into the kitchen and create new dishes.

Ah well. *When she had her own restaurant…*

She sighed, and got to work. She put a short white apron over the uniform of black T-shirt and black mini skirt that the waitresses all wore at Driftwood. It was, she knew, little more than a modern, and somewhat sexist, take on the traditional French maid outfit. But despite this, Senara admitted that she loved the freedom of bare legs. It was the best thing about living by a beach, whether it be Cornwall or Greece; the sense of feeling like a child, forever playing in the rock pools. In tandem with Giovanna, Senara began to arrange the champagne glasses onto silver trays.

Before long the place started to fill up. Olly's sailing pals were first to arrive, dressed in what Senara supposed could only be described as 'nautical leisurewear'; crisply pressed shorts, polo shirts and deck shoes. Greying hair and bald patches were borne by way of impeccable haircuts. They were tanned, groomed, and doused in aftershave. They wore expensive wristwatches. Senara struggled to think of anyone of her generation who still wore a wristwatch. They were considered redundant; a symbol of slavery to the clock, to time as money. And besides, they had their smart-phones.

There were a couple of wives, equally well-presented and oozing opulence. They were dressed almost identically in white slacks and loose floaty tops, and were heavily adorned with gold jewellery. They barely acknowledged Senara as they lifted the champagne flutes from her tray, but talked loudly about how St Ives fared in comparison to St Mawes. Even as a long wavy strand fell from her ponytail across her face, Senara wondered how these women kept their hair, expertly cut and bleached, so pristine and sleek in the salty sea breeze coming in from the beach. It was not Cornish hair. Cornish hair was wild, and tangled by wind and sea.

A younger girl arrived. She was alone, but not, Senara sensed, out of place. She wore a cropped, striped Breton top and a pair of red, high-waisted shorts. With her long hair worn loose and her scrubbed face, she was more in tune with the Cornish 'vibe' than the other guests, but there was still something about her; something immaculate, confident, and...*entitled*, that made her worlds apart from Senara.

'That's Daisy, Olly's daughter,' Denny informed her in passing, and breathing down her neck. 'Down for the holidays. She stays with her mother up near the moors somewhere.'

Stepping away from Denny's close proximity, Senara watched as Daisy flitted from guest to guest, chatting gaily. 'She seems nice,' she said.

'Yeah, I've heard she's *very* nice,' said Denny with a wink. 'Very obliging.'

'Don't!' said Senara, appalled. 'She's a young woman. You shouldn't talk about her like that.'

'Takes one to know one, eh Senara?' Denny said, nudging her with his elbow.

Senara's heart sank. She should have known it was only a matter of time before Denny stuck his oar in. What was it about this place that no one could mind their own business?

'So what?' she said fiercely. 'She can do what she likes. You don't talk about your male friends like that, do you?'

'Calm down, I'm only kidding you,' said Denny cheerfully, but with shark eyes. 'Gotta learn to laugh at yourself, Babe. Come on now, get those canapes out doing the rounds. Jump to it!'

Senara wished the night was over. She didn't belong here, with these people. But where did she belong? Once again, she had that strange sensation of being in a beautiful place, a place that she knew and loved, but of being cast adrift. There was a big hole in her life and she knew neither what it was, nor how to fill it.

She dutifully delivered the canapes to the increasingly large and babbling crowd.

'I'll have one of them, if that's all right,' said a familiar voice.

Senara turned to see Kit, beaming at her. Beside him, with a less enthusiastic expression was Astrid. And behind them, almost hiding, if it were possible for such a large lad, was Dan. They had all already acquired champagne.

'Kit!' cried Senara, resisting the urge to kiss him, as she would usually. 'And... it's Astrid, isn't it?'

Senara ran the gamut of emotion. Happiness for the appearance of a friend; alarm at the potential for further confrontation.

Astrid nodded and smiled weakly. 'Pleased to meet you,' she said.

So that was it. No mention of their prior encounter; no apology for lack of civility.

...But it was enough. Astrid was Kit's girlfriend and Senara had no desire to continue hostilities.

'Likewise,' she said, with a smile. All the same, she prayed that Pepper was not going to show up.

'Hi Dan,' said Senara, with a small nervous wave. She still didn't know how many others held a grudge. But Dan just waved back timidly, as if he were afraid of being caught uninvited.

'I didn't expect to see you guys here tonight,' continued Senara. 'Not your usual environment.'

'Olly likes to parade a few locals, for entertainment,' said Kit.

'It does feel weird,' said Senara, with a giggle. 'Like, you're all out of context, or something. Is Zack here?'

'He meant to come,' said Kit. 'But he's not allowed out to play.' He shoved a canape in his mouth, then took another.

'You mean, spending quality time with his family,' said Dan, disapprovingly.

'Didn't expect to see you here, either,' said Kit, to Senara.

'Oh, you know me,' said Senara, as Kit reached for another canape. 'If there's a low-paid bit of drudgery to be had, I'm your girl. And stop that! They're hors d'oeuvres. You're not supposed to eat them all.'

Kit flashed his eyes at her and took a couple more. 'I'm hungry.'

Senara shook her head at him and then offered the tray to Astrid. 'Canape?'

'No, thank you,' said Astrid, then knocked back her champagne.

'Is there any beer?' whispered Dan, popping his head between the other two.

Senara laughed. 'I think I saw some in the fridge. I'll sneak you a couple out.'

'Cheers, Senara,' said Dan. 'And er, good to see you again, mate.' He plonked his empty champagne glass on Senara's tray and indicated the kitchen with his eyes.

Senara laughed again. 'Okay, okay. I'm on it...mate.'

She turned to Kit and Astrid. 'I hope you enjoy the party.'

'Don't address the guests, wench,' said Kit. 'Get back to drudging.'

Astrid stood silent, inscrutable, a practised smile on her lips.

Senara decided it would not be wise to continue the banter. She merely smiled and left, deftly diverting the tray of nibbles from within Kit's grasp.

She returned to the kitchen and covertly pilfered a couple of bottles of beer from the fridge. The beers weren't strictly on offer, but it was hardly a crime to give guests what they wanted, she reasoned. She delivered them together with a bottle opener to Dan, who lurked nearby. The delight on his face was palpable, and he thanked her profusely.

Senara returned to her duties with purpose. She picked up another tray of food and began to circulate amongst the crowd again. As she approached a group in the corner, she stopped abruptly. There was no mistaking it this time. Even if she had been uncertain about his exact features, she could tell from the look in the man's eyes that he recognised her. It was Brian.

He looked edgy, she thought, as though he had been caught out in some way. But immediately she dismissed this ungenerous notion; he was just surprised, that was all.

'Brian!' she said, brightly, approaching him. 'Fancy running into you here. Small world.'

'Yes,' said Brian quickly. 'I didn't know you'd be here.'

She thought he seemed nervous, and Senara's instinct was to put him at ease.

'It's good to see you again,' she said, smiling warmly. 'How come you're here?'

'I know Olly,' he said. 'I met him in The Sloop. I might be doing some work for his company.'

'Cool,' said Senara, smiling. 'You should have said you were in St Ives. We could have met for that coffee.'

'I'm just here for business,' said Brian. 'It might not look like it, but this is networking. I won't be staying long.'

'Okay,' said Senara. 'Talking of business, I'm supposed to be working. Would you like...' She held out the tray of food.

'No. No thanks. I really have to get going,' said Brian.

'Well, it was nice running into you,' said Senara. 'Let me know about coffee if you're in town for a while?'

'Will do,' Brian smiled and nodded, before slipping away into the crowd.

Shortly after, the partygoers gathered by the windows, and crammed onto the balcony to watch the sunset, cocktails in hand. Everyone declared that it was indeed spectacular, and *much* better than the sunsets in St Mawes. In time, becoming chilly, they drifted back inside, and the rest of the food was served and cleared away.

Eventually, sensing a lull, Senara stole away to the briefly vacated balcony. She needed a minute to digest the meeting with Brian. There were still unanswered questions, but in her confusion, she had sought to reassure him; to be friendly. She had no doubt that he would explain all when they met for coffee.

* * *

Daisy found Dan skulking on a blanket chest in the laundry room, which was on a mezzanine level between the bedrooms and living area.

'Hey, Dan, you made it. Awesome!' she cried. 'I thought I saw you arrive, but then you disappeared. Sorry, I was involved in a really tedious conversation, otherwise I'd have said hi straight away.'

It did not seem to faze her in the slightest that he was sitting alone, away from the party.

'Yeah, I was just having a quiet beer. You know. Parties can get a bit noisy.'

'For sure,' said Daisy, putting her drink on the counter, and happily sitting alongside him. 'And they're all so old, apart from *your* lot. I mean, I really like Daddy's friends, but they can be a bit stuffy sometimes.'

'Are you not enjoying it then?' said Dan.

'Oh yes, for sure. And the sunset was awesome. But I missed you, Big Bear.' She slipped her slender arm around his waist.

A vague memory of their previous, drunken conversation stirred in Dan's mind, triggered by the words "Big Bear". Something to do with him talking about bare feet? That's right. After a few drinks he had loosened up, and admitted that he hated having to go barefoot into the water to launch or tether the boats. How it was worse at low tide, with all the little pools left behind, and where danger in the form of weever fish might lurk, their venomous spines hidden beneath the sand. He had tried wearing aqua shoes once, but Zack and Kit had teased him ruthlessly. And besides, they'd rubbed his skin raw, and given him a rash.

But Daisy hadn't been listening to all that. All she heard was that he hated his "bear" feet.

'Well, I like your bear feet,' she had said. 'And I like your bear hands, and your bear tummy!' At this point, she had grasped his midriff in a cuddle.

Much as she was doing right now.

'Do I get a bear kiss?' she purred in his ear.

Dan, though petrified, somehow managed to oblige. Once more, he couldn't quite believe his luck, but his enjoyment was tainted by anxiety, as he feared she might at any moment push him away in abhorrence.

But she did not push him away. Instead, after several minutes of intense snogging, she stood up and took his hand. 'Come on!' she said happily.

She led him downstairs to where the bedrooms were, although Dan had not taken this fact on board when he had arrived, but rather had followed Kit and Astrid in a state of blind angst. They arrived at a door that said 'Cabin Boys'. Daisy led him inside and shut the door behind them. The room was laid out in a long narrow shape, with a row of cabin bunks built along one side, sleeping up to six in single beds. The other wall was lined with shelves and cupboards, and there were little hooks for coats, and pegs for wellington boots by the door. A teddy bear dressed in a yellow sou'wester and hat sat on a painted wooden chair in the corner.

'This is where my cousins and I all used to sleep when I was growing up,' said Daisy. 'But there's no children staying at the moment, so less chance of being disturbed here.'

'Disturbed?' said Dan, starting to break a sweat. She really was far too pretty for him. Much prettier than any girlfriend he had ever had. 'What if we are? Someone might come in.' There was no lock on the door.

Daisy, it appeared, continued to be ignorant of his condition. 'No one's going to come in, silly.' She pulled him down onto one of the cabin bunks, then lay back and hauled him on top of her.

Something about the situation felt wrong to Dan. Maybe it was the teddy bear staring at him from the corner chair.

'I'm not sure I feel quite comfortable,' he said.

'What's wrong, Big Bear?' said Daisy, whilst snuffling around his neck, and licking his ears.

'It's just...it doesn't feel quite right. This is meant to be a children's room. And we're about to...'

'Yes?' said Daisy brightly.

'Desecrate it,' said Dan.

She laughed, a light, fairy giggle. 'Oh, you are a silly Big Bear. I've done it here loads of times with cousin Digby.'

'Your cousin?' said Dan in horror.

'Oh, he's not a real cousin,' said Daisy. 'Something complicated like Daddy's uncle because of Grandpa's third marriage. We just call everyone cousin. It's easier.'

Dan frantically tried to calculate the relationships, but giving up, said: 'That just makes it worse, somehow.'

Daisy pouted. 'Don't you like me anymore, Big Bear?'

'No. I mean, of course I do. Only... Maybe we should go back to the party?'

'In a while,' said Daisy, pulling him close and kissing him again.

There was nothing else for it. Dan did not have the skill to extract himself, and it was not as if the situation was entirely unpleasant. So, he sank into Daisy's embrace, and lost himself in the moment; consoling himself, that he was after all, getting laid.

‘Just a minute,’ he said, stopping abruptly.

He stretched out to reach the teddy bear, then hurled it onto one of the top bunks where it could no longer torment him with its affronted gaze.

‘That’s better,’ he said. ‘Now. Where were we?’

* * *

Leaning on the balcony railing, Senara listened to the waves break on the darkened beach, and breathed in the sea air. As stars became visible in the clear night sky, something like a silent prayer began to form in her heart. The party had started badly, but now she felt a little hope. She was grateful for Kit, and for Dan. It did not take so very much to anchor her, it would seem; just a little kindness meant so much. Even Astrid had been polite, at least.

‘I thought perhaps you could do with one of these.’

Senara turned to see Kit holding two large tumblers, rattling with ice. Strips of orange peel permeated the drinks with subtle flavour.

She looked at him in delight. ‘Rum, old-fashioned? My favourite.’

‘I know,’ said Kit, handing her one of the glasses.

They look pretty good too,’ said Senara. ‘Noah’s doing an amazing job.’

‘As are you,’ Kit replied. ‘Who was that guy, by the way? The one you were talking to in the corner?’

‘Oh, that was Brian,’ said Senara. ‘I sat next to him on the train from London.’

‘Is he from St Ives?’

‘No, Truro, I think. I didn’t know he’d be here to be honest. It was a surprise. We talk on social media, but he didn’t mention being in town.’

'Wait, he followed you on social media?' Kit pulled a face. 'After sitting next to you on a train?'

'Well, there was a bit more to it than that,' said Senara. 'We talked. You know, had a laugh.'

'And now he shows up in St Ives,' said Kit. 'Sounds like a stalker to me.'

'Oh, don't be ridiculous,' said Senara. 'We chat, that's all. We get on.'

'He looked shifty,' said Kit. 'Why did he leave like that, in a hurry? And more to the point, why are you wasting time with a guy like that?'

'What do you mean?' said Senara.

'Well, he seems...' Kit hesitated.

'Go on,' said Senara.

'Really, really boring,' said Kit. 'You can do better, and you know it.'

Senara laughed. 'Just because he's not some beardy hipster dressed like a lumberjack, doesn't mean he's boring. Besides, maybe I want someone a bit boring, someone... *Normal*. You know; easy-going and well-adjusted. I'm tired of drama. And he's really nice, honestly.'

'Hmmm,' said Kit. 'If you insist. I'm just looking out for you Snow.'

'I know,' said Senara softly. 'And thank you. Thanks for always being there; for being a friend...'

'Oh god, you're not going to get all sentimental, are you?' said Kit. 'Hand me that drink back.'

She moved it swiftly from his reach. 'No chance! And I mean it. It was so good to see a friendly face earlier tonight.'

'Please don't get all teary.' He feigned a long-suffering expression.

'I might!' laughed Senara. 'You know me.'

'That's what I'm afraid of,' said Kit. 'You cry at anything.'

'Not anything,' said Senara. 'Just important stuff. Anyway. Cheers.'

They clinked their glasses together and took a sip of delicious rum cocktail.

'Boy, that's good,' said Senara. 'But...shouldn't you get back to Astrid?'

Kit stared at her for a second, shaking his head. 'Honestly, you women. Am I supposed to be harnessed to her side? I haven't *left* her. She went to the bathroom. So, I thought I'd come and say hi. What are you so terrified of?'

'You know what.'

Kit turned to face the sea, shaking his head again. 'Yeah, I suppose,' he said wearily, his expression obscured in the darkness. 'I'm not sure I'm cut out for all this.'

'All what?'

'All this... Togetherness. Being in a couple. I liked my freedom. I liked just being me.'

'But... You must have wanted it at the time?' said Senara, although panicked at the dangerous territory she was in. Astrid would not appreciate their conversation one bit. 'Otherwise, why do it? Why move in together?'

Kit continued to stare out to sea. 'It wasn't an actual, you know, decision. There was no discussion. It just kind of happened.'

Senara fell silent. He sounded different, and serious, almost melancholy. It was not like Kit. And what could he mean? She wanted to know more, to be there for her friend, to listen to him. Yet although she owed Astrid no loyalty, to discuss their relationship while she was nearby, felt wrong.

'Hey, did you see that?' said Kit suddenly, his mood returning to normal. He had instinctively raised an arm to point at the night sky.

'No, what?'

'A shooting star. Did you miss it?'

'Yes. I was looking at you.'

'Ah, that's a shame. I wonder if it's the start of a meteor shower? Although a bit early for the Perseids, I would have thought.'

'It is a beautiful night. I want to see one too now...'

'I'm going home,' Astrid's voice interrupted from the doorway. 'Are you coming?'

Kit looked at his still full glass. 'Can I finish my drink?'

'Of course,' Astrid smiled. 'What are you both drinking? Cocktails?'

'Yes,' said Senara. 'Old-Fashioned. It's heavenly.'

'Perks of the job, eh?' said Astrid. 'I don't suppose Olly and his friends will notice you're gone, now they're all sloshed.'

'Hopefully not!' said Senara.

'Perhaps I could have one too?' Astrid said to Kit. 'Since you're not ready to leave just yet?'

'Yeah, sure,' said Kit. 'But wouldn't you prefer something with vodka? That's your usual preference.'

'No, I'd like to try one of those,' she said, indicating their drinks. She turned to Senara. 'What is it? Whiskey?'

'No, rum,' said Senara. She was happy that Astrid was being sociable at last, but still felt somewhat uncomfortable after what Kit had said.

'Coming up,' said Kit. He dived back into the throng inside.

The two women stood silently in the dark. Astrid was looking at Senara, with that same fixed expression, that betrayed nothing.

Awkwardly, Senara gestured to the sky. 'We were just...' She had been about to say 'looking at the stars', but stopped, realising how inappropriately romantic it would sound. '...talking about meteors. Kit thinks he saw a shooting star.'

Astrid said nothing, but just stared at her blankly.

Senara took a gulp of rum. 'I hear you work in a jewellery shop? Selling gemstones and the like? I'll have to come and take a look one day. So many new places have opened since I was here last.'

Astrid inspected her nails, but still said nothing.

'Anyway,' said Senara, increasingly uncomfortable. 'I should probably get back to work. Lots of clearing up to be done before we're let off.'

Still Astrid behaved as though she were alone on the balcony. As if she could neither see nor hear Senara.

Kit returned with Astrid's drink. 'Here you go. Enjoy.' he said.

'Thanks Sweetie,' said Astrid, and gave him a peck on the cheek.

Senara stood like an apparition in the corner as Astrid tried the cocktail.

'Urgh, no,' she said, frowning, and handing the glass back to Kit. 'That's disgusting. Really sickly.'

Kit sighed and put the rejected drink down on a nearby table. 'Should have had the vodka.'

'Can we go, please Kit?' said Astrid. 'I'm really tired and have things to do tomorrow.'

'Okay, sure,' said Kit. 'Here.' He handed his own drink to Senara. 'You can finish mine. It's all looking under control in there, you won't be missed for a bit longer.'

'Thanks,' said Senara, quietly.

Astrid turned to Senara, miraculously aware of her presence again. 'It was so nice to meet you properly at last. You must come and visit the shop where I work. It's near the old Drill Hall.' She leaned forward and air-kissed Senara on both cheeks, continental-style. 'See you again soon.' Then she linked arms with Kit and drew him towards the balcony doors.

He looked back over his shoulder and smiling, mouthed goodbye.

Senara stood alone, with a rum in each hand, not quite sure what had just happened. The remnants of the party were still going on behind her: loud conversation and jazz music. She should indeed probably be stacking the dishwasher and cleaning the surfaces. But Senara felt numb, confused. It was then that her phone bleeped, indicating a message. She placed the drinks on the table and opened it.

It was from Brian: *No time to chat longer, or I'd miss my train. You'll have to catch me next time I'm down in St Ives x*

So, he was back in Truro? Why had he not said he was returning that night?

Bewildered, Senara did not reply, but turned off the phone. She poured the remainder of Kit's drink into her own glass. Then sliding to a seating position in a corner of the balcony floor, she gazed up at the stars and slowly drank the lot.

CHAPTER 25

Coast Path

Malory ambled down the steps to West Beach in some trepidation. She had enjoyed the few walks along the coast path that she had taken, but Senara had made her somewhat nervous about the trek to Zennor. On top of which, she was afraid that she might encounter Jago himself, on his way to or from a surf. But the sea was flat, with barely a ripple breaking on the shore. She wondered if Jago had confided in his sister; had told of her rejection of him. It was possible that she might be hostile; might not even show up.

But she need not have worried. She found Senara seated in the café with a coffee and adjusting her bootlaces. She had tied her long blonde hair into a fishtail plait. She wore the same light sleeveless shirt and khaki shorts that she had worn the day they had first met at Paddington station. But today her long and lean brown legs ended in chunky socks and walking boots. She looked amazing, thought Malory. She herself looked more prepared for a London gym, in pedal-pushers, a vest and running trainers.

'Morning,' said Senara, seeing her. 'Going to be a fine one, by the look of things.'

'I do hope so,' said Malory. She did not tell Senara that she had become anxious about howling gales and muddy, slippery footpaths on treacherous cliff edges. But the day was still, and the sky a clear, indigo blue.

'Gonna be baking out there,' said Senara. 'Hope you've got sunscreen? I have some if not.'

Malory bought them both another coffee, and then they studied Senara's map.

'These are the bits where it gets a bit hairy,' said Senara, pointing. 'There's a tough ascent here, and the path becomes a clamber over boulders here...' She saw the furrow on Malory's brow. 'But it will be fine, honestly. There's practically no wind. We'll just take it at our own pace. As you said, one step at a time.'

Malory smiled and tried to relax. Truthfully, she was excited, for there was an air of anticipation to the day. *Look at me*, she thought, as she took in the beautiful scenery, and the comforting smell of roast coffee. *Me, setting off on a hike.*

They bought bottles of water from the café, repacked their small day rucksacks, then set off, along the path past the bowling green. Towards Man's Head the giant planted hydrangeas gave way to hedgerow flowers.

Before long, the tarmacked section of path ended and became a track; a narrow, stony and uneven passage that cut through the thick undergrowth. Malory became ever more aware of the presence of wildlife. The foliage, profuse with wildflowers, was alive with the buzz of insects. There were bees, and butterflies, and beetles. Malory kept spotting little snails with beautifully coloured shells, and she tried hard not to step on them, even as she worked to place her next careful footstep. Senara appeared to be strolling at leisure.

Occasionally, they'd meet walkers coming the other way, and one or other party would have to balance on the verge to let them pass, so narrow was the path. But once they reached Clodgy Point, the way dispersed into several worn trackways across the grassy hill of Burthallan Cliff. They stopped by the cliff edge to take some water, with the sun hot against their backs. The view along the coastline of the headlands was sublime; the colours intensified in the bright light. A sailing boat in the distance made its way out to sea, a vision of tranquillity. It did not seem quite real, for there was no wind, at least on the land, where they stood. It floated on the ocean, an unearthly mirage. Malory wondered who was on it, and what kind of life you had to have lived, to be on a sail boat heading out to wherever.

'Look!' cried Senara, pointing. 'Over there.'

'What is it?' said Malory.

'Dolphins!' said Senara, just in time for Malory to see the pod breach the water

'Oh yes, I see them! That's incredible. I find it increasingly hard to believe I'm still in England.'

Senara gave her that look again, the one she had given on the train from St Erth.

Malory laughed. 'Yeah, I know, I know. Cornwall is a *country*.'

A boat laden with tourists passed by, far beneath them. Senara waved frantically. The man at the helm looked up, and shading his eyes from the sun, waved back.

'It's Kit,' said Senara. 'He probably can't tell it's me from this distance, but nice of him to wave back anyway.'

'Kit?' said Malory. 'Jago...mentioned someone called Kit.' She was sure her voice sounded odd when she said Jago's name.

'Yes, he's a friend of ours,' said Senara. 'He's a fisherman, but he does boat trips too. You might have seen him if you're up early in the morning.'

Malory strained to observe the man in the boat.

'Oh, *him*,' she said, taking in the long hair, tied back from his face, and dressed in what appeared to be a boiler suit. 'Yes, I've seen him around. Isn't he on the lifeboats as well?'

'Yes,' said Senara.

'He's very handsome.'

Senara sighed. 'Yes, he is. Please don't tell him that though, he doesn't need any more confidence.'

Malory looked at Senara. 'Are you and he...?'

'No, no. He's just a mate. He has a girlfriend.'

'What's she like?'

Senara looked hesitant for a second then said, 'Odd.'

'But I don't really know her very well,' she added hastily.

Before Malory could ask her to elaborate, Senara went to sit upon a nearby rock. Malory joined her close by, and they both watched in silence as Kit's boat made its way around the rocky coast.

'Right,' said Senara, after a while. 'You ready?'

They gathered up their rucksacks and set off again, with Senara leading the way. They had not gone far, when Malory stopped, and looked unsure. They had reached a point where the path was dangerously close to the edge of a deep gash in the cliff face, a crevice with a sheer drop onto treacherous rocks and the churning sea below.

'Are you okay?' said Senara.

'Yes. I mean no. It's just...'

Senara waited.

'I've never gone further than this point before,' said Malory. 'It's a bit scary.'

Senara looked down over the cliff edge at the precipitous zawn. 'Yeah, you wouldn't want to fall down there. But it'll be fine. It's only a short distance, and there's no wind. Just watch your step.'

Still Malory looked hesitant.

'Look, we can go over the top of the hill if you want, and re-join the coast path again further along,' Senara suggested. But

Malory thought she looked disappointed. 'So long as you realise that it's all going to be a bit like this from here on in.'

Malory looked at the hill behind them. Traversing it would add to their journey length, but at least you couldn't plunge to a watery grave. Yet something about Senara's look of regret made her ashamed. She was probably thinking that Malory was going to be a pain in the arse all the way to Zennor. But more than that, Malory was dismayed at her own lack of courage; that she was too afraid to do the things that she wanted to do. An errant vision of Jago Berryman's smile and the touch of his lips came unbidden into her consciousness. She pushed it away.

'No,' she said. 'Let's stick to the coast path.'

'You sure? The point of no return...' But Senara was grinning.

'Yes,' said Malory. 'The point of no return. Let's do it.'

Senara strode confidently around the ledge, but waited for Malory at the most crucial, threatening bend.

Malory made baby steps, inching her way along, and as far from the cliff face as was humanly possible. She wondered if perhaps she should crawl on her hands and knees... 'Oh my god, oh my god, I'm going to die,' she shrieked. 'Why can't you have proper bloody pavements, that aren't littered with death-trap loose stones to send you falling to your death!'

Senara chuckled. 'You're not going to die.'

Then she danced a little jig, right on the precipice.

'Stop that!' screeched Malory. 'Seriously, it's not funny!'

'Come on!' Senara laughed. 'Take my hand, or we'll be here all day,'

'Don't rush me!' Malory cried, but she couldn't help but laugh too. She took the outstretched hand and held on tight as Senara guided her around the bend. When they reached a place of relative safely, the two women were giggling like teenagers.

'I'm so embarrassed!' said Malory. 'Promise me you won't tell anyone what you just witnessed.'

'No need,' said Senara. 'They probably heard you back in St Ives. Come on. Only about six more miles of heart-stopping danger and you can have a well-earned pint in The Tinners.'

Malory didn't know whether to laugh or cry. 'I'm such a bloody townie.'

Senara reached out and touched her on the arm. 'Nonsense. You did it, didn't you?'

Malory nodded like a child.

Gradually they made their way along the coast path. Malory was grateful for stretches where the path was level, weaving amongst yellow gorse bushes, but for the most part it was a roller-coaster of soaring cliffs that plunged into deep valleys and coves. Malory's thighs began to ache from the effort of balancing where the track descended, and then hauling herself up where it rose steeply again. In places it appeared that the granite stones had been deliberately arranged in steps, presumably, Malory thought, to ease passage up the sheer cliff face.

'But they've made them for giants!' she complained, as she heaved herself, panting and sweating, up yet another rocky staircase.

At the top, stopping to catch her breath, she gazed up at the moorland peaks. She could feel the spirit of Barbara, whose sculptures revealed a pagan heart, climbing to the top of Rosewall Hill. She saw her sit atop of the carn to sketch. Surveying her domain, she embodied the locals' nickname for her: *The Witch of St Ives*. Inspired, Malory felt her heart fill with desire to equally conquer this wild, untamed land. She pressed on.

They saw Kit's boat make its way back home again to St Ives, but Malory did not dare look too much in case she lost her footing and went tumbling down the treacherous route. She keenly felt the sense of remoteness. The further they went from civilisation, and the constant drone of traffic, the stranger the quiet ambience of the day became. The hum of wildlife, and Senara's voice as she chatted, seemed extraordinarily amplified.

In time, they descended into a valley, where the undergrowth appeared to Malory to be even more lush, and she could hear the sound of running water.

'River Cove,' said Senara.

It looked more of a stream, or a waterfall, than a river, cascading over the rocks and boulders to the sea. An age-old clapper bridge traversed it.

'We have to go over that?' said Malory, looking warily at the narrow flat stone.

'Yep,' said Senara. 'Unless you want to wade through the water?'

Malory took a look at the slippery rocks and conceded that the bridge must indeed be crossed. 'Why can't they put up handrails or something?' she moaned.

'Where would be the fun in that?' said Senara, and then turning, picked her way through the boulders and deftly walked across the little bridge.

Malory noted that immediately on the other side, the route ascended again in another 'enhanced' staircase. 'More bloody steps!'

She made her way carefully across, then flinging her rucksack from her back, threw herself down onto the small grass verge.

'No more,' she said. 'I need a rest.'

'Sure,' said Senara. 'No problem. We're about halfway, anyway.'

'Is that all?' wailed Malory. 'It feels like we should nearly be there by now.'

'Yeah, it's a strenuous walk, all right,' said Senara, sitting down next to Malory and reaching into her rucksack for her water bottle. As she leaned forward, Malory noticed a tattoo on the back of Senara's shoulder.

'Oh, that looks pretty,' said Malory, after glugging from her own water. 'Your tattoo, I mean. What I can see of it, anyhow.'

'It's a snowflake,' said Senara, pulling back her shirt so Malory could see.

'Oh yes, I see now, it's lovely.'

'It's because of my nickname, Snow. At least that's what Kit calls me, ever since we were kids.'

Kit again, thought Malory, but said nothing.

Senara looked thoughtful as she stared at the gurgling water. The heat was intense in the valley, but the sound of the bubbling stream, rendered it deeply peaceful.

'I got it to celebrate my eighteenth birthday,' said Senara. 'Pepper... Pepper got one too, in the same place, when her eighteenth came around. Only she got a red chilli pepper, because, well that's what she was calling herself by then.'

'Pepper?'

Senara turned to look at Malory. 'Tina. She used to be Tina. But she changed it to Pepper.'

'Why Pepper?' said Malory.

'I don't know, just liked the idea I suppose. I think we were all at a beach party—a group of us—and she was dancing to the Red Hot Chili Peppers, and it sort of came from that. But now I think about it, she asked Kit—I think she may have had a *thing* for Kit at the time—why he called me Snow. Then she said something about being the opposite of snow; that she was fiery and red-hot.'

Malory laughed aloud. 'Nice chat-up line.'

'Well, she'd had a few drinks, I expect,' grinned Senara. 'Anyway, that's when she announced her new name; Pepper.'

'You can't give yourself a nickname,' said Malory. 'It should be given *to* you.'

'That's what Kit said, at the time,' said Senara. 'In his own inimitable way, of course; something about self-anointment, I think. Anyhow, she wouldn't answer to Tina after that, and so eventually, it stuck.'

'And she got a tattoo? In the same place as your snowflake?'

'Yeah, she did.'

Malory raised an eyebrow.

'Yeah, I know. But we did everything together back then,' said Senara. 'Looked the same, wore the same clothes. You know. Like young girls do.'

'But not anymore?'

Senara gave Malory another searching look, before apparently deciding to continue; to trust her.

'Pepper is married to Grady O'Keefe, at least now. But when they first started dating... I had an affair with him.'

'Blimey,' said Malory, and took another sup of water.

'I know, what can you say to that? I was a cow, and I cheated on my best friend. Inevitably, I got found out, and I ran away to Greece, in shame. And now I'm back, and she still hates me.'

'What did *he* do?' said Malory, recalling Senara's reaction at Atlantic Arts. 'What did Grady do when you were... Found out?'

Senara made a small scoffing noise. 'He dumped me of course.'

'Did you have feelings for him?'

'Yes. At the time, I did,' said Senara sadly. 'And I think I convinced myself he felt the same. But he abandoned me. It was horrible. Suddenly I was an outcast. I felt so…isolated and alone. I had never experienced anything like it before. I'd always had friends. I was confident and happy. And then I did this shitty thing, and I still don't really know why.'

'And do you still have feelings for Grady?' asked Malory.

'Maybe I do, in a way,' Senara looked thoughtful. 'He still makes me uncomfortable, at least.'

'He makes *me* feel uncomfortable,' said Malory drily. She shook her head. 'I'm sorry if you still like him, Senara, but I have to say I think the man's a player and a creep. I can't believe he's married.'

'Yep. Couple of kids too.'

'Really? Well, I feel sorry for this Pepper woman. I don't mean because of what you did, but because she has to be married to him.'

Senara smiled crookedly. 'Yeah, I suppose.'

Malory looked at Senara's sad expression. 'You know, you shouldn't beat yourself up. You must have been very young when it all happened.'

Senara still looked downcast. 'Maybe.'

'It makes me mad, it really does,' continued Malory. 'It's always the woman who gets the blame. Never the lowdown…' Malory halted mid-speech and stared. 'What the…? Is that…?'

'A donkey, yeah,' said Senara with a grin.

They both stared at the little donkey that rambled down an inland track then stood a few feet away, nonchalantly chewing on some grass.

'Why is there a donkey?' said Malory, giggling. 'Why, out here, in the middle of nowhere, is there a donkey?'

'Why not?' said Senara, but she was laughing too. 'And you're a cute little baby donkey, aren't you?'

The donkey moved a couple of paces away from them but continued to chew the cud.

'It must have come from a nearby farm or cottage,' said Senara. 'We're nearer civilisation here. That track eventually goes back up to the road, if you've had enough? Or we could join The Coffin Path across the fields?'

Malory was sorely tempted. Her feet hurt and her legs ached. But having rested by the beautiful brook, her enthusiasm was restored. 'No, it's fine. We'll carry on.'

'Are you sure? It's your last chance before Zennor, pretty much.'

Malory looked at the way inland and then out to sea again.

'I'm sure,' she said. 'I'm okay. I'm enjoying myself.'

And she realised, as she spoke, that it was true.

CHAPTER 26

Cosmic Things

Jago trudged along the dry mud path with his friends, Josh and Luke, at either side. Banks of wildflowers growing from the hedgerows released their scent into the morning air. The usual herd of cows gazed sorrowfully as the trio passed by the pasture. It was a path they had trodden for many years now, leaving Luke's van at the farmstead owned by Cosmic's parents, and heading through the familiar tracks to the barn.

The barn was undoubtedly a good rehearsal space. In a farmland field on the outskirts of St Ives, they could make as much noise as they liked. But it also meant that not only were they obliged to have Cosmic Ray in the band, but had increasingly succumbed to his leadership and artistic vision. The barn had started out in a decrepit state, but over the years, Cosmic Ray—with more than a little help from his parents—had had it restored and fitted with a small recording studio, so that the band could make CDs to give away at gigs. And there was a small faux stage, with a platform at the back for Josh's drums. Cosmic was the singer, of course, and had set up a camera to record their rehearsals, so that he could examine and refine his performance. Cosmic always stood in the middle, flanked to the right by Luke on bass, and to the left by Jago on guitar. They gave him some space, to allow for the expression of his wild, frantic stage act.

Farmer's son Ray, or Cosmic, as he preferred to be known, slept in a mezzanine area on a futon with his girlfriend Tatiana. Tatty, as she was sometimes known, was originally from London but had followed Cosmic home from Bali where they had met. The whole set-up was puzzling to the other Neutrinos, since, despite his being discreet about his preferences, they had long assumed that Cosmic was gay. Being introduced to Tatiana had been more than a mild surprise.

'Who knows *what* he is,' Luke had said at the time, and observing Cosmic's outfit of baggy, striped harem pants, and leather waistcoat atop of a bare chest. 'He looks like Aladdin.'

'He's a performer, that's what he is,' Jago had reminded them. 'An *artiste.*'

As they approached the barn today, Cosmic and Tatty were relaxing outside on scruffy deckchairs arranged around an unlit firepit. Cosmic raised an arm in salutation as they approached.

'Hey, mis amigos!' he cried, as he always did. 'Welcome!'

A long, wooden bench provided extra seating, and after passing round the beers they had brought, Jago and the others, as always, settled on this.

'Okay guys,' said Cosmic. 'Quick beer, then we'd better get rolling. Rockin' an' a-rolling. Gotta get our vibe on. Big gig coming up.'

Jago tried not to roll his eyes. They had just one gig in the near future, at Driftwood. It was hardly big time; not even the September festival; just an 'open mic'. But Cosmic had persuaded himself that a 'serious' music agent was going to come all the way from London, a belief based purely on the fact that he had badgered the said agent persistently by telephone, and assured the others that they had made a 'connection.'

'I've written a new song,' said Jago. 'It still needs work, but maybe we can try it out today?'

Cosmic cocked his head on one side and smiled indulgently. 'For sure, man, for sure. Always up for something new. So long as it's, you know, in tune with our energy.'

'Our *sound*,' muttered Josh, sardonically.

'Space rock,' added Luke even more sarcastically.

'Hey, I'm feeling some bad vibes man,' said Cosmic. 'Space rock's where it's at, dudes.'

Tatty gazed at him silently, adoringly.

'Isn't space rock more, I dunno, synthesisers and all that?' said Josh.

'And psychedelic,' added Jago.

'I used to think we were metal,' said Luke. 'I'm really not sure about the direction of the band.' He shook his head sadly.

'But that's where the Lady Tatiana comes in,' said Cosmic. Tatty had recently been installed as the keyboard player in the band, even though her skill was rudimentary. Cosmic had provided the instrument, and well, *hey*, she looked the part. 'I'm confident that our little lady will develop those synthetic vibes in good time. But it's not important. Synth is too predictable for a space rock band. We're not about predictable, man. We wanna take that theme and rock the hell out of it.'

'You do know that space rock sounds like, y'know, a *rock*?' said Josh. 'In space. A space rock.'

'Anyway,' Jago sighed. 'It's sort of a ballad. My new song. Like a... *Love* song.'

Cosmic looked at him with a world-weary expression. 'We've been through this before, Yago.'

Cosmic had cultivated the extremely annoying pretension of pronouncing Jago's name, 'Yay-go,' or sometimes even more preposterously, 'Iago'. He acted for all the world as though he were the only one with the wisdom to realise the correct articulation. It drove Jago crazy, but the others told him to get over it, that it was just Cosmic's way, his little idiosyncrasy.

'It's all right for you,' Jago had protested petulantly. 'He doesn't call you Yoshua."

'Why can't we do a ballad?' asked Jago.

'It's just not our thing, man,' smiled Cosmic. 'We're loud, man. We're the loudest damn rockers in town. We can't be getting all soppy with a ballad.'

'Not even a space rock ballad?' said Luke.

'It's just one song,' said Jago. 'I'm all for the heavy stuff too, but I don't think it would hurt to, like, change the texture now and again.'

'Right. Okay,' Cosmic held his hands up in surrender. 'Okay. We'll give your ballad a try. Never let it be said that Cosmic Ray is not open-minded. Just bear in mind that we might have to... *You* know.'

'What?' said Jago.

'You know...' said Cosmic again, with a grin, '...pump it up a little.'

Jago sighed. He was not in the mood for this. Other things preyed on his mind. Malory had made her feelings clear, but somehow, he didn't quite believe her. This in turn made him feel creepy and pathetic. He should get over it. Move on. But he had an itch that he couldn't scratch, and everything else felt redundant, and dissatisfying. He had the overwhelming feeling of not being in the right place; of wanting to be elsewhere. It was true that the barn was a great rehearsal space. They were lucky in many ways to have the opportunities that Cosmic provided. But when he looked around at the surrounding fields, and up at the vast open sky, it sometimes felt like the biggest backwater on the planet, and the band the most colossal waste of time.

CHAPTER 27

Zennor

An eerie sound was carried through the air, ghostly and forlorn.

At the top of Treveal Cliff, Malory stopped in her tracks. 'What the hell was that?'

'Oh, that's just the mermaids singing,' said Senara, matter-of-factly.

The sound came again; louder, haunting.

'Seriously,' said Malory. 'What is it?'

'Over there,' said Senara, indicating The Carracks. 'Seal Island. At least that's how it's become known. That's where Kit would have been taking the tourists.'

Malory looked down at the dark rocky outcrop in the sea. She could just about make out the shapes of the creatures basking in the sunshine. 'You're telling me that *seals* make that noise?'

Senara grinned. 'Or it might be the mermaids. No one really knows for sure.'

They carried on. Malory expected the journey's end around every headland, only to be greeted by yet another cliff with high moors beyond. There was still no sign of civilisation.

'I think it's great what you're doing for Jago, by the way,' said Senara, as they reached the top of another incline and paused for breath.

A feeling like a jolt of electricity surged through Malory at the mention of his name.

'About the paintings, I mean,' continued Senara.

'I'm happy to help,' said Malory. 'I was really impressed by him—by his work.'

'I think he's just as good as some of the more well-known St Ives artists,' said Senara. 'He deserves more recognition. It's wonderful for him to have the opportunity to promote, and maybe sell, his paintings.'

'I agree,' said Malory. 'But it's no big deal, for me. His paintings will look amazing in the shop. I want to make it more appealing, and relatable to the art galleries. I'm using *him*, really.'

'I think you're being self-deprecating,' said Senara, laughing.

Eventually, they reached Zennor Head. Malory trudged up to the craggy point after Senara, and then stopped to look out over Pendour Cove, with the headlands of Carnelloe Cliff and Gurnards Head beyond. She felt roasted in the hot sunshine. Her legs were in agony and her back dripped with sweat.

'It's so beautiful here,' she said.

Senara nodded, and took a slurp of water. 'I spent a lot of time here, as a kid. Jago too. Our Aunt and Uncle have a farm nearby. Pendour Cove is inaccessible but we can go down to the valley if you like?'

'Seriously?' laughed Malory. 'I'm not going down one more bloody cliff face today, thanks very much!'

'Fair enough,' said Senara.

They stood for a moment in silence, taking in the serenity of the vast expanse of ocean. Malory looked up at the crop of rocks that characterised the place. And then she saw it. Two stones, large and almost upright, like toppled menhirs, touched each other lightly, as if in the throes of an eternal kiss.

Zennor Kiss... This was it. The scene in Jago's painting.

Malory had the sudden sensation of being overcome by a powerful feeling of identification with the land. It was a feeling that had been creeping up on her ever since her arrival in Cornwall, but it struck her powerfully now. And this was the land that had made *him*; had shaped and formed him from birth. He was part of it, and it reflected in his art.

Malory turned away to hide the emotion that threatened to reveal itself. How could she ever dare to equally be part of it? Of all this? To be like him?

'Come on,' said Senara. 'Last stretch, and it's easy all the way inland to the pub.'

Malory took one last look out over the entrancing seascape, then turned and followed Senara.

The trail soon became a path, and before long they arrived, at last, in Zennor Churchtown. Malory took in the small village. Beyond the pub, the church, and conversions of the old mill and Wesleyan chapel, it was little more than a handful of cottages, farms and outbuildings, all built from the same granite stone. It had a timeless beauty, enduring and unspoilt. She stopped by the church, and read the inscription on the sign: *Zennor Parish*; *St Senara's Church.*

'Your namesake,' she said to her companion. 'Who was St Senara?'

Senara shrugged. 'There's talk of a princess from Brittany. But she probably came over from Ireland. All the Saints seem to have come from Ireland. Usually in an improbable vessel like a barrel. Or a leaf,' she added drily.

Malory laughed. 'Can we go in?'

'Sure, but let's be quick if you want to eat before the pub stops serving lunch.'

It was immediately cool inside the small and empty church. Senara, familiar with the place, took a rest on one of the wooden pews, while Malory explored the tombstones and the 'Mermaid's Chair.' It was an old settle with the carving of a mermaid on one end, complete with what was considered to be a comb and mirror. She read the story of how the mermaid Morvoren, enchanted by his singing in the church choir, had lured Mathey Trewella into the seas forever.

'Is there time to look around the graveyard?' she asked Senara.

Senara sighed. 'Yes, I suppose so, since we've walked all this way. But just so you know, my stomach's rumbling.'

They went outside, and Malory searched around the small churchyard, which was still and silent in the midday heat. It was bordered by stone hedges and surrounded by ancient fields. Like the rest of the village, it was imbued with a sense of permanence. As she perused the gravestones, Malory once again became filled with a sense of history, of the people who had battled to stay alive in this unforgiving landscape. She was surprised to find that some lived to a great age, but other headstones told of death in infancy, or by drowning.

Once again, Malory felt that she could sense those lives, as if they were still going on around her. Here there was time and space for all souls to co-exist. The place was beautiful, but there had undoubtedly been hardship and sorrow. The land here bore the fierce, determined signature of mining, fishing and farming. But it was otherwise untainted by modern commerce. And there was mystery too, in the surrounding fields and moors, with their megalithic menhirs, quoits and stone circles. This view had not changed for centuries. The ocean and the craggy cliffs had been this way longer still. There was a sense of perpetuity; a connection to the prehistoric, and to the land itself. Malory felt a yearning, and a *belonging*; even as the voice in her head told her that she did not.

It was then that she saw Virginia stroll past the churchyard, on one of her rambles. No longer a young girl, there was a wisdom and message in her eyes, as she stopped and looked up at Malory. But Malory did not understand.

'Patrick Heron's grave?' said Senara, disturbing her thoughts. 'He lived in the house at Eagle's Nest.'

'Yes. I read that he was buried here,' said Malory, looking down at the headstone before her. 'I much admired him as an artist.'

'Makes a change,' said Senara. 'Most people go on about D. H. Lawrence living here.'

'Well, that is a notable point!' said Malory. 'But I believe Heron campaigned to help protect this whole area from development.'

'Job well done,' said Senara. 'Hopefully it will stay like this forever.'

Finally, they shut the gate of the churchyard, and strolled across the way to the pub. The pretty beer garden was tempting, but still hot from their walk, the women opted for one of the old wooden settles in the dark and cooling twelfth-century room inside.

'This is so gorgeous,' said Malory, finally taking the weight off her legs. 'But I'm not sure I'm going to be able to stand again.'

Senara laughed and said she would go to the bar. They ordered cold Cornish cider and food; a fresh crab sandwich for Malory and a vegetable quiche and salad for Senara. They ate hungrily, enjoying the reward all the more for their hard walk.

'I have never tasted a better crab sandwich,' said Malory. 'Or enjoyed a better glass of cider.'

'Nothing like a good hike to make you appreciate the simple things,' said Senara.

'How's your quiche?' asked Malory, in between mouthfuls of sandwich.

'It's really good,' said Senara. 'I make something similar myself, only more of a frittata; without the pastry base.'

'You like cooking?'

'I do. It's something of a passion of mine. I love the creative side of it, and the joy it brings to others.' Senara looked a little shy. 'I know that sounds a bit pretentious, but it's true. I'm a real foodie. A cooking nerd.'

'Wait a minute...,' said Malory. 'The choux buns. Jago gave me a choux bun—I've no idea why—but it was delicious. I mean *heavenly*. Did you make them?'

'Yes, I did,' said Senara, in delight. 'I'm always experimenting. And Jago happily eats everything, so...'

'Have you ever thought of doing it for a living?'

'As a matter of fact...'

And so, Senara told Malory all about working at Nikos's taverna in Greece, and about the net loft, and Isadora Francis.

'Would that be Dora Francis, the artist?' asked Malory.

'Yes,' Senara confirmed, and went on to explain how she would desperately like to make the loft her own, but could not figure out a way to come up with the money. Malory listened with interest, watching as Senara's eyes alternately sparkled with excitement and became dull with defeat.

'That's not an extortionate amount of money,' she said, when Senara told her the cost of the lease.

'Maybe not for some,' wailed Senara. 'But it's completely out of my league. I could kick myself for wasting so much time in Greece. Financially, I mean. I should have been plotting my future instead of lounging about, swimming and sunbathing.'

'It sounds to me, like you worked hard and learned a lot about cooking and catering.'

'Well, yes, I suppose I did. But it didn't translate into anything tangible. Like hard cash.'

'It's good experience. I wish to god I'd had more life experience like that.'

'What did you do before you came here?' Senara suddenly asked. 'Were you always into the art scene?'

Malory paused, taken by surprise. 'Yes, I've always been interested, but I sort of...got on the wrong path. Before I came here, I worked in business...'

'Really?' said Senara. 'What kind of business? Who for?'

'It was for...' Malory hesitated, and frowned. 'You know what, it doesn't matter. Let's just say it was a typical well-paid corporate job. There were clothes and glamorous offices and high-powered meetings. But it was soulless. It meant nothing to me. Even now, I can't bear to define myself by it. And so I won't. It was all incredibly boring. I'm not sure why I went down that road; I felt it was expected of me, I suppose; to maintain a certain lifestyle.'

'There's no better lifestyle than this,' said Senara. 'The sea, the sunshine... A good hike, some grub, and a pint. But don't listen to me,' she added hastily. 'I'm broke!'

'No, you're right,' said Malory. 'I don't think I've ever felt so satisfied with a morning well spent.'

'And you're *here*,' said Senara. 'What happened? Did you just decide to give it all up? The 'certain lifestyle' you speak of?'

Again, Malory hesitated. 'Not immediately. I think I became so embedded in my circumstances that I couldn't see a way out. But then...'

Malory looked into Senara's big blue eyes and decided to trust her. 'I was married. Back in London. My husband was also in corporate business, and expected a high standard of living. I suppose I did too, to start with. I mean, it was nice having money. And the longer that goes on, the harder it feels to give up. You see others struggling and develop a fear of being in that situation yourself. But I began to feel a certain lack. A feeling that there was something missing...'

'I know that feeling,' said Senara. 'But go on.'

'I wasn't happy, but it felt ungrateful to be unhappy. I was comfortable, and secure. And then I found out my husband was having an affair.'

'Oh,' said Senara. 'I'm... I don't know what to say.'

Malory saw the shadow of shame flicker across Senara's beautiful face.

'Oh, I don't blame *her*. She was a co-worker, younger than him. The typical story, I suppose. I'm sure she imagined she was in love with him.'

Again, Senara looked uncomfortable. 'There's still no excuse. If she knew he was married.'

'Anyway. It doesn't really matter,' said Malory. 'Once I found out, it actually came as no surprise. That was the strangest thing. That I wasn't shocked. It was as if I suddenly saw him clearly for what he was; as if I'd always secretly known, but refused to see it. And I'm quite sure there were others, this was just the first time he'd been caught.'

'So, I take it you're divorced now?'

'Yes. I realised that not only did I not love him, but I hated my life. I hated my job. I hated the stupid big house in the suburbs that had no character. I was surrounded by people I had nothing in common with. With few exceptions, I had no real friends, just people I happened to work with; neighbours who had values opposed to my own.'

'You needed to find your tribe,' said Senara, with a small smile.

'Yes!' said Malory. 'Exactly. So, I divorced him and sold the stupid big house and the stupid big car. I sold everything, practically, except the clothes on my back and... The bowl.'

'The bowl?' asked Senara.

'Yes,' said Malory smiling. 'Just a small clay bowl. If anything, if I was still unsure, it was the bowl that tipped me over. I found it on an antique stall in Portobello Road. It was very plain and simple; rustic, but utterly compelling. I liked to imagine it was from The Leach Pottery. I fell in love with, and very quickly bought it. But back home, I couldn't find anywhere to put it, that felt right. I realised that it didn't match its new surroundings. And very soon, it became obvious that it wasn't the bowl that was wrong, but all the rest of it. The modern furniture and fittings; the house, everything. I realised I felt more of an affinity to this one little bowl, than to all of the wealth that surrounded me. It somehow symbolised what my life ought to be, and everything else did not.'

'You *were* the bowl,' said Senara with a grin.

'Quite. And so, I bought a ticket to Cornwall and the leasehold on a little art shop with a *truly* crummy flat above. I have no idea how to run a retail business, but I'm hoping to eventually turn it into a gallery, or find a better space for one. That's where my heart really lies. I love art. That's the world I want to become a part of.'

'Well, you came to the right place,' said Senara, clinking Malory's glass. 'Another? The bus back to St Ives won't be for a while yet.'

'Sure, why not? And yes, I hope so. I hope with all my heart that I've made the right decision. I love it here so much. I feel like I'm meant to be here. But...'

'But?'

'Part of me thinks I'm deluding myself. That it's all fantasy. That I will rue the day I gave up my corporate job and security.'

'For what it's worth,' said Senara. 'I think you have definitely done the right thing. Because now you have freedom. You can do whatever you want. I mean, yes, you might fail, but to have that chance—the chance of the adventure—I'd give anything to be in that position.'

'Of course,' said Malory softly. 'And maybe one day you will be.'

Malory watched as Senara fumbled in her rucksack for her purse. Strangely, she recalled the look in Virginia's eyes, as a reckless idea began to form in her mind. 'Wait a minute, it's my turn,' she said. 'Same again?'

She stood up awkwardly, her muscles now tight and disobedient, and shuffled painfully to the bar. But despite her discomfort, Malory felt unusually happy and relaxed. Senara was right about the Cornish lifestyle. Now that the difficulty was behind her, she realised she had loved the experience of the walk; that she appreciated the food and drink all the more; even the opportunity to sit down on a basic wooden settle was bliss. She had never experienced such a level of satisfaction, of contentedness, after a gym session. She wished that she could keep hold of the feeling, that such moments were not swallowed forever by time.

She returned with a glass of cider for Senara, which she plonked unceremoniously on the table, and an opened bottle of sparkling wine and two glass flutes.

'What's this?' asked Senara, looking puzzled.

'They didn't have actual Champagne,' said Malory, sitting opposite Senara again. 'So I hope you like the Cornish equivalent?'

'Are we celebrating something?'

'I think so, yes,' said Malory, as she poured them each a drink.

'I suppose we did make it in good time,' said Senara. 'You did really well. I needn't have worried you, at all.'

'I'm not referring to the walk,' said Malory. 'I think we should celebrate me thinking about buying the lease for this net loft you talk about.'

Senara looked confused and began to turn pale. 'But... But *I* want it. For me.'

'Yes, I know that. But you can't afford it. And the money is not going to appear by magic.'

Senara looked like she might cry.

'What you need, Senara,' said Malory quickly, 'is a business partner.'

Senara continued to look blankly at her, not understanding.

'You may not have the money, but I do. I will have to take a look at the place of course, check if it seems a viable proposition. And I'll have to sample some more of your dishes, which I'm sure will be a complete ordeal. But if you're willing, I can buy the lease, and you can run the place; handle the cooking and the décor and such. Do all the hard work basically. It will just be a business investment for me. So, what do you say?'

'Are you kidding me?' Senara said with such intensity that Malory could not be sure she was not angry or upset. 'You would do that? Why would you do that? You hardly know me. Wait, is this the cider talking?'

'Like I said,' said Malory calmly, 'we would be partners. I'd expect to see a small profit in time. It's really nothing to be scared of Senara, at least once you're used to it. People invest in businesses all the time.'

'But... You're trusting in me. To get it right.'

'You mean someone who dances on a cliff edge?' Malory grinned. 'True, it's risky. But you have to be prepared to take risks in business.'

Senara's hands were trembling as she reached into her bag for her phone. 'We have to call him, Bob Prowse, the estate agent, right now. I couldn't bear it if somebody else got it first. We have to... Damn it! No signal here, I forgot.'

Malory laughed. 'Relax, I'm sure it will be fine. I'll call him later, and make an appointment to go and see the place. Then we'll take it from there. For now, though, we can discuss your menu, and vision.'

'But what about your gallery?' said Senara. 'That's what you really want. Not a surf café.'

'It won't interfere with those plans. If a suitable gallery space comes up, I can let the shop go.'

'How much money do you *have?*' cried Senara. 'No, don't answer that; that was rude. It's just... I can't believe it, that's all.'

Malory smiled. 'So, here's to business partners,' she said, holding out her glass.

Senara still looked stunned, and tears began to well in her eyes.

'Ever since I met you, you've helped me,' she said. 'First at Paddington, then with Grady. You're already helping Jago, and now this. It's like you're my guardian angel, or something.'

'Huh,' said Malory, amused, but rather liking the idea. 'Maybe I am. It's true I often wonder why I'm here. Perhaps I've been sent to Cornwall for the sole purpose of fulfilling your dream. Perhaps we are all each other's guardian angels.'

'Well then,' said Senara, finally holding out her glass. 'To angels.'

'And partners,' said Malory with a smile, as the flutes of champagne clinked.

CHAPTER 28

Debris

Kit let himself into the house and listened. It was Astrid's day off work but there were no sounds of her being at home, only the now ubiquitous signs of her occupancy. The candles and crystals and jewel-coloured cushions. A half-finished cup of coffee left upon the granite hearth. The elephant table. The furnishings were not unpleasant he supposed, but Kit's heart always sank a little now when he entered the room. In past times he would spend the long winter nights lingering by the fire in an old easy chair with a book, a glass of rum, and his peace. The only other furniture then had been a dark oak high-backed settle and table, inherited, along with the house, from an older relative.

'It looks like a pub,' Astrid had said, and had one day moved both items to the kitchen, where she deemed them to be more practical. They had been replaced—at her own cost, she reminded him—by a more customary plump, comfy sofa.

Kit took the abandoned cup to the kitchen, swerving, as usual, to avoid the dangling stones in the doorway. He took a beer from the fridge and went to tend to his plants on the terrace. But outside, he was met with a scene of disarray. Two sun loungers had been left out in a disordered manner, surrounded by magazines, bottles of suntan lotion and empty cocktail glasses. From the cigarette butts stubbed out on the floor tiles, he surmised that Pepper had been over, and that she and Astrid had taken advantage of the privacy of the balcony to top up their tans. He knew, from experience, that they had probably got restless and hungry, and somewhat inebriated, gone for burgers in town. Sighing, Kit began to clear up the mess. He was tired and a little sunburnt from a long day at sea, and longed to relax. Once the debris was removed, the sun loungers folded and packed away, and the floor swept, he returned his attention to the herbs.

With the sun in the west, they had some shade now, but Kit could feel them gasping from the day's scorching heat. Lovingly, he fed and watered them, then sat down to finish his beer. He gazed out across the bay towards Godrevy lighthouse and the coast beyond, then closed his eyes and listened to the soothing rhythm of the sea, crashing onto the rocks below. When he opened his eyes again, they came to rest on a butt that he had missed, stubbed out in the soil of the lemon-tree pot.

He tried not to be irked. This was what it was like to share a house, he reasoned. You couldn't have everything your own way. But there was something so bad-mannered about the cigarette butt that caused the anger to swell in him. It felt not just an afront to him, but to his precious plant itself. Kit reminded himself that he did not believe in control. He believed that you should go with the flow, and take life as it came. Yet once again he had that uneasy sensation; a peculiar sense of loss.

He had not noticed it at first; that day when Astrid had turned up unexpectedly and in distress on his doorstep, laden with luggage. Tearfully, she had explained that the flat above had flooded her own, causing immeasurable damage. Luckily, she had quickly managed to pack just a few essential items and escape. Kit had looked askance at the huge suitcase, and overstuffed holdall, but said nothing.

And what was she to do? The landlord had said that it would take weeks, months perhaps, to make the repairs. She could not stay with Pepper, of course, because of the children, and had nowhere else to go. So naturally she had come to Kit; her *boyfriend*.

They had only been dating for a couple of months. Kit had met her at a gig; a band from Penzance that, unlike the Neutrinos, were popular enough to warrant advance ticket sales. Pepper had announced that she had a spare one going for free and perhaps Kit might want it? Kit had shrugged and said, "sure, why not?". In the bar before the concert, he had met with Pepper and Grady and been introduced to their friend Astrid, who appeared to be immediately taken with him. All night long, she stayed by his side, singing and clapping along with the songs, and with a permanent happy-go-lucky smile on her face. She gave him her full attention, and he was flattered. She was, after all, pretty, blonde, and had an amazing figure.

Pepper and Grady had left early, with the excuse of relieving the babysitter, leaving Kit and Astrid alone. After the concert they had shared some chips and caught the train home to St Ives together. The evening had gone so well that it felt only natural to extend it to a goodnight kiss.

Kit had awoken the next morning in Astrid's flat pleasantly bemused. It had been a fun, if unexpected evening. And when Astrid had casually suggested they see a movie that night, it had not felt like an imposition. Rather than ponder the wisdom of turning a one-night-stand into an entire weekend, he had followed his life's philosophy, and gone with the flow.

So, any alarm that Kit might have felt when Astrid had arrived on his doorstep with all her worldly belongings, had given way to his better, more generous nature. *Of course,* she could stay, he had said. He wasn't going to leave her on the street, after all. Even when Pepper had shown up later with a further car-load of Astrid's belongings, including furniture, rugs and lamps, he betrayed no outer signs of dismay. Yet he had paused to wonder at how an entire collection of vinyl records had survived such a devastating deluge, dry and intact.

The weeks slipped by. At the beginning she had apologised constantly, assuring him that once her flat had been made good and redecorated, she—and her belongings—would return. In the meantime, she was eternally grateful to him; and for having such a wonderful boyfriend whom she adored so much. But over time the declarations had waned, and now, almost a year since Astrid had moved in, the flat was not mentioned at all.

Kit got up, picked the fag-end from the lemon-tree pot, and conscientiously took it to the waste-bin. He washed his hands at the kitchen sink. Then, with no sign of Astrid's return, he wondered if Zack might be up for a pint. He scooped up his phone from the kitchen table, and turned to go into the living room.

It was understandable of course, but even Kit was surprised at the extent of the loud profanity he emitted as the pink and blue quartz stones smacked him, goliath-like, right in the centre of his forehead. Yet somehow, he resisted the urge to rip them from where they still swung in the doorframe and hurl them into the depths of the ocean.

CHAPTER 29

Isadora

Malory stood in the centre of the old net loft and felt her heart sink.

It had already been an anxious morning. Jago had arrived early, before customers were out and about, to deliver a selection of his larger paintings to the shop. A friend, introduced as Luke, had helped deliver them in the back of his van, and initially the mood had been cheerful, full of pleasantries and jokes. But, being only temporarily parked for dropping-off purposes, Luke had had to hurry away, leaving Malory alone with Jago.

Together, over coffee, they had discussed where to hang each painting. They measured and adjusted, rearranged and replaced. It was a supreme exercise in civility, that was not without amusement and laughter; yet Malory felt a strange sadness. She missed his impoliteness; the forthright attitude and startling cheek that she had previously found so alluring. At one point he had climbed up on a small stepladder and stretched to reach with hammer and nail, causing his T-shirt to rise, and exposing his smooth and tanned midriff.

Malory had been almost consumed with lust and regret. Turning away, she had stared maniacally at another one of the paintings, in an effort to gain her composure. It had not been an entirely successful endeavour, given the passion and expression contained in the artwork. For it was still *him*. Too late, Malory realised that she had stupidly surrounded herself—had filled her workplace—with him.

They finished up, agreeing that the paintings looked good in place, and he had presented her with his 'business cards', which were of postcard-size and showed one of his works on one side, and his contact details on the other. She put them on her desk, and at various strategic points around the shop, and finally, in the window, splayed out in a fan shape in her beloved bowl.

'There,' she said. 'I think we're done. The paintings look amazing. And the shop is so much more inviting for them.'

He looked her straight in the eye. Those pale blue eyes that spoke of summer mornings; clear and fresh and vital.

'Malory,' he said, almost whispered, his tone an urgent plea.

She turned away again. 'I'd better tidy up, before customers start arriving.'

He was silent for a few seconds, and Malory felt sure he must sense the thump of her heart.

'Sure,' he said, at last, and once again she ached at the sad change in his tone and manner, a change that she might be responsible for. 'Thanks again, for doing this. I'm...grateful. I guess I'll leave you to it.'

Malory looked at him, forcing an amiable smile. 'No problem.'

'I'll see you around then.'

And then he had turned and left, leaving Malory foolishly waiting for the cheeky remark that never came.

And now, gazing around the atmospheric space of the net loft, she found herself also the protector of his sister's hopes and ambitions.

It was not because the place was not worthy of the rash commitment that she had made, but rather that her more selfish instincts threatened to sabotage all of Senara's dreams. Because the truth was, she wanted it for herself. Yes, the bar area and kitchen would have to go, but otherwise, it might have become her gallery. A gallery that she could afford...

'I can't believe it has managed to escape development,' she said to Bob Prowse, who had offered to show her around personally.

'That would be because of the owner, Isadora Francis, sadly deceased now,' said Bob. 'An artist, you see, and rather eccentric. Not interested in making money. It was she who stipulated that the bar be let on a leasehold basis. Wanted to see its glory days return, I imagine. Oh yes, she was quite the troublemaker. But all that may change when the lease expires. The new freeholders may have other intentions.'

'The freeholders?'

'Yes. Whoever buys the pilchard cellar will own the freehold to the entire building. I suspect very much that they will wish to profit from their purchase going forwards.'

'I'm sorry,' said Malory, 'but what do you mean, pilchard cellar?'

'Downstairs,' said Bob. 'The cellar forms the other half of the property. Didn't you know?'

'No, I did not,' said Malory, with a peculiar excitement beginning to buzz in her.

'This building,' said Bob, 'is one of a very few remnants of the days of the pilchard fishing industry in St Ives. The cellar would have been a salt house, for preserving the fish. Structures like this once took up the whole of this stretch of the beach. Of course, what is now Porthmeor Studios was saved thanks to the artists and fishermen, but many were converted into holiday apartments. This is a rare find, and I expect it to go at a considerable price.'

'Can I see this cellar?' asked Malory.

Bob Prowse scrutinised Malory for a moment, as if assessing her potential as a buyer.

'Of course,' he said.

Instead of exiting via the stone steps by which they had entered, he took her to a door in the small corridor that led to the toilets. Unlocking it, he revealed an internal staircase, which Malory followed him down. Bob was chattering about how Dora Francis originally used the net loft as a painting studio, and later installed a bar for entertainment purposes, '...but down here, in the old pilchard cellar, is where she established her pottery.'

Malory stood at the bottom of the dusty wooden staircase and tried to absorb what she was seeing, while Bob prattled on; something about how the floor was slightly inclined so that the oil from the pilchards in barrels, weighed down with pressing stones, could run off.

It was a huge space, interspersed with columns of supports that held up the loft above. Most of the columns were granite, but some were wooden. Bob described how they had been salvaged from old mine shaft props, and the masts of wrecked ships, having been built at a time when nothing went to waste.

'Of course, it would have been an open courtyard originally,' said Bob. 'This wall would have been a later addition.'

He gestured to one side of the building, where a row of windows, which, despite in need of a clean, flooded the room with light. Arched double doors, made of wood, and painted in the same dark green of the net loft, led onto a separate cobbled yard on the other side of the building. Malory noticed that some of the heavy round pressing stones with iron hooks still lay in one corner. She saw the ledge in the granite wall where the pressing beams had been placed. She saw the abandoned potter's wheel, the old kiln in the corner, and a couple of workbenches. It was a scene of some melancholy; the remnants of a life no longer lived. If Malory had been impressed with Dora's studio upstairs, her heart now began to beat wildly at the discovery of her pottery. This place felt authentic. It had space, light, and atmosphere. It had not had its history demolished in the name of progress.

'How much?' she asked Bob Prowse. 'How much would it cost to buy the freehold?'

He told her.

'Wow!' Malory exclaimed unashamedly; her expression aghast. 'That's incredible. I mean, *really?*'

'It is indeed a high asking price,' said Bob. 'But think of the size and location. This will make someone a lovely state-of-the-art beachside home, with more space than you could hope for in a typical Downalong cottage. There's room, even, for an integral garage, if access can be made. Parking comes at a premium here, as I'm sure you know.'

'But... It would be such a shame to change it,' said Malory. 'Especially if there are few survivors of its kind. What about the heritage?'

Bob Prowse shook his head. 'It would require a certain type of investor to preserve the building's integrity, given the incentive for profit. Can't see it happening myself. It's the way of the world.'

'Would you mind if...? Could I have a minute alone? To think about things?' said Malory.

Bob Prowse tried to hide his irritation. 'Of course. I suppose I'll wait outside.'

'I won't be long,' she said.

Just as on the coast path, Malory felt as though she stood upon a precipice. No; she would not betray Senara. Yet if she took the lease, it could only guarantee them seven years. That might be time enough to establish a reputation, and a business that could be moved to other premises. But if she bought the freehold...

In her mind's eye, Malory could see it all. Down here, in the old pilchard cellar, would be her gallery, and upstairs, adjoining, and as part of it, would be Senara's vision of the café. She saw Jago's paintings upon the walls, and the cultural mix of surfing, art and heritage. This was it. This was everything that she had professed to want; part of the fantasy that had persuaded her to sell everything and move to Cornwall.

But it might break her, financially. She had, she knew, existing responsibilities, and buying the freehold would take almost every penny she had left. Sure, if the business failed, she could always sell it on, to the developmental fate that Bob had predicted. But Malory knew in her heart that if she took the place on, that she would become its guardian. She could almost feel Dora Francis handing her the reins; chuckling even, at her predicament. Malory could not in all conscience, take on board such a building only to eventually sell-out its soul for profit.

And more than that, such a huge undertaking would require her personal commitment; to St Ives and to Cornwall. At the moment she had options. But there would be no quick escape from *this*. She thought also of the connection, and close association with the Berrymans. If she bought the leasehold alone, then she could play a background role. Senara would be in charge, and to all intents and purposes, it would be her business. Buying the freehold would change all that. She would be entirely involved. She saw a different vision of her future, one full of potential, but also of danger.

She saw eyes the colour of the morning sky.

And so, Malory Black stood with everything she had ever claimed to want, right in front of her, and there for the taking, only to find her courage fail her.

CHAPTER 30

Dan the Brave

The unmistakable whiff of manure rose in the breeze, as Dan stood observing the view from the high moor. The fields blanketing the land cascaded down to the sea in a patchwork of glorious colour, thwarted only by the abrupt and jagged cliff edge. Dan zipped his hoody up a little further, and shoved his hands back into his pockets. Nervously jiggling from foot to foot, he noticed the mud on his trainers.

They had come to Hendra Maen, the farm where Daisy's mother Joy lived with her partner, and where Daisy lived out of term time. It had started as an innocent enough plan, and quite a pleasant one at that. She would show him around the farmyard, and, from a safe distance, the animals. Then they would have a cream tea in the little farm-shop there. But things had since escalated.

As Daisy led the horse from the stables, Dan felt the fear heighten, and looked around shiftily for means of escape.

'Here you are,' said Daisy cheerfully. 'This is Meg, the oldest mare we have. But she's strong. And very placid. You won't have any trouble with this one. Say hello.'

'Hello?' said Dan.

'To Meg,' instructed Daisy. 'You should always get to know your horse. Earn its trust.'

'Look, I really don't think this is a good idea after all,' said Dan. 'I told you, I've had no experience. I don't have a clue about riding. Or horses. Or animals, come to think of it.'

'There's a first time for everything,' said Daisy, still beaming. 'It will be great. You'll love it. We have young children on our treks all the time, who've never ridden before. Don't be a baby.'

Dan looked suspiciously at Meg, who gazed back with a cynical eye. 'I will get a hat and all?'

'Yes of course,' said Daisy, patiently. 'We'll only be trotting anyway. Most of the time. You remember what I taught you?'

Dan could see across the stable-yard to where Freddie and George, two of the farm labourers, were leaning on a gate and watching him, with amused expressions. They were both young, strong, lean and fit. Doubtless *they* would have no issue with successfully straddling a four-legged beast; one that was much, much, higher in real life than you might think. Dan felt a fresh terror engulf him as he imagined not even being able to mount the horse. How they would laugh, Freddie and George; they with their easy confidence in slim jeans, wellies and checked shirts, rolled up to the elbows. They reminded him of Kit, with their carefree outgrown hair and their stupid trendy beanie hats; their tanned, wiry muscles and surfing-strong balance. *They* would not end up being dragged around the farmyard with one foot caught in the stirrup.

Yet he wished with all his heart that Kit were with him now, in the hope that some of his confidence and charisma might rub off. That, by way of association, he might be regarded with some respect. As it was, the farmworkers appeared to have taken a tea-break with the sole purpose of watching the fat boy that Daisy had—inexplicably—brought home, humiliate himself on a horse.

'Dan!' Daisy snapped, with a grin. 'Wake up! Do you remember? The basics?'

'Umm, yeah, I think so,' said Dan. 'I have to lift my bum off the saddle if the horse starts to go fast.'

'It's called a gallop, Dan,' said Daisy. 'But don't worry, Meg won't gallop unless you let her have her head. She's far too old and lazy. But we might have a little trot here and there, at which point you should...?'

Daisy looked at him with a querying eye. Dan's mind was a white-hot blaze of screeching static.

'Rise and sit?' said Daisy.

'Rise and sit. Right got it,' Dan mimicked her words.

'Like this, remember?' She turned one palm over and hit it firmly with the other. 'This is the saddle, and this is your bottom. You rise and fall to meet the saddle, by tilting your pelvis; like this.' She clapped her hands together in a rhythmic manner. 'Rise up, sit down. Rise up, sit down. Do you see?'

'I think so,' said Dan, only now starting to foresee a new cause for discomfort.

'You'll get the hang of it,' she said. 'You'll mostly just be sitting anyhow. That's easy. You just go with the roll of the horse as she walks. Come on now, you'll be having fun in no time. I'll just go and fetch the hats.'

'There's just one more thing,' said Dan upon her return, as he buckled the riding hat in place with the face of a condemned man. 'How the hell do I get on it?'

Daisy laughed. 'Don't worry, you can use the step-stool, as it's your first time.'

She yelled instructions to Freddie and George, who went into the stables and reappeared with a device designed to only add to Dan's mortification. While Daisy went to fetch her own horse, they helped Dan, using the added height of the stool, to secure his left foot in the stirrup and swing the other leg over the animal. With no means of retreat, Dan did as he was told.

Amazingly, he found himself seated and upright in the saddle.

'There you go Mate,' said George. 'No problem.'

'Don't worry about Meg,' said Freddie. 'She's the oldest, tamest, cob horse in the stables. You'll have no problems with her.'

Their kindness almost made Dan feel worse. Yet, he had to admit, he felt better now that he was in the saddle, and having a bit of a sit-down. Daisy led her own steed, a tall black stallion named Merlin, into the stable yard, and swiftly mounted him, unaided.

'Come on, let's join the others,' she said. 'Gather your reins, and just give a little squeeze with your legs to get her moving. Meg knows what's going on. She's done this trek hundreds of times, and will probably just follow the other horses.'

Dan squeezed his thighs lightly against the side of the animal. He felt bad enough to be burdening the poor mare—the oldest one, as they kept reminding him—with his bulky load, and was anxious not to hurt her in any other way. But Meg did not move. She stood silently surveying the middle distance. Dan didn't think he had ever seen a horse so still. Perhaps he had done something wrong? Perhaps she didn't like him?

'Come on, give it some welly,' called Daisy. 'Everyone's waiting in the lane.'

Dan squeezed his legs again, with what he hoped was more authority, and leaned forward in the saddle in a pressing motion, as if the momentum might kick-start the rigid animal. Still Meg stood defiant and disinterested.

Daisy walked Merlin back towards him. The stallion looked haughty and outraged, Dan thought. It was clearly unaccustomed to this sort of imbecility. With one hand, Daisy took Dan's reins, and immediately, Meg allowed herself to be led out of the stable yard into the lane where the day's trekking party waited patiently. Dan could only cling awkwardly to his saddle as Freddie and George chuckled and called after him.

'Whoo-hoo! And he's off!'

'Yee haw, ride him, cowboy!'

Dan closed his eyes and made a silent prayer. It didn't matter that he closed his eyes, for his horse was being led obediently to the waiting party. The fact that it was made up of two families; holidaymakers who had booked a pony trek, should have reassured him. Yet in Dan's current state of mind, he could only see the stage being set for yet more indignity.

This too shall pass, he told himself, solemnly. *This too shall pass...*

The team of horses and ponies walked in file at a leisurely pace along the country lane, and after a few minutes, Dan began to relax. This wasn't so bad, after all. It was fun to sit up high on a real beast, and not the stuffed, toy rocking horse that he had loved as a child. If he let himself, he could almost imagine he was indeed a cowboy surveying his ranch. Daisy's mother Joy led the parade, with Daisy in the middle of the group, dispersing advice and information. His fellow trekkers appeared to be perfect nuclear families, glossy with health and prosperity. Dan soon ascertained that the children were called things like Tarquin, Pandora, and... Was that little one really called *Figgy?* Dan was happy to trail at the back, and imagine that he was in charge of his steed, and that Meg was not merely habitually following the other horses.

In time, the party began to turn off the lane into a field. Dan, who had just been getting the whole 'American Indian brave' routine going in his head, was dismayed to find that once again, Meg had decided to stop moving. As the others entered the field one-by-one, Dan's trusty mare had decided that she would much rather chomp on the gorse that lined the hedge.

Dan made a clicking sound with his tongue. 'Come on! Come on Meg!' he pleaded.

He pressed her sides with his legs again and tried, using the reins, to drag her head away from the gorse bush. But the stubborn horse did not budge, and—he was sure—lunged at the gorse with even more intent. Dan looked around in distress. When would they notice he had been left behind? Daisy would miss him, surely? Again, he tried to coax the animal away from the hedgerow, but again, Meg made it perfectly clear exactly who was in charge.

When Daisy finally reappeared, a puzzled look on her face, and enquiring what he was up to, Dan was sitting, arms folded, in the saddle, his cheeks turning a furious red.

'*I* don't know!' he gestured at the recalcitrant animal. 'Ask *her!*'

For the first time since they had met, Dan noticed a change in Daisy's optimistic demeanour. For a fleeting few seconds, he saw in her eyes, first confusion, then irritation, before she scolded Meg into action. Immediately, the mare stopped feasting and recommenced her walk; turning, with no instruction from Dan, into the field, where the others waited. As Daisy urged her horse past him, Dan was sure that Merlin looked him right in the eye with a contemptuous sneer, before kicking his back legs in the air, making Dan start.

'Mummy, why was that man so slow?' asked Figgy. His high-pitched voice had a bell-like quality, clear and resonating across the moors.

'I think his horse was hungry, Darling,' said Figgy's mother.

Dan could see the sly smiles, and sense the politely repressed laughter, as the other riders turned their steeds to continue the trek. He gripped his reins tighter in an attempt to assume authority, but stared sullenly at the back of the aloof Meg's head.

'Nag,' he whispered.

He saw the horse's ears twitch, and felt her muscles tense; and for a fearful second, he thought she might rear up and throw him from her back, before trampling him with her hooves, in an equine hissy-fit. But Meg, on some unseen signal, had merely joined the others in a trot across the field. Dan bounced along in an ungainly, and frankly, quite painful manner, until he remembered Daisy's brief tuition. Abruptly, he stood up, balancing on the stirrups, then promptly slammed back down into the saddle. He did this a couple of times, wondering how the hell he was supposed to keep this up, and swearing aloud in the sure knowledge of how much this was going to hurt in the morning.

'Dan!' cried Daisy, pulling Merlin alongside again. 'That's too much! You don't have to stand up straight. Good grief!'

'What?' said Dan, sweating profusely now from the effort of his movements, but too afraid to stop them.

'That man is funny!' Dan heard Figgy's crystalline tinkles of laughter from behind him.

'Less rise,' said Daisy, 'You only have to lift a little way off the saddle. Copy me.'

'Oh, I see,' said Dan, feeling foolish, but relieved, as he reduced his bouncing motion.

'And don't forget to guide her,' said Daisy. 'Don't let her have her head. And watch your language! There's children here.'

His relief was short-lived, for the repetitive motion was still rather tiring, and he suspected used muscles that he did not know he possessed. But all the same, he began to think that perhaps he was getting the hang of this horse-riding malarkey. Suddenly Dan saw a whole new slant to his personality, previously undiscovered. Horses would become his thing. Let Kit and Jago have their surfing and skateboarding. He would be the essence of cool; a romantic hero galloping along the beach towards the lighthouse at Godrevy in a billowing white shirt, with his dark hair blowing in the wind.

Just as Dan was imagining how he would have to grow his hair long, the group came out of the field and onto a vast stretch of open moorland. He saw Merlin buck his back legs again before taking off at speed. The other horses, and even the children's ponies followed suit. He heard laughing and hollering and cries of delight. Without warning, as if suddenly liberated, Meg broke free into a wild gallop.

Dan was aware of the sensation of the rough moorland earth moving rapidly underneath him; of the thundering of hooves and the sound of a loud scream that appeared to emanate from somewhere deep within his being...

'FUUUUUUUUCK!'

What was happening? Why did no one come to help him? This horse was clearly unbroken and had bolted. *Tame old mare, my arse*. It was only a matter of seconds before he would be thrown to the ground and killed. Desperately clinging on to the animal's mane, the reins entwined therein, he tried to calm his mind and think. He could barely see the other riders through the beads of sweat that dripped into his eyes, and the only sound that matched the thump of hooves on the landscape was the drumbeat of blood pumping through his veins.

Somewhere from the depths of his terror he conjured up the image of a jockey, which somehow seemed to correlate with Daisy's advice. It felt like the act of a madman to follow it through, but Dan knew that he would not stay on the horse much longer otherwise. Summoning all of his courage, he lifted himself from the saddle, and leaning forwards, rode using only his feet in the stirrups.

Somehow, it worked.

Dan had the strange sensation of being on horseback, riding across the Penwith moors and also watching himself from somewhere above. It took every ounce of strength he had to stay upon his steed. Stray thoughts rampaged through his mind in tune to the rumble of horse's hooves. Thoughts like: *who designed bloody reins?* There was no security in a rein whatsoever. Something firm to cling on to and steer with, that's what was needed. *Where were the fucking handlebars?!*

And yet he was flying.

His confidence grew once more and he began to wonder again if perhaps he might be some kind of equestrian prodigy. In his mind's eye he was suddenly a jockey winning races at The Derby. There was still relief when the horse decided to slow, and terror when it picked up speed again, but somehow, he remained mounted.

Later, when they were all trekking along the lane back to the farmyard again, Dan's mind was at peace with the world. A small smile stayed fixed upon his face as he listened to the chatter of his companions. There was sunshine and birdsong and wasn't the world particularly beautiful this fine day? He even began to entertain the thought that he might do this again some time.

Daisy rode alongside him. 'All good?'

'Fantastic,' said Dan. 'That was great.'

'Awesome,' said Daisy. 'I was a bit worried. What with all the shouting and swearing.'

'Ah, yes. Sorry about that,' said Dan. 'I'm not saying it wasn't a little...*tricky*, to start with. But I soon got the hang of things.'

'Awesome,' repeated Daisy, and Dan was pleased to see that she looked a little less peeved, and more her usual uncomplicated self.

They arrived back at the stables and Dan gratefully slid from the back of the horse the way he'd been told. He was starting to feel a bit queer, and extremely ravenous. Immediately he began to fantasize about the meal he would have that evening. Pizza perhaps. A large juicy pizza, or maybe nachos. At that moment Dan felt he could devour both. Oh yes; pizza, nachos, and a movie, in the blissful comfort of his den. It was a most soothing thought; and for once, he realised, he might have earned it.

Daisy had offered to show him how to rub down his horse and clean his tack.

'Come on Dan, over here,' she said, leading Merlin towards the stable.

But something happened. Or rather, didn't.

Meg turned her head and looked Dan in the eye, knowingly.

'Dan! Come here,' Daisy beckoned impatiently.

But Dan could not move. The message from his brain to follow Daisy into the stables appeared not to have been received by his leg muscles.

'What's happening?' he cried in dismay.

'Are you okay?' called Daisy, giving Merlin's reins to a stable hand, then walking back towards Dan.

Dan tried to move again, but still his legs would not work. He looked desperately around the yard, only to see Freddie and George lurking nearby, pointing and laughing at him.

'Looks like we've got a stretcher case,' yelled Freddie, good-naturedly.

As Daisy reached Dan, her pretty features twisted in concern, and some disbelief. 'Is that true? Can't you walk?'

Dan, still gripping on to Meg's saddle for support, could only nod and simper in deep shame. 'Nope. Can't move a muscle.'

Daisy pulled another face and beckoned to Freddie and George to join them. The two strong lads strolled across the yard with huge grins on their faces.

'Ah, mate! Hit the wall, did you?' said George, slapping him on the back.

'Dear old Meg,' said Freddie, patting the horse's neck affectionately. 'What did you do to poor Dan?'

'Can't have been much,' said George. 'She's too old and slow.'

'She's *not that* fucking slow!' Dan rasped in misery.

As Daisy gave him a look of utter disapproval, all 'poor Dan' could think of was that she had not called him 'Big Bear' once, all day. Beginning to shake, he rested his head on his arms which lay across the saddle, fully expecting Meg to trot away and leave him stranded. He could only listen in horror as the others made plans. Daisy would see to Meg, and Freddie and George would take Dan back home in the van.

'Come on then, Mate,' said George, 'Let's get you sorted.'

Standing either side of him, the two men supported him under the arms with their shoulders, then each grabbed a leg under the knee. Then, carrying him gracelessly, they stumbled towards a transit van parked nearby, giggling as they went.

'Phew, you're a big lad, aren't you?'

'Gonna need a lie-down myself after this.'

As they struggled to carry him from the stable yard, Figgy and the other children congregated by the stable doors to watch the funny man being silly again. Dan, in his wisdom, twisted his head awkwardly to look back at Daisy.

'I'll call you?' he asked plaintively.

Daisy's expression was unnaturally stone-like; chilling to behold.

There was an old smelly rug in the back of the van, and they threw him onto it, groaning with the effort. Then Freddie and

George jumped into the cab, which was open to the back. Turning in their seats, they asked him where he lived, and if he was comfortable, and gave him a bottle of water to drink. They did all of this in the greatest of humour, so that Dan did not know whether to cry in gratitude or despair. As the bumpy journey began, he stared at the metal roof and tried not to think, since all thoughts circled around to his utter humiliation. The sad truth dawned on him that it was not to be. He was not a horse-rider extraordinaire, but rather had had to use practically every muscle in his body just to stay on the damn thing. It was all rather disappointing.

When they arrived at his home it was, unfortunately, still daylight. Dan could feel the eyes of his neighbours, sniggering behind curtains, as he was again lifted and carried in an ungainly fashion along the side entrance of the house to where his log cabin stood. Luckily Zack did not appear to be about, but he'd hear about it all the same, as Dan spied his two young nephews gazing in curiosity from the bedroom window that overlooked the garden.

Finally, assured that he was comfortable in his king-size bed, with the tv remote and a takeaway menu close at hand, Freddie, George, and their irrepressible bonhomie, left him. Dan closed his eyes, and decided that a hefty dollop of self-pity was most definitely in order.

He would not be seeing Daisy again; he knew that much. Something about the glazed-over look in her eyes when they had parted assured him that the fantasy, for her, was over. He was no longer her Big Bear, but a weakling sloth dangling from the branches of her much stronger, more youthful, stable boys.

Oh well. He sighed.

Two hours later, refreshed with the promised pizza and nachos, all washed down with a large bottle of Coke, Dan began to feel himself again. His muscles hurt and he still had trouble moving much, but was sure it would be all right in the morning. He tucked himself in with his duvet and large tartan blanket. Then, safe and cosy once more, he settled back to watch a movie.

CHAPTER 31

Sea Fever

As the weeks progressed into high summer, the streets of St Ives became alive with activity. Each train from St Erth brought with it a fresh supply of tourists and day-trippers, and there was a steady increase in the amount of traffic that wove its way along the wharf, in search of parking or some elusive, tucked away cottage. Fridays and Saturdays, which were 'changeover' days for most of the holiday lets, brought the rumble of countless suitcase wheels over cobblestones, and the frustrated shouts at drivers who had accidentally turned into a traffic-free zone, or blocked the way as they attempted to unload luggage into a tiny cottage with no parking. An increasing number of businesses offering boat trips set up along the wharf, along with buskers, and street-vendors offering hair-braiding, or other knick-knacks to entice the tourists.

It was not quite the mighty swarm that would descend once the school holidays began, and Porthmeor Beach would become littered with beach tents and territorial windbreaks. But still, Jago took his stall out almost every day, despite the fact that several of his paintings had already been sold from Atlantic Arts. It was an encouraging sign, and he wished that he could devote all of his time to his art. The rented part of the cottage that opened onto Carncrows Street was fully let for weeks to come, but he knew that this alternative source of income would be short lived, and would fall away after the September festival. There would be a brief reprise in the

October half-term holiday, but after that there would be long months of quiet streets and little opportunity. And so, he rose early each morning, and, provided there was no surf, of course, devoted as many hours as possible to painting. Then in the late afternoons, he would take the barrow out to the harbour, and charm the passers-by into buying his wares.

Malory had appeared as delighted as he, that the paintings had sold. 'You must go to more gallery shows and private views,' she had said, as she handed him his earnings. 'Take your business cards and make yourself known.'

'Come with me,' he had said. 'You feel at home in these places. I wouldn't know where to start.'

Malory had produced that familiar expression; a small squirm of her features, as if she were being pinned like an insect to a board. She appeared torn between her willingness to help him, and her apparent abhorrence at spending any time with him. Jago knew that he had messed up by asking her out, but he didn't quite understand how. He had been sure that there was a natural chemistry between them; that he had caught her dark eyes return his own desire. His head, not to mention his pride, told him to leave it alone, that it would be unwise to persist. Yet when they were together, it felt as though his heart was screaming a message to not give up.

She had nodded in agreement. 'I suppose I should.'

Again, that odd mixture of enthusiasm and reluctance, as if there was something covert that she was not telling him. It had come as a surprise to discover that she not only possessed some wealth, but had previously been married. But after confiding in Senara, she had reverted to reticence on the matter. So Jago respectfully withheld his advances, and made himself busy with art, and with squeezing out a summer income.

One afternoon, headed back from the studio, he returned to find a stranger lurking on his doorstep. The man was about the same age and height as himself. His hair was longer than Jago's, but the same golden, sunkissed brown. He too was tanned and lean, and with a similar surfer's physique of strong, broad shoulders and toned limbs. But there the similarities ended. This man wore a black hat—a fedora, Jago thought—at a jaunty angle, and a long feather earring hung from one ear where he'd pushed his hair behind his ear. He carried a tan satchel over one shoulder and trailed a large duffel bag, signifying a recent arrival in town.

'Can I help you Mate?' said Jago, seeing the stranger's puzzled expression. He was probably a tourist lost in the maze of narrow streets. 'Looking for somewhere to stay, maybe?'

'I am,' said the man, in what Jago took to be a Mediterranean accent. 'But I was given this address. I'm looking for Senara...'

* * *

Not so far away, another story was unfolding. In the late afternoon sunlight that flooded through the large window of the net loft, Senara surveyed the newly painted walls and cleaned-up wooden beams and once more felt like she was enjoying a perpetual hug. It was still hard to believe that it was actually happening; that her dream was being realised. But everywhere around her, everything sparkled with freshness, and sang with promise and joy. Brian, having heard the news, had just sent another message of support.

She had initially been cool with him, after the beach house party. It still seemed strange that he had not said at the time that he was leaving that night. But as the weeks progressed, she could not allow her excitement to be marred with ill feeling. He promised they would catch up in person soon. She had invested time in their chats, and felt that he at least deserved the benefit of the doubt.

Malory stood nearby, with clipboard and pen in hand, surveying the work that was still required, and making notes. Malory had told Senara about the cellar below, and the risk involved with a new freeholder. Nevertheless, she had purchased the lease, and things had moved alarmingly fast. They had come to a business arrangement, and together had raised a small bank loan to get started and undertake the refurbishments. They had advertised for more waiting and bar staff, and a local lad called Charlie had already been hired as an extra chef.

But even as she stood in painter's overalls, brush in hand and a smudge of paint on her cheek, Senara could not quite believe her good fortune. To think that all this had come about because she had fainted in Paddington station, and had chanced to make a friend, whose kindness, and faith in her, was quite overwhelming. She knew it was an opportunity not to be wasted, and vowed to make it the best damn surf shack in Cornwall. But more than this, Senara experienced an emotion that had been missing for too long. It was as though her gears had been stuck, but now her wheels were carrying her forward at speed. It was exhilarating.

From the smaller back room, she heard Kit singing loudly in time to a song on the radio, enhancing the air of excitement. He had offered his carpentry skills, more usually applied to boatbuilding, to help with the repairs and decorations. That morning he had been making a couple of low-level benches with storage underneath, that doubled as seating around a second wood-burning stove. Having taken a break from her own work, Senara ambled over and leaned against the door jamb.

'I swear you're just making your own personal little gang hut,' she said, when there was a break in the singing.

'Yeah. Going to be great, isn't it?' said Kit, beaming.

'Are you sure this will work? I mean, won't people nick stuff?'

Kit frowned exaggeratedly. 'Of course not! Don't know what kind of custom you're expecting, Snow. But no one from round here would abuse the situation.'

'I knew it,' said Senara. 'It's just going to be a hang-out for you and your mates.'

Kit's idea had been to fit the back room out with surfboards and a rail of wetsuits, so that if the surf kicked off, anyone happening to be in the café would be able to grab a board and a suit and go surfing.

'I'm not so sure,' Senara had said at the time. 'There'll be people hanging around all day just watching the surf, and not buying much more than a coffee.'

'You might be grateful for that come the winter months,' Kit had replied. 'When the tourists have all gone home.'

Besides, he had explained, it was more for display; to give the impression that you could, if the mood took you, suddenly get changed and go for a surf. Looking through the glass panels from the café the immediate sight would be of a line of surfboards, and retro surfing posters and paraphernalia. It was all about creating atmosphere, he said. About being authentic.

Senara had raised her eyebrows, but with little other idea what to do with the room, conceded to give it a try. With Kit spreading the word, several of their friends had donated old boards and wetsuits, as had one or two of the surf shops in town, in return for advertising posters on the walls of the room, and flyers on the counter by the till. They had sourced an old metal set of lockers via the internet, and would supply any potential surfers with a key on a bootlace to be worn around their neck.

'Anyway, Chef,' said Kit, downing tools and standing up. 'How about some grub?'

'Again?' said Senara. She had brought in limited supplies to the kitchen, to keep them going. But Kit was working his way through them fast.

'Can I remind you about the free labour?' said Kit. 'The least you can do is keep me fed and watered.'

'And you have been fed and watered,' said Senara. 'Stop griping and get back to work.'

Kit eyed her mischievously, then brushing past her, headed to the kitchen and started exploring. Senara turned and watched him, with one hand on hip, and her paintbrush still in the other.

After a quick rummage, he found the tin containing the walnut cake that she had made.

'Don't even think about it,' said Senara. 'It's for later, when we've finished work.'

'But I'm hungry now,' said Kit, taking the freshly made cake from the tin and eyeing it ravenously. He found a knife and cut a huge slice.

Senara eyed him critically as he stood right in front of her and took a large bite.

'Umm. Yum,' he said. 'You should try some of this, it's delicious.'

Without a word, Senara raised her paintbrush and flicked it at Kit. He was splattered with paint.

'Senara!' he said severely, and shielding his purloined snack. 'Think of the cake!'

Senara flicked the paint again.

'I see,' said Kit. 'Gonna be like that, is it?'

He put the slice of cake on the counter, then scooped the coffee-flavoured butter icing from the top with his fingers. He raised his hand and moved towards Senara, who ran away giggling and screaming.

Malory, who had only just met Kit formally, watched in resignation. *This*, she thought. *This is what I've signed up for*.

As Kit grappled with Senara by the window, attempting to smear butter icing on her forehead, the doors flung open and Jago entered, followed by the traveller he had found in the street.

Senara looked up in surprise, then wriggling from Kit's grasp, she bounded across the room to greet the newcomer in a warm embrace.

'Teddy!' she cried. 'You came! I didn't think you would.'

'I'd had enough of the Australians,' said Teddy, in perfect English, but with his Greek accent. 'There's only so much partying a boy can do. It was starting to affect my beauty sleep.'

'But, how did you get here?' said Senara. 'The train? And why didn't you call or text me?'

'It was an impulse,' answered Teddy. 'I wanted to be spontaneous. So, I packed my bags and caught the night-sleeper. It was quite the adventure. Lots of strangers getting together at the bar. I didn't call because I wanted to surprise you. I spent the morning in Penzance, and then caught the train here, where I ran into your adorable brother.' He gave Jago an appreciative look. 'How is it, that we have not met before?'

Jago looked back in bemusement.

'I didn't know you when he last visited Greece,' explained Senara.

'And who is this?' said Teddy, looking at the man who recently appeared to have been grasping Senara from behind, and was now licking cake icing from his fingers.

'I'm Kit,' he said, with a friendly wave.

'Ah, the famous Kit,' said Teddy, giving Senara a loaded sideways look. 'I've longed to meet you. Senara has told me many stories.'

'Not *many*...' said Senara, grimacing.

Malory remained shyly at a distance, pretending to be distracted by her lists.

'How long are you here for?' continued Senara. 'Do you have a place to stay? You can stay at the cottage, of course. That is, if it's all right with Jago? But it will be extremely cramped.'

'Yes, I've seen the hole in the ground that you live in, *agapi mou*. Jago kindly let me leave my bag there. But like your brother it has great charm, and believe me, will be a refreshing change after sharing with the crowd from Oz. If it is not a problem? I have a sleeping bag.'

Jago nodded. 'It'll be fine.'

'But what of all this?' said Teddy, with an extravagant wave of his arm. 'Jago told me all about it on the way. How wonderful! Your own café.'

'But of course!' said Senara, suddenly. 'You couldn't have come at a better time. If you're here for the summer, do you want a job? We'll need help with the tables, in the kitchen, at the bar...'

'I would be delighted,' said Teddy, giving Senara another hug. 'It will be the old team, back together again.'

'Hurrah! And—forgive me—this is my new partner, Malory. Although, she's not so much a partner in crime as you!' Senara was bubbling with excitement, as Malory finally stepped forward to greet Teddy with a handshake. 'Malory,

Teddy is an excellent chef and genius mixologist. We worked together in Greece. I'm so thrilled!'

'I'll put some more coffee on,' said Kit. 'Cake, anyone?'

'I never say no to cake,' said Teddy, 'But I think this might be more appropriate, if you have any flutes in the house?' And he pulled a bottle of champagne from his oversized satchel. 'Otherwise, we can use cups, I suppose, if we must.'

As they all stood by the window overlooking the surf, Senara felt that her heart would burst. Everything was starting to work for her, and she was surrounded by amazing people. Real friends, with good hearts. For the first time since arriving home, she felt loved and safe. The champagne helped to break the ice for the others with Teddy, and as she looked at their smiling faces, it felt like an intimate, quiet celebration of her new beginning.

She could not know, that although he was grinning with delight at a joke—one of Teddy's Greek tales, told at Senara's expense—that Kit was secretly wondering how Astrid would react to their private party. She had already fumed at his offer to help Senara, and he, of course, had been characteristically stubborn about it. It was a matter of principle, for Kit. He would not be coerced into behaving outside of his nature. But he was becoming sick of the argument. And the promise of the row to come had the insidious effect of threatening his enjoyment in the moment.

The champagne did not last long between them, but the mood was still alive with the sense of celebration.

'Let's go to The Barque,' said Senara. 'It's happy hour for cocktails.'

'I'm in,' said Jago. 'We need to get some rum inside Teddy; christen him in Cornish ways.'

'Shouldn't that mean a pasty and a pint of Betty Stogs?' said Kit. 'What's particularly Cornish about rum?'

'Are you kidding?' said Jago. 'It's the smuggler thing. And the pirate thing. And you know full well that The Barque's own brand is the business.'

'Ah, Sea Fever,' said Kit, as though suddenly spellbound. 'That truly is a delicious rum.'

Malory looked unsure. 'What about the decorating?'

'We've done enough for the day,' said Senara. 'And besides, we haven't celebrated properly yet. Now Teddy's arrived, it's perfect. All my favourite people are here...' She slung an arm around Malory. 'C'mon, Mals. Don't be the big boss-woman.'

Malory cast her eyes around the mess of the room, before returning them to meet Senara's pleading blue eyes.

'Oh...all right then!' she grinned. 'We do have to wet the baby's head, so to speak.'

'That's the spirit,' said Jago. 'Got to launch this ship properly. Let's go.'

Only Kit was quiet as he followed the jubilant gang along the winding streets to The Barque.

* * *

'I still don't understand why this bar is 'Aft', and the other one 'Fore',' Malory babbled as they filed up the stairs to the snug bar of The Barque.

'Why's that?' said Jago, who was behind her.

'Well, it means the back, doesn't it?' said Malory. 'The back of a boat? The front, the Fore end, should be facing out to sea. It's obvious.'

'Not necessarily,' said Jago. 'And I think you mean the stern and the bow.'

'Yes, necessarily,' answered Malory, ignoring his correction. 'It drives me nuts, actually. It's irrational.'

'It's not irrational for a ship to face into harbour when it docks,' said Jago. 'And besides...' he pointed towards the other bar through the open door. 'That way...is *Fore* Street,' he intoned drily.

Malory blushed as the penny dropped. 'Of course,' she muttered, remembering the alternative entrance she had since discovered on the busy thoroughfare. 'How silly of me.'

'Now you can sleep nights again,' said Jago.

Behind them, Senara and Kit entered the bar, engaged in a very different discussion.

'...I understand what you're saying,' said Senara. 'I get that it would provide a few jobs locally, but I'm not convinced that would be worth the impact on the environment. Not to mention jobs in tourism and hospitality.'

'I hear you. But are you sure this isn't just nimbyism?' said Kit. 'These minerals are needed for technology and have to come from somewhere. Why not here?'

'Are you serious?' said Senara. 'Because it's beautiful here. Call it what you like, but I'd fight tooth and nail against them plundering St Ives Bay for profit. And I think you would too. You're just playing devil's advocate.'

'Maybe,' Kit grinned.

Teddy trailed in last, his eyes taking in his new surroundings, but his senses nonetheless highly tuned to his companions' conversations.

The group managed to secure a table to themselves, and Jago approached Tamsin at the bar. 'All right, mate?' he grinned. 'We'll have a bottle of Sea Fever, five glasses and some ice, please. Put it on a tab?'

'Bottle of rum, on its way,' he said upon his return, sliding onto the bench next to Malory. Teddy was on her other side, and Senara and Kit sat opposite.

'I thought we were having cocktails?' said Malory.

'You cannot dilute this rum with other flavours,' said Jago with authority. 'It's got to be ice, and ice alone.'

'That's not what they suggest on the menu,' said Malory, tapping at the long list of rum cocktails.'

'Trust me,' said Jago.

When Tamsin brought the order over on a tray, Kit very quickly necked a small glass of the rum. 'I'd better let Astrid know,' he mumbled, reaching for his phone from his back pocket. 'She should be finishing work soon.'

'Great,' said Senara, 'The more the merrier.' Although frankly, the thought of Astrid's presence made her feel uneasy. She topped up the glasses. 'Okay, here's to... The Surf Shack?'

'Been done already,' said Jago.

'It is kind of predictable,' murmured Kit, as he tapped out a message on his phone.

'I've been racking my brains,' said Malory. 'Everything has been taken. Every business or cottage in town has already been named after some nautical or beachy reference. Everywhere there are cabins, cuddys, lofts and decks.'

'I think... The Secret Spot,' said Kit, twirling the ice in his refilled glass of rum.

'Curious,' said Teddy. 'Isn't that a woman's special place for orgasm? I really wouldn't know...'

Everyone chuckled.

'That's the 'G' spot, Teddy,' said Malory.

'If such a thing exists,' said Kit.

'Oh, I can assure you, it does,' said Malory, taking a slurp of rum.

'Really?' said Jago. 'Interesting.'

His eyes looked into Malory's brazenly, and he flickered his eyebrows suggestively. Malory smiled but quickly looked away.

Kit addressed Teddy. 'It's a term for a surf break that's not generally advertised, especially to tourists. Keeps the crowds down. It's not the done thing to reveal the whereabouts of secret spots. People have been run out of town for less.'

'Except there are no real secret spots left anymore,' said Jago with a wry grimace. 'Too many surfers posting pictures and surf reports online. Nothing is sacred.'

'It might work...' said Senara. 'What do you think, Malory?'

'I like it,' answered Malory. 'The 'secret' element could have the reverse effect of making people actively seek it out. Which we'll need being stuck down an out-of-the way alley. And it sounds kind of exclusive.'

'My thoughts exactly,' said Kit.

'Well then,' Senara raised her glass. 'The Secret Spot it is. Here's to our new adventure.'

'The Secret Spot,' everyone chorused.

'And all who sail in her,' said Jago as they all clinked glasses.

Senara turned to gaze from the window and admire the view of Smeaton's Pier. It was a hazy, early evening. A family were playing a makeshift game of cricket on the sandbanks left in the harbour by the receding tide. Small pale green waves lapped at the shore, and further out, leisure boats drifted at anchor on the aquamarine sea. Seabirds cried and swooped overhead. As she listened to the murmur of the others' chat, the rum induced a fuzzy warm feeling in her body and a blissful stupor in her mind. Even at this time of day the St Ives light was dazzling, so that when she turned back towards the room, it appeared darkened, and intimate. Kit, who had also been drinking in the view, met her eyes, and smiled.

'Thank you for all your help,' said Senara. 'I don't know what I would have done without you.'

'I'm sure you would have figured it out,' said Kit. 'But happy to help.'

'I mean it,' said Senara. 'You... Malory... *Everyone* has been so wonderful. I feel quite overcome.'

'Oh, here we go,' said Kit, grinning. 'We can always rely on the rum to activate the mushiness.'

'Leave me alone,' said Senara, returning his grin. 'I don't see what's so wrong with mushiness anyhow. What's wrong with showing affection? Life's too short.'

'You're a sap, Berryman,' said Kit. 'You let people trample all over you and then beat yourself up about it. I know you.'

'Well, no one's trampling on me now!' protested Senara. 'Can't I just say something nice about a friend—about *friends*—without appearing weak? You're too cynical.'

'I am not!' Kit snorted. 'I'm just... Discerning. That's it. And right now, I discern that this...' he held his glass of rum up before him, entranced as the light from the harbour twinkled in the ice. 'This is truly the finest rum in the land.'

'Agreed,' said Senara. 'It's so sweet. And yet sort of...piquant? What is that?'

'Salt,' said Kit, replacing the glass on the table, but still appearing to study it keenly. 'It captures the briny essence of seaweed, samphire, and sea-salt, tempered by the sweetness of local honey.'

'Right,' said Senara slowly, holding her glass before her in equal reverence, before taking another sip. She closed her eyes and let the dark elixir tantalise her taste buds, and then warm her blood.

'Yes,' she said. 'I get that now.' Opening her eyes, she looked at Kit again. 'It tastes of the sea...' she said wistfully.

Kit emitted a spluttering laugh. 'No, it doesn't,' he said, shaking his head in jest at Senara. 'It doesn't taste of the sea. That would be fucking horrible!'

Senara looked at him in indignation. 'But you said...'

'Yeah, I was just reading the description off the bottle,' he smirked.

Senara hit him playfully on the arm. 'You know what I meant. I meant the spirit of the sea. The unpredictability. The wild, untamed romance and freedom of the high seas.'

'The fish,' said Kit. 'The crabs.'

Senara chuckled loudly. 'The seagull poo...'

'Sounds like you're having fun,' said Astrid, sitting down on the other side of Kit. Senara had not seen her arrive.

Kit turned, still with a grin on his face. 'Hey there,' he said. 'You made it. Let's get you a glass and...'

'It's fine,' said Astrid. 'I've ordered a cocktail at the bar. I don't like rum.'

'No, of course not,' said Kit.

'What are we talking about?' said Astrid.

'Well...the rum, mostly,' said Kit, apologetically.

'You have paint on your face. And in your hair,' said Astrid to Kit. Her eyes flitted briefly over Senara's overalls.

'No doubt,' said Kit. 'This is Teddy, by the way,' he said, gesturing. 'A friend of Senara's from Greece. Teddy, this is Astrid.'

'Yassou,' said Teddy, raising his glass across the table. 'Pleased to meet you.'

'You too,' said Astrid, brightly. 'And congratulations, Senara; you too Malory, on your little venture.'

'Thank you,' said Senara and Malory in unison.

Astrid turned to Kit. 'Have you finished work there now? You know I've been asking you to build a storage unit for some time.'

'There's just a little more to do before the opening,' said Kit. 'We got waylaid today...'

'It's just I could really use the extra space for my excess stock,' said Astrid. 'You know that.'

'I haven't forgotten,' said Kit.

'We're very grateful for Kit's help,' said Malory.

'I suppose a real carpenter would have cost you,' said Astrid. 'Although I think Kit's boatbuilding qualifications make him as good as any proper tradesman. You're lucky to get him for free.'

'It was kind of him to offer,' said Senara meekly.

'I think it is a wonderful thing for all concerned,' said Teddy. 'And this rum is divine. I think I am going to like St Ives. Especially if everyone is so delightful and attractive…' He glanced at Kit, before catching Senara's eye playfully. Alarmed, she gave him a warning look. He was not averse to stirring up trouble for fun.

The sky darkened and the night set in. The small group drank rum and cocktails as if the following day would never come, becoming ever more boisterous. Despite her initial unease, Senara felt relieved that Astrid appeared to be relaxed and joining in. Perhaps she had got it wrong, and had imagined her strange behaviour at the beach house party. And so, she buried the ungracious feeling that had arisen when Kit had invited Astrid; the feeling that the group had been somehow sullied, and the dynamic spoilt. She was clearly a horrible person for having such thoughts. And so, she smiled brightly and waved them goodbye, as Astrid kissed Kit suggestively on the lips and then dragged him away into the night.

* * *

Senara left shortly afterwards with Teddy, announcing that they had sleeping arrangements to consider in the poky confines of the cottage cellar. After Teddy bade them *kalinychta*, Malory found herself alone with Jago. Somewhere in the recesses of her mind she knew that she too should be making her excuses; that she should scurry home like a frightened mouse. But the rum had made her woozy with comfort, and all caution was drowned in a warm sea of cordiality. And it was a such relief to see the return of Jago's former boldness, that Malory could not help but feel endeared.

She glanced around at the nautical paintings and prints that adorned the granite walls; vintage images of luggers and seine boats and sea creatures.

'Did you know,' she said, 'that this building was probably once a boathouse?'

'Is that so?' said Jago.

'Yes,' said Malory. 'I've studied it. Well, not studied, exactly, but I've read a lot. The history of St Ives and its old buildings is absolutely fascinating. There never used to be a wharf road, you see. They would just drag the boats up straight from the shore, and Fore Street would have been the main thoroughfare down to the harbour.'

'You don't say,' said Jago, smiling. His eyes were warm, if slightly glazed.

'Yes,' said Malory. 'There would have been big doors right underneath here, where we're sitting, opening out onto the beach. This part would probably have been a sail loft or something.'

'Used to be a chip shop,' said Jago, in a deadpan tone.

'A *chip shop?*' said Malory in dismay.

'Best fish and chips in town,' said Jago, with a nod.

'Well,' said Malory, uncertainly. 'Imagine that. But I'm talking about *originally*; I'm talking about long before the tourists came, looking for chips. They would have used the side alley and the basement hidden under the stairs for smuggling purposes. Who knows what scurrilous deeds went on?'

'Well, it is called Dead Man's Alley…' said Jago, hunching over his drink.

'Really?' said Malory, her eyes widening.

'Yeah,' said Jago. 'It's where the pirate Billy Bones died. They say his spirit still haunts the alley.'

'More ghost stories?' said Malory. 'Go on then. How did he die?'

'Suddenly and mysteriously. But they say it may have been the rum.' He lifted his glass and eyed it dubiously. 'Maybe he drank too much, or maybe it was poisoned. But it happened not long after he'd been given the black spot by a blind beggar…' He turned to look at Malory, his expression serious.

'The black… Wait a minute,' said Malory. 'Isn't that *Treasure Island*?'

Jago grinned maliciously.

'Fine, mock me,' said Malory. 'But I know I'm right. I love these old buildings; they're steeped in history and romance. When I walk the streets of St Ives, I feel like I'm there, in the past.'

'With the pirates and smugglers?'

Malory chuckled. 'Yes, with the pirates and smugglers. And with the fisherfolk and miners…'

'It was a tough life for the fisherfolk and miners,' said Jago. 'They were dependent on the sea and the land for a living. When the pilchards went away and the mines closed, they had nothing. I doubt it was as romantic as you like to imagine.'

'I know that,' said Malory. 'But I do feel a resonance here that we've lost elsewhere in the land. Something of the old ways has been preserved.'

Jago drained the remains of the rum into their glasses. 'Yeah, preserved in quaint holiday cottages with a level of luxury that no fisherman could ever have afforded. Preserved in souvenir lobster pots and porthole mirrors; in strings of painted wooden mackerel and other crappy trinkets...'

'*You* sell trinkets,' said Malory. 'And don't you have a holiday let?'

'This is true,' said Jago, clinking his glass against hers. 'But I don't have blue sofas.'

'Blue sofas?' said Malory.

'You know... Blue sofas. Cushions with prints of seagulls and lighthouses. Nautical bunting. I'll have none of it.'

'What, not even a hanging piece of driftwood that says 'Gone Surfing?' said Malory, giggling.

'Nope. And likewise, none with an arrow pointing 'To the Beach'.

'No mugs that say 'I'd rather be in St Ives'?' Malory warmed to the theme. 'Not a single starfish, anchor, or piece of old rope in the whole place?'

'None.' Jago looked haughty. 'They come to my place they get the real experience. The bare bones. They get a place to sleep and eat and shelter from the weather. A proper fisherman's cottage.'

Malory was almost in tears with laughter. 'Well, aren't you a bundle of fun? Do you make them bathe in a tin bath before the open fire? The open fire that they've built with their bare hands? What's it called, Luddite Cottage? Old Fogey's? Have you been wondering why there's no bookings?'

'I'll have you know, it's very successful,' said Jago, loftily. 'There are still some that appreciate the unpretentious. And no, it's not called Luddite Cottage, Smarty-pants. Although I am quite liking Old Fogey's...'

'What *is* it called?' asked Malory.

Jago looked suddenly bashful. 'I don't want to say...'

'Why not?' Malory, fixed him with a suspicious stare. 'What have you got to hide? It's something really esoteric in Cornish, isn't it? Something that no one can spell or pronounce properly. Go on, tell me.'

Jago turned to look her straight in the eye. 'Okay. It's called... Mermaid Cottage.'

For a split-second Malory looked at him in disbelief, before they both burst out laughing, uncontrollably. Tamsin eyed them in curiosity from the bar.

'No way!' Malory could barely get the words out. 'So, you're telling me...after that...that *diatribe...*'

'Yeah, I know, I know,' said Jago, lowering his head as if in shame. 'It's cheesy.'

'It's the cheesiest,' said Malory.

'I've just always liked mermaids,' said Jago. 'What can I say?'

When their laughter had subsided, Jago looked at Malory intently. 'Do you want another?' he said quietly, indicating their glasses.

Malory suddenly felt too close to him in the dark and cosy room. Oblivious to the other customers on nearby tables, she had been drawn into a warm, intoxicated intimacy with Jago.

'Actually,' she said. 'I should probably go. School night and all that.'

Even as her heart beat faster when she looked at him, she could feel the smile fade from her lips and her spirits plummet, in the knowledge that their communion must end.

'Yeah, sure,' said Jago, although she could sense that he hid his own disappointment.

'Well then,' he said, getting up. 'I'll walk you home.'

Before Malory could protest that it was unnecessary, he had turned and moved toward the door. Outside, where he waited in the darkened alleyway where she had first set eyes on him, she felt the night's embrace of chill, salty air. It stirred an ineffable emotion in her; an indefinable yearning for something past; a half-forgotten memory that danced around the edges of her mind. She walked up the narrow, cobbled lane with him in silence.

It was a journey of such ludicrously short distance, that they both smiled in embarrassment as they reached the doorway.

'Thank you, kind Sir, for your gallant escort,' she said.

Jago stood with hands in pockets and twisted to look behind himself in puzzlement. 'Where? Where is said gallant escort? The knave must have run off again. I'll thank him when I find him.'

Malory giggled once more, delighted to have her spirits lifted again. 'I mean, for your gallant *escortment...*' She grinned in bewilderment. 'No that's not right. *Escortingment?*'

'I'm afraid there's nothing gallant about it,' said Jago.

'No?' said Malory. She supposed her confusion to be the rum's influence.

He took a step towards her. Malory backed into the shelter of the alcove doorway.

'Nothing at all,' he said, as his arms encircled her and he pulled her close.

There was nowhere further for Malory to retreat. For a moment, not a soul passed by on the street, and in the darkened recess, the world slipped away. Malory's guard melted into oblivion, and when he kissed her, she did not stop him.

CHAPTER 32

The Anchor Gallery

Malory lay in bed and stared at the ceiling for a very long time. She kept replaying the previous night in her mind, chastising herself for letting it happen. Yet at the same time, she lingered guiltily on the memory of his kisses. Groaning, she put her hands to her head, in despair.

Stupid, stupid idiot! She berated herself again.

At least, she had retained a modicum of wit, in not allowing the situation to develop further. Despite the maelstrom of drunken, mutual desire that had taken place on the doorstep, she had somehow disentangled herself long enough to thwart Jago's passion, and escape indoors. Yet she had been tempted. For a minute she had forgotten why she should not invite him upstairs to her bed. To think, she might have awoken this morning, with not just a mild hangover, but to the silent, inner howl of regret.

Worse still, as her senses returned, she remembered that she had arranged to go to a private view at a gallery with him that evening. The timing could not be worse. All she wanted to do was hide in shame and embarrassment. But if she cancelled now, and even if he had his own regrets, he would surely feel slighted. Malory spent all day at work hoping that Jago himself would call it off; that if nothing else, he would lose confidence in their plan to spread the word about his art.

But when the text message came, it said: *Still on for tonight? I'll meet you outside the place. 7 o'clock, right?*

At least there were no kisses or declarations of love. Perhaps he would be cool about the whole thing, and it only remained for her, Malory, to also be cool. She took a few deep breaths.

Relax Malory, relax. She shouldn't take it so seriously. It was just a rum-fuelled snog, after all.

But later, when she saw him standing outside the venue, her heart skipped a beat at his loveliness. It was then that Malory knew she was in deep trouble.

He leaned in to kiss her, not with the previous night's ardour, but intimately, on the cheek.

'You okay?' he said with a smile.

'I'm fine,' she said briskly. 'What a night though. Phew! I should probably steer clear of Sea Fever in future.'

He looked at her uncertainly. 'I thought it was fun.'

'Let's go in,' said Malory. 'Did you remember to bring your business cards?'

'Of course,' said Jago, his voice somewhat subdued.

'Okay then, let's do this,' said Malory. 'Only remember, be discreet. It's not your show. Just make conversation, and only give your card if asked.'

She turned to enter the building, but he took her by the arm.

'Are we not gonna talk about last night?' he said, his face now firm, unreadable.

Malory faltered, then said softly, 'I'd rather not. It was a mistake, Jago.'

'I see,' he said.

'I'm sorry.' Malory shifted uneasily.

'I thought you liked me.' His eyes were resolute, unyielding.

'I do. I really do,' said Malory. 'It's just...'

'Yeah, I know. You think I'm too young.'

Malory did not reply.

'Okay,' said Jago. 'It won't happen again.'

He turned and marched into the building, leaving Malory, in turn, to feel deflated, as she followed in his wake.

The Anchor Gallery was strategically lit, with paintings hung expertly on whitewashed walls, and beautiful ceramics on pedestals. Rather than cold and intimidating, like other galleries could be, it felt welcoming and personal; and Malory felt she liked it, despite her miserable mood.

It was a joint exhibition, shared by two artists. The first, a young man named Alex Summer, was everything she might expect of an up-and-coming artist. He wore strategically ripped jeans and the ubiquitous black T-shirt, both splattered with paint, as if to suggest that he never abandoned his work, for something so banal as a private view. On his feet, worn canvas trainers and odd socks became artful insouciance. His hair was short, spikey and bleached blonde. Oh yes, he was definitely 'in character', thought Malory as she swiped a glass of the champagne being offered around. His paintings were large and abstract, portraying striking geometric shapes, and their labels bore cryptic descriptions.

The other artist was an elderly woman, whose silver hair was cut into a neat bob. She was slender, and wore comfortable loose-fitting jeans and a printed shirt, with the sleeves rolled up. Her name was Marion Wills, and her paintings were mostly still lifes of flower vases, fruit bowls, and interiors. But there was a charm in her stylised forms and chalky colours that appealed to Malory. She strolled around the paintings, with Jago brooding silently at her side.

'I love the gestures she makes with her brush,' said Malory, in an effort to break the discomfort between them. 'And how she doesn't feel the need to overwork things.'

Malory was serious; she adored the confidence of character that showed in Marion's work. But while Jago nodded appreciatively, he did not reply.

After a while, they found themselves standing in a circle with a group of other attendees, each, apart from Jago, clutching a champagne glass by the stem. They all wore 'artistic' garb: William Morris-print scarves, and handmade brooches; corduroy jackets, red trousers, and improbable hats. Jago stood, disparate in the same black skinny jeans and grey T-shirt that he had worn when Malory had first met him; his tattooed arms incongruous amongst the middle-class orderliness. The group all, naturally, praised the exhibition and the artists; although Malory felt that some were being cynically, calculatingly, obsequious.

'Marion has earned her place, I suppose,' said a woman, who in the course of the introductions and conversations Malory had learned was named Judith Crutchley.

Judith's greying hair was impeccably cut, with subtle blonde highlights. She dressed her portly figure in wide linen slacks, a silken shirt and the sort of long coloured-bead necklace that Malory never understood. Malory couldn't quite grasp what Judith's occupation was, exactly, but from the way she spoke, assumed her to be prominent in the arts world.

'...She's somewhat conventional,' Judith continued, 'but a large body of work will always bring the buyers. Alex, on the other hand, is so exciting.'

Malory cringed to realise that Marion, whilst appearing disinterested, as she sat perched on a stool surveying the room, was close enough to overhear. Thankfully, another guest soon approached her for a chat, distracting her from further insult.

'Their work is indeed very different,' said a man called Hugh Pearce, who was the gallery owner. 'It's unusual for us to place such contrasting artists together, but I like the juxtaposition of styles. It works, somehow, I think.'

'I love Marion's work,' said Malory. 'Her eye for simplicity, especially.'

Judith eyed Malory over the top of half-rimmed spectacles. 'Do we know you?'

'I'm Malory Black,' she said, 'I'm the new owner of Atlantic Arts.'

'Ah, I heard that the lease had been taken up,' said Hugh. 'I'm pleased to see that you've kept it as it was, in the creative field. We were afraid it might become another clothing boutique, or some such.'

Malory's face brightened. 'No, not me,' she laughed. 'I'll never be 'boutique' in any way. I'm not that sophisticated.'

Hugh smiled, but Judith continued to scrutinise her.

'And who is this young fellow?' she said, casting her gaze upon the man who stood, taciturn, at Malory's side.

'I'm Jago,' he said.

'Jago is a local artist,' said Malory quickly. 'I'm exhibiting some of his works in the shop. Pop by and take a look, any time.'

'I see,' said Judith. Then addressing Jago again, said, 'I don't think we know you either, do we?'

'Depends on who you mean by 'we',' said Jago.

'Are you a member of any of the societies?'

'No,' said Jago.

'I see,' said Judith again.

Malory fought the urge to hit her.

'And where did you train?' continued Judith.

'Train?' said Jago. 'You don't train to be an artist. It comes from within. It's self-expression.'

'So, no education then?' said Judith, with a synthetic smile. 'It appears we have another self-taught genius amongst us,' she addressed the group, who laughed nervously.

Malory looked at Jago anxiously. His expression was stony, but otherwise gave nothing away.

'Well, who represents you, at least?' said Judith. 'I assume you have representation?'

'I represent myself,' said Jago, with a curled lip.

Malory could tell that he was quietly fuming, and suddenly hated herself for putting him in this position.

'Jago is very talented,' she said. 'I can vouch for that.'

'I'm sure,' said Judith, looking her up and down, in undisguised judgement.

It was then that Jago turned, and without a word of goodbye, left the building.

Malory was stunned. He had just *left*. Without a word. She tore her eyes away from the door where his presence was last seen, and cast them down onto her glass of lukewarm champagne.

'Well!' said Judith. 'It seems one cannot handle the heat. There's so many that call themselves artists these days, it's a wonder we can find the valid ones.' Then she turned her back on Malory before she could respond, and started a different conversation with a couple of eager recipients.

Malory wished the world would swallow her up. It must have shown on her face, for Hugh stepped closer and said, 'Don't take it to heart. If your friend is any good, he won't be put off.'

'And what if he is?' said Malory in anguish. 'What if he gets destroyed by such negative response?'

'You can't afford to be, in this business,' said Hugh, kindly. 'You have to have utmost faith in yourself. You can't even begin to think about the reaction of others.'

Malory looked at him appreciatively, but clearly still appeared downhearted.

'Look, do you have any examples of his work?' said Hugh. 'On you, I mean?'

Malory thought for a second. 'Yes,' she said, reaching for the small rucksack that she had taken to carrying everywhere.

She pulled out a handful of Jago's postcards from the shop, which were printed with a selection of his paintings. She handed them to Hugh who looked at them carefully.

'He clearly has talent,' said Hugh. 'But may require nurturing.'

'I don't think he'd be very good at that,' said Malory morosely.

Hugh laughed. 'Perhaps not. I will come and take a look though, I promise.'

Malory's eyes brightened. 'Really? That would mean so much. Thank you.'

When Hugh had meandered off to chat to other guests, Malory was approached by Marion Wills.

'Hello,' she said. 'I couldn't help but overhear your conversation. You mustn't let him give up, you know.'

'I'm not sure it's up to me,' said Malory.

Marion smiled. 'I suspect you have more power than you realise. But if you can't sell a gorgeous boy like that, you're doing something wrong! And don't pay any attention to the likes of Judith Crutchley. She's not an artist. She's a patron.'

Malory smiled, despite her unhappiness. 'I don't think I really know what that means.'

'It means money and time to spare,' said Marion flatly. 'She's an approver. Doesn't have a creative bone in her body, so has to sit in judgement of those who do. Don't let your boy give up. The only reason I'm here today is because I didn't quit. I returned to painting late in life, after my children were grown up. I wasn't part of any 'scene'. I had no friends in societies. But I was persistent, you see.'

Malory smiled again. 'I think you're an inspiration.'

'Hah!' Marion scoffed. 'Just remember. If you want something, never, ever, give up.'

She tipped her glass of champagne at Malory and then returned to the throng.

It was only then that Malory allowed the events of the evening to sink in; only then did she allow the pain and sadness to flow unreservedly through her heart. He had walked away. He had walked away, and everything, everything, was her fault.

CHAPTER 33

Concoctions

Malory did not stay long at the viewing after Jago's departure. The evening was still warm, with crowds milling about the streets of St Ives. She sought out a quiet spot, but struggled to find the words for the message that she knew she must send. What part of the evening's fiasco to mention, and what not? She longed to comfort him, yet had no desire to elaborate on her rejection of him. Again. In the end she simply put: *I'm sorry. That could have gone better. But I gave some of your cards to Hugh Pearce. He seemed genuinely interested x.*

There was no reply that evening, or the next morning. Malory felt torn between guilt and annoyance. Was he going to ignore her forever? She had, after all, had his best interests at heart...

Except you didn't have his best interests at heart when you kissed him wilfully, she reminded herself.

She would see him during the course of the week, she reasoned, and things would return to normal then. She was supposed to be overseeing the hang of his paintings at The Secret Spot, before the launch party next Saturday afternoon. This was to be a celebration; another sort of 'private view' for friends and supporters, before the doors officially opened to customers.

But on Monday morning, Malory was aggrieved to discover that Jago had delivered his paintings early, and then left.

'Yeah, he said he had band rehearsals, or something,' Senara said flippantly from a stepladder, as she hung a string of lights from the roof beams.

Malory spent her spare time during the week hanging the paintings alone, once again becoming immersed in their essence, and sinking deeper into the soul of Jago Berryman. Yet still he did not appear, or contact her; and so, Malory's paranoia at the extent of his injury escalated. Cosmic Ray and The Neutrinos were booked to play at the party, and Malory secretly hoped that the band, or more specifically, Jago, would be dreadful. She desperately needed a cure, an irreversible antidote to this feverish pool that she floundered in. She craved some switch to turn off the drug.

By Saturday morning, Malory decided in frustration that she could not face another day of torment over Jago. It wasn't healthy. What was done, was done, she told herself. She should get a grip and return to normality. She padded back to the bed in her pyjamas and plopped the laptop carelessly on top of the duvet. There was time for a cup of tea and a check of her emails before opening up shop, just for the morning. But first she allowed herself a trawl through social media. It was a habit of Malory's to ensure, before she committed to the day, that the world was not about to end in a ball of flames.

There was a newly opened account on Twitter for The Secret Spot. The word had spread, and it already had a healthy squadron of followers. Ostensibly Senara managed the account, but had enlisted Giovanna and Teddy, her newly appointed team members, to help out. Giovanna had been so excited to be involved with the new venue that she had quit her other bar job especially.

There was an email from Sam. He proposed a visit in the coming weeks.

Malory's heart spun in a mixture of emotions. She longed to see Sam again, in the flesh. They had Facetimed, of course, but it was not the same. Their connection was made awkward by interruption, and by Sam's complete incomprehension as to why she was in St Ives. And now there was this other complication; one that she struggled to defeat, but must, before it was too late.

She almost missed the other email, hidden as it was in the reams of mailshots and bills. Already the company name looked alien, a remnant from another existence. She stared at the message in some disbelief. Why had this been presented to her now? It felt like a temptation; a taunt from the universe sent to test her. It was a proposal from her old employers; a job, offering a much higher salary and a medley of company perks. It was more than she had ever been considered worth, in all the years that she had worked there. Malory could not help a wry smile. Despite having been an asset; supremely efficient and hard-working; despite having produced results, and profits; and despite a more than decent salary; Malory had always been vastly underpaid in comparison to her male counterparts. But now it seemed they had not been able to headhunt anyone suitable to replace her, and were offering all she might desire on a silver platter, if only she would agree to return. Max Patterson, her old boss, suggested an informal lunch meeting to discuss. It was an open invitation, he said. There was no rush, but he was sure that she would take time to consider such a generous proposition.

Malory looked around at the humble flat, which really was perhaps, the grottiest in St Ives. She thought of the luxury she had once had, and the privileged lifestyle. She had wondered enough herself, about her sanity in giving it all up, and didn't need Max Patterson reminding her.

But then she looked up, through the open door to the roof terrace, to the blue sky beyond. She heard the ever-present cry of gulls, and the distant, persistent noise of the sea at Porthmeor. Already that sonance, that energy, was in her bones, filling her heart with expectation for the day ahead. In London, Malory would have dragged herself from bed, a martyr to the duties of work or the gym. But here, she could hardly bear to be indoors. The call of the sea was almighty; it must be seen and felt and embraced and absorbed.

She flipped the laptop shut.

Stepping onto the roof terrace, Malory leaned against the railings, and closing her eyes, basked in the sunshine. She breathed in the fresh salty air, absorbing the vitalising power of the ocean. She might have been completely relaxed had it not been for the secret thrill that pervaded, and disturbed her composure. *The thrill of Jago*. Malory shook her head in despair that her thoughts had once again returned to him. And yet somehow that pleasure, that excitement, was part of it all. It had become knitted to her experience of St Ives and she did not know how to unravel it.

* * *

Senara carried the tray of stuffed baby peppers from the oven and placed them on the counter. The peppers had been cut in half lengthways and stuffed with tomato, capers and fresh tarragon, drizzled in olive oil and balsamic reduction, then slow-roasted until the juices became thick and caramelised, and the pepper skins perfectly chargrilled. She wiped her brow and smoothed her apron, then surveyed the dishes laid out on the counter before her.

She had been up since the early hours, working to provide the buffet for the party, desperate to ensure that she made her mark. It was a casual affair, she knew, but it was still her debut, and her reputation started right here. She felt the gentle pressure of hands on her hips, as Kit moved her aside. He was there, in theory, to put the finishing touches to the surfboard room, but materialised like magic in the kitchen, just as the food was ready.

'Looking good, girl,' he said.

'How opportune that you are here,' said Senara, with deep irony. 'You can be my taster. Or victim. Depending on how you look at it.'

'Always willing to oblige,' said Kit, rubbing his hands together.

Carefully Senara plated up one small half-pepper next to a perfectly roasted smashed potato into an oversized, Mediterranean-style bowl. She drizzled the potato with the rich sauces, then sprinkled the whole thing with a crumble of almonds and blue cheese, and topped with a single olive.

Kit wolfed down the portion immediately, then, still chewing, used his fork to shovel a few more potatoes and peppers into the bowl.

'What are you doing?' demanded Senara.

'That morsel didn't touch the sides,' said Kit. 'It was delicious, but not nearly enough.'

He filled the bowl and spooned more sauce over the top. 'Now that's more like it,' he said.

'Aw, but it's supposed to be minimal,' said Senara. 'You know, like tapas. You've ruined the appeal. It's just peasant food now.'

'I *am* a peasant,' said Kit, between mouthfuls.

'It's probably too messy for the party anyway,' said Senara, looking sadly at the demolished tray of peppers. 'I don't know what I was thinking. What about the rest of it? Does it all look okay?'

'Yes Snow, it looks amazing. Stop worrying. What's this?' he said, putting down his bowl and picking up a crunchy-looking, reddish nibble. 'Hold on; is this the famous beetroot ball that Jago's always on about?'

'Yes,' sighed Senara. 'It's a sort of falafel. With beetroot and hemp seed.'

'Sounds ominously healthy,' said Kit, before taking a bite and chewing thoughtfully.

'Well?' said Senara anxiously.

'It's good. Very good,' said Kit. 'Is that the mint I can taste?'

'It is,' said Senara, with a smile. 'Thanks again so much for the herbs. They all look wonderful.'

Kit had agreed to supply Senara with fresh herbs for her kitchen, but had donated an initial batch as a gift. He had made a wooden box for the sill in the kitchen area, and the breeze from the open window wafted in smells of oregano, thyme, basil, tarragon and mint. He had also given her a large and very healthy chilli plant, contained in its own clay pot. Senara had been enchanted by its delicate and graceful form.

'You're more than welcome,' said Kit, as he returned to finish the peppers. 'But I wish you'd let me supply you with fresh fish too.'

'I know it appears stubborn,' said Senara. 'I get that it would support the local economy and all that...'

'Not to mention me,' said Kit.

'...but I'm vegetarian,' continued Senara. 'It's the principle. Sorry.'

'Yeah, I know. I get it. And I admire you for sticking to your beliefs.' The peppers finished, Kit reached for a stick of fried matter that looked a bit like a chip and stared at it quizzically.

'Halloumi,' said Senara.

'Oh, right,' said Kit, but frowning as he chomped on the crispy titbit. 'And this?' he asked picking up a small cube of filo pastry layers, sandwiching a dark green filling. 'Let me guess... *Grass?*'

'Ha-ha!' Senara laughed nervously as she watched him chew. 'It's spanakopita. Spinach and feta and pine nuts, my own recipe. But I make mine sweet with honey, like baklava, and—oh my god, that's crazy, isn't it? You hate it. Everyone will hate it.'

'It's delicious,' said Kit, as he finished off the sticky little pie, and wiped his hands on a napkin.

'No one's going to come,' said Senara. 'Why did I ever think anyone would care about my café? Nobody likes me.'

Kit gave her a severe look. 'That's the most pathetic, self-pitying thing I've ever heard you say. And stop fiddling with your ear.'

'I know, but I'm a wreck,' said Senara, self-consciously removing her hand from where it fidgeted furiously with her right ear. 'I didn't sleep well, and when I did, I dreamt that Pepper was standing at the end of Pudding Bag Lane handing out leaflets, telling people not to visit The Secret Spot, because I was a... A harlot!'

Kit burst out laughing. 'A harlot? Senara please, get over yourself. People really don't think about you that much. And you're right. Maybe nobody will come. But it won't be because they hate you.'

'What about Eden Rowe?' said Senara. 'Did you ask her? Will she come?'

'Yes, and she says she'll be here,' said Kit, patiently, referring to the local pro-surfer, sometime model, and a personal friend of his. Eden's presence would ensure more attention, including that of the local press. 'But it doesn't matter if it's just us, Malory, Teddy and the band. Oh, and your 'normal guy'. Didn't you say he was coming? It will be enough. Now stop stressing and get yourself ready.'

He reached his arms around Senara and untied her apron. She watched him with fretful eyes as he lifted the garment over her head. Underneath she wore a short floaty dress in a sheer material, navy with tiny white polka dots. He watched her in turn as she untied her pony tail, and rearranged her long hair with her fingers.

'There,' he said. 'Ready.'

Senara shook her head in despair.

'I'm *not* ready,' she wailed, putting her fists to her temples. 'I've been working day and night. I'm exhausted, and my head is swirling with a million things I can still think of to do! I could do with a shower and I need to put some make-up on!'

'You look just fine,' said Kit. 'And there's no sense in worrying now. What will be, will be.' He looked at her more sombrely. And this time when he spoke, his voice was quiet, and gentle. 'It's *time*, Senara.'

She looked into his dark sea-green eyes and saw the seriousness therein.

Nodding, she straightened her back and lifted her chin to the world. 'Right. You're right,' she said. 'It's time.'

'That's the spirit,' said Kit softly. Then he embraced her in a hug and whispered in her ear. 'Enjoy the ride.'

And so finally, still hardly believing her luck, Senara opened the green doors of The Secret Spot. She welcomed each guest with a warm smile and an air of confidence, but her heart was dumbfounded; astonished that this was actually happening. As the room filled up with a happy, chattering crowd, she had to take a moment alone by the sea-view window, to take it all in. Outside, the ebbing tide gushed its rhythmic song, and the happy cries of children could be heard from the beach. It was hours still until sunset, and the cavernous room was filled with warm sunshine. It was just as she had imagined it, when she had sat in the shadows, just a few months before, and dreamed this vision. She watched as surfers, fishermen and artists mingled as one. Over there was Aunt Minnie with her arty and Methodist friends; and at the bar, Olly Down-from-London with his sailor chums. Even Bill Negus appeared to be genuinely enjoying himself. And Brian would be here soon. Their chats had resumed their earlier rapport, and Senara had made sure to invite him to the opening night.

Well, Dora. I hope you approve, thought Senara, with a smile, as she looked up at the Surfer's Store poster, that, despite its dilapidation, she had had framed and re-hung. Then, just as she thought that tears of joy might overwhelm her, she spotted the figure snaking his way through the crowd. She watched as he insinuated himself in a gap beside Malory at the crowded bar.

Grady O'Keefe.

Senara felt her insides churn as she saw him casually strike up a conversation with Malory, with that steady gaze and inscrutable smile.

What is he even doing here? Senara raged silently, at the gall of the man.

Did he even realise that this was *her* place, her venture; and that his presence without Pepper might spark fresh rumours? Senara scanned the room again. Where was Brian? She felt more than ever, that she needed the companionship of someone new; someone from outside of St Ives. Even if it wasn't a proper date, no one would know that, and it would steer gossips away from observations about Grady's presence.

But she could not see Brian anywhere in the crowd.

CHAPTER 34

Road to Discomfort

Dan sat on his usual perch at the bar in The Barque, and browsed the crossword, a reassuring pint on the counter by his side. He couldn't finish the puzzle and Tamsin had been too busy with the summer crowds to help, but he wasn't bothered. There was a deep comfort to be had in just sitting in his customary place, with the sure knowledge of beer and crisps to hand, that eased the sorrow and humiliation over his brief, disastrous love affair with Daisy. Both she and Marta had now joined the long list of exes never to be acknowledged with more than a nod, as each passed the other on a cobbled street. A smile, or a 'how are you?', was totally out of the question. It was the unspoken etiquette of a small town where relationships were tangled, and everyone had some sort of history with everyone else. Better never to speak of it again.

Ed, the local postman arrived, and seeing Dan at the bar, approached him.

'Alright?' he said.

'Alright?' replied Dan.

'Got a parcel here for Tamsin,' said Ed. 'Can you pop it to her, when she gets a moment?'

Tamsin rented the flat in the eaves above the inn, and so usually saved Ed his legs by allowing him to deliver directly to the bar when she was working.

'Will do,' replied Dan, taking the slim package.

'Right on,' said Ed, turning to leave again. 'Don't forget now, will 'ee?'

Dan plopped the parcel on the counter, and continued staring at the unfinished crossword. When Tamsin was free, he called her over.

'Looks like another movie for you,' he said. 'Judging by the shape of it.'

'Ooh, I've been looking forward to this,' said Tamsin in delight.

She tore open the package and took out a couple of DVDs.

'That's made you happy,' said Dan, observing her face light up. 'What've you got there, then?'

'*Some Like it Hot*,' said Tamsin. 'And *The Cat and the Canary*.'

'Never heard of them,' said Dan, taking a sup.

Tamsin looked at him in horror. 'Never heard of *Some Like it Hot*? Are you joking? It's a classic! This is a new copy because my old one got worn out.'

'Let me see,' said Dan, reaching out to take the DVDs. He grimaced. 'Oh. Black and white. That explains it.'

'Explains what?' said Tamsin, although her tone suggested she suspected what was to come.

'Well, it's old stuff, isn't it?' said Dan, matter-of-factly. 'I'm more of your modern-day action movie fan. You know, lots of CGI. Excitement, adventure; that's me.'

'Really,' said Tamsin drily, as Dan took another slurp of his pint.

'No offence,' said Dan. 'I know you like old stuff.'

'If by 'old stuff', you mean classic movies of the golden Hollywood era, then yes,' said Tamsin. 'You should give it a try sometime. You know, be *adventurous*.' She looked at him slyly as she pulled a pint for a regular who had just arrived.

Dan perused the DVDs while she finished serving, his features forming a dubious expression as he read the blurb on each.

'This one here,' he said, tapping one of the films a little aggressively. 'That's Marilyn Monroe, right?'

'Yes,' said Tamsin patiently. 'And Jack Lemmon and Tony Curtis. It's brilliant.'

'I reckon I could give that a go,' he said hesitantly. 'Because of Marilyn. But I don't like the look of this other one. Bit scary.'

Tamsin giggled. 'Aw, is the big brave boy scared of a little old movie. A black and white one at that?'

Dan scowled. 'I don't like horror. It keeps me awake all night.'

'It's supposed to,' said Tamsin. 'That's the thrill. Besides, this is comedy horror,' said Tamsin. 'It has the original pairing of Paulette Goddard and Bob Hope, who is frankly, in his element.'

Dan looked at her blankly.

'Bob Hope? From the 'Road to' movies? With Bing Crosby and Dorothy Lamour?'

Dan pursed his lips and shook his head slowly. 'Nope, Sorry.'

'I can't believe it. For someone who watches so many films, you're sorely lacking in knowledge. You're really missing out.'

Dan plunged into deep thought while Tamsin served another customer.

'Okay, I'll do it,' he said with vigour, when she returned. 'I'll watch the Marilyn one. If you'll lend it to me, that is.'

Tamsin flashed her eyes at him through thick fake lashes. 'Ooh, taking *action*. You are an adventurer, after all. I tell you what. I'll bring them both over. We can make a movie night of it.'

Dan's heart began to thud wildly. He hadn't planned on this. He wasn't used to sharing his den, at least not for movie nights. Movie nights were always a solitary indulgence that he thoroughly relished.

'Oh. Righty-oh then,' he heard himself say.

'I'll come over sometime when I get a night off,' Tamsin said cheerfully. 'I'll bring the films; you can sort the popcorn.'

Dan drained the remnants from his pint, and slammed it down on the counter a little too brusquely, but decisively nonetheless.

'Righty-oh,' he said again, and dismounted clumsily from the bar stool. 'Anyways, I'm off now. Going to this party of Senara's at The Secret Spot. You coming?'

Tamsin's red-painted lips broke into a dazzling smile. 'Maybe later, when I get off.'

'Right then,' said Dan. 'Might see you there. Better get going.'

Tamsin watched as he bumbled his way to the door, where he turned and waved awkwardly before disappearing into the street outside. She allowed herself a small smile before returning to her duties.

CHAPTER 35

The Secret Spot

When Dan arrived at Pudding Bag Lane, he found the narrow alleyway populated with an overspill of people, mostly smokers, and could hear music and laughter emanating from the party further along. He squeezed his way through the crowd and up the steps in some trepidation. With this sort of turnout, it was likely that Marta would be here. Possibly even Daisy.

Thankfully, it didn't take him long to spot friendly faces near the bar, and he gravitated towards the security of Zack, Kit, and Astrid.

Once he had said his hellos and secured a drink, he furtively scanned the room. He saw the band equipment set up in a corner near the window overlooking Porthmeor Beach, and Jago engrossed with something technical to do with the speakers. Directly opposite the bar, a long table laid with enticing food drew his eye. There were familiar faces everywhere, but since none of them appeared to be ex-girlfriends, Dan relaxed a little.

'Place looks smashing, doesn't it?' he said, as he took in the sympathetic décor and ambience of the newly renovated loft.

'Yeah, amazing,' said Kit, and Zack nodded in agreement. Astrid stayed silent. 'Senara's worked really hard,' continued Kit. 'But she's a little nervous, so say something nice when you get the chance.'

'Of course,' said Dan. Then, noticing that only Teddy and Giovanna were on bar duty, added: 'Where is she?'

'Over there,' said Kit, indicating. 'She's being interviewed for the local paper.'

Dan looked and saw Senara standing near the large window chatting to a woman holding some sort of recording device. A trendy-looking photographer was snapping busily nearby. Just then a girl in the intervening crowd turned and spotted him. It was Daisy. He hadn't noticed her at first because she had tied her long hair up, for once, in a loose and rather fetching topknot. For a fleeting second, he thought he saw pleasure in her eyes, and the beginnings of a nervous smile begin to form in the corners of his mouth. But Daisy turned to whisper to a friend behind her champagne glass, and then the two of them giggled, and quickly looked away. Dismayed, he turned to Astrid and hastily struck up a conversation about the first thing that came to mind.

'So, Astrid. Still into all that crystals malarkey? Don't know how you get away with having them all over the house, given that Kitto hates them.' He chuckled exaggeratedly.

'What do you mean?' said Astrid, coldly.

Kit stared at Dan with a wide-eyed expression that screamed *'Why?'*

Despite the feeling that he had committed a faux pas, Dan could not seem to stop himself from floundering on. With a wary eye on Kit, he muttered, 'I mean, it's not that he doesn't *like* them, so much, because they're very pretty and all, it's just to do with their...' he struggled to remember a pub conversation with Kit, and the words that he had used. 'Their...*provenance?* Is that it?' he looked at Kit hopefully. 'He said you can't ever tell where they come from. You know, where they've been mined, and the conditions for workers and that.'

Kit shook his head slowly in despair.

'Is this true?' said Astrid, turning to Kit, with a small, hurt note to her voice. 'Is that really what you think?'

'I think it's worth considering,' said Kit. 'I mean, are they fair-traded? From regulated mines? What about child labour?'

'I'm sure all my crystals and gemstones come from trusted sources,' said Astrid.

'But how do you know?' said Kit, with a smile. 'It's not as if they're sourced from local Cornish mines. They're not *cassiterite*.'

'Because... It just wouldn't be *allowed*,' said Astrid. 'And I truly believe that they are here on Earth for our benefit.'

'Of course,' said Kit, still smiling. 'It wouldn't be human not to ravage the Earth for every last scrap of resource. Even for the sake of baubles.'

'They are *not* baubles!' cried Astrid. She touched her hand to the pendant that she wore, a rod of green tourmaline, as if to protect it from such offence. 'They are treasures that the Earth gives up for us; to help us heal, and find our way!'

'But they're not 'given up', are they?' said Kit. 'And what gives treasure its value, but its rarity? Treasures should be *found*. They should be individual, unique, and happened upon by chance. Not blasted and plundered from the Earth in vast quantities, for profit.'

'Plus, they don't work,' said Zack, mischievously.

Astrid shot him a look of wrath.

'Isn't that Daisy?' said Kit, cheerfully, and too loudly. 'Over there, look.'

'Shh!' pleaded Dan. But Kit just smirked, evilly.

'How's that going anyway?' said Zack.

'It's not,' said Dan woefully. 'And I'd rather not talk about it, if that's all right.'

'Talk about what?' said Jago joining them.

'His love life,' said Zack. 'Going nowhere, as usual.'

'I thought you were doing that list thing?' said Jago absentmindedly, as he grabbed a vacant barstool and procured a bottle of beer from Teddy.

'I was. It's not working. Think I'm just going to go back to dating girls who actually like me.'

'Sounds like a good idea,' said a woman's voice from behind Dan.

He turned to see that it was just Tamsin, who must have finished her shift already. She squeezed her way past him to the bar next to Jago, and grabbed one of the free glasses of champagne.

'Daisy liked you,' said Zack. 'But you appear to have stuffed that up.'

'Come on mate,' said Kit, slinging an arm around Dan's shoulders. 'Don't lose heart. We'll find you someone special yet.'

'What about her?' said Zack, with little discretion, and a nod with his beer bottle towards the other end of the bar, where Malory sat with Grady O' Keefe.

'Who?' said Dan, and the whole group turned, with even less discretion, to see whom he meant.

'That Malory,' said Zack. 'Good looking woman. Must have a few bob too, I'm guessing.'

'Wealth isn't on the list,' Kit objected. 'It's not an important factor. But she's certainly attractive, intelligent, into the arts...'

'I don't think that's a good idea,' said Jago suddenly.

They all turned to look at him suspiciously.

'You don't think she's attractive?' said Astrid.

'No, I mean, of course she is. I just don't think she's right for Dan. No offence, mate.'

'Oh, that's right,' said Zack slyly. 'You're pally with her, aren't you? And didn't you get all friendly at The Barque the other night?'

'That's what I thought,' said Astrid. 'I heard you left with her.'

Jago looked peeved. 'There's nothing going on. I have a professional relationship with her, as does Senara. I don't want you lot and your dodgy list meddling with that. Could get awkward.'

'Fair enough,' said Dan.

'I agree,' said Tamsin. 'She seems too nice to be meddled with.'

Jago said nothing, only sat hunched over his bottle of beer. But when they all lost interest and moved on to other gossip, he risked a glance towards the other end of the bar, where Malory appeared to be deeply interested in the wise words of Grady O'Keefe.

* * *

There was a commotion by the entrance. It was the arrival of Eden Rowe, accompanied by a couple of other surfer friends: Gabe, an American, and Salima, were from a nearby village, but as surf instructors, had come to St Ives for the summer season. Relieved that Eden had been true to her word and shown up, Kit held up a hand in recognition. The three newcomers all waved back.

Eden strode across the room with the confidence and charisma of someone used to attention, saying gracious hellos to all as she moved through the crowd. She departed from the usual surfer-girl image of long blonde Californian locks, by having her dark hair cropped in a short, messy, boyish style.

She wore a simple, skimpy black dress with white trainers, emphasising her tanned, and incredibly toned legs.

Kit noticed the photographer become visibly agitated, and nudge the reporter, who was mid-conversation with Senara. Hurriedly they made their excuses and pushed their way through the crowd towards Eden. He watched Senara, hoping she would not feel snubbed. But catching his eye, Senara merely waved cheerfully, before holding her thumbs up, and miming an exaggerated wipe of her brow with one hand. Delighted to see her so happy, he returned her smile, then looked back to where Eden stood nearby, and listened as she professionally answered the reporter's questions:

'Yes, for sure I will be a regular customer at The Secret Spot. I think it's an exciting new venture and a much-welcome addition to surfing culture in the town.'

'Can I get a picture, Eden?' asked the photographer. 'Maybe up in front of that painting?'

'Of course,' replied Eden. 'The painting, by the way,' she said turning to the reporter, 'is by local artist and surfer Jago Berryman. That's Berryman with a 'y' not an 'i'; got it? Jago Berryman. He's playing in the band tonight, if you'd like to request an interview.'

The photographer cleared the crowd directly in front of one of Jago's paintings and shyly asked if Eden would mind striking a pose.

Eden held her chin thoughtfully. 'Wait a minute. Gabe?' she called to one of her friends. 'Can you grab one of those surfboards from the back room? Cheers.' She turned back to the photographer. 'And how about we get the girls in the picture too? Senara and Malory? It is, after all, their opening.'

'Of course,' said the photographer, as though he had committed a severe oversight, and almost tugging his forelock. Kit thought he might drop to his knees and beg forgiveness.

A few minutes later, Eden stood in front of Jago's painting, flanked by Malory and Senara, and the three of them posed holding the longboard that Gabe had fetched from the back room.

Kit watched with an impish smile, and then leaning in towards Zack and Dan, spoke quietly. 'You know what I think?' he said.

'What?' said Dan nervously, still waiting for Kit to berate him for his earlier blunder.

But Kit appeared to have already forgotten the matter. 'I think we've been missing a trick all along.' He nodded towards Eden.

'What do you mean?' said Dan, but with a tremor in his voice as he began to suspect Kit's meaning.

'Eden,' said Kit. 'Look at her. She's amazing. She has enough confidence for the both of you. You should ask her out. Right here, right now.'

'That's a great idea,' said Jago, with enthusiasm. Tamsin eyed him sideways.

'Oh no. Oh, no, no, no.' Dan shook his head. 'You go too far. She's way too hot for me.'

'Agreed,' said Tamsin, then coyly took a sip of her drink.

'Don't put him off,' reprimanded Kit. 'And you shouldn't be perturbed by the all the glamour, she's really nice and approachable. Completely down-to-earth. You'd be pleasantly surprised.'

'I don't trust her,' said Astrid. 'She doesn't hang out with the other girls. Pepper and I have tried to socialise with her a few times, but she always bails on us.'

'I don't know,' said Dan. 'What about that Gabe fella...'

He cast an anxious look at the tall dark American with a small red heart tattoo on his cheek. He looked kind of scary.

'They're just friends.' said Kit. 'Come on, what have you got to lose? Just have a chat and see how you get on.'

'Well, she is really fit. And I've never dated a real surfer girl before...'

'Really?' said Tamsin, her voice loaded with dry sarcasm. 'Well, I never!'

'Maybe I will give it a go,' muttered Dan, ignoring her. 'Maybe. In a bit. After another pint.' Then he turned and headed for the bar.

* * *

When the interview was finished, Eden re-joined her friends Gabe and Salima.

'Hey, she's back,' said Gabe, in his laid-back Californian accent. 'Job all done?'

'All done,' said Eden. 'But they'll probably still be taking some candid shots, so be aware.'

'Of course,' said Salima, striking a pretentious pose, and then giggling.

'Don't know why you bother,' said Gabe. 'Pain in the butt.'

'Yeah, I know,' said Eden. 'But honestly, it does me good too. It's all exposure.'

'Whatever you say, Babe,' said Gabe. 'Now, if you'll excuse me girls, I'm gonna go say hi to Kit.'

'No worries,' we'll be over too in a sec,' said Salima.

They watched as Gabe moved across the crowded room towards Kit.

'The truth is,' said Eden, leaning in confidentially towards Salima. 'There's not much I wouldn't do for that guy.'

'You mean Kit?' said Salima. 'I can see why. Didn't you and he once...'

'No, that was just rumour. Not that I would've minded, but I knew he would never be serious. He was always wild. The consummate free spirit. So, I consciously avoided that particular pitfall.'

'Bummer,' said Salima.

'Yeah, it wasn't easy,' said Eden. 'I was crazy about him. I mean, look at him. He's hot! But I kept my head. What's really galling, is that he appears to have settled down anyway.'

'You're kidding?' hissed Salima, in a loud whisper. 'Kit Curnow? Who's the girl?'

'That hippy chick with all the rings. In the floaty dress,' said Eden, directing Salima with her eyes.

'Hmm. Cute,' said Salima, assessing Astrid. 'Very cute. But I would never have guessed. She doesn't look the type. I mean, does she even surf?'

'Nope,' said Eden.

'Seriously?' said Salima, turning to Eden, aghast, and forgetting to whisper.

Eden turned to face Salima, her eyes wide in mock-horror. 'I know, right? That's what I thought. I mean, what the hell is going on there, exactly?'

'Highly suspect,' said Salima, and the two women chuckled profusely.

* * *

As they had posed for the photographs, Malory had tried hard to stop fuming. For, after attempting to impress her with his clearly practised lines, Grady had spotted a fresher victim in the form of Daisy. He had unashamedly followed the young girl with his eyes, as she innocently passed them at the bar.

Then, as Malory was mid-sentence, he had placed a patronising, consolatory hand on her shoulder, as if to quickly curtail their conversation, before diving into the crowd, chasing after the unsuspecting Daisy.

It was infuriating. He had flagrantly dismissed her, practically patting her on the back. As if she cared!

When the photographer had finished, she looked around, hoping that Jago was still at the bar, and that she might summon the courage to approach him. But at that moment she saw him leave the others and head back to the band area.

She spotted Hugh Pearce on the other side of the room, looking interested in one of Jago's paintings. Deciding it was an opportune moment to promote the cause, she wove her way through the mingling crowd, only to find that she had been beaten to the spot by Judith Crutchley. Standing foolishly a couple of paces behind them, Malory could not help but overhear the conversation.

'I think they're rather good,' said Hugh. 'Wayward, but daring.'

Judith laughed. 'There may be some ability there, I suppose. And he is local, we're told, so there is that selling point. Although they all call themselves local artists these days, no matter where they originate from.'

'It does make quite an impression, seeing them all together like this,' said Hugh. 'They've done a good job with the hanging. Perhaps Malory Black has something to offer the community, after all.'

Judith scoffed. 'I think we've yet to see if Miss Black has any other cards up her sleeve, or if the infatuation runs to this artist alone...'

Humiliated, Malory slunk back into the crowd before they spied her.

Deciding she needed another drink, she found herself once again trapped in conversation at the bar, only this time with the man in the posh polo shirt, whom she had met that first day in The Barque. *Olly?* She tried to focus, and listen, without giving the idea that she was at all impressed by his sleek and groomed appearance, or his entitled manner.

'It's good to find another incomer amongst the locals,' Olly was saying. 'Another 'emmet', so to speak,' he grinned.

'Well, I hope I'm not always regarded as an incomer,' said Malory. 'I really feel an affinity with this place. Like I belong here. It's quite odd, really, how familiar it all feels to me.'

Olly sighed. 'My dear, I've been coming here for decades. Since I was a boy. My family always visited in the summer hols, at least after the obligatory jaunt to hotter climes. It was always my desire to have my own house in the town, and I've succeeded. *I* feel an affinity, as you say. And despite losing my wife to one of the locals, I still love the place. Wouldn't be without it. But they still treat me like an outsider.'

Beneath the jolly bluster, Malory could sense the note of sadness in his voice.

'Olly just-down-from-London, they call me,' he said. 'Oh, I know they do. Even after all this time. Even though I own a house here, and consider it a home from home.'

'Maybe that's the problem,' suggested Malory, kindly. 'Perhaps you should make it a permanent move.' Second homes, she knew, were not looked on favourably, especially if left empty for long periods.

'That's the plan, long term,' said Olly. 'Once I can set myself up for early retirement. But for now, I need London to run my businesses.'

Malory had tried to avoid asking what business he was in, sensing earlier in their conversation that he was dying to tell her. But at this further mention she realised it was not to be averted. 'Your businesses?'

'Real estate. Property. Lettings...' Olly visibly cheered up. 'I've been meaning to compliment you on acquiring this little earner.'

Malory thought of the extortionate rental prices in London, and how they were almost impossible for ordinary workers to afford. But it was a conversation she did not want to have; and had he known her views, she was sure, neither would he.

'Thank you,' she said. 'But it was Senara who found it. She's the one who will make it a success.'

'Clever of you to get in on the action though,' said Olly. 'Although you might have to find yourselves a new home when the lease expires,' he said blithely.

Malory shifted uncomfortably. What did he know of the lease? 'I'm sure things will work out,' she said.

'You do know that the freehold for the building is up for sale?' continued Olly.

'Of course,' Malory nodded, but felt increasingly wary. Instinctively, she knew what was coming.

'Thinking of putting in an offer myself,' confirmed Olly. 'This will make a great conversion project. Huge profit potential. I've already consulted my usual firm of architects.'

Malory's blood ran cold. She felt a little dizzy and struggled to keep her composure. 'Is there much competition for it? The freehold, I mean?'

'A few others sniffing around,' said Olly. 'But they'll need the dosh. The price itself isn't too great, but it's the cost of the conversion that'll eat away at your pennies. Not to mention the planning permission. Might need to grease a few palms there.'

He grinned as though there was nothing remotely wrong with what he had just said.

'What would you do with the building?' said Malory, with a sick dread in her heart.

She listened in dismay as Olly described a picture of demolition and destruction; then of steel, and mezzanine levels, and huge glass frontages.

'Of course, it's not settled yet,' said Olly, still smiling confidently. 'I'll have to speak with my business partners. But I don't see it being a problem. It's going for a song, really.'

Malory longed to protest, to remind him of the history and heritage of the pilchard cellar, but knew she would be wasting her breath. And she feared that he might detect the panic in her voice; that he might suspect her as a rival.

'Anyhow,' Olly continued jovially. 'Got some pesky lessees to be rid of first. Could hold things up for a while, so no rush.' He winked at her.

Malory smarted at the brazen cheek. To discuss their eviction on the day of opening was incredibly rude. She forced herself to find some fighting talk.

'Well, we'll see,' she said. 'Perhaps the new owner will be sympathetic. Maybe even renew the lease.'

Olly laughed aloud. 'I like your spirit, my dear. And I would love to discuss the matter further. Perhaps over dinner one day? Our sort should stick together.'

Malory hoped she did not look as taken aback as she felt. She gave a small laugh that she hoped would fend off his proposals.

'Well, perhaps another drink, for now...' said Olly, clearly not discouraged, and already summoning Teddy with a coarse click of his fingers.

Malory shot Teddy an apologetic look. And then her eyes wandered, as if seeking home, in the direction of her longing.

The band were discreetly beginning to tune up, in preparation for their set. She watched as Jago strummed his guitar and then reached to adjust a dial on the amp. Even these small motions she found agonising. There was a beauty and elegance in the way that he moved and held himself, and she felt lured by this agility and poise. How could Olly, or Grady, hope to compare? And yet these were the men she found herself with, at her own doing. When Jago turned again, she thought he met her eyes, and felt an errant shiver of pleasure flow through her body. But the moment was brief, elusive, as he went about his business, so that she decided she had imagined it.

Her eyes darted back to Olly, who was still paying for the drinks, and thought of what he had said; that she was an incomer like him. He had implied that she was one of his kind, and that they should stick together. Malory felt the horrible twist of doubt and fear begin to gnaw at her heart. For Olly represented everything that she had tried to break away from; was everything that she no longer wished to be. But in the deepest part of her lurked the dread suspicion that she was deluding herself, and that Olly's words might be true.

* * *

As she worked her way around the room, mingling with the guests, Senara tried not to watch the door. She had been knocked off-kilter at Grady's presence, and prayed that Brian would soon arrive. At the bar area, she thanked Eden for her support, then turned to speak to Kit and Astrid, who appeared to be having a protracted argument about crystals.

'...I'm not saying there's no placebo effect, or something, going on,' Kit said. 'Maybe belief alone can heal. But there's no intrinsic quality. There's no *magic*.'

'You're such a cynic, Kitto,' said Senara, laughing. 'Belief *is* a kind of magic.'

'I'm not a cynic,' said Kit. 'I'm just not gullible.'

'I think you like to be contrary,' grinned Senara. 'There's power in plants, right? Like your herbs? So why not crystals? It's all nature. And your necklace is so pretty, Astrid.'

'But...' Kit started.

'How about the healing power of the ocean?' continued Senara. 'Are you really saying you don't feel restored after a sunset surf? Or a dawnie?'

Kit appeared to give up the fight. 'Okay, fine,' he said, raising his hands in surrender. 'Crystals are magic. Now can we please drop it?'

Senara smirked in victory, but decided not to goad him further. 'I hope you both enjoyed the food?' she asked.

'The food was delicious,' said Astrid, without hesitation. 'I ate so many of those mini rhubarb and custard tarts, I'm going to be so fat tomorrow!'

'I'm so glad you liked them,' said Senara cautiously.

'Getting a bit low in supplies, though,' said Kit. 'Time you got back in the kitchen, maid.'

Senara shot him a look and a grin, but once more in Astrid's presence, thought twice about continuing the jest. When Kit broke apart to talk to Eden, Senara stood awkwardly with Astrid.

'Thanks again for coming,' she said politely. 'I hope you're having a good time?'

Astrid said nothing, her eyes focused somewhere beyond Senara.

Senara felt the flush of embarrassment and confusion creep over her. This could not be happening again... Perhaps Astrid had not heard her, above the chatter and commotion? She saw Jago wave at her, indicating that the band were ready.

'Forgive me,' she said to Astrid, 'I have to go and introduce the band.'

Again, Astrid stood stony-faced and seemingly oblivious to Senara's presence. And then Senara knew, for certain, as she scanned Astrid's frosty features, that it was deliberate, and that she had been wrong-footed again. The feeling was akin to being slapped in the face. She struggled for the words, to plead or question. But what was the point? Astrid would continue to ignore her.

She turned and walked away.

* * *

With a break in the conversation, Dan sensed, too late, what was about to happen.

'Hey Eden,' said Kit. 'I don't think you've met Dan before, have you?' He placed a hand on Dan's back, and gently but firmly guided his friend from where he had been skulking on the perimeter of the group. 'Dan, this is Eden.'

Dan visibly squirmed.

'Hi,' he said shyly. 'I'm really pleased to meet you. Your, erm, fame travels before you.' He gave what he hoped was his most charming smile.

He thought that Tamsin, who stood nearby, had tutted loudly. But when he glanced at her, she was staring absently around the room, clutching her glass of champagne to her bosom, exposed by the neckline of her clinging black dress.

Eden laughed. 'Relax, I'm just a local girl. How come we've never met, since you're a friend of Kit's? Do you get out back at all?'

'I'm sorry; outback?' Dan looked puzzled. 'No, I've never been to Australia.'

This time Tamsin definitely appeared to have emitted a groan. Was she all right? Was she ill? Dan looked at her momentarily with a frown. But Kit's hearty laughter drew his attention back again.

'Hey, I'm sorry,' said Eden, with a grin. 'I forget I'm talking surf slang sometimes. I meant, do you go out back in the waves? Do you surf?'

'Er, no. No, I've never ventured, myself. I'm more into...'

Tamsin cocked her head on one side, as if she simply could not wait for Dan to elaborate. It was rather off-putting. He searched his brain for an answer.

'Didn't you say you'd taken up horse-riding?' said Kit, with a quizzical expression.

'...horse-riding,' said Dan, eying Kit suspiciously. 'Yes, that's right. I'm better off with solid land sports, I reckon.'

Tamsin stared at him before turning her head with equal interest towards Eden.

'Hey, that's cool,' said Eden. 'But if you horse-ride, you must be fit. You must have a strong core.'

'Yes Dan, you *must* have a strong core,' Kit parroted, with a glare of delight.

What was he doing? Whose side was he on? It dawned on Dan that perhaps Kit had not forgotten his little mishap, after all.

'If you have a strong core, you should be able to handle surfing,' said Eden.

'Strong as an ox, this boy,' said Kit, punching Dan playfully on the arm. A little too hard, in fact. 'He'd be great in the water.'

'Well, I'd be happy to take you out,' said Eden. 'Give you some instruction, if you'd like to give it a try?'

For a second Dan was not sure what was happening. He only knew that Eden Rowe had apparently just offered to take him out, and give him some instruction. He felt his mind melting.

'Er, yeah. Great. That would be cool,' he spluttered, but remembering to grin amiably again.

Tamsin made an odd flapping motion with her hands, and then turned and walked away.

'Is she okay?' said Eden.

'No one can ever really tell,' said Dan.

* * *

Sullenly, Jago waited with the rest of the band as Senara stood at the mic and formally thanked everyone for coming. It was not altogether their usual crowd, he mused. Some of them might be a little shocked by the level of noise and general mayhem. But at least in the confined space Cosmic would be unable to perform his usual frantic stage routine. Once again Jago's ballad had been vetoed from the set, but for once Jago had not complained. He was not in the mood for love songs. Not when he could see, from where he stood, that Malory was still engrossed in conversation with Olly-down-from-London. It had been bad enough to watch Grady O'Keefe prowling around her, and even Dan had been tempted to give it a shot. But a middle-aged man from up country? What was she thinking? He conceded that they had London in common, but still, he couldn't understand what Malory might see in Olly.

Except perhaps for his *money*, he thought ruefully. But in truth, he did not think Malory the sort of person to have her head turned by riches. She was kind and giving, and more to the point, independent. And far too gorgeous for that old man.

It was no use. He could not reason himself out of a tormented attack of jealousy. That Malory had rejected him, yet appeared to be content in the company of Olly—of all people—was almost too much to bear. When Senara had finished the introduction, and re-joined the crowd, he was more than ready to begin the set. As the first number began, he attacked the noisy guitar riff with extra venom. No; there would be no love songs tonight.

* * *

Senara leant against the bar, and watched as the band performed, grateful for not having to talk to anyone for a while. Her evening had been sullied not only by Grady's appearance, but by Astrid's hostile behaviour, and she perversely found some peace in the loud music. She had messaged Brian again, worried that he had been unable to find the venue, and suggested she meet him somewhere nearby. But so far, there had been no reply. She could not understand why he had not come, when he had promised her that he would; had said he was looking forward to it; that he could not wait.

It's your big day, he had said, by text. *Why would I let you down?*

Something must have come up, she reasoned. But she was disappointed all the same.

She saw, in another part of the room, that Grady appeared to have given up on Malory and latched on to Daisy instead. It gave her some small, wicked pleasure to note that if Astrid had been requested to spy and report back to Pepper, that this time, she, Senara, could not be accused as trespasser, and only Grady's behaviour, not to mention his presence, considered suspect. Yet she worried for Daisy. Someone should warn her.

Her eyes found Kit and Astrid, enjoying the band. She watched Astrid smile happily into his face, as Kit put his arm around her shoulder. There was no way she could reveal anything, least of all to Kit. She already had a reputation, and to expose Astrid's false behaviour would only make Senara appear a troublemaker, or even a liar. She tried to focus on the success of the party, and the promise of the life to come; she must not let her mood sink any further.

She noticed that towards the end of the set, Jago appeared distracted by something outside. He kept turning to face the window, as he continued playing. It might have appeared some sort of rock-star affectation, but Senara began to suspect the reason. Sure enough, as soon as the set was over, and Cosmic could be prised away, Jago took the mic and made an announcement.

'Hey everybody,' he said. 'I don't want to spoil the party or anything, but some of you might wanna know....The Boiler's working.'

After a second of digesting this information, Kit, Eden, Gabe and Salima all rushed to join Jago at the window, where they checked out the waves, and appeared to have a brief but highly serious discussion about this news. Then they all turned and hurried to the back of the venue, where the surf room was; Jago hastily downing his guitar. Only Kit stopped quickly by the microphone this time, and confirmed: 'He's right, it's on...', before rushing to join the other surfers.

'You coming, Snow?' he said as he passed her by.

He did not stop long enough to see Senara's uncertain expression, or indeed Astrid's glare of disapproval. Senara wavered. She had no desire to stoke Astrid's dislike of her. But the thought of a surf right now suddenly felt like the best cure in the world for her malaise.

Malory approached her.

'Go on,' she said. 'I'll help Teddy take care of things here. We'll be shutting up soon, anyway.'

Something inside Senara snapped. She had been nothing but nice to Astrid, but being nice had got her precisely nowhere in life. It never had. She suddenly remembered Pepper telling her, on more than one occasion, that she was 'too nice.' Senara had never really understood what that meant, but right now, the need for rebellion was stirring in her.

'Fuck it,' she said, and ran to the surf room, where the others were already getting changed.

The rest of the party watched in amusement through the glass panels, as the surfers, without reserve, quickly changed into wetsuits, and selected boards.

A few minutes later, Malory watched from the window with a collection of interested guests, as the small band of surfers ran excitedly across the sand towards the waves. She thought they probably had about an hour before sunset, but already the sky was being painted in red and pink and gold, with drifting purple clouds. It was a fitting end, she thought, to the opening of The Secret Spot. She only hoped that the pleasure was not to be short-lived, and that Olly would not have his way with the building.

But it was another source of distress that saddened her heart, and diminished the success of the launch party. As she saw him take off on his first wave, Malory conceded that despite their close association, Jago had successfully, and deliberately, managed to avoid her all night.

CHAPTER 36

Boat Trip

'Please, Malory,' Senara beseeched over the phone. 'You have to come. I need you there. I need some back-up.'

'I sprained my wrist a couple of days ago,' Malory explained. 'It's still quite painful.'

'Sorry about that,' said Senara. 'But you don't need your wrist to sit on a boat.'

'Thanks for the concern,' said Malory, drily. 'But what about the café? You've barely just opened, and you're already taking time off?'

'It's one day, and Teddy can handle it,' said Senara. The Secret Spot had begun to build a steady trade in the relaxed atmosphere that Senara had imagined. 'I wouldn't even go, but it's Kit. How can I say no, especially after all the help he's given us?'

Malory sighed. It was Kit's birthday, and he had organised a boat trip on the old lifeboat to celebrate. They had both been invited, but Malory had declined because of her work commitments. Senara had not done the same, but was nervous about Astrid.

'Are you sure you're not imagining things?' said Malory. 'I can't believe she would be that weird with you on purpose.'

'Maybe,' Senara faltered. 'But what if I'm right? Please don't make me go alone.'

'Who else is going?' asked Malory.

'Gabe and Salima I think, maybe Eden. But they're more Kit's friends than mine. Please come, Malory. It'll be great.

Apart from the Astrid thing. The weather is going to be beautiful today.'

Malory rolled her eyes in exasperation. 'I'll have to check if Giovanna can cover at the shop...'

'Thank you!' cried Senara. 'I knew you wouldn't let me down.'

A short while later, Malory found herself walking along Smeaton's Pier dressed in shorts and a vest on top of a bikini, as Senara had advised. In her rucksack she had packed sunscreen, sunglasses and a hoody, in case the weather report proved unreliable. Her feet were water-ready in flip-flops, and Malory smiled to herself at the complete change in her everyday wardrobe. She waved at Senara who was waiting for her at the end of the pier with Teddy. At her feet was a large dry-bag full of supplies.

'I thought Teddy was running the café?' said Malory, after she'd greeted them hello.

'Oops,' said Senara. 'I forgot Kit had invited him too. But Charlie and the other staff know what they're doing, I trust them.'

'*Lots* of back-up, then,' said Malory, raising a cynical eyebrow.

'You too?' said Teddy.

Malory nodded.

'What *are* you on about?' said Senara craftily, and linking arms with them both. 'I'm just glad I have two of my best friends here today.'

'I'm not stupid,' said Teddy. 'I see what you're up to.'

'I don't know what you mean,' said Senara.

'I've seen how she treats you,' said Teddy. 'That Astrid. People forget the barman sees everything.'

'So, I'm not imagining it then!' said Senara. 'That's a relief to know. Seriously guys, I'm very grateful you're both here. I don't think I'd have the confidence otherwise...'

'Are you lot coming or what?' Kit's head and shoulders appeared at the top of the steps leading down to the water.

Senara approached him and bent down to give him a hug.

'Happy birthday, mate,' she said.

The others greeted him in a similar fashion, and then followed him to board the boat. Malory was halfway down the granite steps when her heart lurched. At one end of the boat, the woman called Salima sat chatting with Astrid. And at the other end, locked in conversation with Gabe the American, was not Eden, but Jago. Even as she felt the urge to turn and run, he looked up and met her eyes. Malory read in his squinted expression the same horror that she herself was feeling. But it was too late. He had seen her, and so she would have to endure the ordeal. Cursing Senara, she forced herself down the now seemingly endless stone steps, fumbling against the wet granite wall with her bandaged hand. Finally, she reached Kit, who helped her on to the rocking boat.

'What happened to your wrist?' he asked.

'Oh, plain idiocy,' said Malory, aware of the others listening. 'I was trying to shift some stock in the storeroom. Imagined myself to be stronger than I am.'

'Well, it's good to see you,' said Kit, kindly. 'Hope you're not in too much pain.'

When they were all safely on board, Kit addressed the gathering.

'Thank you all for coming, it means a lot,' he said. 'Zack couldn't make it, so he owes me a couple of pints in The Barque later. Dan, as we all know, doesn't like the water, so that'll be another couple of pints.'

'Eden sends her love,' said Salima. 'But she has a surf competition today.'

'Pathetic excuse,' said Kit, with a wink. 'There's barely a wave on the ocean today. But let's all wish her well. I know she'll smash it. And I'm so happy to be sharing this heavenly day with you all.'

'Hear, hear,' said Gabe, who had already started drinking. He raised his bottle of ale towards Kit. 'Let the party begin.'

'Yay!' said Astrid, beaming at the assembled party, for all the world as though she adored each and every one of them. 'Who wants prosecco?'

As drinks were passed around, Senara declined, saying 'Maybe later.' But Malory, despite the painkiller she had taken earlier, eagerly took the flute of bubbly, hoping it would help anaesthetise the worst of her condition. Teddy went to join Gabe and Jago in a beer, but Kit abstained, for now. Senara helped him to untie the mooring ropes, and then he took the helm.

The *James Stevens No. 21* slowly turned in the harbour, and then made her way out into the bay. Malory estimated the boat to be perhaps thirty-five feet long, and could easily hold their small party with room to spare.

She sat close to Senara and said quietly: 'You didn't say Jago was coming.'

'Jago?' said Senara, too loudly. 'Of course, Jago was going to come, silly! Does it matter?'

'Of course not,' said Malory quickly. 'I was just surprised, that's all.'

Senara looked at her, suspiciously. 'What's the deal with you and my brother?'

'There's no deal,' said Malory, frantic to keep her composure. 'I just forget he's a friend of Kit's too.'

As the boat rounded The Island, Malory saw the dark caves that were hidden from the coast path, and where smugglers were rumoured to have once stored their illicit trade. She imagined the secret tunnels leading to St Nicholas Chapel, where they might have entered and exited by nightfall.

She saw the bench on the path where Jago had kissed her...

Feeling that she had somehow entered into a dream world, that could not possibly be her own life, she turned away to look out to sea, where a seemingly unending body of water stretched out towards the vast horizon. Kit had been right, there was very little motion that day; the sea was calm and there was virtually no breeze. Even out on the open water, the day felt hot and still.

Malory knew little about Salima, but felt she seemed nice, and confident in the gorgeous yellow bikini that she had already stripped to. She had the same olive skin colouring as Malory, and dark hair; but she wore hers cropped in a boyish, gamine style, that suited her petite stature and build. Astrid appeared to be doing her utmost to befriend her.

'It's such a shame Pepper couldn't come today,' she was saying. 'You'll have to meet her. She surfs too, only she has her hands full with the children at the moment.'

Remembering her duty, Malory turned to Senara, and engaged her in a conversation about the landscape. As they passed beyond Porthmeor Beach, Senara revealed her intricate knowledge of every cliff and headland, and Malory was pleased to realise that she too, now recognised some landmarks, although all looked different from the sea. They passed by River Cove and The Carracks, where seals basked on the rocks, and Pendour and Veor coves near Zennor Head, where the shy mermaids hid from their view.

'Where exactly are we headed?' Malory asked Senara.

'It's a secret spot, further around the coast,' said Senara. 'Not for surfing, although it has been known. It's great for swimming, diving and fishing. It's really beautiful; you'll love it.'

When Salima went to join the men at the other end of the boat, Astrid smiled briefly at Malory and Senara, then said, 'Time to top up the tan, I think.'

She stripped to her bikini, then after a quick slap of sunscreen, lay back on the bench and bathed in the hot sunshine. Sunglasses shielded her eyes, a barrier between herself and the two other women, although she was close enough to hear their conversation.

Malory glanced towards where Salima was chatting with Jago. He looked engaged and at ease, his smile open, warm, and genuine. It occurred to Malory that he might never again be that way with *her*. Her rejection would always mar their friendship. When Salima giggled at something he said, and touched him lightly on the leg, Malory looked away again. She knew, of course, that he would be with other women; that their fleeting entanglement would become an anomaly, a bump in the road of his love life. But right now, trapped on a boat on the ocean, with another woman touching him—*in a stupid yellow bikini*—was unbearable.

Who was this Salima woman anyway? She thought jealously.

When they neared the spot, Kit stopped the engine, leaving the boat drifting on the gently rolling ocean. The plan was to catch fish to cook and eat on the rocks. Sometimes, Kit explained, he would use a cast net, but since they only required a small catch for lunch, he handed out pole fishing lines to those individuals who wanted to give it a try. Gabe, Salima and Jago were all up for it, but Senara of course, refused. Astrid turned over onto her stomach but remained absorbed in a paperback. Malory felt paralysed with indecision. She did not object to giving it a go; it felt churlish not to join in, given it was meant to be a birthday celebration. But the thought of interacting with Jago rooted her in terror; for he might be bitter, and hostile.

But she was happily distracted from these negative thoughts by what happened next. Teddy had stripped off his shirt, revealing a toned, muscular physique. In just his boardshorts, he stood skilfully balanced, on the bow of the boat. Raising himself onto the tips of his toes, he held up his arms, as if summoning his concentration, before performing a perfect dive into the sea. He resurfaced briefly to leisurely applause, before taking a breath and diving once more under the water. He did not come back up.

'Is he okay?' said Malory, leaning over the side of the boat, looking for Teddy.

The others exchanged looks, wondering if they should become concerned. Kit lowered a rope ladder over the side of the boat.

'He's fine,' said Senara. 'He's free diving, that's all. Or to put it another way, showing off. We called him The Dolphin, in Greece, because he's so at home in the water.'

Despite Senara's reassurance, the gathering began to feel uneasy as the seconds went by.

'Senara, are you sure...?' Kit began.

But in the next instant, Teddy returned, breaking the surface of the water in a flurry of foam. He shook the sea from his long hair, then prepared to once again plunge into the shimmering depths. The others attempted to remain nonchalant, as they lazed by their fishing lines, and watched as Teddy's upended feet slipped once more beneath the ocean's expanse. After several dives, Teddy, The Dolphin, emerged triumphant from the deep, with a struggling fish held aloft in his hands. Grinning, he lobbed the fish onto the deck of the boat. Astrid screeched in alarm, as the unfortunate creature flapped on its side.

'Hey man,' called Gabe to Teddy. 'That was radical.'

'It's a sea bass,' said Kit, moving to dispatch the struggling fish. 'I can't believe he caught a sea bass with his bare hands.'

'I told you,' said Senara, grinning. 'Showing off.'

'It's making our few mackerels look a bit lame,' said Jago.

Teddy continued his underwater forage near the rocks, where he plucked mussels from below the tide line, depositing them on a rocky ledge. Senara too, now, stripped to her bikini and dived into the water. Then she turned and called to the others to throw her the dry sack that she had brought with her. She hauled it, swimming through the water, and then climbed up onto the flat stony plateau, where Teddy had piled up the mussels. She opened the sack and removed a stove, a series of stacking billy cans, a few utensils and the food that she had brought, and began to make a makeshift camp.

On the boat, Kit was considering how best to manoeuvre the boat closer to the rocks.

'So, drop anchor here,' said Gabe, somewhat fuelled by beer. 'We can swim across. He turned to the others still on the boat. 'Come on, everyone in,' he called.

Jago and Salima did not need a second request. Malory watched covertly as Jago stripped to his shorts, and dived into the water after Salima, guiltily absorbing his perfect frame, and tanned, tattooed skin. Malory had not thought herself a fan of tattoos; they were clichéd; banal. So, it befuddled her that a silly octopus and other marine doodlings on *his* skin, could be so alluring. Kit threw the swimmers some more bags to take to the rocks. Malory looked at the rope ladder and hesitated. Her wrist was still painful, and she was not sure if she would be able to climb back on board again.

'I think I'll stay on the boat,' said Astrid.

'Really?' said Kit, with a touch of annoyance.

'Yeah, I just want to sunbathe and read my book, if that's okay?' said Astrid.

Kit looked out to where the others were assembling on the rocks. 'You'll miss all the fun,' he said.

'Well, I'm not having that,' said Gabe.

He moved towards Astrid, and before she had time to defend herself, scooped her up in both arms, and threw her struggling and screaming, into the cold water.

She emerged, spluttering and shouting, 'You idiot! My sunglasses! I was wearing sunglasses!'

Malory watched nervously as Astrid, furious and red-faced, made her way to the rocks.

'That was a bit unnecessary,' said Kit to Gabe.

But Gabe was unperturbed. 'It was totally necessary. Not having any party-poopers on the trip. Right then,' he said rubbing his hands together in glee, and eyeing up Malory. 'Who's next?'

From the glint in his eye, Malory knew she wouldn't have time to explain the intricacies of her sprained wrist to Gabe. But there was no way she was going to be thrown in, in the same ungainly manner as poor Astrid. She stood up and quickly removed the shorts and vest. Then, after a warning glare at Gabe, she climbed up onto the side of the tilting boat and, with no time to think about it, jumped. She felt the shock of the cold water after being in the hot sunshine so long, but when she began to swim, it immediately felt warmer. She stroked her way through the salty sea, praying that she would be able to climb up the rocks when she reached them. She found a spot, and, with her support bandage now wet, began to haul herself up on hands and knees, wincing at the pain in her wrist. At the last part, an outstretched hand came to help her. It was Senara.

She thanked her, and then looked around at the others. Jago and Salima lounged on the flat stones, drying in the sunshine. Teddy had miraculously retrieved Astrid's sunglasses before they sank forever in the briny, and so she looked a little appeased. Senara already had a pot of sea-water boiling on the stove. Malory tried not to be ungrateful that it was Senara who had helped her, and not Jago, who appeared for all the world not to care, or even have noticed her predicament.

She looked back to the boat, where Kit and Gabe seemed to be having a discussion. Kit was pointing to an overhanging ridge of rock. Senara stood shielding her eyes against the sun, and seemingly trying to ascertain what their plan was.

'I think Kit's going to bring the boat over nearby under that overhang,' she said, with confidence. 'They'll be able to unload the rest of the gear onto it, and we can carry it down.

It transpired that Senara had in fact, read Kit's mind. He steered the boat towards the overhang, and dropped the anchor. It would be easy to reach up and deposit the remaining beers, picnic blankets, and Kit's acoustic guitar. It meant a tricky climb up another, narrower ledge, for the others to retrieve the items, and again, Malory hesitated because of her injury. When they were satisfied the boat was secure, Kit and Gabe finally swam the new distance to join the others on the rocks.

'Dickhead,' said Astrid to Gabe, who merely shrugged, unapologetically.

'Gotta get with the vibe, Babe,' he said.

Malory did not approve of Gabe's bullying tactics, but she did wonder that Astrid had truly intended to stay on the boat. It was her boyfriend's birthday, after all. But all acrimony was soon forgotten, as the drinks were passed around once more, and the group fell into an easy camaraderie. Kit and Jago cleaned and gutted the fish, and Teddy washed the mussels. While the fish were cooking on a portable barbeque, Senara cooked potatoes in a lidded pot, in a shallow combination of sea water, olive oil, fresh lemon juice and oregano. When they were done, half-boiled, half-roasted; she blanched some samphire then dressed it in butter. Finally, Teddy cooked the mussels in a simple garlic and shallot broth, with a hefty slug of white wine. Senara unpacked the cheese, watercress and sunflower seed quiche she had made early that morning.

Astrid had brought a birthday cake and lots more prosecco. When the feast was ready, she held up her drink and announced a toast. 'To Kit, my lovely boyfriend. Despite your taste in friends…'

Malory glanced at Senara, before realising that Astrid had meant the gibe for Gabe, whom she was glaring at, with a sardonic grin. Yet Senara looked a little shaken, all the same.

They all laughed, somewhat nervously, and joined in with birthday wishes. After they had eaten and cleared away the debris of the meal, Kit picked up his guitar, and finally succumbed to a beer. He sang folk songs; some old, some of his own composition. Malory lay back on the hot rock and closed her eyes. Kit's voice was perfectly attuned to the genre; there was a slight rasp to it that suggested rugged mariners who had witnessed sea monsters, and other strange things from the deep. Still slightly feeling the movement of the boat, Malory imagined that she was alone on a wooden raft drifting out to sea, and away from the others.

Opening her eyes, she sat up again, shielding her sight from the dazzling sunlight with her hand. For a second Malory almost believed that she had awoken in the Mediterranean. The dazzling blue sea and barren rocks transported her to another life, when all too briefly, she had gone roaming. Or perhaps she had leapt into a secret island cove in the Bay of Naples, sometime in the mid twentieth century, where the wealthy and carefree would while away the summer in a bohemian paradise. She imagined Daphne sitting on a nearby rock, dreaming of Monte Carlo, and the stirrings of Rebecca beginning to form in her mind. It was idyllic. But despite the beauty and splendour, despite the company of friends, Malory had the jarring sensation that all was not right. There was a thorn in her soul that cast the entire scene askant.

Shaking off these feelings, she turned to speak to Senara.

'It's so hot,' she said, with a laugh, whilst simultaneously wondering why people rarely spoke their minds; never revealed the complex thoughts that truly occupied them.

'Yep,' said Senara. 'I'm going back in the water. Coming?'

Malory paused. She had managed to climb up the rocks before, with a little help. And the water did look so enticing... But there was something in her make up that held her back; something that made her afraid of looking foolish.

'I'm up for it,' said Kit, getting up.

'Me too,' said Jago.

Malory saw that Salima also got up, and stretched her limbs. Immediately Malory became angry with herself. She did not want to be like Astrid, who was only interested in sunbathing, and reading her book. She did not want to be that prissy girl who was afraid of adventure; of breaking a nail or getting her hair wet. She stood up and followed the others. They made their way to another part of the plateau that was high enough to jump or dive from. There was a cave at the base of the cliff, and the rocks jutting out to sea opposite formed a rugged sea wall for a small pool of crystalline green water.

Senara was first to jump, followed by Kit and Salima. Malory found herself alone for the first time with Jago, as the others hollered and frolicked in delight in the water below. She knew she had to speak; to try to break the tension between them.

'It's so beautiful here,' she said. 'If you made a painting, and coloured the sea that blue, no one would believe it. It would look fake.' She glanced at him, in hope.

He looked at her for a second and then said. 'Depends how you go about it. But every painting looks different anyway, depending on the artist. If each of us made a painting right here and now, no two would look the same. It has to come from you… Or rather, go *through* you…if you know what I mean?'

'I think so,' said Malory, grateful that he was at least talking to her. 'It's all about perception. It's like, how do I know that what you call blue is the same as what I call blue? It's just a name given to what we're seeing, but there's no way of knowing if we see the same thing.'

'Exactly,' said Jago.

'So… How would you approach it?' she asked. 'What paint colours would you use to describe it?'

Jago looked down at her through scrunched eyes, and then said: 'Well…I suppose I might incorporate veridian and aqua greens; maybe some ultramarine violet, and pale gold sparkles. But let's face it…' The edges of his lips curled. '…It's just *blue*, isn't it?' He held out an arm to indicate the expanse of cerulean ocean. 'It's just one great big slab of blue.'

He laughed, and Malory's heart leapt.

'I mean, look at it,' he said, grinning. 'It's just so…fuckin' *blue!*'

The laughter escaped her, spluttering, spontaneous; and suddenly, the sun came out for Malory. Despite the intense heat of the day, the world had been awry, and there were dark shadows beneath the rocks that had threatened to creep over her. But now, everything slotted magically back into place. Back in the picnic area, she saw Salima climb out of the water, go towards Gabe, and plant a kiss on his lips. She looked back at Jago and saw the merriment in his eyes, a look that she had missed; had pined for the return of. Laughing with him, she turned and looked out to sea again; the sea that was so fuckin' blue...

Then, with her heart aglow, she leapt off the rocks into the glimmering water below. She swam, luxuriating in the joy of the moment. Everything was right in the world again, because she knew now, that he had forgiven her.

* * *

Senara swam through the clear aquamarine water of the rock pool, into the cave at the foot of the cliff. Turning, she saw that Kit had followed. His wet hair looked even longer trailing down his back, as he parted the water with long graceful strokes. He stopped when he reached her, a beatific smile on his face.

'Isn't this great?' he said, as they trod water in the flickering light and shade of the cave.

'Amazing,' said Senara. 'It's been a long time since we did something like this.'

They fell silent for a moment, as their bodies lifted and fell on the cool, undulating water, each taking in the beauty of their surroundings.

'That was some surf last week,' said Kit. 'At The Boiler. Good to see you out the back again.'

'Yeah,' said Senara. 'I needed it. What with all the stress of opening the café.'

'What happened to that guy?' said Kit. 'The normal guy. I thought he was supposed to come?'

'You've *got* to stop calling him that,' said Senara. 'It was all a misunderstanding. He said he got the dates wrong and was double-booked.'

'For what?' said Kit. When Senara didn't answer, he gave her that stern look. 'He didn't say, did he?'

'Does it matter?' said Senara. 'I'm hardly going to interrogate him, am I?'

'No...' said Kit, thoughtfully. 'But what's weird is that he didn't offer an excuse. He's barely explained at all.'

'I don't know why you're so against him,' said Senara. 'It's really no big deal.'

'If you say so,' said Kit, unconvincingly.

'Let it go,' said Senara. 'It's your birthday. We're here to have fun.'

She splashed his face with sea water.

'Gonna be like that is it?' said Kit with a wicked grin.

Senara squealed and began to swim away fast, out of the cave. But Kit quickly caught her up, and lunging, dragged her under the water. She came up spluttering, but laughing.

'Okay, I'm sorry; no more,' she begged.

But Kit still had hold of her, and there was an evil glint in his eye. There was no choice but to retaliate. The others in the pool looked on in amusement as Senara leapt out of the water, pushing down on top of Kit's head, in an attempt to submerge him. But Kit kept a firm hold, and took Senara under with him.

'We're too old for this,' said Senara, gasping, when they surfaced again. 'Can we just go back to elegant stuff, like diving and swimming, please?'

Kit nodded, with grace, knowing not to take it too far. He smiled and then turned away from her, swimming underwater. Senara felt an odd comfort in seeing him so happy, and at ease. She wished he wouldn't be so quick to judge Brian, but this was not a day for contention. As she looked around at the other smiling faces, Senara knew that this was a day to enjoy the fleeting pleasures of life; to capture and store the memory of a day well spent in the sun. Pushing all uncomfortable thoughts from her mind, she swam back to the rocks, and climbed up, ready to dive back in again.

* * *

Only later, when it was time to leave, did Malory remember the pain in her wrist, and how she would struggle to get back onto the boat. She voiced her concern to the others.

'Rope ladders are difficult enough to climb as it is,' she said.

'Hey, no worries,' said Gabe. 'We'll get you back on somehow. I'll push and Kit will pull; right Kit?'

Malory looked aghast at the thought of being manhandled up the ladder in a bikini.

'There must be some other way...' she said.

'I have an idea,' said Jago. 'Come with me.'

Malory followed him, picking her way over the rocks towards the overhang. When there was a need to clamber, he took her good hand and helped her up. When they reached the narrow ledge, he walked behind her protectively, as she negotiated the jagged stones underfoot. All the time Malory wondered what his plan was. They reached the precipice and studied the drop to the deck of the swaying boat below.

'What are you going to do?' said Malory. 'Throw me down like baggage?'

'Hmmm,' Jago appeared to contemplate. 'Can you jump?'

'I guess so,' said Malory, frowning in consternation. 'Although the deck may be slippery...'

'Yeah...' agreed Jago. 'If you slip you might damage your wrist more. But it's okay. I'll catch you.'

'Catch me?' said Malory.

But even as she spoke, Jago jumped lithely from the rock onto the deck below. He made it look easy, thought Malory, yet she wavered at the thought of making the leap herself.

'It's fine, I'll catch you,' he said again, and reaching out an arm.

Malory saw that the others had congregated in the water by the rope ladder at the other end of the boat, and were already boarding. She looked down into Jago's morning-blue eyes, and trembled. But there was no time for dithering; for thought, even. She would not be a burden; the one to hold them up, out of fear. She jumped.

As she landed on the deck, she faltered, but Jago caught her in his arms. Malory could feel the strength of his body, and the heat from his skin against hers. She looked up into the blue eyes again and forgot everything else in the world. It was not fear of the jump that had made her tremble, it was this. At that moment she felt it impossible that he could not feel her desire, nor read her mind. It was not just her near-nakedness that made Malory feel exposed, but the sure belief that in that instant, he knew her heart.

'Okay?' he said, still meeting her eyes.

Malory nodded. 'Okay.'

Quickly he released her and moved towards the others. As Kit drew up the anchor, and they settled down for the journey home, Jago sat on the opposite side of the boat to her, and appeared silent and contemplative.

Malory leant her head on her arms against the gunwale, where its shape dipped lowest to the water. Mesmerised, she watched the foam gurgling and swirling as the boat coursed its way through the shimmering sea. It had been an amazing day, in the end; and she was glad that Senara had swayed her. And at the other end of the journey, who knew what joy was yet to come? Even the thought of St Ives filled her heart with love, because for the first time, Malory sensed that it was home. She was going home, to St Ives.

But she knew that she could no longer ignore these other feelings. She did not have the strength to fight them, nor could she bear to hurt Jago again. Something would have to be done. A decision would have to be made.

A decision would have to be made about Sam...

CHAPTER 37

A Kook

Dan stood at the top of the steps that led down to Porthminster Beach from Pedn Olva, and surveyed the pristine stretch of white-gold sand, and idyllic, verdant headlands beyond. The rough stone hurt his bare feet. He tugged at the neck of the too-tight wetsuit he had hired, without first trying-on. It had been an enormous struggle to change into the wetsuit in the car, and now he sweated as the neoprene stretched around his belly. His legs felt like sausage-meat, filled into skins. But since he had agreed to a surf lesson with Eden, it felt wise to get in a little practice at the whole business first.

He had borrowed a bodyboard from one of his nephews to start with. A bribe of chocolate and the loan of an unsuitable computer game had been required to ensure his mission remained secret. He had selected this beach, in particular, since he knew it was unlikely for Kit and the other surfers to hang out here. And sure enough, the occupants appeared to be mostly families enjoying the sunshine. But now as he stood staring at the expanse of water, his confidence rapidly waned.

Concluding that the effort to get into the wetsuit should not be wasted, he bravely made his way down the steps hewn into the rock, trying not to drop the bodyboard as he did. Once he reached the sand, things improved. It really was a beautiful beach, with the sea resplendent and crystal-clear.

Inviting, almost. Near the brink of the shore, he carefully attached the leash to his ankle, as he had seen his surfer friends do oftentimes. It should have made him a little more confident to be connected to a large float, but to be honest, the short leash made it hard to walk properly and carry the board at the same time. Gripping it close to his chest, he hobbled closer to the water's edge. But as he stepped into the lapping foam, he nearly lost faith. It was freezing.

Some children were playing nearby in an inflatable dinghy. Seemingly oblivious to the cold, they wore only boardshorts or swimsuits, exposing glowing, evenly tanned skin. Dan could hardly walk away now after getting all dressed up. He waded bravely onwards, and tried not to wail aloud as the painfully cold seawater embraced his calves. He had made it to thigh-deep when one of the children suddenly jumped from the dinghy, shocking him with a large salty splash.

Dan screamed and gasped. 'Oy! Be careful!' he yelled at the perpetrator.

The boy looked at him for a second in that blank, unfussed way that children did; a mere second being all it took to realise that Dan was no threat, no fun, and generally a loser; before swimming back to his friends, and throwing himself bodily back onto the dinghy.

However, the uninvited initiation had oddly helped. The cold water that seeped inside his wetsuit began to be warmed by his body heat, and his legs already didn't feel so cold. Feeling inspired, Dan bent down to scoop some more, splashing it over his arms and chest in an effort to acclimatise. That was better. Bravely, he strode in deeper, repressing all fear of crabs and weever fish; of sharks and other bitey-things. When he was waist-deep, his board floated reassuringly, and his body began to feel quite toasty in the wetsuit. The sun warmed his face, and he started to think that this wasn't so bad after all. No wonder Kit and Jago liked it so much. It was quite pleasant to be out in the water, surveying the landscape in all its glory. All he had to do now, was 'catch a wave'. He waited, bouncing slightly in the gentle ebb and flow. Oh yes, this was quite fun!

The children had stopped their more boisterous games, and now lay sprawled lazily in the dinghy, observing him curiously.

Bloody nosy little sods, thought Dan.

He moved a bit further away, but the inflatable boat appeared to drift along after him. Its occupants continued to regard him steadily, like inscrutable, malevolent piskies. It was rather unnerving. A fleet of stand-up paddleboarders on a lesson with the surf school glided past him, dipping their paddles smoothly in the sea to manoeuvre. Dan recognised the instructor as Gabe, Eden's American friend. He tried to hide his face but it was too late. Gabe, remarkably, appeared to remember him from the party.

'Hey, Brah,' called Gabe, with the widest of grins. 'Good to see you in the water. You might want to grab a paddle though...'

The group of paddleboarders snickered, but were already, mercifully, sliding away from him. The children in the dinghy were chuckling too now, and slowly, very slowly, the awful truth began to dawn on poor Dan. There was a reason why Kit and Jago rarely surfed at Porthminster. He gazed towards the lighthouse on the smooth horizon, and then back towards the families on the beach; the little children frolicking safely on the shoreline; the group bobbing in the inflatable boat.

There were no waves.

The children in the dinghy paddled it closer to him. One of them leaned over the edge of the boat and rested her chin on one tanned arm. Steadfast eyes appraised Dan.

'Excuse me, Mister,' she said. 'You're supposed to tie it to your wrist.'

'What?' said Dan in irritation.

'Your wrist,' the boatful of children all said together, pointing emphatically to their own arms.

'Bodyboard leashes go on your wrist, not your ankle,' said the bright-eyed girl, with a pleasant smile.

Dan felt himself redden. 'I know that,' he snapped. 'Mind your own business!'

The children all looked at each other, then burst out giggling again. But thankfully, they decided to steer the inflatable away from the weird man.

Mortified, Dan considered his options. He could either do the walk of shame and exit the water mere minutes after entering, in full view of the audience on the beach. Or, he could lark about a bit on his board as if he were trying something new and experimental. Neither option was appealing nor convincing. He looked about, trying to read his surroundings. He thought, or perhaps prayed, that the tide was going out. If he waited, and bounced his way over a bit towards the rocks at Pedn Olva, he should be able to wade across to the harbour beach and exit the sea that way. But it would be a bit of a walk back to the car in a tight wetsuit, and he had no idea if this plan—given that it involved a receding tide—might be life-threatening. Dan thought of the shame and humiliation of having to be rescued by the lifeboat crew, particularly if Zack and Kit happened to be on the shout. With a heavy sigh, Dan folded his arms on the bodyboard and lay his head to rest atop them. He closed his eyes against the dancing glare of sunlight on water, and listened to the ocean sounds of distant voices and the call of birds.

He thought of Eden and how gorgeous she was; how all this effort would be worth it in the end. He was imagining what a fabulous, quirky couple they would make, even as a large seagull fluttered down to settle on the end of his board.

CHAPTER 38

Date Night

At precisely five-thirty in the afternoon, Malory turned the 'open' sign hanging on the back of the door window to 'closed'. She locked up the shop and dashed upstairs to the flat to get ready. Her heart leapt at the thought of seeing Sam again. She wondered what he would make of St Ives, and her new life. He wanted to see the harbour, but she did not arrange to meet at The Barque, for once. After only living in St Ives for a short time, she knew enough to realise that there would be prying eyes, and minds all too willing to speculate on her private life. The Sloop wasn't much safer, to be fair, but she had to draw the line of paranoia somewhere.

He was waiting outside at one of the picnic tables. He stood up to greet her with a hug, and she thought he looked thinner, if still beautiful; exquisite. She had not, until that moment, realised how much she had pined for him, for his company. Everything had changed so much that it felt strange to meet him like this, in a new context. Malory suddenly realised in shock that there had been a hole in her life these past months. A pain so rare that she had had to fill it with new experience. But now they were back together, and that place in her heart became filled again.

* * *

Across the cobbled street near the slipway, Jago looked up after serving a customer and felt a shockwave of emotion pulsate through his body. He felt as though he had been punched in the stomach. He watched as Malory greeted the strange newcomer. The man was somewhat exotic looking. Tall and lean, he towered over Malory as he embraced her with affection. He wore his long dark hair loose, and had the neatly groomed beginnings of a beard. He was dressed in a white cotton tunic, jeans and sandals, and his arms displayed silver bangles; his neck, amulets. His facial bone structure made him impossibly beautiful, so that his aura was both yogi and male model.

He looks like Jesus, though Jago bitterly.

He watched as Malory's face lit up in a way that he had not seen before, and suddenly Jago realised his mistake. The reason why Malory had rejected him was standing right there, in the harbour. He felt a flush of shame that he had not considered a more fitting rival than Olly-down-from-London. But now it all seemed perfectly clear. Why had he thought he was the only suitor for her attention, or at least, the foremost candidate? He watched as Malory and the man linked arms and entered the pub.

Jago had been sure that there had been a spark between himself and Malory. But she had never looked at him the way that she had looked at the stranger. He had foolishly, romantically, thought that they had a special relationship, but it was now clear that Malory had just been fooling around. Yes, she had backtracked, a couple of times, but she had not been honest with him. Her reticence could not have been because of his age, as she had claimed, because this Jesus-guy did not look any older than he was. He turned and began to pack up his barrow. He was done. Done for the day, and done with this.

* * *

It had been a mistake to choose the new Mexican restaurant. Senara had wanted somewhere private, where they would not be overlooked by local eyes, or subject to gossiping mouths. So, she had chosen a small, cosy nook of a place, with intimate booths. But as she ordered her second glass of wine, and the waiter asked once again if she was ready to order, she conceded her blunder. If she had, instead, opted to meet at one of the beach cafés, it would not have appeared so strange, to be supping a glass of wine alone, admiring the view. But who went for a Mexican meal on their own?

She checked her phone again. Still no word from Brian. She should probably message him, but hesitated, reluctant to appear pushy. The date had been Brian's suggestion, to make up for missing the Secret Spot party. Yet there was a chance that he had forgotten all about it. Or perhaps he was stuck in traffic and unable to call?

Eventually, after taking a large glug of wine, she tapped out the message: *Still coming?*

She knew she should probably add a 'smiley face', to show that she absolutely wasn't concerned. Senara hated the language of emojis. Smiley-faced was definitely not how she felt, but rather was obliged to feel, and furthermore to express, lest her message be deemed in any way aggressive. She added the stupid happy face and pressed send.

The reply could only have taken a few minutes, but it felt like an age to Senara. It read: *Hi, yes, I should probably make a move soon.*

Senara felt a strange sensation rise up from her heart to sit lodged in her throat, a bilious mix of confusion, fear and shame.

You haven't left? She tapped the reply, appalled to notice that her hands were shaking. *Are you still in Truro?*

Twenty-five-miles-away Truro, Senara calculated. It would take him the best part of an hour to drive to St Ives and park.

Yes, I've been busy with work, came the response.

Senara struggled not to allow the awful feeling to turn to rage: *Are you still coming? We can leave it, if you like?* Once again, she added the happy smiley face.

He did not reply straight away. Senara took another foolhardy drag on the wine, and began to feel flushed. *Keep your head, girl. Don't over-react*, she coached herself.

But he wasn't coming. Somewhere deep in the darkest depths of her heart, she knew he wasn't coming. A part of her soul was aware of the reality of the situation; even if Senara, the young woman physically sitting alone in a Mexican restaurant, the one at the very frontier of her being, refused to acknowledge it. A turmoil of emotions began to swim, unbidden, from the core of her, to become a tumult of recriminations in her mind. This was to be her fate. There was something wrong with her. No wonder Nikos had tired of her. No wonder Grady had chosen Pepper. She could not even maintain the interest of the plainest, most average, and easy-going man.

When the message finally came through, it made her jump. *I'm actually feeling sort of nervous*, Brian replied.

Senara's heart leapt with as much enthusiasm as it had just plummeted. It wasn't her fault! How self-centred of her to assume so. The poor man was just anxious. It was true that he had not appeared skittish when they had first met on the train; but this was different, she supposed. It was a first 'proper' date, and he was feeling intimidated. It was actually quite endearing.

Senara smiled as she tapped her answer: *There's no need to be nervous, it's only me*. This time she meant the emoji.

Again, the minutes passed, before he replied: *I know, but it looks like I'm going to disappoint you again.*

Where was the apology? The voice deep inside questioned. Where was that small word, 'sorry'? Senara quickly repressed the thought; a mean-spirited gibe from an untrustworthy friend.

Ok, no worries, she replied. *I don't want you to feel uncomfortable. Honestly, there's no pressure. But if you change your mind, you know where I am.*

She waited for the silly, self-deprecating response; for the return to good humour that usually characterised their messages. But there was no reply.

With the waiter hovering nearby, Senara reluctantly ordered a plate of nachos, and another glass of wine. He might still come. Was probably just thinking it over. The waiter returned with her drink, and a large platter, heaving with food, which he placed in the centre of the table. Too late, Senara realised that it was a 'sharing plate'. She stared at the gargantuan mound of corn chips, dips, refried beans and cheese. Her first instinct was to protest, but seeing the waiter's cynical eye, she merely nodded in thanks, hoping to ensure his fast departure. Thankfully, her humiliation was somewhat contained by the high backs of the booth, but as she looked around the restaurant, she still observed surreptitious glances from those nearby, and—oh *no*. Sitting on the other side of the room, with his poor unfortunate wife, was Denny. But it was too late, he had spotted her. His eyes lit up in scornful mirth as he only half-hid a smirk behind his hand.

A new fury found her. Why should she not be allowed to sit here in quiet solitude and enjoy some food? She admonished herself for thinking that she had no right to be here; that she should have chosen somewhere more appropriate for a lone woman. A man in a business suit on a nearby table suffered no such ignominy as he guzzled another forkful of burrito. Still churning over her conflicting emotions, she forced herself to eat, determined to act for all the world as though she often got dressed up and went out for nachos alone.

When she could consume no more, she paid; smiling brightly at the waiter's sly enquiry: 'I hope everything was all right?'.

'Perfect,' she replied, and left a generous tip.

It was still daylight when she left the restaurant, which somehow added to her mortification, as if the whole world knew she had made herself look nice for nothing. Rather than return to the poky cellar flat to lick her wounds, she decided she may as well head to The Secret Spot, where she had left Teddy in charge, and see how things were going. As she strolled through the busy streets, she tried not to allow the black cloud to engulf her. After all, she had done nothing wrong. She tried to persuade herself that she had taken the high road; that she had been kind and understanding; noble, even.

But the shadowy spectre of rejection stalked her best endeavour to keep her spirits up. She thought of Brian consumed with panic in his—*she didn't even know where he lived*—Truro home. It would be vanity to assume that this attack of nerves had been brought about by the scale of her formidable beauty and general awesomeness, and by his subsequent intense feelings. And it wasn't as if she were all that attracted to *him*, but rather had formed an affection through their messaging, and had believed a certain character of him. But now she felt insecure. The rug had been pulled from under her, and Senara lay sprawled and bruised in the dirt, with mud on her face.

CHAPTER 39

Surfers

The Secret Spot was fairly busy when Senara arrived, with many customers lingering, awaiting the impending sunset view. A string of pretty globe-shaped light bulbs followed the line of tables, where candles illuminated happy, contented faces. Giovanna and the other waiters danced like bees around flowers, while Charlie was on kitchen duty.

'You're back early,' said Teddy, taking a moment from tending the bar. 'Where is your guy?'

Kit was sitting on a bar stool at the counter cradling a beer, and Senara wilted further at Teddy's indiscretion.

'Oh, he couldn't make it,' she said, breezily. 'Got held up or something.'

Teddy made a 'pfft' sound. 'He stood you up? How rude!'

Senara marched behind the bar and put her apron on. 'I may as well give you a hand in the kitchen, since you're busy. I've only had one drink,' she lied.

'You had a date?' said Kit.

Still with her back to the bar counter, Senara raised her eyes to heaven. It seemed there would be no escape. She turned to face him.

'Sort of. Not really,' she said. 'It was just grabbing a bite at that new Mexican place.'

'And he didn't show?' said Kit, frowning.

'It's no big deal,' murmured Senara, avoiding his gaze by busily wiping the immaculate counter.

'Who was this numbskull?' said Kit.

Senara did not answer, but could keenly feel Kit's mind prowling around her own.

'It was that 'normal guy', wasn't it? I told you I didn't trust him.'

Senara turned to face him in irritation, ignoring Teddy's raised eyebrow and pursed lips. 'It's not like that. He said he felt anxious. That's a thing, you know; social anxiety.'

Kit looked disbelieving. 'Whatever,' he said sardonically, and reached for his beer.

'I told you,' said Senara, in annoyance. 'It's not important.'

Teddy and Kit exchanged glances.

Senara had been about to further scold them, when her phone pinged, and she grabbed it, a little too quickly. But it still wasn't a message from Brian, just an Instagram notification. Instinctively, she clicked on the button and opened the App.

As she stared at the picture before her, she had the strange sensation of sinking, as if she were falling slowly into a gaping pit.

'Wait,' she said aloud, her voice unsteady. 'I don't understand.'

'Are you okay?' said Teddy. 'You've gone quite pale.'

'This post,' she stuttered, transfixed by the Instagram picture. 'It's a picture of the sunset. Overlooking Porthmeor. It's Brian's account.'

She showed them the picture of the sun dipping down behind the rocks at the edge of the headland, the sky alight with orange embers. The caption read: 'A beautiful evening in West Cornwall'.

'Maybe he came after all?' said Senara, frantically. 'Oh no! What if he went to the restaurant and I'd gone? Maybe I should have stayed...'

'No,' snapped Teddy, his features arranged in disgust. 'You cannot be expected to sit there all night. If he came to St Ives, he should have messaged you.'

Senara frowned in contemplation, and then suddenly brightened.

'Oh, I know,' she smiled. 'Silly me. It's probably an old photo. He could have taken it the last time he was here...'

'Let me see,' said Kit, holding his hand out for Senara's phone. Something in his voice made it hard for her to refuse.

Kit looked at the post for a good minute, before he handed the phone back to her.

'Block him,' he said. 'Unfollow and block him on everything.'

'I think that's a bit...' Senara started to mumble.

'Block him,' said Kit again. He stood up and drained the remains of his beer and then promptly left.

Senara turned to protest to Teddy, but found her gaze met by a look of deep sympathy.

'He's right you know,' he said kindly. 'You should block him.'

* * *

Kit burst through the green gate that led to the beach. It had become accustomed to more use of late, but still quivered in response to the harsh treatment. He strode quickly along the length of sand, past the studios and the café and the surf school. When he reached the cliff edge he looked up, and, his worst suspicions confirmed, felt a flood of anger engulf him. He jumped across the small river of water that escaped the rock face in a waterfall. When he reached West Beach, he sprinted nimbly up the series of granite steps to the clifftop car park. Unhesitatingly, he marched straight to where

Senara's 'normal guy' was standing by the barrier overlooking the beach, still snapping pictures with his phone. Brian looked up, and on seeing Kit, instinctively took a step backwards to lean against the side of his car.

He knows why I'm here, thought Kit, observing the man's horrified, panicked expression. 'You look like a man who's been found out,' he said.

Brian emitted a giggly, high-pitched, but smile-free laugh. His eyes flashed with what Kit knew to be fear. 'Can I help you, mate?' he said. 'Weren't you... Weren't you at Olly's party?'

'Leave Senara alone,' said Kit. 'I don't want you to contact her in any way, ever again.'

Brian's expression changed to a dark malevolence. 'Who the hell are you?' he snarled. 'And what's it got to do with you?'

'It doesn't matter who I am,' said Kit. 'Stay away from her, and I don't want to see you around here again.'

Even as a flush of rage crept over Brian's features, and his eyes grew deadened with hatred, curiously, he giggled again.

'Ooh, get you, big tough guy,' he said in a mocking tone. 'And what if I decide to ignore you?'

Brian cried out in alarm as Kit grabbed him by his shirt and slammed him against the side of his car. The shouts and altercation attracted the attention of others in the crowded car park. A number of surfers emerged from nearby vans, to see what the commotion was.

'What are you going to do about it?' said Brian, looking around for help, and seeing many eyes upon them. 'You touch me and I'll sue your ass. There's plenty of witnesses.'

Kit unhanded him, but laughed aloud. 'You'll do what? Sue my ass? What kind of non-American speaks like that?'

'I could sure as hell sue your ass,' said Gabe, emerging from behind the open back door of his van, his wetsuit stripped to the waist and dabbing himself with a towel. 'What's goin' on? This guy bothering you?'

Salima popped her head out of the open roof window of Gabe's van in curiosity. Brian looked around nervously as Gabe and several other surfers formed a semicircle of onlookers around his car.

'Yeah, he's bothering me,' said Kit. 'Been an itch in my side for a while now. He's been gaslighting Senara.' He spoke without removing his eyes from Brian's.

'Well, that sucks,' said Gabe, still drying himself, but slowly taking in Brian with a long gaze of disapproval.

Brian looked in appeal to the other surfers. They were mellow, unthreatening, but mimicked Gabe's expression of repugnance.

He turned again to Kit, now trembling with fury. 'Does she know about this? Senara? I wonder how she'll feel when I tell her you threatened me?'

Kit snorted in disgust, and shook his head in disbelief. Then he took a step closer to Brian again, and fixed him with his eyes. 'But that won't happen, will it? Because I told you not to speak to her again.'

Brian edged his way from Kit's unwavering gaze along the side of the car. Nervously glancing at the other surfers, who one by one, stood aside to let him pass, he reached the other side of the car. With trembling hands, he fumbled with the lock before finally managing to get the door by the driver's seat open. With escape at hand, he turned to scowl at Kit again, his features twisted in ugly hatred.

'This isn't the last of this,' he said. 'You'll regret speaking to me like this. You... *Surfers*,' he looked around in contempt at the tribe before him. 'You all think you're so fucking cool...' He appeared to struggle for words, for a more fitting and devastating condemnation, but instead threw himself into the driver's seat, slamming the door behind him. Quickly starting the engine, he reversed recklessly, making one or two of them jump out of the way.

'Hey,' said Gabe, 'Watch it!'

'Idiot,' said another, banging his palm on the boot of Brian's car.

They watched as the vehicle turned and sped out of the car park.

'Did you all get a good look at him? At the car?' said Kit to his friends. They nodded in response. 'Let me know if you see him hanging around here again.'

'Whoa; relax Warchild...' said Gabe, and they all burst out laughing.

'What's he done exactly?' said one of the surfers. 'Something to do with Senara?'

'He stood her up,' said Kit. 'And not for the first time. Gave her a load of bullshit while he's standing here posting pictures to Insta. He can't ever make a date but shows up unexpectedly at other times. I don't know, there's something really wrong about it. To be honest I can't put my finger on it.'

'I can,' said Salima, from her roof-window perch. 'Classic narcissist behaviour. They draw you in until you're close enough for them to stab you in the heart. Causes confusion and self-doubt.'

The surfers murmured and nodded in agreement.

'How come you know so much?' asked Gabe, frowning at Salima.

'Oh, I'm used to narcissism, darling,' she winked at Gabe, then spoke more seriously. 'But this kind is different. Don't worry Kit, you were right. Senara should run a mile.'

'I'm not sure she'll see it that way,' muttered Kit.

'What's Senara doing with a clown like that anyway?' called one of the other surfers as they each made their way back to their respective vehicles. 'She's far too hot for him.'

Gabe remained standing alongside Kit. Nodding towards the departing surfer, he tilted his eyes towards his friend and said, 'He makes a valid point.'

Kit raised his arms in despair. 'I know, I know. She appears to have developed a low opinion of herself. She has this theory that dating someone dull will—I don't know—avoid heartache or something.'

'Except you never can tell who's really dangerous,' said Salima, thoughtfully.

'That's true,' said Gabe. 'And some of us truly handsome folk are just the sweetest, kindest... What?' he said observing Salima's cynical expression. 'I am *not* a narcissist. I'm not!'

Nevertheless, he turned with his arms raised towards the rest of the car park and called aloud, '...And surfers *are* cool, am I right?'

He was met with cheers and laughter and raised shaka signs from all around. A couple of passing tourists on their way down to West Beach likewise turned and called 'Yay!' with thumbs raised.

Kit chuckled and grinned at Gabe's antics. But then he turned towards the sea as the sun's last rays cast golden ladders across the darkening sea, and felt an unusual discord in his normally unshakeable composure. He had acted hotly, impulsively. But now that it was done, he allowed doubt to slowly permeate his thoughts.

What if he was wrong?

CHAPTER 40

Eden

Dan strode nervously across the beach, tightly clutching the hired foam surfboard under his arm, as it was pummelled about by the wind. He didn't think it was a very cool surfboard, being all bright-yellow and spongey. He remembered Kit telling him that they made them that colour so everyone could spot the kooks in the water, and of foam so that said kooks didn't knock themselves out when they inevitably nose-dived. It all did little to reassure.

He carefully picked his way across the bank of small black stones that had accumulated on the beach, and habitually scanned the shallow puddles left by the tide for the treacherous spikes of the weever fish, which surely lay in wait to meet the tender soles of *his* feet alone. He had heard terrible tales of the ferocity of their sting, and was quite sure that *he* would be the rare victim to develop an anaphylactic shock.

His stomach churned with the sludge of decaying 'butterflies' that had troubled him since the early hours, and he thought he might puke. The thought almost made him turn and run, but Eden had seen him, and was waving from where she stood waiting nearer the water's edge. There was no going back now.

She looked absolutely stunning, he thought, in a sleek black wetsuit that emphasised her perfect curves and toned muscles. She was so much fitter than him—fitter than most of the guys he knew, come to that. Thankfully it was early morning, and there were not many people around to witness his downfall, because Dan knew for sure that he was going to drown in a humiliating manner in front of this gorgeous woman.

The excuse that he had nurtured in his mind unfurled in a blind panic when he was just yards from her.

'Hey, said Eden, with a broad smile. 'You showed up. Kudos.'

'Actually,' said Dan, against the clamour of the waves. 'I'm not sure I can do this, after all. Got a bit of a dicky tummy. Spot of flu coming on, methinks...'

'Oh, don't worry about that,' said Eden. 'You'll forget all about it once you're in the waves. Salt water; it's the cure for everything, you know. And besides, it'll keep you focused. You won't have time to worry about anything else once that wave is coming at you. You'll be in the moment.'

'Very zen,' mumbled Dan. Although he didn't feel very zen, at all.

'Okay, first things first,' said Eden. 'Put your board down and we'll run through the basics; safety and all that. Then we'll work on your pop-up.'

'My what?' Dan could hear himself snap, exposing his nerves.

'Pop-up,' said Eden, unperturbed. 'You have to move quickly to your feet from prone position.'

They sat cross-legged on the beach, as Eden discussed rip currents, tides and wind direction. But Dan could barely hear, his mind still fixated on the ordeal of having to 'pop up'.

'You have to learn to read the ocean,' Eden summarised. 'But that will come with practice. Okay then, pop-ups.'

She lay flat on her belly on her surfboard. 'So, when you see the wave that you're going for, you have to paddle really fast.' She made furious paddling motions with her arms. 'And then, in one swift movement, you've got to bring your feet up under you and adopt the stance. Like this; watch.'

Clutching the rails of her board, Eden quickly drew her legs up and appeared to instantly be standing in a sideways-on manner. She held one arm out before her, and the other raised to the side, as if to counter-balance.

'Okay? Now, you try.'

Nervously, Dan lay down on the foam board. Eden had made it look easy enough. He just had to... Dan could envision the movement in his mind, but somehow his brain could not connect the thought to an action. With great effort, he somehow found himself on his hands and knees, wondering what to do next.

'Okay, well that's half-way,' said Eden. 'Now put one foot forward and ease up.'

The instructions she gave sounded simple enough. They were the sort of movements he had surely been doing all his life, yet had suddenly been rendered impossibly difficult. Somehow, he managed to pull one rubber-clad sausage-leg up under him, and stagger to a standing position.

'Huh. Goofy,' said Eden.

'There's no need to be rude,' grumbled Dan, sulkily.

Eden giggled. 'No, I mean your stance. You're goofy-footed.'

'I am?' Dan stared at his feet in puzzlement and dismay. 'What's wrong with them?'

Eden suppressed her chuckles. 'It's more common for people to put their left leg forward. But you lead with your right. It means you'll be facing the wave on a left.'

'That doesn't sound good,' said Dan, 'I don't think I want to be facing the wave at all. And what's a 'left'?'

Eden's features softened, and Dan noticed the pretty freckles on her nose. 'Hey, let's not worry about that now. Let's just practice your pop-up. You'll need to be quicker. It ought to be a fluid, one-two movement. Try and get your front foot here,' she indicated, pointing. 'And your back foot here, knee slightly bent to adjust your weight and balance. Shape your arms like this,' she showed him, 'as if you're aiming a bow and arrow. And eyes forward. Always look where you are going.'

She jumped down flat onto her board again and indicated that Dan should do the same. For goodness' sake, he had only just got up! Silently, he complied.

'Okay, do it with me this time,' said Eden. Remember; one-two movement. Ready? Go!'

Instantly, Eden was on her feet.

Dan once again lumbered to his knees and then upright.

Not bad, he thought. *Much quicker that time.*

'We're going to need more practice,' said Eden.

Many pop-ups later, Dan was sweating in the tight wetsuit, so that even the thought of actually getting wet began to appeal. He shot Eden a pleading look.

'Maybe that's enough for now,' she said. 'Time to warm up.'

'Warm up?' cried Dan in disbelief.

'Yes. Just a quick jog along the beach, some jumping jacks and knee raises,' said Eden, already jogging on the spot. 'Don't want to be going into the ocean without a warm-up.'

'Are you kidding?' said Dan, panting heavily. 'Trust me, I'm warm.'

Eden stopped jogging, and studied his ruddy features. There was a deflated note in her voice when she spoke. 'Okay. Let's just get in the water.'

She gave him some further instructions about 'getting in', and 'paddling out', then leaving her own board on the sand, safe from the reach of the tide, she called 'Let's go,' and began to run towards the shoreline. Dan loped after her, trying his best to keep up, with his board under his arm again. As he neared the breaking waves, the insistent roar of the sea became louder and the biting wind more intense.

Eden stayed dutifully by his side, as he gingerly waded in, floating his board beside him. The waves that had not looked too alarming from the beach, now appeared to be fast-moving, monstrous towers of seawater. What was he doing? Too late Dan realised the seriousness of the situation, and remembered that he didn't even like the water. Hated it, in fact. Could barely even *swim.*

Eden, on the contrary, looked exhilarated, and had a huge smile on her face.

Doesn't she ever get bored of this? thought Dan, with some hope that this might be the day that Eden recoiled at the chill, and declared they should go for a drink instead. He imagined the two of them cuddled up together by the fire in a country pub, safe from the elements outside. But there was no time to entertain such charming thoughts, as he pushed against the power of the oncoming waves.

'This is far enough,' called Eden when they were waist-deep.

'Are you sure?' asked Dan, as the breakers continued to buffet against him. He gazed longingly towards where some other surfers sat bobbing on their boards further out, seemingly without a care in the world.

'I'm sure,' laughed Eden. 'No green waves until you master the white water, Mister.'

Dan had no idea what she was talking about, but duly followed Eden's instructions to lie prone on the surfboard, while she steadied it for him. Eden continued to shout directions and encouragement; something about the next wave. But Dan could no longer hear. As Eden let go, and the board began to move at great speed beneath him, his mind entered a fatalistic mode. Whatever would be, would be.

He was vaguely aware of Eden yelling at him to pop up, but somehow, he felt much safer clinging to the rails of the surfboard for dear life. He closed his eyes and hoped for the best. It was a bumpy ride, more so than he had expected, and he found himself automatically leaning to steer the direction. The next thing he knew he had washed up on the shore like a piece of driftwood, still gripping fast onto the sides of the board. Weirdly, there was a smile on his face.

Actually, that was quite fun... he thought.

Eden was splashing towards him, through the shallow water.

'Hey, you were supposed to stand up!' she called amiably.

'Just getting the feel of it,' said Dan defensively, as he struggled to his knees. The next wave hit and threatened to suck both man and board out to sea again, but somehow, he managed to withstand, and haul himself clumsily to his feet.

'Come on,' said Eden. 'Straight back out again.'

Dan sighed as he battled his way once more through the incessant breaking waves. It was exhausting, and all so much effort. Yet he felt encouraged by the thrill of the ride. This time, maybe this time, he would actually stand up...

The moment came. Dan paddled into the wave, then clumsily rose to a standing position on the surfboard. For a few seconds he saw the appeal. He was surfing! He was riding the waves... Flying, free as a bird...

The next thing he knew he was eating sand. He gasped for air, recovering from the choking salt water that he had swallowed. His bum hurt where he had landed awkwardly against a hidden rock. His surfboard still drifted on the current, the leash tugging at his ankle. But he was still alive. He had survived what Kit would no doubt call a wipe out, or something. He knew he should jump up and try again. But right at that moment, Dan just wanted to lie there and do nothing. He remained motionless on the shore, his cheek pressed against the clammy cold sand, and dreamt of faraway places.

Eden splashed towards him in concern. 'Are you all right? Did you hit your head? Dan?'

At that moment Dan knew he was wasting his time. All his fantasies about Eden evaporated, and moreover, he didn't care. Damn the stupid list. Who needed a girlfriend anyway, hot or otherwise?

'Yeah, I'm fine,' he drawled, but still remained face down in the sand.

Puzzled, Eden sat down beside him in the shallow, ebbing water. She studied him closely.

Reluctantly, he opened one eye to look up at her.

'You know what, Eden,' he drawled, with a sigh. 'I don't think I have a strong core after all.'

Eden appeared to consider for a second.

'You know what, Dan?' she echoed, patting him affably on the shoulder. 'I think you might be right.'

CHAPTER 41

Slipway

It was a balmy, sultry, Saturday afternoon, and a 'changeover' day for many of the holiday rentals, and so the streets were temporarily less crowded before the new holidaymakers arrived and began to explore. Malory decided to shut the shop and take a stroll to the harbour. She was just going for a walk, she told herself. She couldn't help it if Jago should happen to be there peddling his wares. She could hardly hide from him all her life. But when she did not at first spot him, she could not disguise the pang of disappointment. Yet there he was, near the slipway, leaning against the barrow, smiling cordially at the passing tourists.

She stopped for a second and watched him, observing the effortless charm that appealed to all. Elderly ladies flirted. Little children, she had noticed, remembered him, and implored their parents to 'go and see Jago again'. The parents, eager to befriend such a character and a local, would spend yet more money on his trinkets. *Tat*, she had called it, and cringed now in embarrassment. How high and mighty she must have seemed. And yet he had not been resentful, but had tolerated her snobbery.

Her mood had been lighter of late. Sam's visit had cheered her, and Jago had been kind to her on the boat trip. There was no reason to not be friendly towards him. She waved and approached. But when she was halfway across the cobbled road, she almost hesitated. There was something about his demeanour that felt wrong. But it was too late. Her course was set.

'Hey,' she said nervously as she reached him. 'How's business?'

He stared at her for a moment, his eyes dark and inscrutable.

'It's okay,' he muttered before looking away.

'I…I expect it will pick up later,' Malory stammered. 'When the new hordes are settled in?'

He looked at her again, unsmilingly. 'Maybe.'

Malory felt her skin flush and her heart thump. To be excluded from the charm that was afforded to all and sundry felt a particular dishonour.

'Is something wrong?' she said. 'Are you mad at me?'

Jago turned his back to her and made a fuss of rearranging some jewellery.

'Jago!' said Malory, her voice distraught. 'Please talk to me. Have I offended you somehow? I know you might have been upset with me, but I thought we were past that.'

He spun suddenly, angrily. 'Yes, you've offended me. Yes. You have.'

'What have I done?' said Malory in distress. 'I don't understand…'

He gave her a withering look. 'It's nothing. It's not important. Forget it.'

He turned towards the barrow again.

'But you can't leave it like that!' said Malory. 'If I've upset you in any way then I assure you it was not intentional. Please, tell me what I've done.'

He faced her again, still angry. 'I just don't like being treated like a mug. You weren't truthful with me.'

'Oh, just tell me what the hell you're talking about,' shouted Malory, angry too now.

The other street traders looked up surreptitiously at the commotion. Jago took a step towards Malory.

'You made a fool of me,' he said, lowering his voice. 'You told me you liked me. You *acted* as though you liked me. We had that thing after The Barque, which felt pretty real to me. But the next day you just dismissed me. You could have just said you weren't interested, but you didn't. You implied it was only because of my age. You said you liked me.'

'I do like you,' Malory murmured, stunned by the fierceness of his words.

'No,' he said emphatically. 'You were just stringing me along. I saw you, Malory. I saw you with your new boyfriend, off for a drink.' He waved a hand, ludicrously, towards The Sloop, as if he might conjure evidence of her misdemeanour. 'It's bad enough that you flaunted him right in front of me...'

'*Flaunted?*' said Malory, in confusion.

'Yes, flaunted. Just Malory rubbing it in. You said I was too young. But that guy couldn't have been older than me. If anything, he was younger.'

Malory felt a chill course through her body as the realisation hit her. *Sam*. He had seen her with Sam. How could she have been so indiscreet? She realised in that moment that she should have come clean about Sam from the start.

'Well?' said Jago. 'Have you got nothing to say?'

She stood there, shamefaced, not knowing how to find the words, or where to begin.

'Right,' he said. 'I thought not.'

Without warning Jago turned and marched away from her along the slipway. She watched as he kept walking in a straight line across the sand towards the pier. Instinctively she moved to follow; wanting to run after him; to explain. But she stopped as suddenly. He had left his barrow unattended, laden with all his goods. She couldn't just leave it. She looked at his receding figure again. The tide was out but there was nowhere for him to go, it seemed. Yet his meaning was clear. He just wanted to get away from her. When he reached the shore, he stopped for a while, his head down, contemplating the clear water that lapped at his feet. Then suddenly, without a backwards glance, he walked around the other side of the pier and out of her sight.

'Excuse me,' said a voice. 'Where's Jago?'

Malory turned to see a couple of teenage girls. One of them held one of Jago's bracelets in her hand.

'Erm, he's had to go somewhere,' said Malory. 'Can I help? I'm ah...minding the stall for him.'

The girl looked disappointed but held out a banknote, sulkily.

'I wanted to buy this,' she said.

Malory made a quick scan of the barrow, and realised that Jago was still wearing the bum bag in which he carried his profits and loose change.

'Do you have the right money?' she asked. 'Jago's...gone to get some more change. Unless you want to come back later?'

The girl appeared to consider this option. 'Yeah... Yeah, I'll come back later. When *Jago's* here,' she scowled.

When they had left, Malory wondered how many more customers she might have to turn away. And yet it somehow felt like penance. She must pay for the wrong that she had done, and a steady stream of teenagers lusting after Jago seemed fitting. She rummaged in a drawer in the side of the cart, and finding a notepad and pen, made a notice requesting exact money only, which she placed amongst the goods, held down by a stone from the beach. She even managed to sell a few items, putting the money in the drawer, and making a note in the pad; although how she achieved this was a wonder as she knew she must have looked apprehensive. *Where was he?*

For a sick-making second it occurred to her that he might have carried on his resolute march and wandered straight into the sea. But surely his anger—she could still not believe it to be heartache—was not so great that he would be driven to end it all? Still, she anxiously searched the shoreline where he had disappeared, willing his return, yet equally afraid for his animosity.

As Malory waited like a naughty schoolgirl made to stand in the corner, she thought about the stupidity of her actions. She had told herself that she had wanted to start afresh; that she did not want to bring the baggage of her past life to St Ives; to be judged for her character alone, and without labels. But it had taken this moment for her to realise that it had all been vanity. Sheer, stupid, vanity.

The streets began to fill with newly-arrived tourists, scouting, after a long journey, for a takeaway pasty, or fish and chips and a pint in The Sloop. Out of sheer guilt, Malory increased her efforts to make a few sales, by feebly accosting passers-by; although she clearly did not have Jago's charisma. She had just finished attempting to sell a hat to a hesitant woman by modelling one herself, when she saw him approach from the south along Wharf Road. He had been gone for hours. His gait was no longer forceful, but shuffling, as if in defeat. She imagined that he had walked all around the peninsula, past Bamaluz and around The Island, along Porthmeor and perhaps beyond. She saw him, in her mind's eye, climbing the hill above Clodgy Point, through bracken and brambles, and skipping through muddy streams. He might have come back down into the town by road and eventually into the harbour. She felt her heart lurch when she saw his features were still harsh at the sight of her.

'Why are you still here?' he demanded, without meeting her eyes. He began to aggressively pack away the necklaces, bracelets and rings.

'I couldn't just leave your barrow unattended,' she answered feebly.

'One of the others would have minded it,' he said curtly, indicating the other street sellers. 'I don't need your help. You can go now.'

He eyed her sideways on, briefly settling on the hat that she still wore. She whipped it off quickly, and handed it to him, smoothing down her messed-up hair.

'Jago, please listen,' she pleaded. 'I do owe you an apology. But it's not what you think.'

'Make it quick then,' he said. 'I've got to get going. Got a band rehearsal.' Again, his voice was cold and taut.

So. Quick then, thought Malory. *Just do it. Just say it.*

'Sam—*Samir*—is not... He's not my boyfriend. He's my son.'

Jago stopped studiously packing the jewellery away, and turned to stare at her in apparent shock.

'That's right,' said Malory, appalled at the shake in her voice. 'He's my son. And I'm not twenty-nine Jago, I'm thirty-nine.'

CHAPTER 42

Wave Collapse

A warm breeze from the open door to the roof terrace lifted the sheer voile curtain. Outside, seagulls called, and a glimpse of blue sky heralded another beautiful day in St Ives. Malory sat on the edge of her bed with her head in her hands. Try as she might, she could not stop revisiting the previous day's events; churning over her stupidity, and the terrible decisions that had led her to this place. But most of all she could not shake the look on Jago's face when she had told him the truth. She had held the smallest of hopes that he might not care; that, as before, he would say, 'So what?'.

But instead, he had looked shocked and confused. She could have borne this; it was to be expected. He clearly had had no suspicion until that moment. But his features had softened into something else. Not the carefreeness and good humour that would have been her greatest hope, nor even understanding and sympathy. Instead, Malory read the look on Jago's face as shame and embarrassment.

'I'm sorry,' she had blurted. 'I should have told you before. I don't know why I didn't.'

Then feeling the tears well, she had turned and walked away, still somehow hoping that he might follow; might catch her up and explain that everything was all right. But of course, he didn't.

And now she could do nothing but brood in anguish about how foolish she had been. What had never been a crime in the first place, had become a deceit, and it was all her fault.

Malory knew she looked young for her age; it was often commented on when others realised. But when Jago had made the usual assumption, she had not corrected him.

She wished that she could explain everything to him now. How she had become pregnant young, and felt compelled to marry; how she had forsaken further study, at first to look after her baby, but later because of the pressure to earn an income.

Ash, her ex-husband, had wanted a larger family, but equally, for her to contribute financially. Ash's philosophy was based on a strict, strong, work ethic. Anything that did not resemble progress and prosperity was, in his opinion, shamefully squandering time. In the beginning she had been attracted to these qualities. She had thought him driven, hard-working, and at the time, principled. But it had soon become clear that they were incompatible in other ways.

Malory loved art, music, nature, and travel. Before meeting Ash, she had spent a gap year backpacking around Europe and the Mediterranean, visiting all the major art galleries, and ancient, historic, and archaeological sites.

But such pursuits did not fit in with Ash's requirement for ever-escalating achievement, and more importantly, financial wealth. And so, Malory's interest in the arts was dismissed as 'a waste of time'.

When Ash had found an opening in a friend's company for her—it wasn't as much money as he would have liked, but if she 'worked hard', she could 'move up the ranks',—Malory had initially baulked at the suggestion. She knew nothing about finance or corporate business and cared even less. She had been relatively happy at home with Sam, indulging in the luxury of caring for her own child, whilst secretly plotting a degree in History of Art. When Ash had discovered her university applications, he had been angrier than she had ever seen him. He accused her of selfishness. How were they supposed to raise a family if she did not earn enough money to pay for the childcare costs? Was he supposed to provide for them on his own? His most damning criticism had been that he might never have married her had he known he would be supporting her egoistic fantasies, and not the large family that he hoped for.

Malory had envisaged the fleet of equally-driven offspring, consumed with achievement and gain, and decided that a job might well be the safest place to hide, before maternity was inflicted upon her once more. Without any higher qualifications, she was obliged to take the one open door; the job that Ash's friend had offered. Yet she made sure as Sam grew, that alongside all the school tests and examinations, and his father's demands for excellence, he was allowed to pursue his creative instincts.

Malory had, she realised, used work as a distraction; climbing the corporate ladder, and achieving some success. Even as Ash had become increasingly morose at his perceived failure to produce a large family, Malory had used the pretext of her workload to evade the matter. She suspected that this was the reason—or excuse—for his infidelity; but equally suspected that he would have been unfaithful whatever their personal situation.

And finally, because he had supplied her with a predicament that she could no longer ignore, postpone, or rationalise, she had found her freedom. Sam had added insult to Ash's injury by deciding to study acting at Falmouth. Her son had been there less than a term before Malory, unable to bear the distance, and harbouring a long-held dream of being part of an artistic colony, decided to relocate; to at least be within travelling distance should he need her. Yet it was not Falmouth, but St Ives, with all its long history and romance, that had called to her; St Ives that had sent her signs and signals, and infected her with a yearning that she could not quite explain.

But she had allowed her ego and her vanity to trip her at the first hurdle. She had allowed the attentions of a young man to turn her head from her real responsibilities. It was, in part, the freedom in being able to express herself differently; to start over, and reinvent who she was, that had caused her to omit the finer details of her history. And why indeed should she be defined by age? By motherhood? But equally Malory knew that she had hidden the full truth of who she was because she had been flattered; and because she knew deep within her heart that Jago might not have paid her more than a passing glance, had he known the reality.

It shouldn't change the picture, but it did.

Just as she had covertly, but ultimately denied Ash further children, so she might have done the same to Jago, had their relationship developed. He was at an age when he should be dating his contemporaries, and having the life experiences expected for the young. It had been self-indulgent of her to allow his feelings to endure only to ultimately be disappointed. Her honesty from the start would have put her in a different category, and he would only ever have seen her as an acquaintance.

And yes, it *was* selfish, for she had loved the sensation. The electrifying feeling that had added irresistible flavour to the already exciting experience of her new life. But now everything was askew. Malory felt like an outcast, a poison that had contaminated a previously happy gang. Even her collaboration with Senara, she now perceived as somehow tainted with deception. And she felt all the more keenly the rejection from Judith Crutchley, and the snobbier elements of the art crowd. They had made it perfectly clear. She was not one of them, and she didn't belong.

She flipped open her laptop and went to her emails. There it was; the lure of a safe return to London, and to forget that all this ever happened. To run away and pretend that it had all been an anomaly. But mostly to try to forget the pain in her heart that was unlike any she had experienced before. She had thought that flirting with Jago's attentions was unfair to him, and she was right. But there had been an equal danger to her own heart, an intuition that she had acknowledged, but not responded to with appropriate defence. Her sword should have been drawn, ready to cut down any bloom of danger, and stamp it into the ground. Instead, she had surrendered to passion in a shop doorway.

She answered the email to Max quickly and ruthlessly. She would return to London at the earliest opportunity for the job interview, should it still be open.

CHAPTER 43

Turbulence

The weather had turned, and St Ives was blanketed in a cloud of grey Cornish 'mizzle', a misty rain so fine and vaporous that it felt like walking through a cloud. It came upon you suddenly, so that you might not at first notice that your jumper or hoody had become slowly sodden.

Jago had tidied up the mess of clutter and belongings, and for once, the cellar apartment felt cosy and welcoming, like being deep in the bowels of a boat. Exploiting a moment of solitude, he lay back against the cushions on the sofa and gently strummed an acoustic guitar. The words of the song played in his mind but he could not sing them aloud. They had flowed forth like a spring when he had written the ballad, but now he felt unsure. The world had gone skew-whiff and the song's premise now felt false; its sincerity hollow. He should probably write a new song to express this new feeling, if he could only pin down exactly what that was.

A rapping sound distracted him, and putting the guitar to one side he got up and strolled to open the top half of the stable door. Kit stood outside, damp from the drizzle, but with an expression that Jago instantly recognised.

'Hey Brother, is it on?' he said, although his voice did not sound as enthusiastic as it should have at the prospect of a surf.

'Not yet, but it will be tomorrow,' said Kit. 'Looks like a big swell is coming our way.'

'Cool,' said Jago, although again he could hear the despondence in his own words.

'Are you okay?' said Kit. 'Thought you'd be more excited...'

'Yeah, sure, I'm, um, stoked.' said Jago. 'Come on in, have a brew. You can tell me all about it.'

He unlocked the bottom half of the door and let Kit into the compact space, then moved to put the kettle on the stove. Kit threw himself onto the sofa and picked up the guitar.

'Thought I heard you playing a tune,' he said. 'It sounded good. Something new?' Instinctively he strummed the guitar strings, as if getting a feel for the instrument.

'Yeah,' sighed Jago as he prepared the teapot. 'For what it's worth. Cosmic keeps intercepting my attempts to include it in the set.'

'Sounds like Cosmic,' laughed Kit. 'Are you playing the September Festival?'

'Yep. And the open mic at Driftwood. You?'

'I am.' Kit smiled. 'Maybe *I* should sing your song.' He stopped strumming abruptly and folded his arms on top of the guitar. 'You know, you don't always have to let him have his way. Stand up for yourself.'

'The truth is...' said Jago, '...I'm not sure my heart's in it anymore. And I think the others may feel the same. Josh and Luke, I mean. Tatty will do whatever Cosmic says. But I don't think the others can be bothered to argue, or support me.'

'Sounds like the band's days are numbered to me,' said Kit. 'And you could always do your own thing. Go solo. Or get your own band together.'

'I guess.... But no one wants to be the one to implode it,' said Jago. 'I dunno. Maybe after the festival...'

The rattle of the door opening again disturbed their conversation, and they both looked up as Senara entered the small room. She appeared to hesitate, and her expression cloud over, at the sight of Kit.

'Hey, Snow,' said Kit regardless, and with a wide grin.

'Just in time for tea,' said Jago, reaching for another mug. But when he turned to look at Senara, he knew something was up.

She was staring at Kit with an expression of rare fury.

'What did you do?' she said.

Kit features instantly became subdued. He sat, silently awaiting the inevitable.

Jago's eyes darted between the two of them. Something was definitely up. 'What *did* you do, Kit?'

'I had a message from Brian,' Senara was hardly able to contain her indignation, 'saying he's sadly unfollowing me on social media because some surfer friend of mine bullied him into it. It was you, wasn't it?'

'Look, I can explain...' said Kit.

'How dare you?' cried Senara. 'Brian won't even speak to me now, and I feel terrible. What gives you the right to interfere? You're supposed to be my friend, but how can I trust you if this is how you behave? Hell, I know surfers are territorial, but you only get to do that with waves, not with people. Not with me!'

Both men appeared stunned by the violence of Senara's accusation.

'It's not about territory,' said Kit, looking up at Senara. His countenance, although still uncomfortable, began to reciprocate her anger. 'That's a ridiculous assumption. The guy was gaslighting you.'

Kit stood up, discarding the guitar, and took a step towards Senara. 'I was doing you a favour. You're too... You wouldn't see what he was doing...'

'Too what?' said Senara in a rage. 'Too dumb?'

'Too nice,' said Kit.

'That means the same thing,' Senara fumed. 'Did it ever occur to you that you'd got it wrong? You're always so fucking arrogant. Brian is just shy, and socially anxious. And *you*... You scared him away. How could you? It's just so mean!'

'*Mean?*' said Kit, incredulously.

Jago, who had abandoned the tea, stared helplessly as the shouting continued.

'*Mean?*' said Kit again. 'I was protecting you. You're the arrogant one, Snow. You think this guy is so fucking terrified because he's just *so* ordinary, and you're so fucking beautiful. You think he's shy, because you secretly know that he's not good enough for you. You're like...like some Lady Bountiful throwing out morsels to the peasants. But he doesn't think you're too good for him, Senara, he was just using you to feed his ego; to see how many times you came running.'

It was Senara's turn to recoil from the onslaught. 'Well, aren't you the expert...?'

'You think,' said Kit, unstoppable now, 'that just because you've deemed someone to be 'normal' that they must automatically be a nice guy. Well, that's bullshit. Creeps come in all shapes and sizes. That guy was a super-creep and you should be thanking me for scaring him off.'

Yet again the stable door flew open, this time from the arrival of Teddy, back from his shift.

'What on earth is going on?' he asked, perplexed. 'I could hear you all halfway down the street.'

'It's not me,' said Jago holding his hands up in protest.

'Kit told Brian to back off,' said Senara, turning to Teddy for support. 'He took a gang of mates and confronted him. Practically told him to leave town and never return...'

It appeared that Kit could not resist a snigger. 'Is that what he said? It wasn't a *gang*. I acted alone. Gabe and some of the others just happened to be there.'

Senara glared at Kit. 'You acted like a thug.' She turned to Teddy again. 'Behind my back. Can you believe it?'

Teddy made a shrugging expression. 'Well…'

'What's that supposed to mean?' asked Senara, beginning to redden.

Teddy led Senara to the sofa, and sitting her down beside him, held her hand and looked her in the eyes. 'My dear friend,' he said softly. 'I'm very sorry to have to tell you this, but I think Kit was right.'

'Thank you!' said Kit.

'I'm not saying I approve of the method,' Teddy eyed Kit reproachfully, before returning to Senara. 'But I did not like the way this Brian behaved towards you. You should not allow yourself to be treated in that manner. You should not have such low self-esteem.'

Senara looked as though she might cry. 'I just wanted a nice, ordinary, relationship for once,' she sobbed pitifully. 'And now he's been scared away.' She held her head in her hands and let the tears flow.

Teddy put an arm around her shoulders. 'That's almost the point, my dear,' he said kindly. 'The man who deserves you would not have been scared away, but would have fought for you.'

'Oh, right!' said Senara with venom. 'My knight in fucking shining armour. That's exactly the kind of stupid fairy-tale crap I was trying to avoid.'

The darkening room fell silent at last. Teddy looked concerned, whilst Jago leant against the kitchen counter with a countenance of gloom.

Kit shifted uncomfortably in the confined space. 'I should go. I'm sorry I've upset you, Senara. But I'm not sorry about what I did.'

When Senara did not look up or respond, he turned and left the cottage.

Teddy continued to console Senara, with kind words and sympathy.

Jago took a look around at the encroaching shadows and suddenly felt fully the creeping claustrophobia that he had tried to ignore over the weeks and months, and that had now culminated in this drama being acted out in the small confines of the cottage underbelly. Or perhaps it was the feeling of despondence that had grown since Malory's rejection, compounded by her recent revelation. The others did not seem to pay much attention as he knelt and found a thermos flask from under the kitchen sink and poured the contents of the pot of tea into it. Neither did they appear to notice as he slowly gathered the things he would need from the bedroom, and pack a large rucksack. He flung the bag by the doorway before turning to face the room again. This time Teddy and Senara were looking at him in curiosity.

'I'm...gonna take off for a few days,' said Jago, 'Not far, just need some space.'

Senara leapt up and ran to her brother, as the words tumbled out. 'Oh Jago, no. I'm so sorry! I didn't mean to drive you away. I know it's been difficult sharing with us, and now *this*. It's my fault, I was thoughtless. I was just so mad, and when I saw Kit...'

Jago put a hand on her shoulder. 'It's not you, Honey, honestly. I just need to clear my head. Only for a few days. It's all good, I promise.'

He picked up his things and left, before there could be further argument or persuasion.

At the studio, he picked up the surfboard; his favourite one that he had shaped and painted himself. For a second, he considered hiding out there, where he could work on his paintings, hidden away from the world. But right now, he needed freedom, fresh air, and surf. Carrying the board under one arm and his rucksack on his back, he locked up the studio again and headed towards Porthmeor Beach. Outside Norway Stores, he hesitated. Suspecting that tea would no longer suffice to restore his mood, he dived into the shop to pick up some beers and snacks.

He followed the road until it met the start of the coast path and set off towards Man's Head. Passing the sign that said 'No Camping', he continued further along the path, as it wove its way through the thick summer bracken and wildflowers, until he could no longer hear the sounds of St Ives. Miraculously, just this short distance away from the town, there was no mizzle, and the air was clear and warm. At Clodgy Point he chose a spot to the west of the giant, monolithic stone that had always reminded him of The Sphinx; proudly guarding this ancient land, and all its secrets.

In the gloaming, he unfastened the small two-man tent that was attached to the bottom of his rucksack. When it was set up, he carefully placed the precious surfboard inside, alongside his unfurled sleeping bag. Then sitting cross-legged in the small doorway to the tent, he cracked open a can of beer, and watched from his high perch towards the west, where the sun began to set on the distant horizon of the sea. Below him the waves crashed remorselessly against the cliffs, and above him seabirds wheeled and called. Stars began to appear in the darkening sky, as the sunlight faded.

Breathing deeply now, Jago drank in the cool night air and the beauty of the landscape that surrounded him. This was how he would restore his serenity. Here, immersed in wonder at the Earth, he would find peace. As the sun finally fell from sight, he could swear, just for a second, that he had seen the 'green flash'; that rare, almost fabled, last encore from the departing sun, which the older townsfolk decreed a sign of good fortune.

It was a perfect zen moment. He was in his element: outdoors in nature, surrounded by mystical ingredients and signs, and with the promise of a swell on the way. And yet despite these symbols and reassurances; despite his removal from stress and conflict; Jago somehow could not free his mind from the thought of Malory, and from the look on her face when they had last parted.

CHAPTER 44

Changeover

The temperature had dropped and the mizzle become more persistent. A blustering wind whipped around the corners of the lanes and alleyways. Malory zipped her jacket up further, even as she took off her flip-flops to walk across the harbour sands, weaving around the boats that lay beached in the low tide. There was something mournful about their air of abandonment; something forlorn in the sea-worn paint, rusted anchors and seaweed-strewn mooring ropes, that artfully matched her mood. She wondered what St Ives was like in the winter, when the crowds left and the sky darkened and the sea rose in fearsome gunmetal waves. She wondered now if she would ever know.

She had packed her bag that morning. Her ticket awaited collection at the station. She would email Senara from the train assuring her that everything had been left in order, and that she would still be available at any time to discuss business matters. Until it could be sold, she had given the spare keys to Atlantic Arts to Giovanna, permitting her to open on a part-time basis, when the hours suited her other commitments. To close completely, she knew, would deprive the girl of much needed income. While it was impossible to leave no trace of her foolish experiment, she had at least tidied up the loose ends as much as she was able, for now. Yet she could not resist one last walk around the town. So passionate had been her calling to St Ives that even now, some part of her hoped for a sign; a message that all had not been in vain.

But it was a different St Ives that Malory observed as she wandered the rain-wet streets and sodden beaches. It was Saturday, a changeover day, and the tourist crowds left silently, sullen at the sombre end to their holiday. Those that remained fled to the shops on Fore Street, or steamed up the windows of the cafés, where they ordered cream teas, and stared miserably at the improper weather. Restless children in newly-purchased rain ponchos were herded towards the book shop, their parents muttering encouraging platitudes; or fobbed off with pancakes or chips, under the ever-watchful eyes of the seagulls.

Malory wandered amongst them like a ghost, deep in contemplation. Under her waterproof jacket she wore only shorts and a T-shirt. Her bare legs felt clammy in the rain, but it was a climate they had become accustomed to. Her dark hair, grown long now, was curled into strands by the damp air and twisting wind, and only a beanie hat held it from blowing wildly across her face.

With a heavy heart, she took a last, melancholy walk around The Island. She halted for a moment by the bench where she had sat with Jago, and absorbed the view of the vast Atlantic once more, desperate to commit every detail to memory. The tide was at its lowest, and revealed the treacherous spiky black rocks that had sent ships to their doom. Malory felt that she had never seen it so low, as if the Earth was summoning some powerful energy that would rise up and be unleashed with untold ferocity upon the turning tide. She closed her eyes and tried to repel thoughts of how a beautiful young man had kissed her, right on this spot.

It was not Jago's spirit that she sought to capture, but that of St Ives itself. But it was a foolish endeavour. *His* essence was everywhere. It was in the sky, the rocks and the sea. It was even in the smell of neoprene, which conjured the image of a half-worn wetsuit, and octopus tattoo. When she stood in front of one of Willie's paintings in The Tate, or lost herself in a Peter Lanyon, she could see the spirit of the land that had been inherited by Jago, and reborn in his own artwork. In Barbara's studio and garden, the carved forms with their curves and concavities embodied the waves that he surfed. He was entangled with St Ives, and would forever be part of her memories of the place. She continued along the coast path until the grand sweep of Porthmeor Beach came into view, almost stripped naked of beach tents and body-boarders. With the strange low tide, the prow and boilers of the *Alba* were fully visible.

That'll be working later, thought Malory, allowing herself a small smile at the fact that she knew this thing.

She passed by Pudding Bag Lane. Somewhere down there was a fanciful dream; the fantasy of her own gallery. But she saw no one she knew; no friendly smile that might draw her back to that false existence. Walking through the backstreets, and along The Digey, where she had first felt the touch of magic, Malory told herself that there was no hope. She would not see him. He would not grasp her in his arms and make it all right, and he would not kiss her, ever again.

It did not matter how long she wandered the backstreets or hung around the harbour, for everything was changed. Everywhere she saw unfamiliar faces; morose, in a hurry, and stressed. This was not the St Ives she had arrived into, where the blue waters had glittered in a golden otherworldly light. Now only the scent of sea air stirred the remnants of enchantment in her. Even in the grey skies and the rain, she felt the yearning. For a moment she tried to catch its coattails, but it was too late. It was time to go.

Slowly she made her way back to the flat and finished gathering her belongings. Even now she hoped for a message, or a call, but Jago appeared to have disappeared from the face of the earth. At one thirty, she knew she could wait no longer, or would miss the train. With a heavy heart she left Atlantic Arts and made her lonely way to the station. At the top of the granite steps leading up from The Warren, she paused by the same wall where she had stood long months ago, and once again took in the view of the sandy peninsula. The tide was racing in now, and the wind had picked up. But still, St Ives was an artist's dream.

A dramatic, Payne's Grey sky contrasted beautifully with the ochre, lichened rooftops. Phthalo Green waves charged a Pale Umber beach. Malory felt a spasm of anguish at what she was leaving behind. The little art shop, The Secret Spot, and the dream of more... But an overpowering despondency prevailed. Her sadness at leaving was overcome by the more prevalent conviction that she was unwanted. Judith Crutchley and her art-crowd cronies did not want her. Jago did not want her. And St Ives did not want her.

CHAPTER 45

Cabin Fever

Dan Hosking was feeling distinctly uncomfortable. He was not used to having the privacy of his log cabin invaded. But the bad weather meant no business on the boats that day, and so, having time to kill, he thought he may as well tidy up. He cleared away his dirty clothes, strewn with abandon to the floorspace around the bed, along with the empty beer cans, coke bottles and pizza boxes. He washed the dishes in the small kitchenette area, and even cleaned the surfaces and shower room. Glancing at the plethora of dubious 'lads' magazines', he had a mild panic attack. He had always been of the opinion that a bit of titillation was normal—healthy even—for a virile man; but he was quite sure that Tamsin would not appreciate them one bit. He made the speedy decision that they could be lived without. Stuffing the indelicate material into a bin bag, he hid it outside around the back of the cabin, praying that his nephews, or worse, his mother, would not find it.

Back inside, surveying his filth-free domain, he had the brief sensation of virtue, as though he had reached a milestone in maturity. But there was something not quite right... His mood plummeted at the slow realisation that despite his efforts, and new-found morality, the cabin stank. Too late now to ask his mother to change his bedclothes. Too late to trace the source of that pungent odour. In a fit of desperation, Dan succumbed to the last resort. He opened the window.

Shivering in the draft of cool afternoon wind, he pulled a hoody on, then stood waving his arms frantically, in an attempt to speed the circulation of air. For a second his mind filled with the horror that the pong might actually be him, and he sniffed his underarms warily. *No*, they were fine. *Weren't they?* Then he remembered the popcorn. Hastily, he scuttled to the kitchen area and produced several large bags from the cupboard, only to stare at them blankly. Which would she prefer? Sweet or salty? What if she had only been joking about the popcorn? Would he look foolish for taking it seriously?

Dan sank to sit on the stool at the breakfast bar which separated the kitchen from the living quarters, head in hands. What was wrong with him? Why was he getting all hot and bothered? It was only Tamsin. But maybe he should cancel. Yes, he could still cancel. It was no big deal, after all, and he really did not care for being made to feel this anxious. A loud rap at the door startled him to his senses. What the...? Was she *early?* How rude! How would he be able to cancel now? For a second, Dan considered just sitting quietly. She might go away, and end this ordeal.

'Hiya!' Tamsin's face popped up at the open window. 'Are you going to let me in? It's getting chilly out here.'

'Yeah sure,' said Dan, still cemented to the stool. 'I'll er... Right.'

Forcing his leaden legs to the door, Dan was aghast to discover that his hands shook as he lifted the latch and opened it to the menace that lurked outside.

Tamsin bustled merrily in to his den, laden with bags. Today she wore cropped black trousers and a fitted top in a print of large red roses—*everything she wore seemed to have been made from a pair of curtains,* he mused—and instead of the usual heels, she wore soft black ballet shoes. For once, she had let her dark hair down, and it fell in luxuriant curls over where the cut of her top revealed her shoulders. Except, that is, for where she had clipped it back behind one ear with some silly flower thing—another red rose. Her fringe was fashioned into a sort of quiff that dangled in a funny little curl over one side of her forehead. Dan watched in consternation as—without a 'by your leave', mind—she entered the realm of the kitchen and began unpacking the bags, chatting incessantly.

'Oh, I see you got the popcorn after all,' she said. 'I wasn't sure if you'd remember. Just in case, I brought some other stuff. Nachos, dips. It'll be just like we're at the cinema, and I'm feeling inspired by the new Mexican place in town. I'll make fresh guacamole if you like...' She held up an avocado in each hand. Her nails were painted that bright cherry-red again. 'I brought a baking dish as I wasn't sure if you had one. Oh crikey, you do have an oven, don't you? Ah yes, you do. Great. We can heat the nachos with cheese first and then dollop the dips on top.'

When there was a small pause, Dan felt that it must be his turn to speak. 'I, um, yes. Was just doing the popcorn. Wasn't sure which you'd prefer though. Sweet or salty?'

Tamsin looked him directly in the eye. 'I like them sweet. And... Maybe a *little* salty.'

Dan was boggle-eyed with confusion. *What did she mean?* He had no idea what was going on, because it seemed he had turned into a great big wobbly blancmange.

Chuckling, Tamsin turned and rummaged around in the cupboards, eventually finding a giant salad bowl. Dan registered mild surprise. He owned a *salad* bowl? Who knew?

'This will do,' she said. Ripping open a bag of sweet, and then salty popcorn, she emptied both into the bowl, then shook it to mix them together. 'See? Easy. And what's more...'

Dan watched in fascination as she dived into one of her goody bags and brought out a large packet of Maltesers. She tore it open, emptied the entire contents into the bowl of popcorn, then gave it another shake.

Dan was agog. 'Popcorn with Maltesers?' he said. 'But that's... That's *genius*.'

Tamsin winked. 'I know, right? So anyway. I got some beers; I hope you like the Mexican-style ones. I was on a bit of a roll with the nachos theme...'

Dan's mood brightened somewhat as she hauled the beers from what looked like a cooler bag.

'...but first I thought...' This time Tamsin produced first a bottle of orange liqueur, which she placed on the counter, then a bottle of tequila which she coyly displayed with one hand, along with a fresh lime in the other. '...We could make margaritas?'

Her smile was dazzling; perfect white teeth framed in soft red lips.

'I um, don't think I have any ice...' muttered Dan.

Diving down, Tamsin briefly disappeared to forage in the cooler bag, before popping up again and slamming a bag of ice cubes on the breakfast bar.

'Sorted,' she said.

Twenty minutes and a margarita later, Dan felt profoundly more relaxed. It wasn't *so* bad having his kitchen invaded. And it was really kind of her to bring the beers and whatnot... He watched as Tamsin removed the nachos from the oven and expertly arranged the dips, then brought everything in on a tray.

'So...we just sort of camp out on the bed, is that right?' she queried, surveying Dan's set-up.

He had no sofa or chairs, only the bed which was positioned to best view the large television screen which had been fixed to the back of the breakfast bar.

'Er, yeah,' he said, breezily. 'That's right. Just, you know... Jump on.'

'Okay,' said Tamsin, not waiting for a further invitation. She plonked the tray on the end of the bed and then curled up by one of the pillows, margarita in hand. 'You can put the films on. This is such fun.'

Dan picked up the Marilyn DVD that Tamsin had brought. He would have preferred to watch the scary movie first, before it got dark, but he didn't say so. When it was ready to play, he moved to take his place on the other side of the bed. Those nachos looked so good, and he had a deliciously fuzzy feeling from the cocktail. Perhaps she was right, and this would be fun, after all.

'Just a minute,' he paused by the window and peered out at the grey skies gathering overhead. The glass rattled in its pane as the wind gained in strength. Out there the world was grim and cold and uninviting, but here in Dan's shelter, there was warmth, and blankets, and beer.

'Better shut this,' he said. 'Looks like there's a storm coming...'

CHAPTER 46

The Storm

On Saturday morning, Jago had moved the tent to Carrick Du. It was somewhat impudent to be so flagrantly breaking the rules, but he wanted to keep an eye on Porthmeor and the approaching swell. He pitched it near Man's Head, behind the old shelter so as not to be so immediately visible from the town, but it was still a bit cheeky. Hungry, he had ventured into town, but only far enough to grab a takeaway croissant and bananas; a coffee and some water. Then he had returned to the tent and eaten breakfast overlooking Foxholes.

'Foxholes' was the local name for Clodgy Beach, the not-so-secret surf spot on the other side of the headland. It was difficult to access—especially when carrying a cumbersome surfboard—and involved knowing covert paths through the undergrowth, or scrambling down the rocks from Clodgy Point. But Jago knew this place well. He had grown up jumping with his friends from its craggy edges into the deep high tide water below, and then climbing up the precarious cliff face to do it all again.

The beach itself was rocky, rugged, and considerably treacherous, only revealing pristine sands at low tide. It was reputedly a good break when it was working, but a somewhat mythical one in Jago's experience. He had only surfed it properly once, when the tide was low, and the conditions, it seemed, magically aligned with the stars. Here, on the clifftop, was another perfect spot to watch as the sun set beyond the long tail of rocks that stretched out into the sea from Clodgy

Point, or spot dolphins breach on the deep blue expanse of ocean. But today the sky was livid, and a brooding ocean huddled on the outgoing tide, as though conspiring, plotting its coming attack on the shore. But when the onslaught began, Jago intended to be ready. In fact, he had never felt more primed for a rough, difficult surf. He sought the deep purge and restorative effect of the waves to free him from other, troubling emotions.

After breakfast he attempted to distract himself in the tent with a book, accompanied by the sounds of the wind blowing against the sides of the thin material, and the gentle drumming from occasional pockets of mizzle. Later, he left the tent and climbed up onto the rocks at Man's Head. He stood in the wind; watching and waiting for the tide to turn.

At the other end of Porthmeor Beach, The Island and St Nicholas Chapel braced to face the threat of storm with the resilience of years. Jago's thoughts turned to the woman whom he had kissed there not so long ago, with the ocean serenading them on the rocks below; back when it had all felt so natural and somehow inevitable. He wondered how you could be so sure of a thing; be so confident as to how it would unfold; only to have an outcome so warped, and ultimately dashed. With hindsight, he knew he should not have been resistant to the signs, but instead had trusted his instinct and emotions, even in the face of Malory's hesitance. He could have withdrawn from the path at any time; there had been countless opportunities. But now he lived with the knowledge that he suffered from a self-inflicted wound; a disappointment that he had not yet experienced in his young life.

Morosely, he returned his gaze to the sea, grateful for its healing power. Observing closely the way the water was moving, he knew that it was going to be wild, and with the practised skill of a surfer, he replaced his negative feelings with those of excited anticipation.

Later, Jago stood at the shoreline and faced the massive waves. They were not uniform clean lines, but an onslaught of towering walls that rose and fell in angry offshore crosswinds.

So, you want a fight, Mother 'Meor? he said to himself. *Well, I'm ready for you...*

It would be better to wait, he knew, but Jago wanted some action before the crowds arrived. The lifeguards had fielded off the more intrepid—or foolhardy—of the holidaymakers by putting up the black and white flags. However, it would not last. He knew that as soon as word got around, the entire surfing tribe of West Cornwall would show up. But for now, the ocean was his. He spotted a rip, where the fast-moving current—dangerous for the inexperienced swimmer—would help him paddle out. Seconds later, he was in the water, driving his way out back. There was to be no languorous bobbing around on the water between sets, admiring the landscape; the waves were raging, relentless.

It was not long before Jago scored his first ride, speeding along the length of the wave as it broke to the left. When he saw it was about to collapse, he turned and attempted an aerial over the shoulder. The force was such that both he and board went soaring, somersaulting in the air. Time slowed down as he flipped above the stormy seas, knowing that, inevitably, he would soon be plunged into the turbulent chaos below. But Jago didn't care. With practised ease, he arched his back into a beautiful curve, ready to greet the water. For a few precious, time-warped seconds, he was flying. And it was just what he needed.

CHAPTER 47

High Tide

The surfers stood by the barrier in the car park and watched Jago test the waves as the huge swell surged. Senara was the only one who had not changed into a wetsuit, but stood leaning against Gabe's van, quietly thoughtful.

'Looks gnarly,' said Gabe.

'And big,' said Kit.

'It's pumping!' said Eden.

'I'm not sure,' said Salima. 'I don't need that stress in my life.'

'It won't feel stressful once you're out there,' said Eden. 'It's gonna be amazing. Look at the power. We're wasting time.'

'Eden's right,' said Gabe. 'Let's go.'

The surfers headed towards the series of steps that led to the beach. Only Kit hesitated, and then turned to Senara. 'You not coming Snow? Looks epic.'

Senara looked at him sideways, then refocused on the pounding surf. 'I'm going to give it a miss. I'm working later, and I've got things to do.'

Kit's reply was terse. 'Suit yourself.'

He turned and followed the others. The look in his eyes had almost made her relent. She wanted to forgive him. He had until now, always been there for her. He had not judged her over the affair with Grady, and had welcomed her warmly on her return to St Ives. But she was still mad at his interference, and embarrassed too. Tearfully, she had begged Brian for forgiveness, but her pleas had been universally shunned. He refused to engage with her on any level, and her sense of guilt had risen accordingly. But it was Kit. She couldn't hate him, or treat him unkindly, despite his crime. To do so would be to treat him with less generosity than he had her.

Senara watched as he charged across the beach with the others, then as they duck-dived their boards under the seething onslaught of breaking surf. The storm waves were ferocious and unforgiving, and Senara wished she could be out there, cleansing her troubles with salty sea-energy. But she was concerned about Malory's message. It had come as a shock to discover that she intended to return to London; and she wanted to speak to her before she left, to find out more before letting Teddy and the other staff know. Sighing, she put up her hood, and pulling the zip of the cotton jacket further up against the wind, made her way to Fore Street.

At Atlantic Arts she found the door locked and the lights out. Giovanna, she knew, was working at The Secret Spot, so it looked like Malory had shut up shop on a Saturday, in season. It did not bode well. She checked her phone again but there was no reply from Malory to her text message. Senara began to fear the worst; that Malory had indeed closed the shop and returned to London; suddenly, mysteriously, and with scant explanation. She frowned, wondering what could have caused her friend to change course like this.

'Senara?' a man's voice said her name.

She closed her eyes and said a silent prayer: *Not him; not now...*, before turning, reluctantly, to face him.

Grady leaned against the doorway jamb of his shop with a glass of champagne in hand. 'I thought it might be you. Wasn't sure.' he said with that practised, confident smile.

What did he mean, he *thought* it was her? Was she so irrelevant to him now that he failed to recognise her quite completely? Was she so faded in his thoughts and memories that he must do a double take upon seeing her? But instead of the sarcastic words that formed in her mind—*No, it's someone else*—, instead she offered the apology, 'Yeah, it's the hoody.'

'It looks cute on you,' he said, with a grin.

What was that supposed to mean? Senara felt unnerved.

'Come in,' said Grady, 'I'm having an open studio. Have a glass of champagne.'

Senara peered beyond Grady to the studio beyond. There were a handful of people moving around, scrutinising the sculptures that lay strategically placed in artful positions. It did not look like a huge gathering. Senara recalled how she had once been in awe of Grady's work, thinking its complexity too abstruse for her limited artistic knowledge. But now, she allowed herself to see just ugly totems of chalk-white plaster. Her mind strayed beyond this shop-floor room to the one upstairs, which Grady used as a studio; or worse still, to the grim, messy, office that he kept in the cellar. Both were scenes of their affair, and Senara felt sick and tawdry at the idea of returning to them.

'Is Pepper here?' she said.

Grady stood sideways-on as if to let her pass. 'No. She has the children,' he smirked. 'The coast is clear.'

'That's not what I... I didn't mean that,' stammered Senara. 'It doesn't matter. I'm busy anyway.'

'Hey, don't be like that,' said Grady. 'We need to catch up. It's been a while.'

Something in Senara snapped. 'You really have no conscience, do you? *It's been a while?* Is that all you think the problem is? Do you seriously think we can ever be friends? After what happened?'

'Ah, come on,' said Grady. 'That was years ago. And of course, I think we can be friends. Pepper was never this uptight. You just need to be a little more...'

'What?' said Senara, her cheeks burning.

'Discreet,' said Grady, with a grin.

Senara was fuming. That smile that she had once found so seductive was now so clearly insidious, and false.

'What's wrong?' she said. 'Did Daisy turn you down?'

Infuriatingly, Grady just chuckled. 'Don't be jealous Senara. It's not pretty.'

'Jealous?' Despite knowing that she was falling for his deliberate provocation, Senara could not stem her rage. 'I'm not jealous, but I am furious that you had the nerve to show up at my opening party. I don't recall inviting you.'

'In that case I apologise for the intrusion,' said Grady. 'I had no idea that I still had such an effect on you. But we can chat another time. As you can see, I have guests to attend to.'

He made a little fluttering motion with his hand, as if to suggest that she had permission to move along. Further enraged, Senara realised that to do so would appear that she acted on his approval. There was nothing else for it. Senara could no longer maintain a dignified manner.

'Screw you, Grady,' she said, gesturing with her fingers, before turning and walking away; knowing that he would remain unperturbed, and still be grinning at her departing back.

At the harbour, with each push of the high spring tide, the sea was flowing up the slipway and spilling onto the street. The tourists gasped and jumped out of the way. With no particular place to be, Senara made her way around the wharf and along Smeaton's Pier, scattering the Turnstones with her wrathful approach. When she reached the end, she looked down as the high seas boiled and raged below, threatening to engulf the harbour wall. Across the water, she could see the waves boom against The Lambeth Walk, sending high sprays of spume over unsuspecting pedestrians, and showering over the seats by the Arts Club. The sea was wild and unpredictable, and it felt to Senara that her mind and emotions had been made manifest; that they had materialised to cause the water to swell and churn in turmoil. Deliberately, she lowered her hood. She stood by the railings at the end of the pier doused in sea-spray and with her hair lifted by the wind, like a witch summoning all the wrath of the ocean.

In the midst of this unrest, an idea began to brew in her mind. It might not be a wise move, but Senara was beyond caring. She was tired of living under this affliction; this disease of guilt. She needed to explode, to shatter it, once and for all, and cast its fragments to the wind and sea.

CHAPTER 48

Damage

The house was not what she might have envisioned for Grady and Pepper, despite the spectacular views over the beach and towards The Island. It was not a chic, arty, St Ives cottage, or modern, minimalist apartment, but a prosaic bungalow to the west of the town, off Porthmeor Hill. There was a neat front garden to one side, with a small lawn bordered by uniformly planted marigolds. On the driveway was parked a large, practical, family car replete with child seats, sunshades and soft toys.

Pepper was at home, Grady had said, with the children. And she knew, from word of mouth, where they lived. Her intention had been, while Grady was absent, to at least try to make peace with Pepper. But standing in front of their home, Senara felt a flare of misgiving. The timing was bad, for one thing, as she was due at work soon. She should turn around, or just keep walking by, as if, by chance, on a stroll that happened to take her right past Pepper's house.

But then the anger returned, at Grady's insolence. And more than that, Senara was convinced that her cowardice only compounded her feelings of guilt. She had reached the point where to do nothing was causing her more suffering than to act. She made herself approach the door and ring the buzzer. Her heart fluttered at signs of movement inside. But it was too late. The door opened and Pepper stood before her with one small child balanced on her hip.

Once again, Senara was struck by the difference in her appearance. It was as if she were either a different person now, or had somehow previously been in disguise, in the days when they had been friends.

Pepper stared for a second, as if she could not believe her eyes. 'What do *you* want?' she said. She did not sound angry, but cold; deadpan.

Once again Senara doubted the wisdom of her mission. This was their family home. She was unwanted, an intruder. But she and Pepper had once been close. If they could only communicate as they used to, it might clear the air. She had to try.

'I thought we should talk,' said Senara, horrified at the tremble in her voice. 'You haven't returned my messages. I thought perhaps...just on the off chance...you might have a new number?'

Pepper looked at her in disdain, but was distracted by a young voice behind her.

'Mummy, who's that lady? Has she come to play with us?' said Molly, peeping at Senara from behind her mother.

'No, not to play,' said Pepper. 'She wants to see Mummy, that's all.'

'Why can't she play with us?' said Molly. 'She's pretty.'

Senara thought that Pepper might explode with anger. But instead, she said, 'You'd better come in.' She turned and fielded her daughter into a room at one side of the house, leaving Senara to gingerly enter the hallway and shut the door behind her. She could hear Pepper give instructions to Molly to play with Liam for a while, while Mummy spoke to the lady. Too late, Senara realised that she had not thought this through. She had taken Pepper off-guard by invading her home, and put her at the disadvantage of having the children to cope with.

'I'm sorry,' she said, when Pepper re-entered the hallway. 'I can come back when you're less busy... Or we could go for a coffee? I just wanted to break the ice...'

Pepper said nothing but turned and walked into the kitchen at the back of the house, leaving the doors open so that the children were still within earshot. Not knowing what else to do, Senara followed. Pepper took a couple of mugs from a rack and put the kettle on.

'I guess we could have a coffee,' she said. 'But here. I'm not going out with you. I think you've got some nerve coming over. What if Grady was here? Or perhaps that's who you really wanted to see?'

'I don't. Want to see Grady, I mean,' Senara stuttered. 'And I knew he wouldn't be here. I saw him at the shop, having some kind of event. I came to talk to you, Pepper.'

While Senara spoke, Pepper spooned some instant coffee into the mugs, filled them with the hot water, gave a quick stir, and then went to the fridge. She poured the cow's milk into each cup. Perhaps Pepper had forgotten that she was vegetarian, but Senara did not dare ask if she had any soya, or oat milk. Her position was tenuous enough. Reluctantly, she took a sip of the insipid brew that was handed to her, before placing it on the side. Pepper was silent throughout her actions, although had slammed the fridge door with a little more force than necessary.

'Come on then,' said Pepper, cradling her coffee cup as she leaned against the counter. They were not to sit, it seemed. 'Get it off your chest. What have you got to say, more than has already been said?'

Suddenly Senara was lost. What *did* she want to say? It was as if all her theories and meditations on the whole scandal had suddenly flown away, like startled birds.

'That I'm sorry,' she muttered.

'You already said that,' said Pepper. 'Is that all?'

'I just wanted... I hoped to make you understand that it was never my intention to interfere with you and Grady,' Senara blurted. 'I was stupid, and young, and I thought I was in love with him. I thought I had some...prior claim. I know that sounds pathetic, I know it does, but it's genuinely how I felt at the time. I felt that I was already in deep, and I couldn't get out.'

'Is that it?' said Pepper. 'Is that the best excuse you can come up with? That you were in love?'

'I thought so, yes.'

Pepper sipped her coffee, regarding Senara all the while with her brown eyes.

'The point being,' Senara continued, 'I made a mistake. A terrible mistake, and I'm sorry. I wasn't trying to undermine you. I just felt that Grady and I were meant to *be*, at the time. Like it was something too powerful to ignore. But I want to make up, Pepper. I don't want any more bad feeling between us. I wish you would forgive me.'

Pepper carefully placed her coffee cup down, and stood with one hand on the counter and her other on her hip. She looked at Senara with utter contempt.

'You really do believe in all that shit, don't you?' she said.

'What do you mean?' said Senara, nervously.

'All that 'meant to be', bullshit,' said Pepper. 'And now you're begging me for forgiveness because your pathetic little soul can't bear the guilt of the bad thing that you did. Do me a favour...'

'I do feel guilty, it's true,' said Senara, 'Of course I do!'

'You know what Senara, just get over yourself,' said Pepper. 'You think you're the only person in the world who's screwed over a friend? Who's got off with someone else's man? And you're still beating yourself up about it five years later. You just can't admit you're flawed, can you? That you did something crap. Senara has to be perfect, and Senara must be forgiven, because she was *in love...*'

'I was...' said Senara feebly.

'Let me put you out of your misery,' said Pepper. 'You know that day when Grady rode into town and you thought he only had eyes for you?'

'Yes,' said Senara. 'But you said, quite rightly, that you were there too. It was vain of me, I know, but it's what I felt. But I was wrong. You were there too. He was looking at both of us.'

'No, Senara, he was looking at you. Of course, he was. They always looked at you. Grady didn't give me so much as a glance. Even though there wasn't much to tell us apart, at the time. I *saw* him, Senara. I saw the way he looked at you. And I saw you become infatuated as the weeks went by.'

'I don't understand,' said Senara. 'You knew?'

'Yes, I knew,' said Pepper. 'And I waited for you to tell me, but you didn't. You kept your little secret all to yourself.'

Senara felt her cheeks burn, as if enraged, but could still not quite understand what she was hearing. Then something Grady said came back to her...

Pepper was never this uptight, he had said.

Shaking, Senara stumbled to sit, unbidden, on a nearby kitchen chair.

'You knew,' she said quietly. 'You knew we were becoming involved and you deliberately went after him.'

Pepper laughed. 'You left me out of it. And since I wasn't supposed to know, I reckoned that made him fair game. Yes, I deliberately went after Grady. You thought that Princess Senara was the only one who could ever get the guy. It annoyed the hell out of me. But then you always thought you were better than me.'

'That's not true.' said Senara.

'Yes, you did,' said Pepper, wagging her finger aggressively. 'Don't try to deny it. *You* had to be the prettiest one, with your long legs and blonde hair. *You* had to be the best surfer. I was just your dumpy sidekick. I could have forgiven you all that, but not when it came to Kit.'

'What?' said Senara, becoming angry at Pepper's manner. 'What's this got to do with Kit? And you talk about forgiving me for being who I am? Did you *ever* like me?'

Pepper grinned maliciously, but did not answer the question.

'Again, what's it got to do with Kit?' said Senara.

'You knew I liked him,' said Pepper. 'You could have helped. You know, maybe put in a good word; paved the way for me. But no, he was *your* precious friend; your toy. You kept him to yourself, just like everything. You deliberately wound me up by hanging out, just you and him, when you could have invited me. It's not as if you ever wanted him for yourself, you just kept him away from me, like a spoilt child.'

Senara had never seen Pepper so angry. When the affair with Grady had been discovered, she had been icy and distant, only to exacerbate Senara's great anguish. But this was a face she had not seen.

'I think Kit can make his own decisions,' she said coldly. 'He's a grown man.'

'But if you were a friend to me, you would have encouraged him,' said Pepper. 'You never did.'

'So, when you saw I liked Grady you decided to get your own back,' said Senara.

'Yes,' said Pepper, bluntly. 'I did. And you know what? It was easy. Do you know how delicious it was to see you so confused? To see all your romantic dreams crumble? It was hilarious, to be honest.'

'And did you know?' said Senara. 'About the affair? All along?'

Pepper shrugged. 'I suspected. I certainly wasn't surprised. It's exactly what I would expect from him. He's a dog, Senara. That's what made it so funny watching you build your delusions.'

'I don't understand how you can be married to someone like that,' said Senara.

Pepper scoffed. 'And there's the biggest irony. I thought I'd won, finally. But look at this. Look at my life. I'm picking up shit, and ironing, and making baby food. Oh sure, I've got the kids, and they're great. But I also get Grady. So, you win again, it seems.'

'I'm afraid I never saw it as a competition in the first place,' said Senara. 'And truly, I didn't realise you were so hung up on Kit.'

'Well, it doesn't matter anymore,' said Pepper. 'He's with Astrid, now. You won't be able to get your claws into him again.'

'Kit is my *friend*,' said Senara.

'It won't last,' said Pepper. 'Not if I have anything to do with it. Honestly Senara, you are so dumb. Truly naïve. Who do you think got him together with Astrid in the first place? Did you think I was going to wait for you to return and get him back for yourself?'

When Senara looked flummoxed, Pepper continued: 'We set him up, stupid. Grady and I deliberately set him up with Astrid, and he fell for it. Astrid was in on it of course, but Kit just arrogantly thought he'd pulled. He thought it was all down to his good looks and charm, but we dangled her before him like a toy. It was priceless!'

'You seem to enjoy laughing at the expense of your friends,' said Senara.

'Well, there's no harm done,' said Pepper. 'It doesn't really matter how they got together, so long as they're happy, right?'

'No, I suppose not,' Senara said coldly. 'So long as they're happy.'

'And even if they're not, that's life, right?' said Pepper, gesturing to her own environment with one arm. 'Is anyone ever really happy?'

Something inside Senara snapped. 'I can think of some who might be a lot happier without your spiteful interference,' she said.

Pepper laughed. 'Oh, grow up, Senara.'

'You let me suffer for years, all because you were...'

'What?' said Pepper. 'Go on, say it.'

'Jealous,' said Senara quietly. 'You were jealous.'

Pepper looked uncomfortable. 'Typical response. Everyone must be jealous of Senara...'

'No. You were,' said Senara, firmly, but with sadness. 'You wanted me to suffer, and now you want Kit to suffer. I'm surprised you're telling me all this. Why now?'

Pepper shrugged. 'I dunno. Bored, I guess.' She smirked.

'I see,' said Senara. 'You had your fun watching my downfall, but now can't resist letting me know you planned it.'

'I thought you came here to apologise,' said Pepper.

'I did. But I'm fed-up apologising,' said Senara. 'And besides, you're right. You got what you wanted; got what you asked for. Maybe I did too. But Kit doesn't deserve to be manipulated like this.'

'It's a done deal, Sweetheart,' said Pepper, smiling. 'Get used to it.'

Senara stood up, suddenly feeling a strength that had been missing for too long.

'Thanks for the chat. Good to clear a few things up, but I'll be off now.'

She turned and made for the hallway, where she stopped and popped her head around the door of the living room, and smiled. 'Bye Molly, bye Liam!'

'Bye,' the two children chorused in delight.

When she opened the door, the wind blasted her in the face, whipping her hair into a wild dance. Exhilarating, refreshing, it felt like a greeting to Senara; a *welcome-home-at-last*, and a *where-have-you-been?* Turning to face Pepper who had followed her along the hallway, she stood for a second, surveying the mundane interior of the bungalow, before alighting on the other woman's embittered expression. And then she smiled, and shook her head in disbelief that she had been such a fool. And in that moment, Senara forgave herself.

'Goodbye,' she said. 'Tina.'

CHAPTER 49

Marooned

As the train rolled slowly across the Royal Albert Bridge, Malory listened to the rhythmic clicking of the wheels on the track, and felt the emotion claw at her heart. It had felt like years since she had made the journey out to Cornwall, but now as she crossed back over the river into Devon, she felt that time condense. The whole episode would soon become compartmentalised. It would recede, and be filed away in her memory as any other holiday would. It would become a once-time adventure, dreamlike and unreal. It would be over.

The boats far below on the Tamar stirred, restless in the wind. Malory had not anticipated how difficult this symbolic transition would be, but almost as soon as the train departed the Cornish borderland, she felt her dream fade, and her old life, with all its habits and preoccupations flood easily back into every pool of her mind. This. This was reality.

The crowded platform at Plymouth slid into view, a small reminder of the teeming hordes of London. Malory strived to find a positive sentiment, but her melancholy held sway. Soon she would be deep in the heart of a land of striving, competition, and worship of the god 'Economics'; back in a world where people were herded from one must-do expenditure to the next via a series of conditioning rituals. Christmas was followed by Valentine's Day, then Easter, and a de-rigueur summer holiday. And all the while the bills and mortgage, or rent to be paid. On it went in an endless repeating cycle, until all the days and years had been consumed. There could be no more assumption of waking to the sound and smell of the ocean; no expectation of walks across lonely moors, or cliff tops with stunning vistas; only day trips to swarming Brighton or Box Hill.

Malory thought of the day that she had walked to Zennor with Senara. It had been the most memorable of times, and she would try to cement its memory forever. But even so, she had felt set apart; a stranger. Despite her deep connection to the land, and to the past, she had felt a melancholy precognition that it would never be hers, and that she would never belong. Perhaps she had always known, deep down, that she would return to London, and had intuited some psychic message from her future self, urging her not to fall too deep; a warning to ease her pain.

Despite the dark skies, the full extent of the wind was not felt until the train passed through Teignmouth, and the English Channel became visible. It was high tide, and Malory gasped as huge towers of steely-grey waves rose and then thundered against the sea wall ahead, collapsing onto the railway track. The train slowed its pace again to a careful crawl, as if assessing the way for danger. The lack of momentum made the carriages feel more exposed than if they had simply charged along this bold stretch of railway. Watching in awe from her window seat, Malory flinched as the mighty waves crashed onto the southbound line, assuring herself they could not possibly reach this far...

Yet this was no sea spray but the venting of a powerful surge, showing its contempt for this petty wall. Time and again the sea flung increasingly mountainous waves upon the track. They appeared to Malory vengeful, hostile; as if intent on claiming back their right of way.

To her left, imposing and sodden sandstone cliffs threatened to break their bonds of protective netting, and avalanche down onto the lumbering train. Malory began to feel afraid. She knew that the line had been breached before; that the sea had been known to demolish the wall and destroy the tracks. As they approached the first tunnel, Malory just had time to see the reddish spectres of The Parson and Clerk rock stacks, cloaked in a watery shroud of grey gauze, before the seas rose and covered them. As the gigantic wave reared up like a silver wall, Malory held her breath, yet could not help but watch in awe. Time slowed. The wave soared and loomed, until it appeared to be waiting, trying to balance in the air.

It hit the train with a force that left it shuddering on the tracks. Instinctively Malory covered her head with her hands. She could hear people scream, and the sound of breaking glass. And then they were in darkness. For a second, she feared that the wave had taken them into the sea, before reason told her that they were in the tunnel. But there were no lights, and voices around her murmured in consternation. Yet the train appeared to still have the power to move, and so she held her nerve, and did not entertain thoughts of the sea-soaked sandstone that might entomb them.

As soon as the train left the tunnel, another wave drowned them in a heavy blanket of salt water. At least she could see now, but there was still a way to go and more tunnels lay ahead. Feeling somewhat ridiculous, but acting on some essential instinct, Malory began to pack her belongings. As wave after wave pummelled the battered train, she collected those precious items of notebook, pen and phone, and then put her rucksack on the empty seat next to her, ready for whatever action might be required, but praying that none would be. Others in the carriage appeared to follow suit, whilst a few brave young souls stood by the windows enthralled, and cheering on the ever-approaching waves.

'This is wild, man,' said one long-haired surfer-type.

'Awesome!' agreed his friend.

Malory stared from her window, gripped by a strange fascination. They were right. It was sublime. Despite her fear, something inside her was excited by the presence of an immense power, a force that could not be reckoned with. She stared, mesmerised, as the swell advanced with what felt like increasing resolve. Another train passed by on the southbound line, and as the next wave struck, Malory feared that they would be smashed together like the toys of a tempestuous child. But, to her relief, the trains passed intact. Emerging from the darkness of the last tunnel, Malory knew that soon the ordeal would be over; that after Dawlish Warren the line would turn along the River Exe and away from the fury of the sea.

But as they approached the station at Dawlish, the train began to make disturbing noises. It crept ever more slowly along until it stopped, clunking and screeching. The Engine could be heard humming for a while before falling into silence. The passengers were on their feet, murmuring and unsure. What was going on? The train wasn't scheduled to stop at Dawlish. Another wave hit Malory's carriage, rocking it frighteningly.

The loudspeaker crackled, and the guard's voice could be heard in intermittent spasms over the passenger conversations.

'Be quiet!' a man further ahead demanded. When the passengers continued to mutter their grievances, the man raised his voice. 'Shut up, everyone, listen!'

From the little that Malory could make out, they were to move along to the front carriages of the train, where they could alight on the platform at Dawlish. Malory stood up and donned her rucksack, but found herself stuck in the narrow aisle as her fellow passengers reached overhead for bags and clustered in a jam at the end of the carriage, where they attempted to retrieve heavy, overloaded suitcases.

The woman from the seat in front of her turned to Malory and spoke anxiously: 'What do you think is going on? This train isn't supposed to stop here. I have to get to Exeter for my connecting train.'

'I'm sure all will be well,' said Malory, 'if we just follow instructions.'

'But I'll miss my connection to Barnstaple at this rate,' said the woman. 'It's not right! There'd better be a refund for all this.'

Malory smiled, but decided to remain silent.

Gradually, the line of people in the aisle began to shuffle slowly forward, encumbered with their luggage. Malory could hear snippets of conversation; rumours of engine failure, of debris on the line, or more fantastically, that the sea wall had collapsed entirely once more. She watched the woman in front as she struggled to squeeze her enormous suitcase along the passageway. Her eyes lingered on the tight dress and heeled shoes, unsuited for travelling. The woman's hair was lacquered in such a way that it was immovable. Instinctively, Malory brushed aside a stray lock of her own, that had fallen from the loose side-plait that she had woven, absent-mindedly, on the journey, noticing how golden the ends had become.

Eventually she found herself in the first-class carriages at the front of the train, where the doors had been opened and passengers could finally reach the platform at Dawlish. Escaping the oppressive confines of the seemingly stranded train, Malory felt almost grateful for the gusting wind that greeted her. They were corralled into the station car park where the guards instructed that there would be no more trains going direct to London that day, but that there would soon be a replacement bus to take them to Exeter, where they might use their tickets on other services. Malory looked at the discontented faces of the crowd. There were hundreds of people. It could take hours to ferry them all to Exeter by bus. Scanning around, she spotted a taxi-cab rank, but saw that others had had the same idea. Not wishing to wait around for a potentially mythical bus, a small mob rushed to form a queue for the taxis, which very swiftly departed.

As the beating wind continued its assault, Malory looked around and considered her options. She estimated that Exeter was only about twelve miles away. If she could get a cab, she might still catch a train to Paddington before too long. But she could not guarantee a seat, especially given the rest of her fellow travellers would be fighting for a place. As the queue awaiting taxis grew ever longer, it seemed that whichever journey she chose, she was in for a long night of uncertainty. The wind continued to whip against her bare legs, as if forcing her to action; to move, lest she be carried off. She looked down at her feet, and the slippery, wet flip-flops. Still in shorts, she noticed how tanned her legs had become. How different was her attire from all those months ago, when she too, like the woman on the train, had struggled with heels and handbags.

Who was she, this strange woman stuck between worlds? It had been hard enough to force herself thus far; to override her heart and do the best thing; the sensible thing. And so it was excruciating to have her escape suspended; to have to dwell once more on the wisdom of her judgment, and all the associated emotions.

Malory made a decision. She turned and eased herself away from the disgruntled, milling crowd and left the car park via a side entrance. She had never been to Dawlish before, but felt sure it was the sort of seaside town that had hotels. It seemed her flight had been curtailed, for now. She would do better to find a room for the night, and in the morning, embark upon the long journey to London afresh. And so; a lonely, almost barefoot backpacker, she dodged the seawater that surged onto the road from under the railway bridge. Then she made her way uncertainly along the stormy seafront, and into the unknown.

CHAPTER 50

Storm Watchers

The last to leave, Kit and Jago dragged themselves from the water, then together carried their boards to a safe distance on the beach, where they turned and stared back at the ocean. Their expressions were those of the happily stoked, their minds washed clear by salt water. Both of them were still fired up, reluctant to leave, and eager for some small sign that more fun was to be had. But the high tide had rendered the swell an angry shore dump; spectacular, but almost un-surfable.

'Just as well,' said Jago. 'I've got noodle-arms. Don't think I could paddle another stroke.'

'Me too, and I'm ravenous,' said Kit. 'Time to call it a day, alas.'

'Look at that,' said Jago, nodding further along the beach, to where a wetsuit-clad young man strode bravely towards the waves with a bodyboard. 'Do you think he's going in?'

'Looks like it,' said Kit.

'Is he nuts?' said Jago.

'It's Saturday,' said Kit. 'Probably fresh in town, itching to get into the water.'

'Don't do it, mate,' called Jago, although they were too far off, and the wind and sea too deafening.

They watched, along with the wave-watchers in the café, as the man plunged confidently into the rough sea, with all the air of someone who'd done this sort of thing before. And they watched as the surfer was obliterated, lost in the heavy wall of water, before being pounded unceremoniously back into the shallows, and then swallowed once more by the next wave.

'Oooh,' said Kit, wincing.

'That's gotta hurt,' said Jago, grinning lopsidedly.

To his credit, or perhaps conscious of the onlookers in the café, the young man appeared unbroken. He walked, if somewhat less enthusiastically, back into the seething, frothing turbulence.

'I think he's gonna cry,' said Jago.

'It's not worth it, man,' called Kit, grinning, although he too, knew he could not be heard. 'Take the walk of shame. No one will judge you!'

They were still laughing about the kook as they ran up the steps to the car park, where they once more surveyed the waves as they stood by the side of Kit's van.

'I expect he's been here before,' said Jago. 'Caught a few ankle-snappers and thinks he's a surfer.'

'It fails me, though,' said Kit, 'how you can't just use your eyes and see what's going on. Nobody in their right minds would go into that high tide shore dump. Let alone in a storm.'

'Yeah, well, looks like he's seen sense now,' said Jago, staring at the pitiful figure who appeared to have finally given up, and was walking with head downcast towards the far end of the beach, as if to suggest that he might still get in, further along. But more importantly, it would distance him from the eyes of the café.

Kit frowned, and swore. 'Look at that,' he said pointing towards the rocks below Man's Head.

A couple of boys appeared to be watching the storm waves from a ledge, dangerously close to where the waves smashed against the land, sending huge spumes of heavy water, showering over them. The boys appeared to be laughing and daring each other on.

'Idiots,' said Kit.

'Do you think they're local?' said Jago.

'If they are, they should know better,' said Kit. 'We should probably alert the lifeguards...'

'They've gone,' said Jago. 'It's past five-thirty.'

'I'd better...' Kit was interrupted by the sound of his pager, which was on the dashboard of the van. He met Jago's eyes and swore again. 'It's a shout. I have to go.'

Jago had never seen anyone get changed so fast. Unconcerned for propriety, Kit stripped off his wetsuit and pulled on his clothes in seconds, all with one eye on the boys on the rocks.

'Don't worry,' said Jago, on impulse. 'I'll go now, and have a word with them.' He was still camped up on Carrick Du anyhow.

'Okay,' said Kit, patting Jago on the shoulder. 'Go.'

Jago nodded, and immediately ran off in the direction of the coast path that led to the headland. As he bounded up the steps from the car park, he saw Kit's van speed up Porthmeor Hill. His board felt heavy, and his legs weak. He had stayed too long in the water, and his energy was depleted. But using what reserves he could muster, he sprinted along the path until, panting and sweating in the wetsuit, he reached the cliff at Man's Head. At low tide, the rocks were a steep clamber down to the rockpools below, but today the high water immersed all the lower levels, and surged dangerously close to the wet rocks where the two boys were still larking about.

Stopping momentarily to catch his breath, Jago called out to them: 'Oi! You two! Get off the rocks. Now!'

The boys turned, but appeared to ignore him, as if his warning had not been meant for them. Looking out to sea, he felt a shiver of dread as a fresh set of massive waves moved stealthily towards them. Quickly, Jago analysed his options.

He made his way further down the rocks to where the boys played, still gripping his board under one arm, and using the other hand to grasp the slippery cliff face where he could. The rocks were jagged under his bare feet, but he had endured worse to reach remote, promising waves before. When he was closer, he called again, and this time the boys appeared more heeding of his warning.

'Climb up, now!' he yelled. 'It's dangerous. Look!' he said, pointing in alarm at the approaching wave.

The two boys turned to observe, and for the first time appeared to acknowledge their predicament. Both turned immediately to head towards where Jago stood nearby, halfway down the series of footholds that had not seemed so hazardous on their way down. Jago could see the fear in their eyes as one by one, they clambered, hand and foot, up the perilous staircase.

But it was too late. Jago watched in horror as the wave struck. Momentarily blinded, it was all he could do to clutch at the rock with whatever strength he possessed, and wait for it to recede. With his heart racing, he saw that one boy still clung to the rockface, but the other was now in the water, and already being swept away by the current.

'Come on, get up,' shouted Jago, extending his arm to the frightened boy below him.

When the boy grasped, he somehow hauled him up to where he stood and gripped him by the shoulders.

'Run!' said Jago, looking into the boy's shocked face. 'There's no time. Get back up there and run as fast as you can. Tell the first person you see, to call the coastguard. Tell them what's happened. The first person. Do you understand?'

When the terrified boy nodded, Jago released him, and without another thought to wounding his feet, jumped down to the lower rocks, and then, after quickly reattaching the leash of his surfboard, he leapt as far as he could from the cliff into the deep, ominous waves.

CHAPTER 51

Exposed

The instant Jago hit the water he knew things were bad. The current had already carried the boy far from the cliffs, and the same rip would make it difficult, if not impossible to paddle back to the beach. But he couldn't think about that now. The crucial thing, he knew, was to get to the boy. His arms were still leaden from the surf, but he paddled as furiously as he could, using that same current to power the board along. On seeing him, the terrified boy struggled to swim towards Jago. It was to no avail, but at least stopped him from drifting further for a while. And at least he was still moving... But Jago knew the boy's energy would not last; that without a wetsuit the risk of hypothermia was great.

When he finally reached him, the boy lunged desperately, wordlessly, at the surfboard, his eyes wide in panic and fear. Thankfully they were clear of breaking water, but the huge swell rose and fell in fearsome billows, the surfboard no more than a bit of flotsam on its surface. Jago vaguely recalled Kit describing how to rescue someone on a surfboard; something to do with flipping the board twice, but he hadn't really paid attention. He would have to improvise. With one arm, he grasped the boy under his shoulders, and using what little strength he had left, hauled him onto the surfboard in front of him.

'Sit up, like me, like you're riding a horse,' Jago raised his voice to be heard above the wind and waves, and encircled the boy's waist with one arm. 'And don't worry, I've got you.'

Nervously, the boy obeyed. 'What's your name?' said Jago, seeing the abject terror on his face.

For a second, he thought the boy, who looked about ten years old, might not answer; that unconsciousness was setting in.

'Harry,' came the feeble reply.

'Okay! Harry, my name's Jago. Don't worry, we'll get you out of here. Everything will be all right. You just need to keep a hold until help comes.'

'Aren't you going to help me?' wailed the boy. 'I thought you were going to help me!'

Jago looked around anxiously. The storm was not abating, and there was no sign of a lifeboat or helicopter. For a ghastly moment, he worried that the boy's friend had not managed to raise the alarm, or deliver the urgency of the message. That no one had been made aware of the emergency.

'Of course, I'm going to help,' he said. 'Here's what we're going to do, Harry. You're going to cling on really tight, and I'm going to try and paddle us back to shore, okay?'

Harry nodded with more surety.

Jago eyes scanned the dark cliffs at Foxholes, before settling on the rocks beneath Clodgy Point.

'You see those rocks over there?' He pointed. 'I'm going to try and get us there, and then we can climb up over the rocks, okay?'

Jago had no idea if this plan would work, or was even wise, in the circumstances.

Oh well, he thought, a lousy plan was better than no plan. They had drifted too far to paddle back to the safety of Porthmeor, but Jago knew that if they strayed out past Clodgy Point and into the deep of the Celtic Sea, they would be in very serious trouble.

'Lie down flat, on your stomach,' he instructed, 'That's it, move back a bit, we have to get the balance right.' Jago positioned himself at the back of the board between the boy's legs, helping to keep him pinned down. 'That's it, good. Now hold on tight to the rails—that's the sides—and whatever you do, try not to let go.'

Jago began to paddle. 'Have you climbed those rocks before Harry? Harry?'

Again, Jago was afraid that Harry had lost consciousness, but he lifted his head weakly from where he had lain it on the surfboard and muttered, 'Yes.'

'Good boy. So, you know it'll be easy.'

Jago continued to paddle with all the power he could summon, but with the extra burden it was slow progress, and after long minutes, the rocky beach at Foxholes appeared no closer. Frowning he asked the boy: 'Have you ever surfed before, Harry?'

Harry shook his head.

'You've body-boarded though?'

This time he nodded.

'Okay, well I'm going to give you your first surf lesson. Do you think you can paddle, in time with me? We might get to the shore quicker.'

'Okay,' said Harry timidly, but the second he released his grip on the rails the water slipped under his body, causing him to panic. 'I can't, I can't let go!'

'It's okay, I've got you,' said Jago. But it was true that he could not risk the boy being swept away again. Frowning, he thought quickly. He reached down and untied the leash from his ankle and reattached it to Harry's. 'I won't let you go, but just in case I'm going to give you the leash, so that you will still be attached to the board. If you do come off just relax and you'll float back up and can grab the board again. But it won't happen, it's just in case. Now, do you think you can try to paddle again?'

Harry looked close to tears, but nodded, and once again attempted to paddle the surfboard.

'That's it, you're doing it! That's great,' shouted Jago above the blast of wind and waves. 'Remember, in time with me.'

Jago wondered if he should encourage the boy to sing, a distraction to raise moral and help keep time. But again, realised that his knowledge of potential hypothermia victims was close to non-existent. He decided to leave the boy's lungs alone, to commit to the act of breathing. He hoped that if Harry kept moving, he might just keep warm enough, but knew he was equally likely to become exhausted and pass out.

As they continued their bold attempt to reach the shore, Jago tried not to let dark thoughts enter his consciousness. He had to believe that rescue would come; that the lifeboat or coastguard would be there soon. He had to believe that the alarm had been raised. For there were no boats in sight on the stormy sea; no hiker braving the cliff-top winds, who might spot their struggle. They were all alone. He noticed Harry's paddling become weaker, and his head droop nearer to the board. He tried to coax him with words of encouragement, but began to fear that the boy would pass out. A terrible dread crept through Jago's soul, at the damning realisation that he did not know what to do for the best.

Suddenly there was a different noise above his head, as though the howling wind had decided to dance to a powerful, rhythmic beat. Looking up, Jago had never felt so overwhelmed with gratitude to see a helicopter. He stopped paddling and waved frantically, hoping they had spotted them.

'Harry, look; it's the coastguard!' He sat up on the board again, hauling the boy to sit close to him. But Harry's body was limp and barely moving. 'Wake up Harry, you're going to have a ride in a helicopter!'

Harry stirred, and looked up, but Jago could tell that he was struggling to stay conscious. The minutes felt interminably slow as the helicopter found its position and lowered a crew member on a winch. As the man was lifted and lowered between waves, Jago began to despair that he would ever reach them. Harry did not have time on his side. But finally, the boy's weak body was attached to the man's harness. The crewmember barely had time to look into Jago's eyes, but it was long enough to wordlessly ask the question...

'Go!' cried Jago, gesturing emphatically. 'I'll be fine, I'll surf to shore! Get him to hospital.' Harry was in a dire condition, and they should not waste another second.

The winch man nodded and made a thumbs up, before receding up with the exhausted boy to the safety of the helicopter, which then turned and disappeared as quickly as it had manifested.

Only then did Jago's relief return to anxiety. Luckily, he was somehow out of the snatch of the current, and should be able to ride the waves to the rocks. But he was exhausted. The adrenalin that had helped him survive this far, had rapidly dissipated the moment the helicopter had shown up. Now his limbs were heavy with fatigue. If only he hadn't surfed for so long earlier... But there was nothing else for it. He reattached the leash, and forced his aching arms to paddle towards the cliffs.

CHAPTER 52

Wreckage

The call out had been in response to a personal locator beacon; a distress signal that had been received somewhere past the headland at Godrevy, near Hell's Mouth. But Kit and Zack had both arrived too late to man the crew. Instead, they helped with the launch along the slipway into the choppy high tide water, and the Shannon Class All-Weather Lifeboat was soon speeding her way out to sea, the water-propulsion jets moving her powerfully through the turbulent water.

Kit had barely had time to gorge on a chocolate bar from his van when Jeff, the operations manager approached them.

'There's been another communication,' he said. 'An abandoned kayak and oars have been spotted floating off the rocks at Hawkes Point. No sign of anyone in distress, or reports of missing persons, but we should check it out.'

Withing minutes the Inshore Lifeboat was launched with Kit at the helm, and only Zack as crew. It sped, as fast as the storm waves allowed, out of the harbour, in the wake of its big sister. Beyond Porthminster Point they advanced across Carbis Bay and around the Carrack Gladden headland, slowing down as they approached Hawkes Point, and scanning the water for the kayak. They found it, floating upturned in the relatively sheltered seas beyond the headland. It was a one-man craft; a wretched sight, as it rose and fell, without its paddler, on the heaving swell. When they could see no signs of a stranded kayaker on the cliffs, they methodically, intensively, searched the rocky inlets and caves around the point, in case an unwise exploration had led to being cut off by the tide. All the while Kit dreaded the worst. It was something you got used to, over time; even with the best efforts of all, the sea was a cruel adversary, and lives were often claimed. But you never got over the sadness for the tragedy.

When they had exhausted their search, Kit radioed the station.

'It's probable the vessel was left on the beach at low tide,' he said. 'It's been carried off by the incoming water and damaged by the storm.'

'Roger that,' said Jeff. 'There's still no missing person's alert, so report back. It's been a busy afternoon. The coastguard helicopter was scrambled for a search and rescue just off Carrick Du.'

Kit looked at Zack, with a chill in his heart. He had been surfing Porthmeor only an hour ago. He had laughed at the bodyboarder for attempting his high-tide storm surf. But he hadn't considered his actions life-threatening. Yet since that time a search and rescue operation had taken place? Surely no one else had tried to go into that water?

And then he remembered the boys on the rocks. Might it have involved them?

'Was anyone hurt? Do they need assistance?' he said.

'One casualty has been airlifted to hospital for emergency treatment,' said Jeff over the radio. 'There are reports a surfer was involved, but the casualty was a young boy who'd been swept off the rocks.'

Kit's blood ran cold. *Jago*, he thought. He had left Jago to deal with the boys. And to think that he had left the scene for no good reason. He had missed the shout, and the kayak had probably been abandoned by a careless visitor who knew no better.

'We'll go and take a look,' he said. 'Make sure the surfer's okay.'

'Roger,' said Jeff.

They recovered the kayak, then Kit powered up the engine again, and the lifeboat was soon bouncing along through the stormy waves. Time and again, the waves splashed over the deck of the fast-moving lifeboat, threatening to engulf them. They reached the harbour and quickly offloaded the kayak to the hands of the shore crew, before taking off again. They rounded The Island, careful that the formidable waves should not fling them onto the perilous rocks that skirted it; rocks that had claimed the lives of the sailors of the *Alba*, and countless others over time.

Finally, they made it across the expanse of water at Porthmeor, and reached the headland at Carrick Du. Both Kit and Zack scoured the rough seas for signs of anyone in trouble. But they saw no one, and they themselves appeared to be the only ones in any immediate danger.

'Let's check the shoreline, just to be sure,' shouted Kit above the clamour of wind and waves.

Cautiously, they steered the boat as near to the rocky coastline as they dared, once again looking for anyone on the rocks or in the sea. They made their way along the jagged shore, expertly looking for signs.

'What's that?' called Zack, pointing, as they neared the rocks that projected into the sea at Clodgy Point. 'Over there, see?'

Something was floating in the water, and likely to be lost to the ocean if they didn't reach it first. It was not easily identifiable, but appeared to have a brightly-coloured appearance. Kit's heart filled with dread, as his mind's eye allowed him to see a shirt or a dress.

'Let's get nearer,' he said.

All Kit's years of combined training and experience were put to use as he steered the boat closer to the object against the oncoming waves, whilst desperately trying not to run aground on the rocks. After several failed attempts, Zack managed to get a hold of the thing, and haul it into the boat.

The object was hard and sturdy, but broken; what appeared to be a large piece of painted driftwood. At first reassured that it was not a body, Kit's relief immediately turned to anguish. He met Zack's eyes over the sprays of seawater that constantly impaired their vision. For both of them recognised the wreckage to be part of Jago's surfboard.

CHAPTER 53

Jago

As soon as Kit reached land again, he called Jago's mobile, but there was no answer. They informed Jeff, who alerted the All-Weather lifeboat, en-route back from a successful rescue, to operate a further search of the waters beyond Carrick Du.

'Go look for him,' said Zack. 'I'll make things good with the boat.' Then seeing Kit's disturbed expression, he added, 'He'll be all right. He's probably having a beer somewhere, keeping out of the storm.'

When there was no answer from the darkened basement in Teetotal Street, Kit headed for The Secret Spot. A handful of customers sat near the windows, making the most of the last light to watch the storm by. Teddy was behind the bar, while Giovanna and the other staff waited the tables. He moved with familiarity around the bar area to the kitchen, where Senara was preparing food. He looked at her cautiously, wondering if she was still sore at him.

'Is Jago about?' he asked. 'He's not at home, or answering his mobile.'

'He's not here,' Senara looked thoughtful. 'Have you tried Man's Head? He took off with his tent the other day. Crazy to be camping in this weather. What's up?'

Kit looked at her searchingly. He did not want to alarm Senara unnecessarily, but she might not appreciate being left in the dark. Cautiously, he relayed what had happened, as far as he knew, about the boy's rescue.

'And you say a surfer was involved?' Senara asked.

Reluctantly, Kit told her about the shattered board they had found.

Turning pale, Senara grabbed her hoody and keys. She turned to Teddy. 'Can you take care of the food? I have to find Jago.'

'Of course,' said Teddy. 'We're not too busy. But what is wrong?'

'It's probably nothing,' said Kit. 'But I'd like to set eyes on him all the same.'

Kit and Senara sped through the streets, past the beach and onto the coast path. They spoke little, but Kit felt that she emanated a less vigorous animosity towards him. She was too worried about Jago, he reasoned, to continue their feud. The daylight was fading fast now, and the headland had become murky and hazardous. They stumbled around in the gloaming, searching.

'Here,' called Kit, on discovering the strategically placed tent. Hidden off the beaten path behind the old shelter, an outcrop of rock similarly cloaked it from eyes at sea.

Senara looked at him fearfully. The tent, pummelled by the wind, appeared lonely and forsaken. She looked out to the raging sea, where the lights of the lifeboat could be seen, ominously searching the deep dark ocean. Kit knelt and unzipped the door flap. The following seconds felt eternal, as Senara braced herself to confront her increasing concern. When she could bear it no longer, she dived towards the little tent and stuck her head in alongside Kit.

'It's okay,' whispered Kit. 'He's here. He's sleeping.'

Senara let out a moan of anguish. 'Well, that's not good enough! How dare he sleep when we've been so worried?' She shoved the sleeping figure roughly. 'Wake up, Jago. Wake up!'

Slowly Jago stirred, and looked in confusion at the two faces that had appeared in the failing light. 'What's the emergency?' he muttered groggily.

'You tell *us,*' Senara cried. 'What the hell happened today? What happened to your board? We've been worried sick.'

'My board?' said Jago, sitting up and rubbing his head.

'I found a piece of it earlier,' said Kit. 'I came in the lifeboat to look for you after we heard about the accident.'

'I could have done with you getting there quicker, mate,' said Jago.

'Yeah, sorry about that,' Kit grinned wryly. 'It's been a busy day on the water.'

'Ha!' Jago formed a deranged smile. 'Tell me about it...' And then as his senses recovered, he added in panic: 'Is he all right? Harry. Is he...?' He could not bring himself to say the words.

'He's recovering,' said Kit, fetching his phone from his pocket. 'Last I heard he was stable.' As Kit called the lifeboat station to tell them to call off the search, Jago closed his eyes again and exhaled with relief.

'And now, you tell us all about it,' said Senara. Squeezing inside the tent, she nudged Jago to move over, and sat cross-legged beside him.

Kit followed suit, zipping the tent up again behind him, and adding apologetically, 'Bit nippy out there.'

Sighing, Jago fumbled amongst his things for his torch, and flicked the switch.

'Whoa!' said Kit observing the cuts and grazes on Jago's face, hands, and feet. You've got some war wounds there...'

'It's nothing,' said Jago quietly. 'I tore my wetsuit up a bit, but I'm fine.'

The trio were illuminated, like children sitting at the hearthside, awaiting a ghost story.

'You all comfy, there?' said Jago. 'Only, I was, like, having a sleep...'

'Just tell us what happened!' Senara said, impatiently.

'I actually don't want to,' said Jago. 'I'd really rather forget the whole thing.'

Senara punched his arm in frustration.

'Ouch!' said Jago. 'Okay, okay. But there's really not much to say.'

'Tell us anyway,' said Kit.

And so, Jago relented, and relayed the events of the afternoon...

* * *

Jago had hoped to surf to the rocks near Clodgy Point, where access from the beach was easier, but the waves were vehemently against him that day, and he did not have the strength to argue with them. Even then, it took him a while to realise what it meant. As his understanding grew, Jago had shaken his head and laughed loudly into the roaring wind and waves. Foxholes, for once, and inexplicably, was working...

He watched as the waves rolled in left from the point break. It shouldn't be happening, but it was. Depleted of energy, Jago had previously surmised that his only hope was to ride the board prone into the rocks and hope for the best. But he knew he could not let this pass. His predicament temporarily forgotten, he focused on catching the next wave. Fuelled by renewed adrenalin, he summoned the stamina to paddle into the wave, and then, with a level of heroic effort that he did not know he possessed, stood up on the board. For a few fleeting moments, he indulged in the fact that incredibly, and bizarrely, given the circumstances, he was surfing Foxholes.

The energy of the wave smashed him hard against the rocks below Man's Head, and just as quickly threatened to suck him away again. He clung on tight to the slippery granite with his fingers, hoping for a miracle. When the wave receded, he was somehow still there, but knew that he would have to move before the next one hit. Quickly he looked up and scanned the rockface before him.

You know this place, Jago, he told himself. And it was true. He had climbed it a thousand times, only to jump off the clifftop again into the water below, for sheer fun. He knew every nook and cranny, every foot and hand hold. Scrambling up the lower rocks, he took shelter behind a boulder as the next wave hit, using his surfboard as a shield.

The surfboard. There was no way he could climb up with the board. With deep regret, he unleashed himself one final time, and let the board drop onto the rocks, hoping against hope that it would find a secure lodging, perhaps become wedged in between rocks. But within seconds, the wind sent the precious board somersaulting across the rocky terrain, where it smashed and splintered into pieces. He watched, clinging to the boulder, as the sea came and claimed the wreckage; as though it must have some prize for its day's work.

Gathering his courage, Jago began to scale the rockface, trying to protect himself as much as possible from the constant bombardment of waves. But in parts there was no shelter, and he could only clutch in desperation as the giant crashing spumes attempted to grab him from his precarious perch and hurl him back down on to the treacherous rocks below.

It was with some astonishment that Jago finally hauled himself onto the grassy bank at the top of the cliff. Truly, he had not expected to make it, and could not understand what had happened to get him there. It was as if another, stronger hand, had guided his path, and that he himself had not been quite present. Yet somehow, he was there, on the clifftop, shaking and shivering with weakness. Slowly he eased himself up, then cut and bruised, limped and staggered his way to the tent, which mercifully was still standing. Once inside he found his water bottle and drank greedily. He stripped off the wetsuit and dressed in layers. Then wrapping himself in a blanket, he lay down. As he fell into sleep, he half-dreamed, half-hallucinated visions of huge waves looming overhead and then slamming down, sending him deep under the water to drown. He saw his fractured surfboard fly through the sky with him still attached as they rolled and bounced together over razor-sharp rocks. He saw the cold limp body of a young boy, and in his dream, he wept, and was filled with an aching pity. Then the pity turned to horror and self-loathing for the knowledge that people—children—could die because he did not know how to save them.

But as the sound of the sea began to diminish on the turning tide, so the nightmarish visions ebbed away, and Jago's feverish mind sought some comfort to sooth his troubled soul.

He thought of Malory, and wished that she was there to hold him, and sleep with him, and to be there when he opened his eyes.

* * *

Jago did not tell Kit and Senara of his troubled sleep, or of the uneasy feeling that he had miraculously escaped a terrible fate. Instead, he told his tale light-heartedly, and not without some humour: 'You wait years for it to work at Foxholes, then all the big ones come at once...'

But then he became quiet and more serious. 'You know, one thing that frightened me almost more than anything, was how little I knew. I mean, I seriously didn't have a clue.'

'It sounds to me like you did just fine,' said Kit.

'Me too,' said Senara, touching her brother gently on the arm. 'You saved a boy's life. I dread to think what might have happened if you hadn't been there...'

'But it's not good enough,' said Jago, with passion. 'I go out in that ocean all the time; I've been doing it all my life. To not know how to save a person is downright lazy. It's negligent. I mean I did my best, but...' Suddenly tears were in his eyes as he recalled the emotions that had terrorised him on the water. 'I was so... *Scared.*'

Jago put his head down, sheepishly wiping the errant tears with the back of his hand, and sniffling. Kit and Senara instinctively both put their arms around him.

'You did great,' said Kit. 'You did everything you could.'

'It's been a strange day,' said Senara. 'Malory appears to have gone missing too, and I can't get hold of her.'

'What?' said Kit. 'Is she all right?'

'Yes, I think so.' But Senara looked concerned. 'It appears she's gone back to London for a while. But she's not answering my messages. I don't know what's going on.'

'That doesn't seem like her,' said Kit. 'To leave you in the lurch. With the business, I mean.'

'Oh, it's not that,' said Senara. 'It was always the plan for me to be in charge. I just thought... You know; that we were friends. That she'd confide in me if something was wrong.'

Jago sat in silence, but his eyes travelled to each of the others as they spoke.

'Anyway, I can't worry about that now,' said Senara, turning to Jago again. 'Please come home. You can't stay up here like this, not after the shock you've had. Come home and eat. I'll make your favourite. You can even have the bed.'

'No. I'm fine,' said Jago with determination. 'I want to be here, and alone. I've got a lot of thinking to do.'

* * *

After several failed attempts at persuasion, Kit and Senara gave in to Jago's stubborn resolve, and reluctantly headed back into town.

'Thank goodness he was okay,' said Kit, tentatively.

Now that the urgency had gone, they strolled uneasily side by side, their previous conflict trailing after them like a shadow.

'Yes. I'm so relieved,' said Senara.

They fell once more into an uncomfortable silence. The tide was finally on the retreat, as they passed a now deserted Porthmeor. But the restless sea still boomed and rumbled defiantly, pounding the shore with luminous surf. Suddenly Senara stopped and turned to face Kit straight on. The wind blew strands of her long hair across her face.

'Kit, there something else on my mind,' she said, raising her voice above the noise of the waves. 'I'm not sure if I should say anything...'

Kit stuck his head forward awkwardly. 'What's that?' he asked, cocking an ear.

Exasperated, Senara grabbed his hand and pulled him into The Digey. Around the corner was the narrow passage that led to Harry's Court, a cloister of cottages facing into a secluded courtyard. She dragged him into the dark alleyway, a shelter from the clamorous wind and sea.

'That's better,' she said, as she leaned against the wall of Alfred Wallis's old cottage. 'I can hear myself think now.'

'What's up Snow?' said Kit, his voice apprehensive. 'Is this going to be about the thing with Brian?'

'No, not that,' she replied.

A lamp that illuminated the street failed to intrude on their secret refuge, but she could just make out his features in the soft glow from one of the cottages, its curtains drawn against the stormy evening. He felt close, scrutinising her.

'What then?' he asked softly; but hesitant, she thought.

'I went to see Pepper today. I had thought to try to patch things up. But it didn't exactly go that way...'

She felt his sigh in the intimate space.

'Go on then...' he said.

For a second, Senara once again doubted the wisdom of her actions. But since she had already drawn him covertly into a dark alleyway, decided she might as well free herself of the burden.

'It was something Grady said that prompted me,' she said, nervously. 'Anyway, it seems that I've had it wrong all these years. I thought I'd done the dirty on Pepper, but it seems she knew all along about me and Grady, and that she deliberately conspired to get him...'

'Seriously? *This* again?' said Kit, frowning.

'Don't you see?' said Senara. 'I've been going out of my mind. Tormenting myself with guilt. For *years*. I've suffered depression and anxiety. I haven't been myself at all. You know I haven't. But she did it all on purpose...'

'Senara, I don't care,' said Kit, becoming agitated.

Senara was taken aback. This was not the response she had hoped for. She had missed him of late, and craved his reassurance and support.

'I don't care what happened between you and that dickhead in the past,' continued Kit. 'If I were you, I'd want to forget it ever happened. I am sick to death of this childish bickering. I get enough of it from Astrid at home.'

'Oh, *Astrid!*' said Senara, her voice quaking. 'Your girlfriend is so rude to me. Do you know she ignores me completely when you're not looking?'

'Stop it,' said Kit sternly.

'It's true!' Senara declared. 'She's horrible to me. And there's more. Pepper told me today that she and Grady set the two of you up. They all think it's a big joke that you don't know about it...'

'That's enough,' said Kit, leaving the confines of the alleyway, and turning back towards The Digey. 'This is beneath you, Senara. I'm disappointed to say the least.'

'But it's the *truth*,' cried Senara, following him.

'It doesn't matter!' shouted Kit. 'I'm sick to death of the whole thing. You're no different to them, it seems; just bitching and stirring up trouble.'

'That's not fair...'

They were interrupted by the sound of Kit's pager going off. He stopped walking, took it from his pocket, and stared, in disbelief.

'Great,' he said. 'Another shout.' He shook his head at her sadly. 'I have to go.'

He turned and marched quickly along The Digey, heading for the harbour. Senara hurried after him.

'Kit wait,' she appealed. 'Please don't go like this. I'm sorry. I don't want us to fight anymore.'

He stopped dead in his tracks, and glared at her, his expression full of anger. 'Senara, it's a shout. I have to go. Just... *Go home*.'

And then he turned again and broke into a run. Senara stood alone in the empty street as the wind tore around her, and watched as he disappeared into the night.

CHAPTER 54

Tamsin

It had grown dark in the cabin, and the wind that prowled outside the timber walls gave a haunting moan. But Dan was too afraid to move, even to put the bedside lamp on. Clutching a cushion to his chest, he stared in horror at the tv screen.

As Paulette Goddard laid her head upon the pillow unawares, a wooden panel opened in the wall behind the bed, and slowly a mysterious hand appeared; a terrifying, gnarled claw, that reached out towards the sleeping figure...

'Arrrrrgh!' Dan screamed as he felt the talons grasp at his own shoulder. He jumped up in fright, leaping from the bed to cower near the door. Tamsin knelt on the bed, and edged her way towards him, making a growling sound, with one hand stretched out, her red-painted fingernails splayed.

'That not funny!' said Dan. 'You nearly gave me a heart attack. Stop it!'

Tamsin threw herself back against the pillows, chuckling. 'Sorry, I couldn't resist.'

'I won't watch the rest, if you keep that up,' said Dan sulkily.

'I can't promise,' said Tamsin, with a cheeky grin.

Dan lowered himself back onto the bed next to her, still looking warily at the wooden panelling behind the bedhead, and even more warily at Tamsin.

'Seriously,' he said. 'Please don't do that again. Give me nightmares now, that will.'

'Oh Dan,' said Tamsin, regarding him, as she relaxed with her head propped up on one hand. 'You're not exactly...'

'What?' said Dan, gruffly.

Tamsin smiled with earnest affection. 'Sorry to say, but you're hardly courageous, are you?'

'That's not very fair,' he grumbled, grabbing a fistful of the chocolatey popcorn mix. 'I've done a lot of brave things recently, I'll have you know.'

'Really? Like what?' said Tamsin.

'I've been horse-riding,' said Dan. 'And surfing. And I nearly died on the rocks at Gwynver.'

'Goodness! How? Surfing?'

'No... Never mind. The point is I don't think you give me enough credit. Just because I don't like stupid horror movies.'

Tamsin looked at him thoughtfully for a second. 'You're right. And I suppose you've been brave to date all these girls lately. How's that going by the way? The list thing?'

Dan hung his head in shame. He didn't really want to talk about it. But it was a distraction from the scary film that was still playing before his eyes.

'It's not working out at all,' he said. 'I really thought I had something with Daisy, but it wasn't to be. And then I fell for Eden...'

'Eden Rowe?' said Tamsin. 'The surfer? You actually *fell* for her?'

'Well... I mean, sort of. I mean she's really fit. And hot.'

Tamsin huffed. 'If you like that kind of thing.'

'Trust me,' said Dan, still scoffing popcorn. 'Every man likes that kind of thing. But I just couldn't hack the lifestyle. They make it look so easy, and glamorous. You know; Kit, and Eden, and that Gabe bloke. But it's really not. It's incredibly stressful. Even if you manage to learn to surf—which believe me, is not easy—there's all these rules to follow. Surf *etiquette,* if you will. If you get it wrong, they beat you up or something.'

'No!' said Tamsin, eyes wide, in mock horror. 'They don't!'

'Well, maybe not beat you up,' said Dan in a surly voice. 'But you're made to feel a right tit.'

Tamsin looked puzzled. 'I always thought surfing was meant to be about the vibe. You know, laid-back; easy going...'

'I know, right?!' said Dan enthusiastically. 'It's not supposed to be about freezing cold water and tight wetsuits and fucking etiquette! It's supposed to be about being a beach-bum and looking cool in Hawaiian shorts and... The fucking *Beach Boys*, right?'

Tamsin laughed. 'Maybe in California. So, I take it you've given up now? With the list?'

'I dunno. I suppose.' Dan chewed morosely as he stared vacantly at the movie. 'But I can't tell the lads that, or they'll think I'm a loser. And y'know, I really hoped it would work. But it's the same old story. They—the women—don't like me as much as I like them, and that's the truth of it.'

Tamsin sat up straight, looking pensive. 'Perhaps you're misinterpreting the list; not reading it right. Can I see it?'

Dan shrugged. 'I don't see why not. Hang on a minute.'

Finally braving the horrors of the dark, he reached over and switched on the lamp. Risking unseen ghouls that might bite his hand, he fumbled around a bowl on the bedside table that contained his door keys, and other detritus emptied from his pockets earlier in the day. He had long since ripped the page with the list from the notebook, for ease of use. Tamsin took the piece of paper, now crinkled and torn, and unfolded it carefully.

'Hmmm,' she said, after a minute of perusing. 'So, this *paragon* has to be a natural beauty, intelligent, non-judgmental, outdoorsy and creative? Is that right?'

'I guess,' said Dan.

'Well, for a start, we're all outdoorsy round here,' said Tamsin. 'I mean, it can hardly be helped. We're surrounded by the sea and the countryside. And it's so hilly.'

'Really hilly,' agreed Dan. 'We probably get more exercise than most city types just walking up Porthmeor Hill every day.'

'Exactly,' said Tamsin. 'Plus, there's different ways of being intelligent. Some people might have fancy degrees, but can't even finish the crossword puzzle... I'm quite sure your soulmate is somewhere right here in town. She's probably right under your nose, but you can't see for looking too hard. You just need to get a bit more... *Flexible*. With the rules.'

'Maybe...' said Dan.

'Now let's see... Well of course, natural beauty can be enhanced...' said Tamsin, eyeing him through her long mascara-laden lashes. 'Women have always used a bit of make-up to promote their natural looks, from Cleopatra right down through history. I mean, you could say it was *creative*, in a way. You know, creating an image, from what you've been born with. It's *artistic*. At least that's what I think.'

'Funny,' said Dan. 'I never thought of it that way before. But now you mention it...'

'And cooking,' said Tamsin, flinging a careless arm in gesture towards the kitchen. 'Cooking is a form of creative expression. Being able to rustle something up at a moment's notice is quite a skill.'

'Let me see that list again,' said Dan.

Tamsin handed it back, and then watched Dan's expression go through the painful machinations of deep concentration, as he re-read the list. Patiently, she reached and took another sip of margarita.

'You know what, Tamsin,' he said at length, and turning to look at her. 'I think you may be right. I think I know exactly who this list describes; exactly who fits the bill.'

'You do?' said Tamsin nervously.

Dan nodded smugly, beaming with delight at his cleverness.

'Well come on then,' said Tamsin in agitation. 'Who is it?'

Dan smiled happily at her. 'Can't you guess? Isn't it obvious?'

Tamsin put the drink down, and turned to face him again. She rearranged her hair casually with her hand, flicking it down around her bare shoulders.

'Why don't you just tell me, Dan?' she said quietly.

CHAPTER 55

Wretched

Senara walked aimlessly and in gloom, until she reached the harbour. She was just in time to see the lights of the lifeboat as it reached Smeaton's Pier and then headed out into the bay. Although past the breakers, she could see how violently it still bounced on the heaving storm swell. She stood for a while on the slipway, watching as it disappeared from sight, with a strange sense of unease in her heart. She knew that this would not be an easy shout.

The sense of renewal she had felt after leaving Pepper was to be short-lived, it seemed. She had, within a few short hours returned to the usual self-loathing. In her effort to re-bond with Kit, she had only succeeded in lowering his opinion of her, and had foolishly revealed something that might cause him pain. At that moment Senara despised herself. Perhaps everything was her fault after all, for trouble seemed to follow her around.

She took her phone from her pocket and stared at it. There was something she knew she could do in order to try and find out, once and for all, if Kit's behaviour towards Brian had been justified. She had thus far avoided it, judging it undignified, and beneath her. But it might give her some knowledge; some help in understanding just who she had been dealing with all these months.

She could stalk Brian.

She barely looked at his social media accounts these days; their private chats having overtaken them. And then it hit her.

He never communicated to her publicly. There were no jovial chats, or retweets, or comments on Instagram. Their entire relationship had been conducted privately, despite social media being the method by which he had found her. Senara snapped open the app, and found his account.

She scrolled down, even as a flush of guilt crept over her. It all seemed quite ordinary until...

...There it was. A tweet bemoaning his rough treatment by a gang of surfers, and all because of lies told by a spurned girlfriend.

Was that supposed to be her? Was he serious? She flicked quickly to the replies column to see the flood of consoling messages, pitying him for his misfortune. Enraged, Senara kept scrolling back weeks, months, reading the messages, until the picture was fully formed in her mind. For hidden amongst the casual banter with his followers, were occasional messages from other women. Messages that pleaded, and begged, asking why he had stood them up, or not returned their calls. Mostly these messages went unanswered by Brian, but occasionally he made a scornful public comment, or subtweet, indirectly referencing them.

Senara suddenly felt the biggest fool in the world. Of course, Brian had behaved suspiciously. She had known the very first time he had messaged, that there was something amiss. But she had been so intent on believing him a 'nice guy'—to believe that such a thing existed in the world—that she had suppressed her natural instincts. Once invested in the relationship, it had become harder to admit that she had made a serious error of judgement. Senara thought about those other women, knowing that they too, had been duped; and suddenly felt overwhelmed with relief that her relationship with Brian had not gone further.

And Kit... Kit had tried to warn her. He had stood up for her, and instead of gratitude, she had shown him anger and resentment.

Senara could not shake off the unquenchable desire to talk to Kit; to apologise and explain. To tell him he had been right, about everything. She strolled slowly along Wharf Road until she reached the lifeboat house. She wanted to find out about the shout; to know how serious it was, and how long they might be gone. But the shore crew were still busy drawing the tractor up the slipway, and she was reluctant to pester them. Yet she stood there a while, unable to make a sensible decision. She should go back to The Secret Spot, although she knew Teddy would take good care of things. She should go back to Man's Head and persuade her brother to come home. She should do anything that might persuade herself that she was a person of worth. But all she could do was stare out to sea at the darkened horizon, where the boat had been, as though she might invoke its swift and safe return.

A woman's voice called her name. She turned and saw Rosa standing on the patio of Driftwood, beckoning her. She crossed the road towards the pizzeria, head bent in her hoody.

'Whatever's the matter?' said Rosa. 'You look so unhappy.'

'I'm just worried about the lifeboat,' said Senara, honestly. 'It's a terrible night to go out.'

'It is,' said Rosa. 'Those brave men and women, heading out into that storm... No one even wants to sit on the patio, tonight, let alone go out to sea. I don't know how they do it.'

Senara looked beyond Rosa to the warm glow of lights inside the café. 'Looks like you're busy anyway.'

'Oh yes,' said Rosa. 'They all come flooding in to the warmth in this weather. I'd better return. I just wondered if you were okay?'

'I'm fine,' said Senara. 'But do you need any help? I don't feel like going home just yet.'

'What about your own place?' said Rosa suspiciously. 'The Secret Spot. Aren't you needed there?'

Senara squirmed under Rosa's piercing gaze. 'I left Teddy in charge tonight,' she said. 'He's sort of my deputy.'

Rosa looked at Senara and then surreptitiously out to sea. 'Kit was on that shout, wasn't he?' she said.

'Yes. I think so...' said Senara.

'Actually, we *could* do with a hand,' said Rosa, briskly, reverting to industriousness. 'Grab yourself an apron and pad then. You know where they are. Good on you girl, for offering.'

Senara removed her hoody in the staff area, and using a hairband that she always carried in her pocket, tied up her windblown hair in a bun. She looked at her reflection in the small bathroom mirror. Her work make-up had smudged, but she looked passably professional. Yet it was her eyes that let her down. Despite her youth, they carried the look of some terrible sadness, or fear.

She forced a smile and entered the noisy fray. She spent the next couple of hours delivering pizza and drinks to packed tables; yet constantly, compulsively, her eyes drifted to the blackness outside, for some sign of lights on the water; for some sign of return. When the last customers had paid and left, she insisted on helping Rosa with clearing up. Rosa did not argue, but watched covertly as Senara ensured every single salt and pepper pot had been cleaned, and refilled.

When there was absolutely nothing left to do except put out the lights and lock up, Senara knew she could delay no longer. And yet leaving felt harder than ever, for the boat had still not returned.

Rosa emerged from the kitchen, dressed to leave, and carrying a thermos flask. A fleece blanket was slung over her arm. Senara recognised it as one of the colourful blankets that they offered to customers who did, on less fearsome nights, want to sit out on the patio and watch the harbour boats.

‘Here,’ said Rosa, shoving the blanket and flask at Senara. ‘It’s hot chocolate. You’ll get cold out there.’ She nodded towards the patio. ‘Just make sure you lock up when you go.’ She reached in her pocket and then held out a set of keys.

‘Are you sure?’ said Senara, in wonderment, but taking the keys, hoped that Rosa would say no more; would not voice Senara’s fears aloud.

‘I’m sure,’ said Rosa, already turning her back on Senara to leave. ‘But don’t freeze your arse off, will you? And lock the front door after me.’

‘I will,’ said Senara. ‘I promise. And thank you Rosa.’

Rosa made a dismissive wave of her hand and a ‘pfft’ sound, then was gone.

Obediently, Senara locked up the main entrance, turned off most of the lights, and then went outside, sliding the patio doors closed behind her. She placed the flask of hot chocolate on one of the tables, then pulled her hood up, and wrapped herself in the blanket. And then she sat, alone and in darkness, looking out across the harbour. With most of the cafés and bars shut now, and the storm still driving all but the most romantic of wave-lovers indoors, Wharf Road was desolate and ghostly. Senara did not really understand what she was doing there. But she knew that she could not leave; could not return to her warm bed and sleep a dreamless sleep. Not while Jago was in a wind-battered tent on a clifftop, and not while brave souls were out in the dark ocean, saving lives.

CHAPTER 56

The Dark Sea

All the crew on the lifeboat knew that it was going to be a tough shout. A fishing trawler had broken down far out in The Celtic Sea, almost halfway to Ireland. Hopefully, they would find it quickly, and tow the boat and crew back to safe harbour. But nothing could be known for sure until the situation was assessed.

They were fortunate, Kit knew, to be in a state-of-the-art lifeboat. All the crew were strapped into seats that had shock absorbers to ensure the utmost comfort possible, even as they pounded over rough seas at speed. Every member had a digital screen which allowed them to communicate, navigate, and monitor systems. The boat was watertight, and self-righting if capsized. They had every available chance of success, if they found the distressed boat in time.

Yet as Kit looked out of the window into the darkness beyond, he still thought of the victims of the St Ives lifeboat disaster in 1939, when seven of the eight-man crew of the *James and Sarah Eliza Stych* lost their lives. The memory of them still lived, fresh in the minds of their descendants and townsfolk. More recent in time was the loss of the crew of the Penlee lifeboat, the *Solomon Browne*. They had bravely gone out in rough seas to aid the imperilled *Union Star*, when tragedy had struck on the rocks near Boscawen Cliff. Kit never forgot them every time they went on a dangerous shout, knowing that he and his companions could easily succumb to a similar fate. No matter how technological the lifeboat, the sea was a wild thing; unruly and indomitable.

They were far out in the Celtic Sea, when a further communication came through to the coxswain: the stricken trawler was taking on water. A tangible silence permeated throughout the crew. No one need voice the urgency of the matter; every second now was a matter of life and death.

In time, despite the darkness and the storm, they located the vessel. The lifeboat pulled up at a safe distance nearby and the crew evaluated the situation from the deck. The trawler crew, thankfully, all appeared to be wearing lifejackets, and were clearly relieved at the sight of them; waving and cheering through the sound of wind and waves... But there was a definite list to the boat.

'Doesn't look good,' said Zack to Kit.

'No, it doesn't,' said Kit. 'Let's hope we can get over there.'

The coxswain manoeuvred the lifeboat with skill and precision, but it was a dangerous task as the two vessels rolled violently alongside in the rough seas. Several attempts were made to get close enough to grab the sailors and pull them onboard, but the lifeboat soared above the trawler's deck one minute, before being dropped below her waterline in the next instant. The coxswain decided that the situation was untenable, and that they should pull back.

'Let me try and get onboard first,' said Kit.

As the trawler careered dangerously close, Kit knew he would only get one chance. As the lifeboat rose high on the peak again, he made the leap. The crew of the fishing boat grabbed him as he landed on the slimy deck. The lifeboat quickly moved away to a safer distance.

'Where's it going?' cried one of the distressed crew.

'Just a precaution,' said Kit. 'Do you have a life raft?'

The man nodded. 'But we can't leave the boat. The skipper said...'

'Where is the skipper?'

'In the wheelhouse,'

'Get your men into the raft, and make towards the lifeboat, they'll pick you up. I'll find the skipper.'

The man looked chagrined, as if the seriousness of their situation had just dawned on him. 'Right... Right away...' he faltered, and then hurried to organise the crew.

Kit staggered up the incline of the pitching boat to the wheelhouse.

'You the skipper?' he shouted at the man who stood at the helm. He had that look of shock and disbelief that Kit had become accustomed to. With a heavy heart, Kit noted that he was not wearing a lifejacket.

'Where's your jacket?' he said to the man. 'We have to get off the boat. Now.'

'Can't you just give us a tow?' said the skipper. 'We've been through this before. Just give us a tow.'

'It's too late for that,' yelled Kit. 'Lifejacket. Now.'

'But what will happen to my boat?' said the captain. 'This is my boat. My livelihood. I can't just leave her.'

Kit grasped at a rail as the trawler lurched with a sudden groan. He made his way closer to the man until he stood right before him. He looked him in the eyes, and said: 'She's going down.'

'No, that can't be right...' said the man. 'I need this boat. You must be wrong...'

Kit looked steadfastly into the skipper's eyes, and repeated, 'She's going down.'

For a second the man appeared confused, but then looked around, as if for the first time, in realisation. When his eyes returned to Kit's again there was fear in his eyes.

Kit nodded.

Then quickly, he guided the man to the deck, and without time to think, unstrapped his own lifejacket which was still connected by a line, to the lifeboat. He put it on the now docile skipper, expertly fastening it.

'When she goes down, it'll be a shock, but the lifejacket will keep you afloat,' he shouted in the man's ear, hoping that he was paying attention. 'It'll be cold, but you mustn't panic. Stay calm. This line is attached to the lifeboat and they'll pull you in. Can you hear me? Stay calm, and you'll be okay.'

Kit looked on in alarm as he saw another wall of seawater approach.

'Hold on!' he yelled, before the wave struck, engulfing the deck with water.

It was too much for the damaged vessel to take. The boat suddenly tilted, as if tired of the conversation; as though she had been toying with them for long enough. In a second, she was overcome. The bow tilted for a hesitant minute to the grim skies, and then with calm indifference, she sank like a stone.

Kit tried to keep hold of the skipper as they were plunged into the icy seas, but somehow lost his grip in the bubbling froth. For a moment, all was still and silent as he went under the water. Whether he had taken an instinctive breath or not, he could not recall. He could only wait, and hope to surface, hope to not lose consciousness. But there was no fear, or panic, for all was out of his control. He only felt a strange sense of peace as he relaxed his body and waited.

It was when he finally resurfaced that he knew his real troubles had begun; as though he had already left the world, but had suddenly been plunged back into a parallel reality, where once again there was dread and fear; where obstacles had yet to be overcome. Now he would have to fight again. He tried to spot the lifeboat; to glimpse a smear of her vivid orange colour and lights in the all-encompassing darkness; to catch some reflection in the waves. But all he saw was blackness; and all he sensed was the mighty heave of the cold ocean; as though he were in the flooded pits of the deepest, darkest, tin mine. Despite this blindness, he could feel the sea gather momentum and rise up before him. He knew, with the instinct of a surfer, that he would not float easily over the crest; that the size and power of the wave would send him under again.

Once more, he felt a familiar sense of inevitability. He had always carried an elusive premonition of doom that some future-self had sent to forewarn him. Usually, it could be reasoned with. But in that moment, he felt a melancholy sadness for his life; a deep regret for the loss of joy, and friendship, and adventure. But most of all, for the loved ones; for those who were held deep in his heart.

I'm not ready, a voice said in his head, as the wave loomed over him. It was not a desperate voice, but a defiant one. He would not cast his fate to the sea without a fight. *I'm not ready. Not yet.*

CHAPTER 57

The Silver Ball

Senara was aware how strange she would appear, should anyone pass by, but Wharf Road was by now completely deserted. All the same, she could not help but feel self-conscious. This was a crazy thing to be doing; sitting alone well past midnight with eyes fixed on the bay beyond the harbour. But the longer she waited, the more terrifying became the outcome imagined in her worst fears. If only the lifeboat would return. She should have gone home and slept through the night, then awakened to good news, without the necessity for any ordeal. But she had stayed, and so could not now leave. She was stuck; paralysed; committed to her watch.

She replayed, over and over in her mind, the stupid things she had said to Kit. She should have let it go; held her counsel. She should have been wiser. Kit was always so forgiving; was able to go with the flow, and leave yesterday's mistakes behind. But Senara did not seem to be able to stop herself from dwelling on her bad decisions. Ruminating, he had called it. She knew he was right; as he was usually right. Yet she seemed to be incapable of control, or change. Kit saw her better than she saw herself, and it was not a pretty picture.

For fuck's sake, I'm doing it now... she thought in a sudden moment of clarity. There really was no hope for her. But Senara knew something that Kit did not understand. The reason she held herself to account so severely was because she held a deep-rooted paranoia that her mistakes would hurt others; would lead to long-term suffering, or worse—immediate calamity.

Senara touched wood constantly. She saluted whenever she saw a magpie. As a child she would feel guilty at choosing one teacup over another. She would compulsively touch every other cup and send her thoughts—assurance that it was nothing personal. She loved them all just as much, but a decision had to be made. Even younger, on her fourth birthday, she had clung in desperation to a heart-shaped helium balloon that had been handed to her. She loved the balloon, but knew, that unlike all the ordinary balloons, it would fly up into the sky and disappear forever, if she, Senara, were to let go.

The birthday party ended, but Senara would not say goodbye to her friends or make any movement that would require her to let go of the balloon. Even inside, there were windows and doors that someone might thoughtlessly open. She could still remember the distress and terror that she had felt as she clung with her little hands to the blown-up foil heart. She could still recall the image of a unicorn printed on to the surface of the balloon. Even as her eyes began to close, and her head nodded in fatigue; even as her mother pleaded; Senara would not let go of the balloon. The unicorn balloon depended on her. She could not let go.

Eventually, after much encouragement and persuasion, her mother convinced Senara that if they tied the balloon's string to the back of the chair, there was no way that the balloon would escape and float away forever.

'Do you promise?' Senara had asked in tearful desperation.

'I promise,' her mother had smiled.

Senara had watched carefully as her mother wound the string several times around the rail of the wooden kitchen chair, and then tied several knots to secure it. Only when she saw with her own eyes that the balloon did not drift away, had she finally succumbed to exhaustion, and fallen into a deep sleep.

And now, she could not move an inch until she was certain that the lifeboat crew had returned safely.

The night stretched on interminably. It was not often, in her young life, she realised, that she took the time for such unflinching contemplation. There was always a distraction: friends, work, or the drama of a doomed relationship. And if all else failed, she could reach for a glass of wine or rum, and suppress her feelings that way. But sitting in the dark of night, with only a blanket to give her comfort, there was no mode of resistance, or superficial crutch. There was no escape from reality. Gazing at the dark harbour sands, and pier beyond, she recalled the day, long ago, when Kit had hatched a plan to win the prize for the silver ball...

Hurling was a centuries old custom. On the morning of every Feast Day of Saint Ia, there would be a mayoral procession through the town, with accordions, pipes and drums, and the local school children dancing along behind. After a short service at Saint Ia's Holy Well, the procession would move back through the town to the parish churchyard, which overlooked the beach. From the churchyard wall, the mayor would perform the ritual of hurling the silver ball.

The ball was the size of a cricket ball, made of apple wood, and coated in silver. But the game was more akin to rugby; rough, and physical. Whoever returned it by midday to the town hall, would win the traditional prize of a silver coin. All the youngsters of the neighbourhood would congregate on the sand below the church to try and catch the ball. Whoever caught it would then run for dear life to keep it, as the mob of teenagers would chase and tackle them to the ground, all vying to win the prize. It was a skirmish that felt like a battlefield at times, but was a tradition that, the boys especially, endured, in order to lay claim to some sort of notoriety and local fame. It was rare for the initial catcher of the ball to keep hold of it for long, but rather, the poor unfortunate would more likely be instantly toppled into the wet sand, and a bigger, stronger, faster competitor would make off with the precious treasure. When Kit was fourteen, he had had enough of taking this demolishing, and realised that a more artful plan was required; and fast, before he became too old to still be taking part without shame.

Kit had reasoned that he stood a pretty good chance of obtaining the ball on the beach, even if a bit of rough play was required. He was now one of the tallest and strongest, and not the diminutive boy he had once been. In past years, he had caught the ball several times, but only got so far, before being ambushed and robbed of it. The teams of teenagers had plenty of time to maraud around town before the end of the game, and there was constant danger of attack.

Senara closed her eyes and smiled, remembering how nervous she had been at the time. But Kit had persuaded her that it would work. She had watched from the end of Smeaton's Pier as the procedure began, and the mayor, after the usual ceremonies, threw the ball over the church wall. In the opening scuffle, she thought that Kit had lost to one of the other boys, but after a boisterous tussle, she saw him streak away from the crowd across the low-tide sands, and knew then that he had succeeded. It only took seconds for the horde to spot him, and give chase. Terrified, Senara faced the grim fact that Kit's plan now depended entirely on her. She dashed along the pier and then stood in the designated position, behind a wall on the old Rampers pier head. It overlooked the slipway that led down to the low-tide spot known as Breakwater Beach. She laughed to herself now, to remember how she had thought it necessary to don an improbable disguise of large sunglasses and floppy hat, in *February*; as if to fool an entire town that knew her well that she was merely a tourist, wandering around the pier.

Kit raced around the back of Smeaton's Pier, along Breakwater Beach, and then sprinted up the stone steps and slipway. Without even looking at her, but with precision timing, he put the silver ball into her open handbag and then carried on running. Senara quickly edged away to look over the wall, as if just an interested observer. It could not have gone more smoothly, but Senara's heart beat wildly as she watched the pile of youngsters race up the ramp and chase after Kit, who by now was standing at the corner of Wheal Dream, and goading the crowd by brandishing the dummy ball. Another group, hoping to outwit him, raced down Quay Street, in an attempt to cut him off.

Senara chuckled aloud now, as she remembered how they had made the decoy from a tennis ball and some tin foil. It really should not have fooled anyone, and for a panic-stricken moment, she had expected the mob to turn and attack her. But amazingly, it had worked, and she had watched in relief as Kit disappeared from her sight, with the braying mass swarming after him.

Later, Kit and Senara congregated by the town hall, where the mayor appealed, as tradition required, for the return of the silver ball. Both acted aloof, as if each barely noticed the other. But slowly they edged closer, until they were shoulder to shoulder. Carefully, Senara slipped the silver ball from the handbag and placed it in his palm. He placed his other hand over hers to cover it, as if to hide their secret for a little longer. Senara looked at his face, and saw that he had a bruise and scratch on his chin, and a cut on his eyebrow that would leave a scar. But his eyes were full of joy and happiness.

'What now?' she whispered.

'I know,' said Kit. He removed his hands from hers, taking the silver ball. Then he lowered his head to speak quietly to Jago who stood in front of him.

Eyes wide, Jago nodded and took the gift from Kit. Then he raised his hand and yelled: 'Here! I've got it! I've got the silver ball!'

The crowd went wild with surprise, and Jago found himself at the centre of attention, as he was jostled forward to return the ball to the mayor. Kit and Senara were forgotten about as all eyes were on little Jago, who had somewhat improbably managed to acquire and return the ceremonial ball.

Senara had looked at Kit in admiration, as they clapped and cheered along with the crowd. No doubt the truth would come out in time. But for now, he was not interested in acclaim, like the other boys; but rather revelled in the thrill of the game. Suddenly beguiled by his familiar, now battle-scarred face, Senara saw a knight of old: generous, noble, and brave.

So, when he suddenly bent, grabbed her face in both hands, and kissed her on the lips, she did not resist. He wasn't to know that it was Senara's first kiss, or that she had felt her heart leap when he touched her. He could not have known that she had realised there and then that for her it was only Kit; had always been Kit; and always would be Kit.

Senara sighed at the bittersweet memory. For as quickly as he had kissed her, he had turned away again, immersed in the celebrations; but leaving her forever with an ache in her heart. For the truth was, that Kit had gone on to kiss a lot of girls after that, leaving Senara, over the years, confused and protective of her feelings. She concluded that their kiss had meant nothing; that he had just been caught up in the moment. As the years went by, she had reasoned her feelings into abstraction, and almost condemned them as false.

Almost.

Senara stood up suddenly as she saw lights approaching the shore. For long minutes, she waited anxiously, wrapped in her blanket, as she tried to ascertain the validity of them. But in time, it was revealed to be true. The lifeboat had returned on the turning tide, and the tractor was already being driven down the slipway by the shore crew, who had also kept vigil throughout the night. Senara watched as the boat was hauled inshore and up to the boathouse, in what felt like a painstakingly long time. She watched as one by one, Zack and all the familiar faces disembarked. There were strangers too; the rescued, she assumed. She searched, in the dark, looking for Kit. *Where was he?* For a second, she wondered if she had been mistaken; and that he had not made the shout in time. But then, she felt sure, he would have stayed, and helped out the crew upon the return of the lifeboat. Senara's heart felt like it had turned to stone as she observed, in the light from the boathouse, the demeanour of the returning crew. They were all, as one, exhausted and heavy of heart.

No, no, no, no, no. Senara began to fear the worst. *Where was he? Where was Kit?*

Her heart was pounding in her chest and she thought she was going to be sick. She could not face this. Anything but this. She would give anything, do anything, for it not to be true. She wanted to run over there and find him, but was rooted to the spot with fear.

And then, finally, she saw him. He was helped from the lifeboat by a fellow crew member, wrapped in a thermal blanket. Quickly she processed the information; that he had somehow been in trouble, but that he was walking; and that he was all right. Immediately Senara felt overjoyed. She dropped the blanket and climbed over the patio railings, then hurried to stand by the barrier overlooking the slipway. For a second, she watched the milling crew as they went about their business, and was about to run to them, to him, when something caught her eye.

In the dim light she saw the figure pace across the wet sand of the harbour and approach the lifeboat house. She watched in a trance as Kit stood up from where he sat, still wrapped in the blanket, on the slipway wall. And then she watched as Kit and Astrid embraced. Reality struck a painful blow. Astrid would be the one to comfort, and to love him; to voice grateful thanks for his safe return; Astrid, not Senara.

She shivered as a ghost of the past embodied her. Suddenly Senara knew exactly how Nell had felt all those years ago; she knew the deep anguish of waiting for her love to return. She had, thankfully, been spared having to endure the sorrow of his loss; but she must still, forever, hide her heart, and bear the agony of her suffering, in silence.

CHAPTER 58

Dawlish

The minute Malory opened her eyes, she knew that something was awry. As the faded, dated wallpaper of the small bed and breakfast establishment came into view, she was at first confused; and then remembering, confounded that her escape had been foiled. She closed her eyes again and hoped that it would all go away.

When that didn't work, she sat upright and surveyed the room. It was pleasant enough. The furniture was a jumble of vintage styles that might be deemed chic, rather than old and tired, and preferable to a fitted corporate suite. There was an old Persian rug on the wooden floorboards, an Art Deco wardrobe, and the sheet on her bed was covered with a patchwork quilt. On the window sill, a small vase held delicate stems of fresh freesias.

It was indeed quite charming, Malory concluded. But the generally pleasant atmosphere was completely spoilt by the presence of Virginia, Daphne, and Barbara, oozing disdain at her. She saw Daphne leaning nonchalantly against the wall by the door, arms folded, and staring at her. Barbara stood by the window looking out to sea, and smoking a cigarette. Virginia sat in the armchair nearby, with her hands on her lap, regarding her with a with a look of kindly pity.

Malory put her hands to her head and threw herself back against the pillows again, groaning.

'Where's Willie?' she said aloud to the room.

'Stormed off in disgust,' said Daphne, matter-of-factly.

‘Of course she has,’ said Malory, in her head this time.

‘There were lots of Scottish obscenities flying around,’ said Daphne.

Virginia smiled graciously, but Barbara continued to make her contempt manifest by staring out of the window, ignoring her.

‘What was I supposed to do?’ Malory cried out to the universe. ‘I tried. It didn’t work out.’

Virginia, Daphne and Barbara became silent.

Remembering the cab that she had booked, Malory showered and dressed quickly. She had found the Bed and Breakfast quite easily, the day before, after a wander along the parade behind the railway line. While not exactly a four-star hotel, it was clean and unpretentious; and Malory had been keen to get out of the storm. There was no kettle in her modest room, so, gasping for a cup of tea, she decided to go downstairs for the complimentary breakfast; a routine she would have preferred to avoid.

The landlady herself served the breakfast, and Malory could see through an open door from the dining room to the kitchen, that it was all cooked from scratch on an old range cooker. The landlady was a sweet old thing, at least if appearance were anything to go by. She was short and sprightly, with her long grey hair tied back in a bun, and a faded apron covering her summer dress.

‘You’re the first up,’ she said to Malory. ‘So, you can have the table with the best sea view.’

She escorted her to a little square table by a bay window, and handed her the breakfast menu. Malory smiled and thanked her, but once the landlady had gone to fetch her tea, looked in trepidation at the menu. She had only really wanted the tea, but now that she had been given the best table, felt obliged to co-operate.

The menu was typical of such an establishment; full English breakfast and variants thereof. Bacon, sausages, fried bread, tomatoes, and mushrooms. Eggs could be had fried, poached or scrambled. All served with toast, jam, and marmalade, on the side.

Who needs fried bread and *toast?* Malory thought.

And perversely, the only form of egg that she felt she could manage to eat—a *boiled* one—wasn't on the menu. She supposed she could request one, but didn't want to be any trouble. She thought of Senara's breakfast options at The Secret Spot: pancakes with banana, berries, pecan butter and maple; granola with fruit salad, yogurt, nuts and seeds; avocado on sourdough bread with roast balsamic tomato and feta cheese.

Stop it, she told herself. *You can get those things in London too. It's not* all *full English breakfasts.*

The landlady returned with her tea, and asked what she would like.

'Just scrambled eggs, please,' said Malory.

'Is that all?' said the woman in disappointment. 'It's all included. Have as much as you like.'

'I know,' said Malory kindly. 'But I'm really not that hungry. And I have a cab booked, so...'

'Very well,' said the landlady. 'Toast or fried bread?'

Just the eggs, thought Malory. 'Toast please, wholemeal if you have it,' she answered.

When the woman had gone again, Malory sipped her tea and stared at the view of the English Channel beyond the railway. Yesterday's storm had vanished, and all was calm. It was hard to imagine that the deluge of just a few short hours ago had ever been real. Now the sea was peaceful, but it was drab and grey. It was not the clear green shallow waters or deep indigo blues of Cornwall, where even on stormy days, there was an ever-changing drama of slate, emerald and snow-white horses of seafoam.

Malory sighed. *Stop making such a big deal of it. What do you want? To be on holiday for ever?*

She ate her eggs, and not wishing to appear rude, as much of the thick dry toast as she could. She returned to her room to fetch her things and then went to the front desk in the hallway, where she was to settle her bill.

'I hope you had a nice stay?' said the landlady, with her apron removed now, as she processed the payment.

'It was lovely, thanks,' said Malory.

'Remember us if you ever visit Dawlish again,' The woman handed back her card.

'I will, thanks,' said Malory, again.

She turned to leave, but her attention was caught by an object on the window sill beside the door. She stared at it, before asking the landlady: 'That bowl; on the window sill. Do you mind if I take a look at it?'

'No, not at all, Dear,' said the landlady, coming around from behind the desk to join Malory.

Malory picked up the stoneware and studied it in a half-stupor. It was almost exactly the same as her own bowl; the one that she had picked up in Portobello Market. The one that had helped persuade her that she was not living her true life. It was the same warm brown clay, with a chocolate colour in the interior; only this bowl, had a painted design on one side, in the same dark brown pigment. It was two stylised fishes, swimming in opposite directions.

'Pilchards,' said Malory, under her breath.

She turned the bowl over and saw the mark carved into the base; the same whirly pattern as the one on her own bowl. But this time she saw it for what it was. Once she saw it, she could not unsee it. It was lower case and cursive with a stylised curl, omitting the dot on the 'i'. It was the word 'if'.

'Where did you get this bowl?' she asked the landlady.

'Why, it was many years ago now,' said the woman. 'Before my poor Maurice died, bless him. In that place in Cornwall, where all the artists go. Lovely holiday it was.'

'St Ives?' said Malory.

'Yes, that's right. St Ives. We only went for the day, as we were staying with friends in a farmhouse in the countryside. But it was very nice, I remember. The lady who sold us the bowl was lovely too. She had her own little pottery and visitors were allowed to come in and look around as she worked, and all her stuff was on display to buy.'

'Do you remember who she was?' asked Malory, feeling the stir of excitement in her bones.

'Oh, let me see now,' said the woman. 'I should know... What was it?'

'Isadora Francis?' suggested Malory.

'Yes. Yes, that was it,' said the woman. 'Isadora Francis. Charming woman.'

Malory turned the bowl over again. If. Isadora Francis. They were initials. And the same initials were on her own beloved bowl. They had been right under her nose the whole time, and she had completely missed it. Hoping that her bowl might be an original from The Leach Pottery, she had completely failed to recognise Dora's interpretation of the style.

'I'm such an idiot,' Malory muttered to herself.

Virginia, Daphne and Barbara were back, standing in the hallway with the landlady, looking over her shoulders at the pot. Only this time they were joined by Dora Francis, who sat perched on the vacated window sill, laughing at her.

'Golly,' said Daphne. 'I dare say she's finally twigged.'

'Brava,' said Virginia, imperiously.

Even Barbara smiled.

Malory was still turning the bowl over in her hands, staring at it incredulously, when she was interrupted by a message on her phone.

'My cab's here,' she said, reluctantly returning the bowl to the now vacated sill.

She thanked the landlady a further time, and then left. She found the car easily and slid into the back seat.

'Exeter, isn't it?' said the cab driver jovially, already pulling away from the boarding house.

'Yes...' said Malory, distractedly.

'Righty-oh,' said the driver. 'Exeter it is.'

* * *

Sometime later Malory walked into the railway station in a fluster, and purchased a new ticket, hoping she would be able to find a seat on the next train. Luck was with her and she only had to wait a short while before the fast intercity arrived. She found an unreserved seat and waited impatiently for the train to get moving. It was imperative that she should not be swerved from her decision. As the carriages slowly left the station, the train manager made his announcement over the intercom.

'Thank you for travelling on the Great Western Railway...we will shortly be arriving at....' Malory closed her eyes and listened as the announcement listed the journey stops, before it culminated with, '*...Camborne, Hayle, St Erth, and our final destination; Penzance. Passengers for Looe should change at Liskeard; Passengers for Newquay at Par...'* Malory listened as the litany was recited, and then

confirmed: '*...That's Par for Newquay, Truro for Falmouth, St Erth for St Ives.*'

Malory breathed a sigh of relief, and smiled. *St Erth for St Ives...* Such lovely words.

The cab had got as far as Exmouth, before she could stand it no longer. The duel in her mind had been excruciating. She could not envisage Exeter, nor suffer arriving at Paddington station. It no longer made sense. So, before it was too late, she had asked the driver to detour. *That was correct; she no longer wanted Exeter, but Plymouth.* And now she was on the train heading back to St Ives and it could not go fast enough. For now Malory knew in her heart, what she wanted most of all.

She wanted the pilchard cellar. She wanted the gallery she knew she had to make there. And she knew she had to save it without further doubt or delay, before it was lost forever in an amalgam of glass and steel. She thought about the hostility that she had felt from Judith Crutchley, and the snobbier elements of the St Ives art scene. She had allowed them to run her out of town, but now her heart was full of valour.

So what, if they didn't like Jago's work? Perhaps St Ives needed a shake-up. Maybe it needed some fresh talent and new voices. Wasn't that what its entire history of art had been based upon? And she, Malory, intended to be at the forefront. So what, if she was an 'incomer'? So was Barbara. And Willie, and Patrick, and all the rest of them. *She* was no second-home-owner; just-down-from-Londoner; she belonged to St Ives, and she was staying put.

But she was ashamed that she had allowed herself to be cowed. And all because she had had her ego dented by a young man. It was not his fault; she had been vain, and had let her fantasies derail her from what, she could now clearly see, was her true mission. She had felt all along that her destiny was in

St Ives. But she knew now that it was not as Senara's fairy godmother, but as a champion of new art. The bowl had been her sign. She had not immediately grasped its meaning, only that it had meant *something*. But she had been distracted. Suddenly Malory realised that life was a game, full of obstacles, and never simple. The road was scattered with temptations, to steer you from your true course with their siren calls. And yet...

She quickly repressed the image of cornflower-blue eyes, summoned by her traitorous mind. She envisioned her ego coolly shuffling the deck, with a languid cynical gaze; knowing there were plenty more of *those* cards to be dealt, and dealt *with*. In that pack were paintings, and choux buns, and octopus tattoos. But there was also challenge, endeavour, and—if she was lucky—victory.

At St Erth, Malory used the short time available before the connecting train to buy a postcard and stamp from the tea room. She filled the card out quickly on the short journey to St Ives, reluctant to miss any of the scenery from the window. St Ives Bay was glorious in the sunlight, with no trace of the havoc wreaked by yesterday's storm...

Gleefully, she practically ran down the steps to The Warren and along through the streets back to Fore Street, only stopping at the post box on the corner of Ayr Lane to send the postcard. It was addressed to Max Patterson. She re-read it once more, wondering if it was too crude? Too severe?

'Nah,' she said, with newfound confidence. It was concise and to the point. And so, Malory popped the card in the box; a message that simply said:

'Stuff your job. Malory xx'.

CHAPTER 59

A Warrior

The minute Malory had returned her things to the flat, she hurried across town to Bob Prowse's office. She should probably have changed into some of her old, smarter clothes, to appear more professional. But there was no time to lose. She had to buy Isadora's pilchard cellar. Bob was cagey at first. There were others interested, he said, and the property had barely been put on the market. She was of course, free to put in an offer, but he couldn't guarantee...

'Full asking price,' Malory said. 'Cash. I can give you all the information and paperwork.'

'Perhaps you might like a little more time to think it through?' said Bob. 'It's a big investment.'

Malory tried not to show her resentment. He didn't think she knew what she was doing, which, she conceded, was a fair point. She wondered what interest it was to him who might buy the property? She remembered Olly's comments about bribing council officials. Was Bob, too, expecting some sort of backhander, on top of his commission?

'I'm deadly serious,' she said. 'And I'm certain. I don't need more time.'

'Very well,' said Bob, reluctantly. 'I'll inform the owners of your offer.'

'Do that,' said Malory, not moving from her chair and indicating the phone on his desk.

'It's usually the practice to inform the sellers...shall we say, privately,' said Bob. 'I'll get back to you in due course.'

'I'm not leaving until you give them my offer,' said Malory determinedly. 'And please ensure they know my intentions in respect of the building. I'd be happy to speak to them myself.'

Fifteen minutes later, Malory left Bob's office almost giddy with nausea at the thought of what she was undertaking, but with a smile on her face nonetheless. The owners were considering her offer and Bob would inform her soon of their decision.

Come on, Dora's family, she thought. *It's in your hands now. Don't let us down.*

In her mind's eye, Malory envisaged a future where she would save further old buildings in St Ives, preserving them as studios for future generations of artists...

She allowed herself a chuckle at her new-found audacity. *Calm down Malory, First things first...*

It was Sunday, so Atlantic Arts was closed, but she returned there to look things over. Not that it was necessary, since her exodus had been so short-lived. But she wanted somewhere quiet to have a think. She sat on the deep window sill and picked up the clay bowl that had started this whole journey, and turned it over in her hands. There was the inscription on the bottom, almost exactly like the one in Dawlish; its message so obvious, now that she could see it. She cupped the bowl in both hands and imagined Dora crafting it on her potter's wheel. It was such a minor thing, on which to lay the foundation of her entire future. The risk was enormous, but Malory felt an excitement that had been alien to her life this far. Could it really be that she might succeed in her dreams? That she had just taken the first step to making it happen? It felt as though she had come home.

She should call Senara and let her know that she had returned, but she would not mention her attempt to buy the pilchard cellar unless, and until, the offer was, hopefully, accepted.

The doorbell jangled and Giovanna came into the shop.

'Hey, you're still here,' she said. 'I thought you'd already left. I was just going to make sure everything was okay before opening tomorrow.'

'That's good of you,' said Malory. 'But there's been a change of plan. I'm not going anywhere now.'

'Cool,' said Giovanna, clearly not requiring any further explanation. 'Hey, have you heard about all the excitement that went on in the storm? Everyone's talking about it.'

'No,' said Malory. 'Why? What happened?'

Giovanna sat down opposite Malory on the window seat, her eyes bright with excitement. Malory replaced the bowl between them carefully, but Giovanna barely noticed.

Funny, thought Malory. *It's just a bowl to her.*

She listened as Giovanna excitedly recalled the events of the previous day; of how Kit had nearly been lost, and Jago had rescued the boy from the sea.

'He's such a hero,' Giovanna finished. 'They both are.'

'Yes,' said Malory, in a trance. 'They are.'

When Giovanna had left, she locked up the shop and went upstairs to the flat. She went out on to the balcony and leant on the railings. The orange-yellow rooftops of St Ives made an abstract pattern as they stretched away towards Porthmeor Beach and the treacherous cliffs to the west. Malory's heart was beating wildly. It was torture to know that while she was busy running away, Jago had been in real danger. If the sea at Dawlish had not so ferociously ended her flight, she might still not know. She could be at Paddington by now, dodging through the crowds, and working her way back into the mundane. To think that he might have been lost forever, whilst she was hundreds of miles away from him, on some cowardly retreat.

She reached into her pocket and took out her mobile. Should she message him? Just a simple, polite, enquiry. Surely that would be acceptable? But even as her heart yearned to reach out, to show love and compassion, it could neither bear the wound of the reply that she thought inevitable. That he might simply reply: *I'm fine, thanks*.

She felt the stab in her heart just to think of it.

Is this how you're going to carry on? She admonished herself. She was supposed to be Malory the Brave, now. Malory who took risks and created her own future. She was a warrior and a knight. How could she let the small matter of rejection cow her actions? Where was her integrity? She should put her pride aside and do the right thing.

Hi, I heard about what happened yesterday. Hope you're okay? x

She pressed send on the message.

There, she had done it. Malory breathed a sigh of relief. Even if no reply was forthcoming, she felt immediately better for being able to send him some small message of love. She would have to see him eventually, and it was preferable for civility to prevail over avoidance and reserve.

But after an hour had passed with no reply, she resigned herself to the probability that Jago now preferred to keep his distance. It saddened her, yet she still did not regret the message; for it was truth, speaking from the heart. It was the bare minimum of truth—she really wanted to hold him and tell him how much she could not bear to have lost him—but it was truth nonetheless.

And so, when the buzz of the phone finally came, it startled her. Nervously, she opened his reply and read:

I'm good thanks. The band are playing tomorrow at Driftwood. You should come, if you're around. Ask Senara, she has the details.

'Is that it?' Malory cried aloud, directing her frustration at the innocent phone. 'You nearly died, and that's all you have to say?!'

And yet a warm feeling enveloped her. They could be friends. She would be his ally, and advocate for his art. It was better than hostility and so much better than the way she had felt yesterday, when she had boarded the train with all hope lost.

Malory smiled, and was filled with gratitude that she had, so literally, been stopped in her tracks; that she had been shipwrecked mid-voyage, and washed up, back upon the golden shores of St Ives.

CHAPTER 60

In the wake

Kit stood on the terrace and looked out over the bay towards the lighthouse. It was two days after the storm, and already life was moving on. That early morning trip to the hospital for a check-up after his accident now felt like a dream, in which, miraculously, they had said he was okay.

He shouldn't be okay. It didn't make sense to him.

It was the open mic night at Driftwood that evening, and Kit was supposed to be playing. Yet everything felt somehow surreal, as though he were still processing the events of the shout. On that night, the trawler fishermen and skipper had all been recovered safely, but he himself, had remained in peril.

Against the odds, the lifeboat crew had spotted what they desperately hoped might be the reflective panels on Kit's jacket against the darkness of the waves. Zack had been the one to jump in with a line, bravely swimming against the onslaught of waves, to rescue him; Zack, the unassuming family man and quiet hero. Kit owed him his life, and would be eternally grateful. But his mind had not yet recovered from the thought of the potential other outcome; when for a time he had had to contemplate his darkest emotions.

Yet tonight he was supposed to stand up with his guitar and sing romantic folk songs, and ballads of the sea. There was a beautiful irony in there, he supposed. The sea had taught him a lesson: that she was not to be trifled with. But Kit could not become afraid. The sea was his life; his living and his love.

He picked up the guitar, sat down on the patio chair, and began to tune it. When it was done, he started to play one of the songs from his set. However, his voice failed him, releasing only a rasping croak. Perhaps the seawater had salt-scarred his throat. But Kit felt a deeper dissonance; a disconnect with his soul. He sat for a minute in silence, wondering if he might have lost his voice forever; if he might never again sing with joy in his heart; and that in this insidious way, the sea would have her price.

Suddenly fearful, he abandoned the guitar and went indoors, looking for Astrid; hoping for some reassurance. He found her by the fireplace in the living room, peering at her reflection in the mirror above the mantlepiece, as she applied make-up. She wore a flimsy summer dress in a flowered pattern.

'Hey,' he said softly. 'You look nice.'

'Hey you,' said Astrid, with a smile. 'And thank you. I do try.'

He slipped his arms around her waist from behind. 'I'm feeling a little nervous to be honest.'

'Nervous?' said Astrid, looking at his reflection in the mirror. 'Why? And can you not do that when I'm applying eyeliner? I'll smudge it.'

'Sorry,' said Kit, moving away again. 'About tonight, I mean. I'm not sure if I'm up to it.'

'Tonight?' said Astrid. 'What are you talking about?'

'I'm just feeling sort of... Fragile. And that's not like me. I hate it. I'm not sure I can perform.'

'Perform?' said Astrid, holding the eyeliner wand mid-air. 'Seriously, I don't know what you're talking about.'

'The music event,' said Kit. 'At Driftwood, remember? It's tonight.'

Astrid turned to face him. 'Oh that. That's tonight? I'd forgotten all about it.'

'I thought that's why you were getting ready,' said Kit.

'Oh. No, sorry,' said Astrid. 'I'm going out with Pepper tonight. I thought you knew.'

'No, I didn't know,' said Kit, trying to hide his irritation. 'Well, just bring her. The more support, the better.'

'I can't,' said Astrid. 'She wants to go to Penzance. A new burger and beer bar has opened there. I thought I told you?'

'No, you didn't,' said Kit. 'Can't you go another time?'

'It's a bit late to cancel now. It's all arranged for Grady to have the kids,' said Astrid. 'And you just said you didn't want to do it now, anyway.'

'That's *not* what I said!' exclaimed Kit, in frustration.

'Look, we'll try and swing by afterwards,' said Astrid. 'You're not going on until late, are you?'

'Thanks,' said Kit sardonically, before walking away.

'Oh, please don't do this now,' said Astrid. 'I'm already running late. You'll be fine,' she shouted after his departing figure.

'You always are,' she added acerbically, under her breath.

When she had left, Kit mooched morosely around the house, wondering if he should bail on the concert. Increasingly, his heart wasn't in it. Absently he began to clear the clutter of make-up that Astrid had left on the mantlepiece and pack it back into the toiletry bag. He went upstairs to the bedroom, and sitting on Astrid's side of the bed, opened a drawer on her bedside table. He was sure that this was where she kept the make-up bag, but it was so full that he had to clear a space. In doing so, a letter was revealed, stuffed at the back of the drawer.

Kit hesitated. He knew he shouldn't read it. But recognising the name on the header of the official-looking form, he became curious. Slowly, he slid the letter out from behind the rubble. It was addressed to Astrid, from her former landlords. Kit read the words in confusion. He read them over and over, sure that he must have made some sort of mistake in translation. His head was spinning with incomprehension, and a searing flame coursed through his veins.

But no. The letter clearly stated that Astrid's flat had been completely made good, and that she could return at the beginning of the next month. Again, Kit checked the date on the letter, but it had not magically changed. It was dated ten months ago.

CHAPTER 61

Open Mic

Later, Kit sat alone at a table in Driftwood tentatively sipping a beer. He closed his eyes and tried to reconnect with his inner force; that spirit for life that he had always so easily channelled. But all he could hear was Cosmic Ray complaining to Rosa.

'It's ridiculous,' said Cosmic. 'We're by far the best-known band around here. We should be headlining.'

'There are no headliners,' said Rosa patiently. 'Everyone is on an equal footing.'

'For sure, for sure,' said Cosmic, nodding. 'But we should at least be on last, not third. It'll still be daylight, for goodness' sake! Our sound belongs to the *night*. It is the natural finale. A climactic crescendo of sound.'

'That's the trouble,' said Rosa. 'You're too loud. There are noise restrictions after a certain time. The residents would complain.'

'Oh, *well*! We mustn't upset the bourgeoisie,' said Cosmic haughtily. 'It's like punk never happened...'

Kit tried to tune him out, but Cosmic had a way of speaking as though he were projecting from a stage. He was the absolute star of his life, and all must hear his words. Kit averted his gaze to take in the view of the harbour. Rosa had opened up all the glass doors to encourage the attention of passers-by. They were not serving food that night, so all receipts would be from drinks alone. As he stared at the scenery, Kit wrestled with his thoughts, and the source of his disquiet. He knew that it did not stem from the incident at sea alone, but rather was the culmination of a slow discomfort that had been steadily growing; a feeling that he was on the wrong path. For a long time, he had supposed that this was just what it meant to be an adult; that naturally things would change, and not always for the best. Ups and downs were to be expected. But when he had found himself stranded in the black ocean, he had experienced something beyond the aching sadness for his life's end. He had felt a deep terror of having gone astray somewhere; that he somehow could have done better. It felt akin to dishonesty; as though his integrity had somehow been compromised.

I used to feel so free, he thought. *And now...*

At that moment, his reverie was abruptly ended by the arrival of Dan, fresh from the bar with a pint, who casually plonked himself down on the banquette next to Kit. He took a slurp of beer and rubbed his hands together expectantly.

'Alright?' queried Dan.

Kit nodded. 'Alright?'

Dan nodded in turn. 'Should be a fun night. Looking forward to it. You, eh...on your own?'

'Yes,' said Kit, not wanting to elaborate.

'Thought Astrid might be here to support,' said Dan, looking sideways at Kit. 'Especially after what's just happened to you.'

'She can't,' answered Kit. Then after a pause added: 'It's not important.'

'Hey ho,' said Dan, as the first band got ready in the corner of the room, where the tables and chairs had been cleared away, and a small platform erected as a stage. 'I'm glad we have a moment to chat before the music starts. I've had a bit of a revelation.'

'You have?' said Kit, eyeing his friend suspiciously. Dan didn't often have revelations.

'Yes. It's about the list,' said Dan, with a smug expression.

Kit groaned. 'Oh, the list. Are you still doing that? Look Dan I think maybe...'

Dan held a hand up to silence him. 'Hear me out. I admit that it wasn't working out for me. I started to despair that I would ever find the right woman, and that we'd got the list all wrong. But then I took a fresh look at it the other day, and I suddenly realised that it described one person. And she's perfect. I can't believe I didn't see it before.'

'Well, go on then. Who is it?'

Dan leaned towards Kit, beaming like a puppy, and said conspiratorially: 'Senara.'

Kit was flabbergasted. 'Senara?' he spurted.

Dan folded his arms and nodded again, looking very pleased with himself. 'Yep, Senara. Oh look, they're starting.'

Rosa had got up to the mic to introduce the first band.

'So, you're going to ask Senara on a date?' said Kit.

'Like I said,' said Dan. 'She's perfect. Matches everything on the list. Well, *more or less*. Now shush,' he said, indicating the band.

Kit stared wildly at the band as they began to play, but was not really listening. Instead, he tried to assimilate what Dan had said into his already decomposed equilibrium. He did not understand what this feeling was, but it was distinctly uncomfortable, and it was not helping him at all. Three songs later, the band left the stage to make way for the next act; a young singer-songwriter who might ensure a quieter set.

Kit did not know what to say to Dan in the interlude. He shouldn't feel so... So *angry*. Why was he feeling angry? Nothing made sense. Thankfully, Tamsin arrived and came to join them. She wore a red mini dress with a low-cut neck that flattered her curves. Unusually, Dan got up to greet her, and then even more surprisingly, embraced her, and then kissed her. Kit was more puzzled than ever. For it was no superficial air kiss, but a proper one. On the lips.

Tamsin moved a chair to be close to Dan on the banquette, and sat down. Dan laid a hand on her thigh.

Kit eyed them each in term. 'What's going on?'

Dan had an enormous grin on his face. 'Turns out I *do* like breasts. And legs as well. I just do. That's the truth.'

Tamsin slapped his arm, playfully.

'And I really don't mind make-up,' continued Dan. 'Did you know it's really quite an artform?'

'I had no idea,' said Kit, drily. 'But what about Senara? You just said...'

'Yes, I did, didn't I?' said Dan, obviously enjoying himself. 'I did say she was perfect. Only one problem...'

'And?' said Kit in frustration.

Dan produced the crumpled list from his pocket and slapped it on the table.

'I didn't write that list. You did.' Dan paused for realisation to sink in. 'This is a list of the qualities in an ideal woman for *you*, not me.'

Kit stared at Dan, then at Tamsin. 'Is this a joke?' he said.

Dan sighed, then turned to Tamsin. 'Come on my love, let's get you a cocktail. Leave young Kit here to have a little think.'

Kit threw himself against the back of the banquette in consternation and watched them move to the bar area. He remained like that for most of the set. Only his eyes drifted from the singer to the piece of paper that still lay on the table in front of him.

Eventually he grabbed it quickly and read down the list of attributes that he had spontaneously written out months ago.

He read it again, and then stared, transfixed, as though the words were an impossible riddle, or blatant lies.

He looked up again just in time to see Senara enter the venue with Malory.

CHAPTER 62

Heartstrings

Malory and Senara arrived in the interval before Cosmic Ray and the Neutrinos took their slot. The café was, by now, crowded, but they managed to grab a small table near the open patio doors.

'Oh look, there's Kit,' said Malory, indicating where he sat. 'Shame all the seats at his table are taken, we could have joined him.'

'Yes, a shame,' said Senara, although Malory did not think she sounded convincing.

'Forgive me, but I heard you two had had a fight, or something,' said Malory, recalling Giovanna's gossip. 'Is it still going on?'

'Not for my part,' said Senara glumly.

Malory gave her a sympathetic look. 'It will all be okay, I'm sure. You've known each other too long to fall out.'

'I suppose,' said Senara.

Malory spotted Jago across the crowd, as he prepared to take the stage with the band. She hoped to catch his eye but he appeared engrossed in tuning his guitar. She drank in his image guiltily, wondering how any man could be so beautiful. A sadness crept over her as she imagined him being with other women. He would already have moved on, she reasoned, from his infatuation with her, and perhaps felt fortunate at his lucky escape. She turned away to look at Senara's unhappy face again, and decided that this would not do. She was determined for her mood to remain buoyant.

‘It was good of Teddy to hold the fort, again,’ she said. ‘I wanted to talk to you. But wait a minute; you save the seats; I’ll get us some drinks.’

Before Senara had a chance to reply, Malory jumped up and edged her way towards the bar area. She returned with a bottle of champagne and two flutes.

‘Champagne again?’ said Senara. ‘Very nice. Are we celebrating something new?’

Malory poured the drinks carefully, with a grin on her face. ‘We are...’

And so, she told Senara her news. That Dora’s relatives, delighted at her intention to preserve the character of the building, had accepted her offer on the pilchard cellar. And so, she would become the new freeholder of the building, which in effect, would make the lease of The Secret Spot essentially void. She also told Senara of her plans for the gallery downstairs. It did the trick of lifting Senara’s spirits, and she fired enthusiastic questions at Malory. From across the room, anyone glancing in their direction would only see two women happy, excited and enjoying life, and would never have guessed that each carried a sadness in her heart.

All conversation was rendered impossible when The Neutrinos began to play. As the crowd watched agog at Cosmic’s contortions on the small stage, Malory only had eyes for Jago. But he did not appear interested in finding her in the crowd, only concentrated on his performance. When they had finished their allocated three songs, Malory’s ears were ringing from the assault, but she cheered and clapped along with the crowd. The band cleared the stage, and Kit went up to get ready for his set.

Cosmic could be seen prowling through the crowd, scanning for mythical music agents. However, Jago did not join the audience or head for the bar with his other bandmates, let alone come and say 'hi'. Instead, he chose to sit alone at one side of the stage on a stool. Malory tried not to feel affronted. She would have to get used to his indifference, she supposed.

Kit began strumming the intro to his first song. He appeared to step up to the mic to sing, but then backed away again, and repeated the lead-in. He paced around the stage, strumming the same chords over and over, as if practicing.

Malory leaned towards Senara. 'What's going on? Has he started?' she whispered.

Senara looked puzzled. 'He seems nervous,' she said incredulously.

'Do you think he's okay?' said Malory, worried. 'I wouldn't be surprised if he was still in shock.'

'Maybe,' said Senara. 'But he's used to the sea; to being on it, and in it. It would take a lot to shake his nerve, I think.'

Malory watched Senara's face as she stared at Kit in concern. Her brow was furrowed and she had placed one hand on her chest; where her heart was. She followed her gaze to where they met with Kit's eyes. He had seen Senara and it appeared to shake him from whatever gear he had been stuck in. He stepped to the mic more determinedly, and this time, the words came out. He seemed to have overcome whatever resistance was battling him, and regained his poise. Malory could see his spirit grow as the set progressed, and noticed too, how Senara's expression relaxed into a smile, and how her eyes glowed with pride.

Kit finished his last song and then after saying thank-you to the appreciative audience, he made an announcement.

'Okay, we have a little bit of a surprise for you tonight,' he said, looking to one side of the stage.

At the same time, Jago appeared to signal to Senara, who suddenly stood up.

'What's happening?' said Malory.

But Senara merely winked at her, then approached the stage area.

'May I welcome back to the stage,' continued Kit, 'Mr Jago Berryman from The Neutrinos, who you've all just enjoyed...and just about recovered from.'

As the crowd laughed, Jago walked back onto the stage with an acoustic guitar this time, and waved at the audience, who cheered back.

'Yeah, you all know Jago,' said Kit to the local crowd. 'But he has an extra number to perform tonight, and it's something a bit special...'

* * *

Kit was surprised when Senara took the stool that Jago had been sitting on, and hauled it onstage. He looked at Jago in puzzlement.

'Senara's going to play harmonica in the bridge,' Jago explained quickly. 'We went over it last night. Is that okay?'

'Sure,' said Kit, shrugging. 'It's your song.'

But he felt oddly uncomfortable to be close to Senara again, particularly since they had not spoken since the night of the lifeboat shout, when they had once again argued. He knew that there was much that remained unresolved between them; but for now, it would have to wait. Senara settled on the tall stool, and Jago stepped up to the mic.

'Okay,' he said. 'I'm not used to being the front man, so be gentle with me.'

There was a good-natured murmur from the crowd.

Kit nodded to Jago, indicating he was ready. Jago paused, staring down at the floor, while he waited for the chatter to quieten. When the audience became hushed, he strummed the first few chords of the intro. Then, continuing to play rhythm guitar, he stepped up to the microphone and began to sing the ballad that he had written earlier that summer, and that Cosmic had rejected. He began to pour out his love song.

After the first few bars, Kit joined in on guitar, weaving a melodic pattern through Jago's chords. On the chorus he approached his own microphone and sang subtle, harmonic background vocals. At the bridge, he dropped back from the front of the stage, and as he continued to play, watched Senara perform her harmonica part. Kit usually forgot that she even played harmonica. But now, as she perched on her stool, with her long blonde wavy hair cascading over her shoulders and back, he remembered once more how Senara would sit on the rock at Pendour Cove when they were youngsters... When she had looked every bit the mermaid of Zennor playing her lonesome song to the sea.

He could not take his eyes off her.

* * *

In the audience, Malory sat in stunned silence. She wished that she had a pause button, so that she might replay the lyrics to the song; so that she could be sure. But all she could do was listen in real time, as the melody and words unfolded. It felt as though he was singing to her alone, and speaking directly to her heart.

'*...Island kisses in the afternoon...Two hearts beating with the ocean's tune...*' Jago sang his words.

Malory glanced around at the audience, who were all enthralled at the performance, and at Jago's soulful voice. To them, it was just a beautiful song, but Malory knew that it was meant for her, because she understood the meaning behind the lyrics.

'...Don't let us become...a ghost story...' Jago sang in the chorus.

She felt her heart swell, and her eyes well up. She let the emotion flow through her body, and the tears shamelessly tumble down her cheeks.

The song finished on one last, long-held note that left the audience giving the biggest cheer of the night. Malory saw Kit nod his approval at Jago onstage. The clapping went on for some time before Jago took to the mic again.

'Er, that's it,' he said. 'That's all I've got. Maybe next year I'll have another song.'

As the audience laughed again, Malory giggled, wiped her tears and tried to compose herself.

After the set, the chattering revived, and people mingled or headed to the bar. Malory saw Jago make his way towards her, at last. She stood up to meet him, but felt lost for words.

'So,' he said. 'Did you like it?'

'I did,' said Malory. 'I loved it. It was a surprise, though.'

'A good one I hope?'

'Yes, I think so.'

'I heard you'd left town?'

'I did. But I came back.'

He looked at her through narrowed eyes

'Alfred Wallis,' he said.

'Alfred Wallis?'

Jago moved a little closer to her. 'Alfred Wallis married a woman twenty years older than him.'

'That's right,' said Malory. 'So he did.'

'They were together over forty-five years; until she died. Also,' said Jago, 'it's my birthday tomorrow. So technically, there'll only then be thirteen years between us.'

'Well, that doesn't sound so bad at all,' said Malory.

'It's nothing,' said Jago.

Malory closed her eyes, and shook her head. Then looking up at him again, said: 'I'm so sorry. I should never have made a big deal out of it in the first place.'

'No, you shouldn't have,' he said, with a stern face.

'After all, it's not as if you're asking me to marry you, or something,' she said coyly, reiterating what he had said, all that time ago, on The Island.

'Exactly,' said Jago.

'I mean, things probably won't work out once we get to know each other better anyway,' said Malory. 'But that doesn't mean we shouldn't try?'

'Absolutely,' said Jago. 'There'd be no fun in that at all.'

'We'll have...a brief summer of love,' said Malory, beaming. 'A beautiful memory to warm us in old age.'

'Not too long for you to wait then,' he said, pulling her close in his arms, and grinning. 'And yeah, I'll give it a week. Maybe two.'

And this time when he kissed her, Malory did not push him away, but responded with all the emotion that she had tried to repress. She did not care that everyone would see, and that they would become the subject of fresh gossip. She no longer cared what anyone thought. All she could think about was him, and the happiness that she felt right there and then. And that was all that mattered.

CHAPTER 63

Fallout

The day after the concert at Driftwood, Kit and Astrid broke up. Amongst all the shouting and recriminations, Kit knew that it was not just the fact that she had lied to him about the flat, but that he had long felt an unease in the relationship that he had been reluctant to explore. It had never, in the past, been in his nature to delve too deeply into matters of the heart. He took life as it came. He was carefree. But now he accepted that the arrangement of living together had been thrust upon him. It did not feel like it had been a conscious commitment, but rather a lazy neglect to steer his own course.

'I don't love you,' he had said, as kindly as he could; but knowing it to be brutal.

Astrid was furious, and hurled accusations. 'It's because of that fucking Senara, isn't it?'

It wasn't without pause that Kit had answered. 'Nothing has happened. This is about you and me.'

But Kit knew that this was not entirely true. He had stayed up late after the concert, sitting on the terrace with his plants. As he stared out to sea, and up to the stars above, he had faced some difficult truths. Even before Dan had planted the hint; even before he had been entranced by Senara playing harmonica; Kit had already suspected what was forming in his heart, but had denied it. He had run from it, unwilling to accept. But the truth was, that when his life had been in the utmost danger, and he had been faced with the story of his life, it was not the thought of Astrid that had pervaded his soul, but

Senara. Not Astrid, but a longing for Senara, that had caused him sorrow and regret.

Since she had not responded to the landlord's letter, Astrid had long since lost the flat. But despite her appeals, Kit was resolute. It was arranged that she would move in with Pepper and Grady until she found somewhere new. It made Kit feel unnaturally cruel, but he consoled himself with the fact that not once in all her angry tirades, did she mention the word *love*. Her concerns revolved around where she would live—not to mention the impact on her finances now she must pay rent again—and most of all, what people would say. Not once did she claim to love him, or to be broken-hearted, and so Kit had little cause for guilt, or doubt in his decision.

It did not take long for the rumour mill of St Ives to spread the word. Within days the news of Kit and Astrid's break-up was all over town.

Teddy rushed into work at The Secret Spot with eyes shining. 'Did you hear?'

Malory, who could hardly bear to stay away these days, now that she was to become the new owner, had popped in for lunch, and sat forking a salad at the bar. 'What's all the excitement?'

Senara kept quiet as Teddy relayed the 'facts', as he'd heard them. Apparently, they'd split up because Astrid was spending too much time with Pepper, and it had been 'suggested' to him that perhaps Astrid and Pepper had become a secret 'item'.

'It's probably all gossip,' said Senara. 'I wouldn't read too much into it.'

She moved away quickly to help Giovanna with clearing the tables, even though her task was to be in the kitchen with Charlie preparing food. Malory watched with Teddy from the bar as Senara gave one table a thorough, violent, scrubbing.

Teddy leaned in towards Malory.

'*She* should be with Kit, not that insipid Astrid,' he whispered, spitefully.

'I agree,' said Malory drily. 'But tell her that, not me.'

'If I were her, I wouldn't waste a second,' replied Teddy. 'Senara's a fool. Someone else will snap him up.'

'I'll have a word with her later,' said Malory.

'If you don't, I will,' said Teddy, with a determined look.

In the days since the Open Mic night, it had been impossible not to notice the tension between Kit and Senara. Malory had watched, from the sidelines, as they passed each other by, in the street. Each would look on the point of connecting, only to look away. Senara would duck into the nearest shop, or café; while Kit, appearing hesitant, would think better of whatever plagued his mind, before walking on. Sitting at the bar of The Secret Spot, Kit's eyes would travel to Senara as she worked, only to return to his pint when she came near. They were passing each other by in *life*. If each could but read the other's mind...

Later, after she had locked up the shop in Fore Street, Malory headed to The Barque, where she had arranged to meet Senara for a drink. She found her sitting by the window, staring trance-like at the view of the pier, and harbour boats. After they had ordered wine, and performed the usual niceties, Malory broached the subject.

'So,' she said. 'What are you going to do about Kit?'

Senara gave a puzzled look, but Malory could detect the blush in her cheeks. 'What are you talking about?' she replied. 'What about Kit?'

'Maybe you should tell him how you feel,' said Malory, looking unflinchingly into Senara's eyes.

Senara returned the gaze defiantly. 'I still don't know what you mean.'

'Senara,' said Malory, kindly. 'It's obvious. To anyone. You love him. Go on, deny it. I dare you.'

Senara shook her head in exasperation. 'This bloody town. Everyone thinks they know everything.'

When Malory said nothing, Senara continued. 'Okay, what if it is true? It doesn't matter. He's only just broken up with Astrid. What would it look like if I went chasing after him straight away?'

'Who cares?' said Malory.

'You can talk,' said Senara, cynically. She had been filled in with the details of Jago and Malory's erstwhile furtive romance. '*You* cared what people thought.'

'Not really,' said Malory. 'Only one person. You can't let him go, Senara. At the very least, stop avoiding him. Have you even spoken properly to him since he nearly drowned?'

'Don't say that,' whispered Senara, facing away to look out of the window once more. When she turned to look at Malory again, she was almost in tears. 'You don't understand. I can't. Not after everything that happened with Pepper. It would justify everything that people say about me. More than that, it would make me question *myself*, and my morals. And what if he then got back with Astrid, and I'm stuck in the middle, again. I'm tired of being cast as the 'other woman'. I want someone of my own.'

'This is different...' said Malory.

'Is it?' said Senara. 'They're a couple. They've been living together. I am not going anywhere near that. And that's final.'

'Okay,' Malory nodded, conceding. She did not wish to upset Senara further. 'Let's talk about something else.'

But later she messaged Teddy: *We're going to have to go to plan B.*

CHAPTER 64

St Ives Bay Mackerel

Senara stood alone in The Secret Spot, wearing an apron, and with her hands covered in flour. She realised that she had been kneading the pastry dough for an unnecessary amount of time. But they were not due to open for a couple of hours, and she relished some rare time alone. She took a moment to stand back and take a look at her life. It was in silent moments like this, that she felt that she was living in a dream. The Secret Spot would soon be safe, and hers to run, and develop her ideas in. She could not expect more.

She wrapped the dough and put it in the fridge for later, then cleaned herself up. Removing the apron, she went to sit at the window. She let her hair down and gazed upon the beach, drawn to the sound of clear green waves, that ebbed and flowed on the morning tide. It was all so serene, and beautiful, that she knew she should be grateful. Yet she carried an aching pain, as though her heart had somehow discovered how to cry, where her tears had refused.

It appeared that the rumours were true, and that Kit and Astrid had indeed separated. Upon hearing the news confirmed, Senara had felt an immediate sense of guilt. She should not have said anything to Kit about Astrid. At the time, he had not listened, but what if she had influenced him in some way? What if she was responsible, and more, that he resented her for her interference? At the concert, she had caught him glance at her on several occasions, but he had barely spoken; and after the gig, had left quickly, without saying goodbye. It broke Senara's heart to think that her foolish actions might have damaged their friendship for good.

She was disturbed by the arrival of Malory, carrying her usual large black notebook, in which she made plans and ideas about the business.

'Ah, good, you're here,' said Malory. 'I need to discuss something with you.'

Malory sat down at a nearby table and opened the notebook. She took a pen from her bag and appeared to scan her notes quickly, before looking up at Senara again, who had not moved.

'Come on, Senara, this is business,' she said.

Senara sighed and slouched from her perch on the window sill like a sullen teenager, to sit opposite Malory at the table. 'Okay, what's up Boss?'

'Please don't call me that,' said Malory, with a smile. 'Although, I may have to be a little bit bossy today.'

'What's wrong?' said Senara, suddenly concerned.

'Nothing,' said Malory, brightly. 'At least nothing to worry about. I'm pleased with the way things are going, on the whole...'

'On the whole?' said Senara.

'Okay, now hear me out, at least,' said Malory. 'I know how important it is to you that The Secret Spot is a vegetarian café. If anything, we could probably expand to include vegan recipes. There's a great demand these days.'

'Sure,' said Senara, thoughtfully. 'I could do vegan. But I wouldn't want to do it exclusively. I like my cheese dishes too much.'

'No, of course not,' said Malory. 'I wouldn't expect that. But talking of exclusion, you sort of raise my next point...'

Senara looked on expectantly.

'St Ives is known for many things,' said Malory. 'But three of the most intrinsic elements are surfing, art, and fishing.'

'Okay,' said Senara slowly.

'We have two out of three,' said Malory, gesturing at the building with her arm. 'We have surf culture, and we have art. But no fish.'

'Please don't make me put lobster pots everywhere,' said Senara. 'It's so corny.'

Malory laughed. 'No, not that. I'm saying we need to put fish on the menu, Senara.'

'What?' Senara looked stunned. 'But... *No!*'

'Why not?' said Malory.

Senara looked aghast. 'Because it's against my ethos. My principles!'

'Teddy told me that both of you used to prepare and cook fish in Greece,' said Malory.

'Well...yes,' said Senara. 'But it was ethically sourced; caught locally and fresh out of the sea!'

'As much of it is, here,' said Malory. 'I'm not talking about fish and chips on a grand scale, Senara. I just mean St Ives Bay mackerel, or crab, strictly locally sourced. A 'catch of the day,' sort of thing. It's about the customers, particularly the tourists. They come to St Ives expecting seafood. It's part of the heritage.'

'There's plenty of other places in town to eat seafood,' protested Senara.

'Yes, but I want us to compete with those places,' said Malory.

At that moment Teddy arrived, and came to join them at the table. The two women both greeted him and then returned to the conversation.

'You never said anything about this before,' said Senara sulkily.

'What's the problem?' said Teddy.

'Malory wants us to serve fish in the café,' said Senara.

'I see,' said Teddy.

'In a vegetarian café!' said Senara.

'What do you think, Teddy?' said Malory.

'I think it's a great idea,' said Teddy.

'What?' said Senara.

'You know fish is my area of expertise,' said Teddy. 'We could resurrect some of the old Greek recipes. It would be great, in my opinion.'

'Traitor!' cried Senara.

'Oh, don't be silly,' said Teddy, touching Senara's arm gently. 'You cooked fish all the time in Greece.'

Senara let out a deep sigh.

'And besides,' said Teddy with a flip of his hand. 'You're a hypocrite. You claim to care for animal welfare, but you use cheese and eggs all the time.'

'That's not the same!' said Senara.

'How so?' said Teddy.

'Well, I reason that we have to take advantage of animals *somehow*. To some degree,' said Senara. 'If we didn't use their produce then they'd probably become extinct. No one's going to let sheep and cows gambol freely around the fields, or chickens roam at will, if they're not being used... People are too selfish.'

'Pah!' said Teddy. 'Nonsense. It's still exploitative.'

'Abso*lute* traitor!' said Senara.

'Well, Teddy's actually made my point,' said Malory, 'If we use cheese and eggs then why not fish?'

'It's not the same at all!' wailed Senara.

'Okay,' said Malory, 'Let's all calm down. I think we should at least give it a try. If it doesn't impact much on the sales, then we can have a rethink.'

Senara leaned back in her chair with arms folded. 'So much for me being in charge,' she said grumpily.

Malory took a deep breath, but ignoring her, pressed on. 'Now, the fish will have to be responsibly sourced, as we've mentioned. So, I thought Kit would be the perfect supplier.'

'Perfect,' agreed Teddy.

Senara said nothing, but began to feel a little queasy.

'I just saw his boat land down in the harbour,' continued Teddy. 'I was out for my morning run. You could go and chat to him now. We could have fish on the menu by lunchtime.'

'I think that's an excellent idea,' said Malory. 'I'm feeling quite hungry now and I'd love to taste your recipes, Teddy.'

'Except it's not on the menu,' said Senara, indicating the large printed card on the table.

'We can put it on the chalkboard,' sighed Teddy. 'Really Senara, stop causing trouble. And go now or you'll miss him.'

'Me?' said Senara. 'Why do I have to go?'

'Well,' said Malory, peering at Senara like a schoolteacher. 'You *are* the manager...'

CHAPTER 65

On the Pier

Senara thought she was going to be sick, as she slowly made her way along Back Road East towards Smeaton's Pier. She badly wanted to talk to Kit, but was afraid that he would be unfriendly. Yet she forced herself on, reasoning that this moment would come eventually, and that she might as well get it over with. It was a bright sunny morning, but there were not many people about yet, and so she soon easily spotted him in the middle of the pier, by the huts, and the *Silver Star* moored by the sea wall. He wore his usual boiler suit, and rubber boots, and had his hair tied back at the front again, reminding Senara of their first meeting after she had arrived back in St Ives, when he had run to hug her. She did not expect the same greeting this time.

He was sorting his catch of mackerel into different boxes. Senara was acquainted with the task, having seen him perform it many times. The smallest fish were always given back to the sea from the boat. The remainder of the catch were sorted by size into ice boxes; with the largest and medium sized-fish being sent to the restaurants and cafés, and any that were damaged saved for bait. Any surplus or unsold fish were taken to Newlyn market, but Senara knew, that there was not much profit there unless you had a large catch. Not using a trawler, but fishing by line only, all of Kit's morning catch usually went to local establishments in St Ives.

He looked up briefly, as she approached him, but carried on with the job in hand.

'Alright?' said Senara nervously, as she reached him.

'Alright?' he replied, looking at her again, but returning to his work.

'I need to talk to you,' she said, adding quickly: 'It's business.'

'Business?' said Kit. 'Fire away, then. But give us a hand, would you? I've got to keep these on ice.'

'Sure,' said Senara, absent-mindedly. She sat down cross-legged on the granite stone of the pier and picked up a fish from the main box and, after a quick inspection threw it into one of the others.

Following her cue, Kit squatted down on the pier as well, and they continued to sort the fresh fish, to the amused looks of some of the other fishermen. Kit glanced furtively at Senara's downcast face.

'You don't mind doing this?' he said.

'No,' said Senara.

'You're not bothered by the smell?' he said.

She gave him a puzzled look. 'They don't smell, they're fresh. You know that.'

'This is true,' agreed Kit. 'I just thought you might be, like, a bit squeamish.'

'Why, because I'm vegetarian?' said Senara. 'I'm not fragile of mind.'

'Some girls would be squeamish,' said Kit quietly, almost to himself.

He looked at her again. 'You don't mind getting your hands dirty?'

'Not if a job needs doing,' said Senara. 'Look, I'd like to say I didn't come here to talk about fish, but that's exactly why I'm here. Malory wants The Secret Spot to put fish on the menu. More specifically, your fish.'

'I see,' said Kit, as he continued to sort the mackerel. 'And...you're okay with that?'

She looked at him properly for the first time, into that familiar handsome face. Her eyes drifted from the long surfboard-inflicted scar, to the smaller one on his eyebrow, and then to his long lashes and the green eyes that returned her gaze.

'I guess so,' she said, in resignation. 'Yeah, I'm okay with it.'

Kit looked thoughtful. 'Well, I don't know,' he said, rubbing his beard. 'I'm not sure I can let you do this. Isn't it against your principals?'

He sounded concerned, but Senara caught the glint in his eye.

'Fine, mock me,' she said, morosely. 'But since I've been reminded that I willingly cooked fish in Greece, perhaps my principals aren't so high and mighty after all.'

'Seriously, though,' he looked at her more solemnly. 'I wouldn't want to be the cause of any more friction between us.'

On seeing his pained expression, Senara relented a little. 'I'm willing to give it a try, Kit. If it helps the local economy...' She winked.

He smiled at her enigmatically. 'Right then,' he said softly. 'We'll give it a try.' Standing up abruptly he added, 'I think we're done here. Help me load the van?'

'Um, okay,' said Senara, getting up. Something felt weird. They weren't arguing for one thing.

She picked up one box and carried it carefully over to the back of Kit's van, while he swiftly did the same with the other two.

'Can you manage that?' he said. 'Not too heavy?'

'No, it's no problem,' said Senara.

'Thanks,' said Kit again, when they had finished.

The awkward moment came. Senara wondered if she should say something—anything—about all the things that had taken place between them.

'I hope you're okay,' she blurted out. 'After what happened on the shout. And since then...'

'I'm fine, I think... I hope,' said Kit.

It was a strange answer, thought Senara.

'I was worried about you, that night,' she said, suddenly. 'Especially after...'

'I know,' said Kit.

'You do?' Senara's heart began to beat rapidly.

'I spoke to Rosa,' he said.

'Ah,' she said, feeling as though her face was on fire. 'I see. Well, I'm glad you're okay, and um...'

This was torture. It was Kit. She had known him practically all her life. She should not feel this uncomfortable.

'Well then,' she said, thrusting her hand out formally for him to shake. 'Thanks for doing business, I'll talk to Malory and we'll be in touch...'

Kit took her outstretched right hand in his left one, and not in a remotely business-like manner.

'—Oh, that reminds me—' stammered Senara, confused by this action. 'She wants—she and Teddy want—some fish for lunch, if you can spare...'

'Come with me,' said Kit, ignoring her gibbering request. 'I've got something to show you.'

Without waiting for an answer, he pulled Senara back along the pier by the hand. When they reached St Leonard's Chapel, he led her down the slipway and steps opposite, to Breakwater Beach; the same steps that he had run up all those years ago with the silver ball, and where Senara had waited, anxiously, for him. She felt every bit as nervous now, at the touch of his hand in hers.

At the bottom of the steps, anchored alongside the narrow concrete jetty, was a lone boat. The tide was coming in, completely covering the end of the jetty with water, but this did not dissuade Kit. He splashed out into the sea, dragging Senara with him, so that she had to quickly kick off her flip flops onto the sand.

'What do you think?' said Kit, when they both stood, knee-deep in the water by the boat.

'She's beautiful,' said Senara.

'Yes, she is,' said Kit, looking sidelong at her.

Senara's eyes remained fixed on the boat, entranced. 'Who does she belong to?'

'To me,' said Kit. 'She's mine.'

'Really?' said Senara, breaking away from him to inspect the vessel at closer range.

It was an old-fashion wooden Jumbo, painted white, and it had traditional brownish-red sails.

'Red sails...' Senara muttered to herself, with a sense of déjà vu, as the elusive memory flickered in her mind.

'Yes, I've been restoring her over at the boatyard in Hayle,' said Kit. He coughed nervously. 'You...might like to take a look at her name.'

Senara looked at him suspiciously. She didn't think she had ever seen Kit so tense, not even that night at Driftwood. She made her way to the bow, where the name had been carefully scribed in blue paint, in a traditional style. Senara stared at it in astonishment, wondering what it meant. She looked at Kit, who said nothing, but eyed her carefully, as if to try and read her response. Then she looked back at the inscription again.

Senara's Song.

Senara could hardly believe it. It made no sense; he had only just split up with Astrid. And yet...there it was. *Senara's Song*. She dared not read too much into it, but her heart was thumping wildly. Kit moved around the boat to stand beside her. He turned her towards him, and put his arms around her waist.

'What do you think?' he whispered.

'I don't understand...' said Senara.

'Don't you?' said Kit. He moved one hand to touch her cheek gently, and then he kissed her, tenderly, on the lips.

He pulled away again and looked at her cautiously. 'Now do you understand?'

'Not really,' said Senara, in some shock.

'I love you, Senara. I think I always have,' he said. 'We should be together.'

'But... What about Astrid?' said Senara.

'We broke up,' said Kit. 'You must have heard?'

'Yes, and it's my fault,' said Senara, in a choked voice. 'I'm so sorry, I should never have said those things...'

Kit held her more firmly, as the tide swirled around their legs.

'It's not your fault,' he said. 'I don't belong with Astrid. I belong with you.'

'I'm not sure you belong with anyone,' said Senara wryly. 'What about your freedom? I know how much it means to you...'

'You give me my freedom,' said Kit. 'You always have. I will always be free with you; I know that now.'

He kissed her again, more passionately this time.

It was too much to resist. Before she even knew what she was doing, Senara responded with all her heart, and they held the embrace for long minutes. When finally, they broke the kiss, but still held each other close, Kit looked deep into her eyes, and then frowned a little.

'I'm sorry, I, er...I probably *do* smell of fish....' He said sheepishly.

'No,' said Senara, looking at him lovingly. 'Not fish. *The sea*. You smell of the sea.'

Kit threw his head back, laughing. 'I hope that's not as bad as it sounds. We've already established that the taste is not a good thing.'

'No,' said Senara, grinning. 'It's not bad, not at all.' She moved her cheek close to his, and closing her eyes, breathed him in.

'It's a good thing.' She whispered.

* * *

From behind the wall on the Rampers pier head, Teddy and Malory grinned as they watched Senara and Kit climb into the Jumbo, and set sail into the bay.

'I think that went rather well,' said Malory.

'Excellent result,' said Teddy.

'We'd better get some help at The Secret Spot. I don't suppose she'll be back for a while,' said Malory.

'I should hope not,' said Teddy.

'And I don't suppose we'll have fish for lunch now either,' said Malory.

'I don't think anyone will,' said Teddy.

Epilogue

The Spirit of St Ives

Malory and Jago stood together, alone in the large, neglected space of the former pilchard cellar. Jago had just announced that he had started the process to become a volunteer on the lifeboats.

'It's long overdue,' said Jago. 'All I know is I never want to feel that way again; to feel helpless in a bad situation. I want to know I can do something.'

'I think it's amazing,' said Malory. 'I think you're amazing.'

'Yeah, well that's just 'cos you like me so much,' said Jago, grinning. 'One day you'll realise I'm not so special.'

'Nonsense,' said Malory. 'You're wonderful. And kind of gorgeous too...'

She brushed a hand across Jago's chest as she strolled past him. 'It's a great decision. It kind of makes me feel like volunteering too.'

'I think you've already got your hands full. For now, anyway,' said Jago.

Malory looked around the room, taking in the reality of the work and effort that would be required to restore it. Yet she no longer felt daunted, but inspired. She had a clear vision in her mind, and with new confidence in her destiny, was sure she could not fail.

Jago leaned against a granite pillar of the old building with arms folded and gazed at her with affection.

'So, what's it going to be then?' he asked. Then grinning, added, 'I'm still liking Malory's Gallery.'

'Definitely not,' laughed Malory.

'The Pilchard Press Gallery? The Saltings?' suggested Jago.

'Hmm. Maybe,' said Malory. 'I like the connection with the past; with the history of the building. But I don't know... There's something more; something that brought me here.'

'And that is?' said Jago, moving to embrace her in his arms.

It's like... The spirit. The spirit of St Ives brought me here. It's the *essence* of this place that drew me: the ghosts of the past; the history, art, and surf culture. It's all bound together in a feeling that's always there. I need a name that expresses that feeling.'

'It's always there?' said Jago. 'You mean, like the sound of the sea...?'

Malory's eyes lit up. 'Yes! Precisely. The sound of the sea in St Ives is always present. It embodies that *permanence*, witnessing everything. It never fades, and yet it's indescribable.

'Not for the Cornish,' said Jago.

'What do you mean?' said Malory.

'We have a word exactly for that,' he said. 'For the sound of the sea and the surf. We call it mordros.'

'Mordros...' Malory sounded the word carefully, thoughtfully. 'That's it,' she said quietly. 'We'll call it Mordros Gallery.'

'Mordros it shall be, then,' said Jago bending to kiss her forehead. 'And what about Dora? Does she like it?'

Malory looked around the empty space, standing ready for renewal and revitalisation; the gift that she had been charged with creating. Then she leant her head gently on Jago's chest.

'She does,' she said quietly. 'She loves it.'

* * *

Senara had eventually discovered the plot; how Malory and Teddy had conspired with Kit to, as Teddy put it, 'move things along', between the two of them. She had also been made aware of the list, and the part it had played in Kit's own realisation. He had been somewhat aghast when Senara announced that *of course* she believed in witches, spriggans, knockers, and aliens from space. And how could he possibly think she didn't believe in mermaids?

'I guess I can make an allowance,' he had said, tossing the worn-out piece of note paper into the fire grate. 'Since it's only for guidance anyway.'

'And after all,' Senara had replied, curling her fingers around his neck as he held her close. 'It seems that anything is possible.'

She could still hardly believe it. For Kit to love her as she loved him, was a dream that she had long forsaken. Now she realised how foolish she had been to abandon it so early. Afraid of rejection and heartbreak, she had cut free and drifted into hopeless romances. But no matter how hard she had tried to convince herself of the qualities of others, there had been no one to match him. She had felt herself unlucky in love, but it was from her own blind stupidity, and by her own miscalculating hand, that all her misfortunes had been dealt.

But now everything had changed and a new light shone on the world. For she knew that that same foolishness might have caused her to pass him by once more, had she not been saved by the intervention of friends. Rather than unlucky, she knew herself now to be the most fortunate of women. Of course, there would still be gossip, and condemnation, and judgement. But Senara no longer cared, because he was worth it. And because something had changed...

She left the cellar apartment and strolled along the street, hood up and hands in pockets, on her way to The Barque, to meet the man she loved. Autumn had arrived, with the promise of winter swells and empty beaches. When she reached the corner, she stopped, in the mizzle, and looked up at the same street sign that she had stood beneath many months before.

Teetotal Street.

But this time, her emotions were completely different. Back then, she had felt the long-aching sense of something being missing. But now she knew without a doubt what had been wrong; what element had caused this distortion in the world's picture.

It was Kit. Kit had been missing. Kit was her anchor in times of storm, and stood by her side in life's voyage, a true comrade-in-arms. And now that she had remembered this thing, she felt complete, and whole again. As the seagulls wheeled and cried high above her, Senara smiled with joy. Then, with new hope in her heart, she turned away from the sign and walked back into the adventure.

CORA DEVINE

Born in Ireland, 'where the mountains of Mourne sweep down to the sea', Cora mostly grew up in London, but found her spiritual home in the west of Cornwall. Much of her work is inspired by love for this beautiful and wild landscape. When not writing or painting, she tries to escape to cliff paths, lonely moors, and of course, the sea…

coradevine.co.uk

A SEA-CHANGE

'A rich and vibrant tapestry of characters, atmospheric scenery, and relationships, interwoven with such poetic, descriptive yet effortless language to create a beautiful piece of artwork.' *Amazon Reader Review.*

Also available as a three-part e-book series:

THE FOGOU

Who can tell where reality begins and ends anyway...?

...She had been in this awful place too long.

A group of friends are walking the coast path in West Cornwall, intending to end up in St Ives for Christmas. But when they make a discovery in a remote field, strange things start to happen... Unsettling and uncanny, The Fogou slowly unpicks our fragile grip on the narrative of life, and increasingly overwhelms with the disturbing sense of having been left behind. A ghost story in the tradition for Christmas, to be read by firelight, with perhaps a stiff drink and a blanket to hide under.

COMING SOON...

Something is wrong with Riley.

Todd travels north to meet up with two old school-friends, and together they plan to find out what has happened to their mutual friend Riley. Once outgoing and enthusiastic, he has recently become uncommunicative and downright strange.

They assemble at Riley's place of work, a creepy inn set in the heart of the equally eerie town of Laminster. But the straightforward 'intervention' that they imagine soon descends into something far more sinister.

And the snow, the snow keeps falling...

Printed in Great Britain
by Amazon

28500172R00299